THE MORTAL SICKNESS

Also by Andrew Taylor

An Air That Kills

THE MORTAL SICKNESS

Andrew Taylor

St. Martin's Press ⚏ New York

Library of Congress Cataloging-in-Publication Data

Taylor, Andrew
The mortal sickness / by Andrew Taylor.
p.   cm.
ISBN 0-312-14371-0
I. Title.
PR6070.A79M67   1996
823'.914—dc20   96-5197   CIP

First published in Great Britain by Hodder & Stoughton

First U.S. Edition: July 1996

10   9   8   7   6   5   4   3   2   1

For Irene and Shahid

The Principal Characters

JILL FRANCIS – A journalist on the Lydmouth *Gazette*
RICHARD THORNHILL – Detective Inspector
RAYMOND WILLIAMSON – Detective Superintendent, County CID
BRIAN KIRBY – Detective Sergeant
NORMAN WILSON – Detective Constable
PC PORTER – Lydmouth Division; Uniform Branch
SERGEANT FOWLES – Lydmouth Division; Uniform Branch
CHARLOTTE WEMYSS-BROWN – owner of the *Lydmouth Gazette*
PHILIP WEMYSS-BROWN – husband of Charlotte; editor of the *Gazette*
MISS AMY GWYN-THOMAS – Philip Wemyss-Brown's secretary
SIR ANTHONY RUISPIDGE, BT – of Clearland Court
SOPHIA, LADY RUISPIDGE – his wife
JEMIMA OREPOOL – his niece
GILES NEWTON – agent to the Ruispidge Estate; churchwarden
CHRISSIE NEWTON – his wife
THE REVEREND ALEC SUTTON – Vicar of St John's, Lydmouth
MARY SUTTON – his wife
THE VENERABLE SIMON DAVIS – the Archdeacon of Lydmouth
VICTOR YOULGREAVE – churchwarden
MRS ABBERLEY – formerly housekeeper at the Vicarage
IVOR FUGGLE – a journalist on the *Post*
"BOMBER" LANCASTER – manager of the Bull Hotel
MR QUALE – factotum at the Bull Hotel
MRS ETHEL MILKWALL – of Broadwell Drive
JEAN JONES – daughter of Sergeant Kirby's landlady

THE MORTAL SICKNESS

Part One

1

Jill knew at once that the woman was dead. The knowledge struck her like a revelation, absolute and unassailable. Her certainty had something to do with the woman's grotesquely abandoned pose and something to do with the smell in the little room, which reminded her not unpleasantly of compost and incense.

The Reverend Alec Sutton sucked air through his teeth in a lingering hiss. He half-turned in the vestry doorway, spreading his elbows like a pair of wings in an attempt to prevent Jill from seeing what lay inside. His plump face was pale, his eyes huge behind the gold-rimmed glasses.

'There's been an accident, Miss Francis. Would you run across to the Vicarage and ask my wife to ring the doctor?'

Jill craned past Sutton's arm. The woman lay on her back in the far right-hand corner of the vestry. One of her knees was bent, and the skirt of her flowered dress had ridden up. Over the dress was an unbuttoned coat the colour of milk chocolate. You could see the ribbed top of a stocking with a triangle of white thigh above it, and a handful of dark, curling hairs on the skin. Jill glimpsed a pink, lacy suspender – an oddly decorative touch in an outfit so clearly chosen with practicality in mind.

'The doctor, Miss Francis,' the vicar prompted.

The woman had fallen with her head propped against the wall, which gave her an incongruous appearance of alertness. She was wearing gloves. The pallor of her face contrasted sharply with the dull and improbable black of the hair that had escaped from the headscarf. The eyes were open, cloudy blue with dilated pupils. The mouth gaped too, revealing grey fillings, well-brushed teeth and the pink intimacies of the gums and the tongue. On the wall above her was a memorial tablet flanked by smirking cherubs, each with a stone cornucopia balanced precariously on his head.

'Who is it?' Jill asked.

'Her name is Catherine Kymin. Now please hurry.'

Jill blurted, 'But she's dead.'

'Perhaps. But phone for the doctor. Run.'

Sutton probably knew far more about death than she did, Jill realised: in a manner of speaking it was part of his job. She turned and bolted out of the vestry.

It was such a pleasant church, she thought with a sense of outrage – tall, large and well lit, with aisles almost as wide as the nave. The sunlight caught the brass eagle of the lectern and converted it into glittering gold, so bright that it hurt the eyes. Behind the eagle stood the facing rows of richly carved, late-mediaeval choir stalls, stately and silent like disapproving witnesses. One of the stained glass windows threw a patch of reddish-purple like a pool of blood on the floor of the south aisle. She swerved round the font to avoid it. Motes of golden dust danced in the air.

To her surprise she wanted to justify herself to Mr Sutton: to explain that her curiosity had not been idle: it was part of her job to be curious, just as it was part of his to know about death.

The iron latch on the south door was cold to the touch, cold as charity, cold as death. She wondered whether the church was locked at night.

The door closed behind her. She stumbled over the worn flagstones of the porch into the sunlit churchyard. Time seemed to have slowed and the workings of her mind to have accelerated. The warmth of the outside world was a pleasant contrast to the cool of the church. She followed the path round the west tower. The northern side of the churchyard sloped away before her. Everything was so strangely normal. The colours were supernaturally crisp and fresh: the blue sky, the grey stones, the yellow lichen, the green of the cropped grass and the darker green of the yews, and beyond the lych gate the flaking cream façade of the Vicarage.

Jill ran down the path to the gate. Once she tripped and nearly fell, and she managed to graze her hand against the gatepost; it was as if her mind and her body were no longer operating entirely in tandem. A stone angel stared down at her from his perch on a tomb, and for a split second she thought he was smiling at her. *I must be going mad,* she thought, for some part of her mind was still capable of standing aside and observing her thoughts and actions with clinical interest.

The road seemed empty. But when Jill ran across she heard the frantic ringing of a bell. A butcher's delivery boy swerved to avoid her, and the wheels of his bicycle collided with the kerb. He was a fat youth with short red hair and a neck like a ham. He shouted something at her as he rode off but she could distinguish only the outrage.

'Oh, do be quiet,' Jill called over her shoulder.

The panelled front door of the Vicarage had been recently painted yellow, a cheerful colour precisely suited to this sunny June morning. The brass door furniture was in need of a clean, a task for servants who no longer existed. She twisted the heavy handle and charged into the house.

At the time she barely registered what she saw. Her mind, however, continued to record everything with the eidetic clarity of shock. She was in a square, stone-flagged hall. There were stairs to the right with a passage beyond; and to the left and in front of her were four white-painted doors, all closed. Directly opposite the front door was a cast-iron fireplace with a blue-and-white tiled surround.

A small woman with close-cropped brown hair was standing by the fireplace. She was reading a letter on blue paper, and her pale face wore an expression of intense concentration. All this Jill must have observed in a flash because, as soon as she entered, the woman's head snapped round.

'What is it?' She crumpled the letter in her hand. 'Who are you?'

'Mr Sutton sent me.' Jill's voice emerged in a gabble, the syllables clattering together like a goods train rattling over points. 'There's a woman in the church.' She was for the moment unable to find words for the enormity of what was in the vestry. 'He said to fetch a doctor.'

'You must be the journalist from the *Gazette*. Miss Francis, isn't it? I'm Mrs Sutton – Mary Sutton. Sit down while I telephone the doctor.'

Jill sat down more suddenly than intended on the leather chair beside the fireplace. Mrs Sutton opened one of the doors. In the room beyond, Jill saw bookshelves, a desk and a large watercolour of an unfamiliar church. Mary Sutton picked up the phone on the desk. Jill stared down at her hands and stretched her fingers until they hurt to prove to herself that she was still alive.

'Ambulance,' Mrs Sutton said into the phone.

Jill lifted her head. 'And police, I think.'

'And police,' Mrs Sutton echoed, still calm.

'It looked as if she'd been attacked in the church,' Jill went on. 'Hit over the head or something. She's in the vestry under the tower.'

Sentence by sentence Mary Sutton relayed what Jill told her.

'Her name's Catherine Kymin,' Jill concluded. 'I think she may be dead.'

Mary Sutton repeated this last piece of information in an impassive voice. A moment later she came back into the hall. 'I'd better go over to the church. Would you like to stay here? Shall I fetch someone to sit with you?'

'There's no need.'

Mrs Sutton opened another door and went into another room. For a few seconds she was out of sight. Jill heard what sounded like a key turning in a lock. When Mrs Sutton reappeared, she was carrying a handbag.

'Are you sure you'll be all right?'

'Yes, thank you. Would you mind if I make a telephone call? I should let my editor know where I am.'

'Of course. Use the extension in here.'

She ushered Jill into the study and left her alone. The room smelled of pipe smoke and old paper. There was a crucifix on the mantelpiece. Jill felt faint and had to support herself on the desk. She worked her way round and collapsed in the vicar's swivel chair. She picked up the telephone receiver and dialled the number of Philip's private line.

There was a click at the other end. A genteel voice wished Jill good morning and identified itself as the *Gazette*.

'Miss Gwyn-Thomas? This is Jill Francis. May I speak to Mr Wemyss-Brown?'

'I am afraid that won't be possible. He is engaged. Would you like me to take a message?'

Jill thought quickly. It was Monday morning. Philip had his weekly meeting with the advertising manager on Monday mornings. He was almost certainly in the latter's office, smoking cigarettes and talking about the weekend's golf.

'I'm afraid it's urgent,' Jill said, carefully matching Miss Gwyn-Thomas's icy politeness. 'Please fetch him at once. He is not going to be pleased if the *Post* gets this story first.'

There was a short but pregnant silence at the other end of the line. The *Gazette*'s rivalry with the *Post* went back almost fifty years to the first decade of the century. Jill could have invoked no greater threat. As Philip had once remarked with an uncharacteristic lack of charity, Miss Gwyn-Thomas considered herself wedded to the interests of the *Gazette* because she could find no one else to marry her. Jill thought privately that Miss Gwyn-Thomas would really have preferred to be wedded to Philip, but she kept this thought to herself.

'I'll see what I can do,' Miss Gwyn-Thomas said. 'But on your head be it, Miss Francis.'

While she waited Jill stared out of the window, which looked out on the road. There was no sign of the police. Somewhere in the house a clock ticked like a beating heart. She glanced round the room. The furniture in the study was shabby and old, but not old enough to be valuable. How could you run a house this size on a clergyman's income, let alone furnish it as it deserved to be furnished? There was a pile of unread copies of the *Church Times* on one corner of the desk. An overflowing ashtray rested on the minutes of the Parochial Church Council. Directly behind the blotter were two photographs in black lacquer frames: a head-and-shoulders studio shot of a much younger Mrs Sutton wearing a ball gown and staring defiantly at the camera, her fine features drawn into a frown; and a snapshot of two boys in caps and blazers on a railway platform.

At last she heard Philip's heavy footsteps approaching the phone, and the sound of his voice demanding a cup of coffee from Miss Gwyn-Thomas.

'Jill. What can I do for you? Have you got the measurements?'

'What measurements?'

'The chalice, of course.'

Jill remembered, as if across a vast chasm of time past, her reason for coming to St John's: to measure the Lydmouth Chalice. Philip's wife needed the dimensions for her wretched little article. Charlotte was either too dignified or too lazy to obtain the information herself – so she'd told Philip to ask Jill to do it for her. It had not been simply a matter of convenience, Jill suspected: Charlotte's pulling rank was also designed to stress the fact to both her husband and to Jill that she was the owner of the *Gazette*.

'Something's happened,' Jill said quickly. 'Have you got a pad?'

She described as precisely as she could what she and the vicar had found in the church. She omitted a few details – the rucked-up dress and the dyed black hair among them; the dead deserved their dignity.

'I'm phoning from the Vicarage,' she finished. 'I thought I'd go over to the church now.'

'Are you all right?' Philip asked. 'Why don't I collect you in the car?'

'I'd rather stay here.'

'Are you sure you feel up to it?' Underneath the concern in his voice there was a layer of excitement: this was the stuff of journalistic romance, the first hint of a story which might reach the nationals. 'Shall I come over and join you?'

'I don't think there's any point at the moment. And would it be wise? I'm on the spot as a witness. But if you turn up with press written all over you, it may not go down well.'

'With the police, you mean?'

'Yes. Actually, I was really thinking of the Suttons.'

'You know best – but phone me as soon as you can.'

Jill put down the phone and rubbed her forehead. She sensed Philip's excitement and part of her shared it. Another part of her worried that she should be making a living out of other people's suffering.

She picked up her handbag and went out into the sunshine. The road was still empty apart from two parked cars near the High Street end. Church Street itself, though so near the town centre, was a relative backwater. She was tempted to linger in the safe, sun-filled churchyard but forced herself to go straight into the church.

The vestry occupied the ground floor of the tower at the west end, separated from the nave by a heavy wooden partition. The Suttons were sitting side by side on the pew nearest the vestry door. Their heads turned towards her in unison. Mary Sutton's right hand lay on the seat between them, and the vicar's left hand rested protectively on top of it. Apart from the setting, their pose was eerily normal: they might have been waiting for a bus.

'The police should be here soon,' Jill said brightly.

Mrs Sutton nodded. No one spoke. Jill was aware of her heart beating like the Vicarage clock. The thoughts pulsed through her mind. A building as old as this must be full of the dead, row upon row, century after century; some with names, most without; flesh, bones, dust and ashes. Only three or four yards away, Jill estimated, was a freshly dead woman. The knowledge filled her with foreboding. Something had recently gone, someone who could never return; and one day Jill herself would go and not return. She rubbed her arms. *Why me? Why couldn't someone else have found the stupid woman?* The chill in the air had already raised goose pimples on the bare skin. Her eyes drifted towards the closed door of the vestry. She noticed that there were splinters of fresh, bright wood around the lock and on the jamb beside it.

'Someone broke in?' Jill asked, as much to break the silence as to hear the answer.

Sutton's hand tightened over his wife's. 'That's what it looks like.'

'The chalice?'

'It's gone.'

The creak of the latch on the south door took them all by surprise. Two men hurried into the church. Jill recognised the elder of them at once: Detective Inspector Richard Thornhill of the Lydmouth CID. He was a slim man with dark hair and a narrow, intent face. He glanced quickly round the church, saw the three of them by the vestry door and strode towards them with the younger man almost running behind him; their heels clashed like hammer blows on the stone floor.

For a second Thornhill looked straight at Jill. She sensed the anger behind his neat, regular features and knew that it was directed at her. They were both recent arrivals in Lydmouth but they had already discovered a talent for disagreeing with each other. It occurred to her, not for the first time, that if he didn't look so cross, he would be quite a good-looking man. His dark pin-stripe suit was reasonably well-cut and made him look more like a solicitor than a policeman. He was carrying grey gloves and a black homburg hat.

The vicar and his wife stood up.

'Are you the police?' Sutton said.

'Of course he is, dear,' Mary Sutton said. 'He's Mrs Thornhill's husband, remember? He was at the patronal service yesterday.'

'I was expecting a constable. Someone in uniform.' Sutton blinked. 'I'm afraid something terrible has happened.'

'Yes, sir.' Thornhill's eyes darted to and fro. 'This is Detective Constable Wilson.'

The younger policeman tried the effect of a smile. He was indeed very young, with thin, tight lips and small eyes permanently narrowed as though trying to calculate the value of everything they saw.

You know my wife, I think,' Alec Sutton said, clinging to the social niceties like a lifeline in a rough sea. 'And this is—'

'Miss Francis and I have already met. I understand that someone has been hurt.'

'I think you'll find *hurt* is an understatement, Inspector,' Sutton said, his voice suddenly crisp. 'Our chalice is missing too.'

'The mediaeval one?'

Sutton nodded. 'Is the doctor—'

'He's on his way, sir.' Thornhill turned to Mrs Sutton. 'Would you go

9

back to the Vicarage with Miss Francis? I'd like to talk to you later but I don't think I need trouble you now.'

'I'll put the kettle on,' Mary Sutton said to no one in particular.

The two women left the church. Jill was aware of the silence behind them – the men waiting until the women were out of the way before they got down to business; it infuriated her.

A silent command must have passed from Thornhill to Wilson: Jill heard hurried footsteps behind them; the young constable shot across the church like a startled rabbit and reached the south door just in time to hold it open for them.

Neither of the women spoke until they were out in the sunshine.

'So that's Lydmouth's answer to Sherlock Holmes, is it?' Mary Sutton's voice was so dry that it was impossible to tell whether she was joking. 'As a journalist you must see quite a lot of him.'

'I've not been in Lydmouth long,' Jill said, avoiding the question. 'Nor has he, come to that.'

'Quite a formidable man. Just as well, I suppose. Have you met his wife?'

Jill shook her head.

'She's rather nice. We often see her and the children – they've two dear little children, a boy and a girl. He doesn't usually come to church – I suppose his work must make it rather difficult – but he managed it yesterday. Though of course I didn't really notice him, what with the church being so full and worrying about the lunch and trying to remember the names of all the visitors' wives.' She stopped talking and looked up at Jill. 'Sorry. I'm talking too much. It's the shock, I think. I made my husband open the vestry door.'

'Because seeing the reality was better than letting the imagination run riot?'

'Exactly. That poor woman.' Mary Sutton squeezed her lips together as if trying to hold something back. 'It's rather ironic, actually.'

There was a sudden hiatus in the conversation – it lasted no more than a couple of seconds; just long enough for Jill to wonder why Mrs Sutton had used the word 'ironic'.

'Luckily he understood about my wanting to see for myself.' Mrs Sutton held open the gate to the road. For an instant her control crumbled. 'Oh, dear. I know it's selfish of me but I do wish this hadn't happened. Everything went so splendidly yesterday.'

'I know. These things come out of a blue sky. There's no warning.'

'And poor Miss Kymin. That's the real tragedy. I keep forgetting she's – I can't take it in somehow.'

'Did you know her well?'

Again there was a tiny hesitation, a hint of calculation. 'Not really. She was a regular churchgoer but we didn't see much of her outside church.'

They crossed the road. To the right of the Vicarage was a pair of black gates, and on the right of the gates was the gable wall of an outbuilding which butted against a low cottage whose front door opened on to the pavement. A curtain twitched at one of the upstairs windows. One of the neighbours was monitoring the unusual comings and goings at the church.

'Tea,' muttered Mrs Sutton to herself. 'The ritual response to crisis. I wonder what they did before they had tea.'

Jill hesitated in the doorway. 'Mrs Sutton? I should really see my editor.'

'Of course – you have a job to do.' It was a statement of fact, neither approving nor dismissive. 'But what about Mr Thornhill? I thought he wanted us both to stay here.'

'There's nothing I could tell him that you and Mr Sutton couldn't. I'll see him later. In any case I'll probably be back by the time he wants to see us.' Jill added mendaciously, 'I'm sure he'll understand.'

She wondered if she had imagined the flash of amusement in Mrs Sutton's eyes. The two women said goodbye. The door of the Vicarage closed. Jill walked briskly down Church Street.

'Excuse me, miss.'

Jill stopped sharply. The voice was little louder than a whisper. It appeared to come from a vacant spot a few inches away from her elbow.

The door of the cottage by the gates was now standing open. An old woman hovered on the threshold, her face in shadow. She was small, plump and hunched over, with a snout-like nose poking towards Jill; she wore an apron over a long dark dress.

'What is it?'

'Trouble at the church, is there?'

'There's been an accident.'

The old woman stepped on to the pavement. 'If it's just an accident, what's the police doing? I know that man – his picture was in the paper. He's an inspector.'

'I'm sorry. There's nothing I can tell you.'

'You was white as a sheet the first time you come out of the church.'

The woman stretched out a hand with long, horny nails. Jill sidestepped with undignified urgency to prevent the fingers touching her arm. Without another word she walked as fast as she could towards the High Street.

'I was only asking,' the woman called after her. 'No harm in that, is there?'

2

'I suppose you'll have to summon one of those body snatchers from Cardiff,' Dr Bayswater said, turning away from the huddle of flesh and clothes. 'And he'll cut her up at vast expense to the public purse and then turn round and tell you that she died because someone knocked her on the head with a blunt instrument. It's called modern science. Marvellous, isn't it?'

Bayswater had ragged grey hair and a badly shaven face; he wore frayed trousers, a grubby collar and a shirt which had lost at least two of its buttons. He spoke, however, with a beautifully modulated voice which would not have been out of place on a West End stage before the war. His accent and his appearance were permanently at odds with each other.

He paused by the door of the vestry. 'Can't stand churches. If there's a God, why doesn't he stop that sort of thing, eh?' He jerked his thumb at the body of Miss Kymin. 'And in his own house, too. Tut, tut.'

When Bayswater had gone, Thornhill lingered in the vestry. The vicar and DC Wilson were waiting for him in the nave, but he refused to hurry. Soon the building would be full of policemen, talking, measuring, photographing, fingerprinting and taking samples. A little later the journalists would gather outside the church, parasites hungry to feed from the corpse. But for a moment there was peace of a sort, a time to gather first impressions.

He stared down at the body. He didn't recognise Miss Kymin's face, though yesterday morning they had been under the same roof: during the patronal service he could have turned his head and seen her alive. The building had been packed for the celebration of the feast day of the church's patron saint. But perhaps he would not have noticed her even if he had turned his head. She was ugly in death and he did not think he would have found her in any way attractive in life. Why did she have to get herself killed in Lydmouth? For an instant he glimpsed the murky depths of his own arrogance and disliked himself accordingly: self-disgust fuelled his anger at the murder of this harmless middle-aged woman and increased his determination to find the killer. Handbag, he thought, his mind sliding off on a tangent: she must have had a handbag.

He stepped back and looked up at the dusty marble tablet on the wall above the body. It commemorated the virtues of Sir Thomas Ruispidge, who had died almost two hundred years earlier.

> *Under this stone interr'd doth lie,*
> *The Mirrour of true Charitie,*
> *To God, his Friends, & Country dear,*
> *The poores Supporter farr & near . . .*

Thornhill shrugged, an automatic response to Ruispidges past and present, and glanced at the freestanding safe, whose door stood ajar. It was about five feet high and two and a half feet wide and deep. The iron was painted British racing green and the fittings were made of brass, dull with years of neglect.

The excitement was affecting Thornhill like a drug: his mind raced; he felt physically lighter; urgency dominated his mind like a desire to scratch an itch. He went outside. Wilson and the clergyman were sitting at opposite ends of the pew nearest the vestry door. Wilson leapt to his feet when he saw Thornhill. Sutton remained where he was; his lips were moving, perhaps in prayer.

'Can you tell me where Miss Kymin lived?' Thornhill asked.

The vicar looked up. 'A cul-de-sac off the Chepstow Road. I can find you the address if you like.'

'Did you know her well?'

'Not really. We've only been here since January. I believe she and her mother moved down from London about eighteen months ago.'

Thornhill would have preferred to pace up and down but he forced himself to sit down beside Sutton. 'So the mother is the next-of-kin?'

'Was the next-of-kin, Inspector. I'm afraid she died just before Easter. It was very sudden.'

Thornhill glanced quickly at the vicar, wondering if an insinuation lurked beneath the surface of the last remark. Probably not, he decided, though he always found it difficult to be certain what was going on in a clergyman's mind; he didn't entirely understand what made a priest tick.

'Would you mind if Wilson takes notes, sir?'

'Why should I?'

Wilson sat down in the pew in front of the two older men, opened his notebook and licked the point of his pencil.

'Was there any reason for Miss Kymin to be in the church when there wasn't a service?' Thornhill spoke slowly, for Wilson's shorthand was as yet an unknown quantity. 'Did she arrange the flowers or something like that?'

Sutton shook his head. 'But people do drop in, of course. To pray.'

'Quite so.' There was a pause. 'Then when did you last see her? At the service yesterday?'

'Yes, I think so. I'm not sure if she came to the lunch afterwards. My wife would know.'

There was a momentary silence. The church smelled of old damp, new polish and yesterday's incense. This, Thornhill knew, was the lull before the storm.

'You were with Miss Francis when you found the body, I understand? Is she – ah – active in the church?'

'No. She works for the *Gazette*. But of course you know her.'

'What was she doing here?'

'She wanted some information about the chalice for an article they're doing. She telephoned me to make an appointment. I had to fetch the chalice this morning in any case. I was going to take it back to the bank.'

'How big is it?'

'That's one of the things Miss Francis wanted to know. Unusually large for a mediaeval one. Ten or twelve inches high, I suppose, and five or six inches in diameter at the top.'

'Do you happen to know how much it's worth?'

'Not really.'

'You must have some idea. A hundred pounds? Five hundred?'

Sutton spoke slowly, refusing to be hurried: 'It's valued for insurance at twelve hundred and fifty. If it were sold through Sotheby's or Christie's, it would almost certainly go for much more. It's probably late-thirteenth-century, and it's unique. How do you put a price on something like that?'

'When did you last see it?'

'At evensong. As you know we used it for the patronal mass in the morning. Afterwards I put it away in the safe with the collection money. We had another collection at evensong, and I opened the safe to leave the money there. At the same time I put the chalice back in its case. I didn't have time to do that before lunch.'

'You remember locking the safe?'

'No. But I am sure I did. It's a matter of routine. I leave the keys in the lock. Every time I shut the safe door I turn the key before I take it out.'

'Was the collection money gone too?'

Sutton nodded.

'So when did you leave the church after evensong?'

'At about ten to six, I suppose. I was the last to leave.'

'And you locked up?'

'Of course. I pulled the vestry door shut behind me as I left – it's a Yale lock so it engages by itself. And I left the church by the south door.'

'What about the keys?'

'We have three for the south door. I keep one permanently at the Vicarage, and one of the churchwardens has another. The third we leave on a ledge in the porch.' Sutton saw the expression on Thornhill's face and hurried on. 'It's one of those enormous cast iron things about seven inches long. You can't carry it around in your pocket. Besides, sometimes it's convenient for people who need to use the church when it's locked. Authorised people, I mean – our organist, for example, or the cleaners.'

'Are there other doors?'

'Only one.' He waved his hand up the church. 'On the north wall – just before the Lady Chapel. We keep it permanently locked and bolted.'

Thornhill glanced at Wilson, who was breathing heavily as he jotted down his notes; the point of his pencil gouged tracks in the paper. It was rather like watching someone trying to play a piano with a claw hammer.

'Keys for the vestry and the safe: what about those?'

'Three of each. I've a set.' Sutton patted his trouser pocket. 'Both my churchwardens have keys to the vestry, and one of them has a key for the safe as well. We keep the third safe key at the bank.'

'Which bank?'

'Barclays in the High Street. And the churchwardens are Victor Youlgreave and Giles Newton.'

'Mr Newton's the agent for the Ruispidge Estate, isn't he? I've met him. And Mr Youlgreave?'

16

'He has the house with the green railings further down Church Street.'

'And which of them has the safe key?'

'Mr Newton.'

Thornhill looked at his watch and stood up. He walked up the church to the door by the Lady Chapel. It was locked and bolted. He bent down: there were cobwebs in the lock. He turned to face Sutton.

'You didn't return to the church until you came with Miss Francis?'

Again Sutton nodded.

'Did anyone else?' He raised his voice to make himself heard, and the acoustics of the church gave it a disconcertingly unfamiliar resonance. 'Were you expecting anyone? A cleaner?'

'No one.' Sutton rubbed the shiny knees of his trousers. 'I shouldn't have let them keep the church key outside. Probably half the population of Lydmouth knew where it was kept.' He shook his head slowly, his face bemused and sad. 'I imagine someone must have broken in to steal what he could get. And Miss Kymin caught him at it, and he lashed out.' Sutton stared down the church at Thornhill. 'But what puzzles me is why Miss Kymin was here in the first place.'

The latch creaked once more. The lull was over: the storm had begun. Superintendent Raymond Williamson shouldered the door open. Hands in pockets, he stared round the church until he found Thornhill.

'Well?' he said. 'Where's this body, then?'

3

The clock on St John's church slowly chimed the hour as Jill ran up the stairs of the early-Victorian building that housed the *Gazette*. On the eleventh and last stroke she arrived panting in the outer room of the editor's office.

Miss Gwyn-Thomas lifted her head from her tall black typewriter and peered through the fog of cigarette smoke at Jill. The secretary's distinguishing feature was a long thin nose which began in the orthodox fashion at right angles to the rest of her face but swung to the left about two-thirds down. The nose thickened into a small fleshy knob at the end, which was why younger members of the *Gazette*'s staff called her 'Bobble' behind her back.

'You're to go straight in.'

She lowered her head over her typing. From this angle Jill had a view of the long hair piled in a greasy bun on top of the secretary's head. Jill tapped on the door of the inner office and turned the handle. Philip scrambled to his feet and came round the desk towards her, his arms outstretched as though intending to pick her up.

'You look as if you've seen a ghost. Miss Gwyn-Thomas, put the kettle on, would you? Have some tea or coffee, Jill – lots of sugar. Or would you prefer some brandy?'

Jill declined everything. Philip ushered her to an armchair. Jill was aware that Miss Gwyn-Thomas was observing his behaviour with keen and hostile interest. Usually Philip treated Jill with an uncharacteristic gruffness when they were at the office. They were both aware of the risks of attracting accusations of favouritism. After six months neither of them had completely adapted to the fact that the Wemyss-Browns were now Jill's employers as well as friends; nor had their other employees.

When the door was closed, Jill swiftly brought Philip up to date.

'So it's definitely murder?' he asked when she had finished. He was back behind his desk, taking notes.

'What else can it be?'

'And the safe?'

'I didn't get a good look. But Sutton told Thornhill that the chalice had been stolen.'

'Lucky, that.' Philip looked up with a smile. 'Thanks to Charlotte we've all the background information we need. Even a photograph. The chalice makes it a better story in fact: apparently it's a Welsh national treasure.'

'No one mentioned that to me.'

'It's only a theory. Charlotte says there's an entry in Edward I's Jewel Roll. After he'd conquered Wales, he had a chalice made from the seals and plate of the last native prince and his family. One historian thinks it might be the Lydmouth Chalice. No proof, of course, but it makes a damn good story.' He hesitated for an instant, then abruptly changed the subject. 'How did Sutton strike you?'

'Difficult to know. I didn't see enough of him. High Church, the conscientious type, a little overweight. His wife seems nice.'

'They've only been here a few months. Some of his changes have upset people. The smells and bells and so on. Did you ever meet Carter, the previous chap? He was a very different kettle of fish.' Philip was rambling as he often did when he was thinking hard, words and thoughts pursuing different quarries. 'According to Charlotte the parish has split into two camps. There's a lot of bad feeling.' He looked at Jill, his eyes hard and bright. 'In fact I had one of those poison pen letters about Sutton at the end of last week. Nasty things.'

'What did you do with it?'

'The usual.' Philip nodded towards the grey filing cabinet in the corner of the room. 'I lock them away. Often it's a singleton, you know, and after a few months I can throw it out. But if we get more from the same source I pass them to the police. The hardest thing is forgetting what they say.'

Philip pushed back his chair and stood up, patting the pockets of his jacket. The day was warming up and his cheeks were pink and shiny. Jill noticed with a tiny pang of sadness that his body was growing too large for his clothes: his neck pressed against his collar and his stomach bulged over the waistband of his grey flannel trousers. Philip was aging, and so therefore was she. Suddenly cold, she hugged herself, wishing she had accepted the brandy. We all end in the same place, she thought, and her mind filled with an unwanted picture of what she had seen in the vestry.

'Time to call in an expert.' Philip opened the door of the office. 'Miss Gwyn-Thomas – could you spare us a moment?'

The sound of typing had stopped some time ago. Miss Gwyn-Thomas was tidying the stationery cupboard, which stood against the wall close to Philip's door. Jill wondered if she had been listening. The secretary seized her shorthand pad and hurried into the office.

Philip perched on his desk and selected a cigarette from his case. 'It occurred to me that you might be able to give us some background information on St John's and Miss Kymin.' He turned to Jill. 'Miss Gwyn-Thomas is practically the horse's mouth.'

His secretary stared at the carpet. 'I'm not one to gossip, sir.'

'Nor am I. This isn't gossip – it's work.' He flicked his lighter and a pale flame danced on the petrol-soaked wick. 'Did you know Miss Kymin?'

'Not very well. She struck me as a bit of a flibbertigibbet.'

Philip coughed out his first lungful of smoke. 'In what way?'

Miss Gwyn-Thomas rubbed the end of her nose as if trying to straighten out the kink. 'Well – when Mr Sutton first came, she was very enthusiastic about genuflexion and so forth. Especially after her mother died. I think she even went to confession. But recently she's not been quite so pally with him.' She paused and added meaningfully, 'She'd started sitting with Mrs Abberley.'

'The previous vicar's housekeeper,' Philip explained to Jill. 'She lives in a cottage near the Vicarage.'

'I think I saw her this morning.'

'You've probably read one or two of her letters.'

'Letters?' Jill's mind was still running on the anonymous ones.

'Mrs Abberley writes to the *Gazette* at least once a week. Occasionally we print one of her letters. We had one the other day in fact, saying that Sutton's patronal festival was a Papist blasphemy and the Bishop ought to ban it. That was one of the ones we didn't print.'

'Mrs Abberley was a great supporter of Mr Carter and his views,' Miss Gwyn-Thomas said primly. 'And she's not alone in that, I may say.'

'No doubt,' Philip murmured, exhaling smoke. 'By the way, did Miss Kymin have any particular friends? Apart from Mrs Abberley.'

'Not that I know of. She met people through church, of course, but they weren't exactly friends, if you know what I mean. Even Mrs Abberley. Of course Miss Kymin hadn't been here long, and in any case at first she was very taken up with her mother.'

'Who recently died?' Jill interposed.

Miss Gwyn-Thomas flicked a glance in her direction. 'It was very sudden but there was nothing funny about it.' She paused, reluctant to gratify Jill's curiosity any further, but the temptation to display her knowledge was too strong for her. 'I believe it was a stroke.'

Philip tapped ash into the waste-paper basket. 'Where did Miss Kymin live?'

'Broadwell Drive.' She saw the question in his face and went on, 'It's that new road beyond the hospital. A bungalow, I think. I'm afraid I don't know the number.'

'Never mind. Thank you for your help.' He slipped off the desk and held open the door for her. 'As ever, you've been invaluable.'

Miss Gwyn-Thomas left the room, her head held high and her slip showing beneath the hem of her cotton day dress. Jill glimpsed the expression on her face and wondered whether Philip had any idea of the effect he had on his secretary. He shut the door behind her and strolled across the room to the window.

'How proprietorial do you feel about this story?' he asked, his voice soft and conspiratorial.

'Do whatever you like with it.' Jill knew that officially the *Gazette* frowned on linage, the practice of feeding choice stories to the nationals. She also knew the pleasure that such stories gave Philip; he wasn't cut out to be the editor of a staid provincial newspaper and sometimes, Jill suspected, he realised it.

'Thanks.' He coloured slightly, a way of showing gratitude which had survived from his youthful self. He leant forwards. 'Listen, Jill. Why don't we steal a march on all of them?'

4

A flash bulb popped behind them as Thornhill and Williamson came out of the vestry.

'Have a look at her house now,' the superintendent said. 'There's a set of keys in the handbag.'

The handbag – brown leather, much scuffed – had been concealed by the body. On Williamson's orders Wilson was sitting on the step in front of the font and sorting through its contents. So far he had found the keys, a small purse, two bus tickets, a powder compact and a dog-eared ration book. Thornhill thought the decision to delegate the job to him was a mistake, and it rankled.

'I'd like to telephone Sergeant Kirby. Perhaps I could collect him on my way.'

'Kirby's on leave, isn't he?'

'Yes, sir. But he's—'

'All in good time.' Williamson scowled at him. 'You can have Wilson instead.'

Thornhill lowered his voice. 'With respect, sir, does he have the experience for a case like this?'

'The decision isn't up to you, Inspector.' Williamson was never afraid of reminding subordinates of the brutal realities of life. 'How's he going to get experience if we don't give him the opportunity?'

In theory the logic was unanswerable, but Wilson's appointment as a detective constable had nothing to do with logic: his father was a friend of Williamson's and a fellow mason. Thornhill realised that he had blundered: the real issue was not Kirby's merits as a detective compared to Wilson's, but what Williamson perceived as a challenge to his authority.

'Besides, we can't afford the delay.' The superintendent stalked towards the south door, his officers parting on either side to let him and Thornhill through. 'What I'd like to know is what Kymin was doing here in the first place. It was a warm day yesterday, but she was wearing a fairly heavy coat. So that suggests that it was evening or even night time.'

'She might have left something behind at the service. A purse, perhaps.'

'Possibly. Something to bear in mind.' Williamson looked at his watch. 'I'll be at headquarters.'

There were running footsteps behind them. 'Sir!'

Both men turned. Wilson hurried towards them, his eyes screwed into tight little slits. In one of his gloved hands was a sheet of blue paper.

'Sir – I think you should see this.'

He was trembling with excitement and the paper fluttered as he held it out to Williamson. Thornhill's pulse rate accelerated abruptly when he saw the irregular lines of black newsprint on the paper.

'It's a letter, sir,' Wilson gabbled. 'Explains why she was here. Looks like the—'

'Shut up,' snarled Williamson, reverting to type at last. 'And don't drop that bloody letter or I'll see you crucified.'

He produced a large white handkerchief from his trouser pocket, shook out its folds and used it as a makeshift glove. Holding the sheet of paper by the corner, he angled it so that Thornhill could read it too.

There was neither address nor salutation. The letters were in several typefaces and several sizes. Nevertheless the overall effect was one of neatness and care. This was no botched or hurried job. The sender had clipped the cuttings neatly, aligning the blades of the scissors in parallel with the verticals and horizontals of the type. The cuttings had been taken from a newspaper, Thornhill noted automatically, usually in whole words or at least in groups of letters.

You tart. I know what you and Sutton do in church. Filthy bitch. God strike you dead, whore. Go back to London where you belong.

PART TWO

1

The Wemyss-Browns' Rover lurched across Chepstow Road and plunged into Broadwell Drive.

'Whoops,' Philip said, adding unnecessarily, 'Took me by surprise.'

Jill let go of the strap she had been clinging to. Philip allowed the car to roll to a halt at the kerb. Broadwell Drive was a gently curving cul-de-sac with perhaps thirty houses in it. Those on the right backed on to the grounds of the RAF hospital. Beyond the others were open fields. It was a suburban road, yet the setting was misleadingly rural because on two sides the land rose gently to the hills: on the lower slopes sheep moved like miniature clouds in a lush green sky, and along the ridges of the hills were the darker greens of woodland.

They climbed out of the car. It was approaching midday and the sun was high in the sky. Most of the buildings were two-storeyed detached houses. Windows sparkled and the gardens were bright with colour. Several of the chimneys boasted television aerials. Philip stared up and down the road.

'Nasty little place, isn't it? But people are prepared to pay the earth to live here. All mod cons, you see.' He nodded towards the end of the cul-de-sac, where four bungalows were grouped in a semi-circle. 'One of those?'

Philip and Jill walked down the road. A woman watched them from the open window of one of the bungalows. She wore a pinafore and was holding the handle of a Hoover. A domestic prisoner, Jill thought, and averted her eyes; she shivered with sympathetic horror because the woman's fate might

27

so easily have been hers. But perhaps – the old counter-argument rushed into her mind – it wasn't a fate to be avoided, but one to be desired. Was her own life so much to boast about? At least the woman with the Hoover had a home of her own.

'A pound to a penny it's the one on the end,' Philip said.

He had worked it out by a process of elimination: one of the other bungalows had a man's shirt flapping on its washing line; in another, a child's red pedal car was parked outside the front door; and the woman in a pinafore was watching them from the window of the third. The fourth stood a little apart from the others in a trim garden of the almost flowerless variety designed to require the minimum of maintenance.

Jill pushed open the iron gate and they walked up to the Kymins' front door. Attached to the bungalow was a garage with black doors. A dog barked in the neighbouring garden, and the woman in the pinafore shouted, 'Shut up, you!' The dog continued to bark but less loudly. Philip rang the doorbell.

'You won't find her at home,' said the next-door neighbour, who had suddenly appeared on the other side of the fence dividing the two gardens. 'Had a night on the tiles if you ask me – look.'

She waved a duster towards the Kymins' bungalow. There, in the angle of the house and the garage, sheltered from the sun, stood a solitary milk bottle. It was full.

'She hasn't put out her laundry, neither.' The voice was local: not quite West Country, not quite Welsh; wholly Lydmouth. 'The man rang the bell this morning but she didn't answer.'

As she was talking, the woman's head bobbed along the line of the fence towards the road. She came out of her drive, shut the gate carefully behind her and walked up Miss Kymin's drive. She was in her forties, snub-nosed, dark-haired and squarely built. Her pink, unlined face could have belonged to a boy.

Philip swept off his hat. 'I'm Philip Wemyss-Brown from the *Gazette*. This is my colleague Miss Francis. Are we right in thinking that the Kymins live here?'

'Only the one of them does now.' The brown eyes were wary but not unfriendly. 'The old lady died. What's this all about?'

'We think an accident may have happened to Miss Kymin.' Philip peered anxiously at her. 'It's rather difficult.'

Jill was deriving a wry amusement from Philip's technique. The doffed hat and the look of anxiety were calculated not only to reassure the woman in front of them but to make her positively want to help them.

She was in no hurry, however. 'Why?' She settled her left hand on her hip and stared from Jill to Philip.

Philip squirmed, putting on a moderately convincing show of embarrassment. 'It was a very bad accident. I hope this won't come as a shock to you . . .'

'She's dead, you mean? How did it happen?'

'She was in the church – St John's. The vicar found her this morning.'

'But what happened? How did she die?'

Jill came to Philip's rescue. 'No one's quite sure. The police are there now. I hope she wasn't a close friend.'

'That one didn't want no close friends. Listen, why are you here?'

'In the circumstances the *Gazette* will be covering the story. We just wanted to find out some background information about Miss Kymin. We don't have to quote you if you'd rather we didn't.' The woman drew herself up and poked her chest at them. 'My name's Ethel Milkwall and I'm not afraid to admit it.'

Philip had whipped out his notepad. 'Would that be Mrs Milkwall?'

'Of course. I don't mind you printing what I say. Just make sure you get it right.'

'Had the Kymins been here long?' Jill asked.

'They moved down the winter before last. February, I think. Used to live in London but the old lady had a fancy to move down to this part of the world. She'd spent her honeymoon here or something.'

'You must have known them quite well,' Philip suggested. 'Living next-door.'

Mrs Milkwall shook her head vigorously. Her vitality was visibly increasing as she talked, a common side effect of speaking to the press in the wake of a death. 'They kept themselves to themselves. Proper Londoners, look. It's not the way we do things down here.' The woman's eyes studied Jill and Philip: no doubt she was assessing the likelihood that they too were Londoners or something equally alien. 'I popped in a few times after they arrived – just being neighbourly, look – but they didn't want the bother of knowing folks. After the old lady died I went over to see if I could do anything, but the daughter more or less showed me the door.'

Philip tutted with disbelief.

Mrs Milkwall turned down the corners of her mouth. 'Said she was busy. That's a laugh! It's not as if either of them did very much.' She waved her hand dismissively at the tidy shrubs and the neat lawn. 'I mean, look at that – you can't call that a garden, can you? Very keen on church, Miss Kymin was, especially after that new vicar came. Mind you, maybe her mother dying had something to do with that.' Mrs Milkwall suddenly pointed to the path that ran between Miss Kymin's garage and the boundary fence. 'That was theirs.'

Philip and Jill turned. Standing in the lee of the garage was a small cat – a short-haired brown tabby, lightly built and painfully thin.

'She hated cats, the mother did.'

'So was it the daughter's?' Jill asked.

'It was her that took it in. It's a stray. The mother said cats gave her fits, so she wouldn't let her have it in the house. Heard her screaming about it.'

'Sounds as if Mother wore the trousers,' Philip said.

'You can say that again. Should have been born a man. She had the moustache, mind.'

'The cat looks half-starved,' Jill said. 'Didn't Miss Kymin ever feed it?'

'Sometimes. I used to see her carrying a bowl down to the garden shed. It's not the sort of cat that can forage for itself, look. Something wrong with it. You'd have thought she'd have it in the house when her ma died, but no.' Mrs Milkwall's face lit up with mischief. 'Probably thought the old lady was still keeping an eye on her.'

Jill crouched down and held out her hand. The cat stared at it. 'What's its name?'

'I don't know. The old woman used to call it plain cat if she called it anything at all. The young one had a name for it, mind. Alice? Something like that.'

The cat stretched and took two steps very slowly towards Jill. It moved awkwardly: there was something wrong with one of its back legs.

I wouldn't mind feeding it myself,' Mrs Milkwall said defensively. 'Not regularly, mind – just until it finds a new home. But it just wouldn't be practical, what with the expense and everything. Besides, Ollie doesn't like cats.'

As if to emphasise her words, a heavy body flung itself against the other side of the fence. The dog barked furiously. The cat turned and darted clumsily down the path. Jill straightened up and followed.

The path took her down to a paved area which ran across the back of the bungalow and the back of the garage. She glanced through the two windows which looked on to the back garden: a small modern kitchen with clear, gleaming work surfaces and a single chair drawn up to the table; a bedroom, perhaps the mother's, crowded with tall dark furniture.

In contrast with the dull but almost obsessively tidy front garden, the one at the back had been left largely to its own devices. The grass was long and speckled with dandelions. The rose bed to the left was in the process of turning into an impenetrable thicket. A path of crazy paving – a tribute, Jill guessed, to the ingenuity if not to the skill of a previous occupant of the bungalow – snaked down the garden towards a shed leaning against the stone wall at the bottom. Both the wall and the shed were older than the bungalow. There was no sign of the cat.

Jill followed the path down to the shed. To one side of it was what had once been a vegetable garden, now colonised by a clump of nettles. The shed itself was built of creosoted wood under a sloping roof of corrugated iron. The door had been wedged open with a broken haft from a spade or fork. Jill poked her head inside.

An enamel bowl stood just inside the door, its surface licked clean. In the absence of a window the only light came through the open door and through the cracks between the planks. Jill made out a lawnmower, a pile of newspapers, an old chest of drawers. It was a warm day but the shed was chilly; Jill shivered, feeling sorry for the cat.

There were brisk footsteps on the path. Jill turned round. Richard Thornhill was striding towards her with a scowl on his face and his jacket flapping. A complicated emotional charge surged through her like a mild electric shock: professional annoyance, private anger, surprise that he was here so soon, a wish she had had a recent opportunity to check her face in a mirror, and other feelings she had neither the time nor the inclination to identify.

'And may I ask what you are doing here?' he demanded.

It was the sort of pompous question that outraged dignitaries asked in second-rate films, Jill thought. She noted his drawn and weary face and wondered how much sleep he had had the night before: he had young children; perhaps they had been wakeful. *Children* – she pushed the word away from her.

'I'm looking for Miss Kymin's cat,' she snapped. 'Have you seen her?'

'I shall have to ask you to leave.'

'As you wish.'

Philip and Mrs Milkwall had now appeared at the back of the bungalow, followed by the young detective constable she had seen in the church. All three of them looked cross, probably for different reasons.

Thornhill still blocked the path. 'Miss Francis?'

'What is it?' She saw with satisfaction that there were spots of colour in his normally pale cheeks.

He hesitated, and she guessed that at the last moment he had rejected what he had intended to say.

'Well?' she prompted.

'I know you found Miss Kymin this morning.' He was making an effort to be conciliatory but his irritation showed in his face and voice like base metal under old silver plate. 'I know you have a job to do. But we can't allow journalists to get in our way.'

'And vice versa,' she said.

'What?'

'You're in my way. Would you please let me by?'

It was then that she saw the cat. It had regained its natural self-possession and was sitting at a safe distance on the wall that marked the right-hand boundary of the garden.

Jill stepped off the path. 'Alice?'

'Who?' Thornhill said, the irritation now unconcealed.

The cat rose, stared at the humans and jumped down on the far side of the wall.

2

The telephone rang just as Philip Wemyss-Brown was leaving for the saloon bar of the Bull Hotel.

'Would you deal with it?' he asked Miss Gwyn-Thomas as he crossed the outer office. 'I'm going to lunch.'

As he hurried down the stairs, however, he heard her footsteps running after him along the landing. .

'It's Mrs Wemyss-Brown,' she called over the banisters. 'I said I'd see if I could catch you.'

'Oh, lord.' Philip turned and came slowly up the stairs.

Miss Gwyn-Thomas coughed. 'She said it was urgent, sir. I hope I did the right thing?'

'Yes, of course. I'll take it in my room.'

He shut the door, perched on the side of the desk and picked up the phone. 'Charlotte. How's tricks?'

'I hope I haven't disturbed you,' Charlotte said with patent insincerity. 'I just wondered if you knew what Jill is up to.'

'Not precisely, no. She—'

'She promised to phone me. I've been stuck at home all morning. *Entre nous*, it's been more than a little inconvenient. Rather thoughtless, don't you think?'

Philip produced an ambiguous sound, part grunt, part hum. 'The thing is—'

'She was going to measure the Lydmouth Chalice for me, if you remember, so I could finish my article. I asked her at breakfast.' Charlotte left a short but pregnant pause. 'You were there.'

That, Philip knew, was the nub of the problem. When Jill moved to Lydmouth at the beginning of the year, Charlotte had found her a room in Castle Street. But illness brought the house's owner and his family back from Northern Rhodesia before their time, leaving Jill homeless. Philip invited her to stay at Troy House while she looked for somewhere else. She had been there for a fortnight. Extending hospitality to an old friend was delightful in theory, but in practice it had created a situation which Charlotte found increasingly undesirable.

'Well?' Charlotte's voice sounded harsher over the telephone. 'Has she found a moment to measure it yet?'

'There's a bit of a snag, I'm afraid,' Philip said soothingly. 'I'm afraid the chalice has been stolen.'

Charlotte was silent only for a second. Then she poured out a stream of questions. Philip knew the value of a good diversion when he saw one: he told her everything he knew about the theft, Miss Kymin's death and the police investigation; he also mentioned with quiet pride that he had just dictated five hundred words on the subject to the *Daily Mail*.

'You were discreet, I hope?'

'Absolutely, my love.'

'One wouldn't want it getting about that you're sending stories to the nationals.'

'No, indeed.'

'It would undermine your authority completely. Besides, they would all want to do it.'

'Quite so.'

'And where's Jill now?' Charlotte went on.

'At St John's. Or rather outside it. I told her to stay down there until further notice. The *Post* have already got Ivor Fuggle down there, and there are two other chaps – one from the *Citizen*, one from the *Western Mail*. There's probably more by now.'

'You're right.' Charlotte sounded mollified. 'We wouldn't want anyone to steal a march on us. But she'd be better off *inside* the Vicarage, wouldn't she? If that were possible.'

'Yes, of course, my love, but—'

'And what about Mrs Abberley? She's next-door to the Vicarage. Mr

Carter used to say that she knew more about the parish than he did.'

'Not very difficult in his last few years.'

'I shouldn't be surprised if the police haven't talked to her yet. I noticed her chatting to Miss Kymin yesterday. And she spends a good deal of time at her window. If I were you, I'd have a word with Amy Gwyn-Thomas. She might be able to advise on the best way to tackle her.'

'That's a splendid idea.' He chuckled. 'Our Trojan Horse, eh?'

Charlotte was not in the mood for jokes. 'Actually, in one way this theft is rather convenient for Alec Sutton.'

'What on earth do you mean?'

'Chrissie Newton popped in for a cup of coffee this morning, and she told me in confidence that there was quite a scene about the chalice at the PCC meeting last Friday. Giles is the vicar's warden, you know, so he's an *ex officio* member of the council. He said they practically came to blows.'

'Because Sutton wanted to use the chalice at the patronal service? Too Papist for some of them?'

'Nothing like that, dear.' Charlotte tutted at his obtuseness. 'There's nothing Papist about a chalice. No, this was far more serious. It seems that a sizeable minority wants to sell the chalice and put the proceeds into the restoration fund.'

'Whose side is Sutton on?'

'He wants to keep it. According to Chrissie – I don't know if she was quoting Giles exactly, of course – according to her, Alec Sutton told Victor Youlgreave that if they wanted to sell the Lydmouth Chalice, they'd have to do it over his dead body.'

3

'Two cheese and pickle sandwiches,' Superintendent Williamson told the uniformed constable. 'Two cups of coffee, white, two sugars. Two pork pies. Got that, Porter?'

'Yes, sir.' Porter's cheeks twitched as though muscular activity were necessary when committing something to memory. He was in his early twenties, and something about his spotty, earnest face made Richard Thornhill feel prematurely middle-aged.

'No sugar for me,' he said quickly. 'And no pork pie either.'

The room shook as Porter clumped towards the door. He was a big man but his boots belonged to an even larger one. Breathing heavily, he tried to close the door quietly. A hinge creaked. Porter, his face gleaming with a patina of perspiration, darted an agonised glance at the two senior officers. Williamson sighed.

'Standards have dropped since the war,' he said loudly. 'There's no two ways about it.' Porter's footsteps thundered down the corridor. 'Well, what have you got for me?'

'Not much. The *Gazette* were poking around Miss Kymin's garden when I got there. Pumping the neighbour.'

'That Francis woman?'

'And Philip Wemyss-Brown himself. Damned nuisance.'

'Pity.' The superintendent opened the file on his desk. 'Pretty woman, though. And she and the Wemyss-Browns have got good connections.' His thick fingers riffled through the pages, but his hard blue eyes stared across at the desk. 'No point in upsetting them unnecessarily.'

'It means the journalists will be arriving by the trainload even sooner than usual.'

'Can't help that.' Williamson did not seem unduly perturbed by the prospect. 'Now, come on – get on with it.'

Thornhill opened his notebook and passed on the scraps of information he had learned from Mrs Milkwall. 'So after the mother's death, it looks as if Miss Kymin consoled herself with religion.'

Williamson snorted. 'And maybe not just religion. Typical middle-aged spinster – falls for the parson. Is this Milkwall woman reliable?'

'Probably. She's a part-time cleaner at the hospital. Husband's a mechanic. Solid people.'

'How were the Kymins off for money?'

'As far as I could see, they were pretty comfortable. The bungalow was theirs. They lived very simply. No sign of any financial problems.'

'Even after the mother died?'

'Miss Kymin had a deposit account with over four thousand pounds in it. And there are some investments, too.'

Williamson let out a whistle. 'In my book that's more than comfortable. Who gets the loot?'

Thornhill shrugged. 'No sign of a will. Picture of a lad in uniform in the old lady's room, but he seems to have copped it at Arnhem. I'll get in touch with their solicitor. It's a London firm.'

'All right. So what did she do yesterday?'

'Sutton said she went to the patronal service at St John's but he thought she didn't go to the lunch afterwards. Which seems a little odd in itself.'

'Does it? Did *you* go?'

'No, sir,' Thornhill said stiffly, refusing to be drawn. 'Then her neighbour caught a glimpse of her in the garden in the afternoon – feeding the cat. Later, about nine o'clock in the evening, Mrs Milkwall saw her going out. She—'

'Was it normal for her to go out at that time?'

'Not at all.'

'The letter would explain it.' Williamson's often-voiced disapproval of unsupported theories did not apply to his own. 'Say she got it on Saturday. Maybe she and the vicar *were* having a fling together. Or maybe they weren't but she wanted to. Doesn't really matter in a way. So what does she do when she gets that letter? She wants to meet him, sort out what to do. But he's all tied up with this song-and-dance festival or whatever-it-is, so the soonest he can manage is Sunday evening. They meet in church because the neighbours would notice if he came to her. She couldn't go to the Vicarage because Mrs Sutton would be there, and even if there's no truth in the allegation it's still what you might call a delicate subject. Naturally she takes the letter along.'

'There's no evidence that—'

'That Sutton was there? The church was locked, remember?'

'But the key to the south door was hidden in the porch, and that was relatively common knowledge. And why would Sutton want to break into the vestry?'

'To make it seem like an outside job, of course.' Williamson thumped his fist triumphantly on the blotter. 'Point is, the safe was opened with a key. No marks on it at all.'

'Must be fifty or sixty years old, the lock on that safe, maybe more. It's not very complicated. Anyone who really knew what they were doing could get it open without a key.'

'The vestry lock is just a Yale.' Williamson rubbed his chin and added, almost to himself, 'You'd need a locksmith to get that safe open without a key.'

'Or a decent cracksman.'

The two men stared at each other.

'Sutton's got his safe key,' Thornhill went on. 'I'll check with Barclays – they've got one. One of the churchwardens has the third – Giles Newton. I'd better have a word with the other churchwarden too. Chap called Victor Youlgreave.'

Williamson grunted. 'That old woman.'

There was a knock on the door and Porter came in bearing a tray laden with their lunch. He tiptoed across the floor and laid it reverentially on Williamson's desk. One corner caught on a file: the tray tilted and the coffee slopped into both saucers.

'Just go away and leave us in peace,' Williamson murmured, his mind elsewhere.

'Excuse me, sir, I—'

Williamson raised his voice: 'Get out.'

'Sir,' said Porter desperately. 'Sergeant Fowles asked me to say that he hasn't been able to get hold of Sergeant Kirby. His landlady said he went off on his motorbike this morning.'

'All right. Off you go.'

'Tell Fowles to keep on trying,' Thornhill said quickly.

The door shut with another screech, and Porter marched away.

'Just as well we had Wilson, eh?' The superintendent took a bite of his pie, glanced at the clock on the wall and turned back to Thornhill. 'So – early days yet, but it looks as if there are two main possibilities. One, Miss Kymin goes to church, probably to meet the vicar, and surprises someone trying to nick that chalice. Could be the vicar or could be a third party. Or two, Miss Kymin sets up a meeting with the vicar, and he kills her to stop her blurting out that they're having an affair. Agreed?'

'I don't know. That business with the keys confuses everything.'

'No two ways about it, that's how it looks at present. I'll see what the Chief Constable has to say. In the meantime, you had better go and talk to Sutton again. And to his wife. That's where this is all pointing. You agree with *that*?'

Thornhill, who was nibbling the corner of a stale sandwich, nodded.

'Perhaps the scene-of-the-crime boys will come up with something in the church.' Still munching, Williamson stood up and examined the map of Lydmouth on the wall. 'It's a fair old step from Broadwell Drive to St John's. Try the beat constables who were on duty last night. Try the bus company, too. Someone must have seen her. Then there's the crowbar, or whatever it was. Presumably it was the murder weapon as well. We should know for—'

The ring of one of his telephones cut across his words. Williamson seized the receiver of the nearer one – his direct line.

'Williamson,' he barked. A moment later he purred, 'No, sir, not at all.' His features stiffened, and he sat up in his chair, reaching for his pen. 'You don't say. And when was that, sir?'

As Thornhill watched, Williamson's pen began to move: he was not making notes but drawing; he reached automatically for pen and paper when he was on the phone, as other men reached for cigarettes. The doodle was almost always the same: a cat with luxuriant whiskers, a snake-like tail and a broad smile crowded with teeth and menace. When he had finished one, he would begin another.

A cat – Jill Francis had said something about a cat in Miss Kymin's garden. Catherine Kymin. Kitty Kymin. Cat Kymin. Kymin the cat. Jill Francis was much more like a cat than Miss Kymin had been, Thornhill thought. Sleek, self-sufficient and aloof.

Suddenly Williamson's nib dug into the paper and blobs of black ink spurted across the cat's back. 'Not as far as we know,' the superintendent said. A second later he added, still in the same emollient tone, 'No, sir, naturally not. I'll send a man over on a motorbike and we'll get it off to the lab at once.' There was another pause, filled with the sounds of traffic through the open window and the faint, high chatter from the other end of the telephone: then Williamson launched into a summary of the Kymin investigation to date. 'Thornhill's just off to the Vicarage now,' he finished. 'And we should be getting a preliminary forensic report within half an hour.' Another pause. 'Yes, sir. Goodbye.'

Williamson slammed the receiver on its rest. He capped his pen and stared across the desk at Thornhill, his scowl intensifying. 'That was Mr Hendry.'

Thornhill raised his eyebrows. 'A letter?'

'Blue notepaper, newsprint – sounds identical, except for the contents. Bloody cheek, writing to the Chief Constable! Luckily he kept the envelope. It matches the paper. Postmarked Lydmouth, midday Saturday collection. Mr Hendry's address was written in pencil, in capital letters.'

Williamson picked up a sandwich, looked at it and dropped it back on the plate. He reached for one of the pipes in the ashtray.

'This letter says that Sutton's committing adultery with an unnamed woman down here. Miss Kymin? It also claims that he goes up to London to amuse himself with prostitutes in Soho.' The superintendent paused, and Thornhill sensed that he had been saving the best until last. 'The final allegation is that Sutton's finding it hard to make ends meet. Not surprising, with all these fancy women. So, according to our letter writer, he's planning to make a few bob on the side by nicking the Lydmouth Chalice.'

4

'Oh my God,' Mary Sutton said, peering through the crack between the curtain and the side of the window. 'It's the archdeacon.'

Holding an unlit cigarette, her husband joined her at the window. A brown Morris saloon had just parked beside the wall of the churchyard. The driver's door opened. First one gaitered leg emerged, then another; next came the rest of the archdeacon – a thin man whose dark clothes accentuated the greenish pallor of his face. His grey hair was cut very short, like a convict's stubble. He reached into the car and brought out a briefcase and a shovel hat. The journalists flocked towards him.

Alec joined her by the window. 'Look at them. When will it all end?'

She took his arm and hugged it. 'Darling, it *will* pass.'

Even as she spoke she wondered how bad the damage would be. Alec didn't know what was in her handbag: he didn't know how bad the situation really was. She watched the journalists clustering round the small, erect figure of the archdeacon. He held out the briefcase like a sword and passed without haste between them, his face expressionless.

The Suttons went into the hall to meet their visitor. A detective constable in plain clothes – a louche youth, Mary thought, with the face of a hungry rodent – was lounging beside the hall fireplace. He had been stationed there by Inspector Thornhill before lunch, relieving the uniformed constable who had been there before. He was a guard, she knew, though whether he was protecting them or restraining them was unclear.

The constable stared at the Suttons, swallowed and took an uncertain step towards them. The vicar ignored him and opened the front door, revealing their visitor with his hand raised, ready to knock. Three reporters hovered behind him.

The archdeacon said nothing until he was safely inside the Vicarage. He handed his hat to Mary and settled his glasses more firmly on his nose.

'Really. All those reporters – it's like something one sees in the cinema.' His voice was high-pitched and precise; and after thirty years in the diocese he still had a pronounced Liverpudlian accent. 'You must feel under siege, Mary.'

'It's all right,' she said, wilfully choosing to misunderstand. 'We have our very own policeman to protect us. This is Detective Constable Wilson.' She smiled encouragingly at the young man, expertly concealing the dislike she felt for him. 'This is Mr Davis, the Archdeacon of Lydmouth.'

'Good afternoon,' said the archdeacon coolly.

Wilson squirmed slightly. 'Afternoon, sir.'

'Did you have a good drive?' Alec asked, stumbling a little over the words but gallantly pretending that this was a normal visit.

'Rather hot.' Davis had a parish ten miles south of Lydmouth. 'Otherwise much as usual.'

'Would you like some coffee?' Mary said. 'Have you had lunch, by the way? I'm sure we could—'

'I should very much like a cup of tea. If you would be so kind.'

Mary knew that the request was a polite way of dismissing her. 'I expect we could all do with some. Even Mr Wilson.'

Her husband glanced at her as he ushered the archdeacon into his study. He was still holding the unlit cigarette. When she saw the expression on his face, her control almost collapsed. She smiled at him, straightened her spine and set off on the long march to the kitchen.

5

'I need hardly say that the Bishop is deeply concerned,' Davis said. 'He has to be at Lambeth today, but he asked me to tell you that he hopes to be able to see you tomorrow. He or his chaplain will telephone this evening.'

'How kind of him.' Sutton moved behind his desk. 'Yes – how very kind. Won't you sit down?'

'I'd rather stand, thank you.' Davis dropped his briefcase on a chair and walked stiffly towards the window. 'Have there been any more developments since we talked on the telephone?'

'Not that we've been told. We're still in rather a daze, I'm afraid. All this hasn't yet sunk in.'

'Understandable, I'm sure.' Davis stared up at the church and turned back to face the room. 'There's no room for doubt here? No possibility that the woman's death was an accident?'

'I'm afraid not.' Sutton sat down abruptly behind the desk. 'I suppose that the Bishop may want to rededicate or reconsecrate the church. Perhaps in the meantime we should join forces with St Thomas's. Oh dear, there's such a lot to do.'

Davis stared not unkindly at him. 'We must first consider your position, Alec.'

'There's nothing much to it, I would have thought. I found the poor woman's body. She was one of my parishioners – did I tell you? Such a sad little woman. I wonder when the police will let her be buried. I know it's

45

absurdly selfish of me, but I do wish she could have died somewhere else.'

'Have you considered how the police may view this?'

Sutton looked up, frowning. His eyes dropped and he noticed the cigarette between his fingers. Automatically he groped for the lighter on the desk. He lit the cigarette at his second attempt. 'I'm not sure I understand you,' he said through a cloud of smoke.

'I don't know what other evidence they may have. But there is at least a possibility that they may want to make absolutely sure that you yourself are not concerned in this.'

'You can't really think—'

'It's not what I think that counts. Of course I don't believe you have anything to do with this woman's death. That's not the point. It's how the police may think that matters. And then there's the missing chalice.'

'Some of the PCC feel we should sell it. They sprang it on me on Friday. Quite out of the blue. That ass Youlgreave's behind it. I – I'm afraid I reacted rather strongly. It was something I wanted to discuss with you.'

Davis nodded. 'The tower needs underpinning,' he said as if the architect's report was fresh in his mind. 'The timbers in the north aisle are badly infested with death watch beetle. And the whole church really needs a new roof; the longer it's left, the more expensive it will be. And that just covers the items which might reasonably be classified as emergency work.'

'We've looked after that chalice for at least four hundred years, Simon. I don't think it's ours to get rid of.'

'At present neither of us has any say in the matter,' the archdeacon said. He moved nearer the desk and picked up an ashtray which he placed under the end of Sutton's cigarette just before a long coil of ash fell from it. 'Alec, there's something else I have to tell you. It wouldn't be pleasant at the best of times.'

'I keep seeing that poor woman's face.'

'I know. But you must listen to me for a moment. The Bishop had a very nasty anonymous letter this morning. It concerned you.'

6

A watched pot never boils. When Mary Sutton had filled the kettle and placed it on the range, there was nothing to do but lay the tray, find the tea caddy and check that the teapot had been emptied. That took her all of fifty seconds. The kettle, which was large, squat and blackened, sat sullenly on the range and obstinately refused to produce any steam.

Mary was restless, full of an unwanted energy that refused to be directed towards a sensible outlet. The vegetables would have to be done in the next few hours; after all, they would have to have something for supper. She had not eaten since breakfast. Her stomach was empty but the thought of food made her feel queasy.

Instead of doing something useful, she paced up and down the long kitchen. The air smelled of damp even on a sunny day with the window open. Like so many of the rooms in the Vicarage, the kitchen was inconveniently large. A house of this size needed to be full of people. Even when the boys were home from school, they barely impinged on the vast and echoing emptiness.

The boys would have to be told – she made a mental note to telephone their housemaster this evening. Thank God they were away from it all – especially from seeing the effect it was having on their father.

The shock had affected Alec's actions rather than his appearance. He had hardly stopped smoking since he came in from church. All his movements had a hesitant quality, as if he were uncertain not only of his ability to complete them but also of their purpose. And it was all because of Catherine Kymin, so obviously unhappy, yet so difficult to help and so impossible to like; a problem in life and an even worse one in death.

Mary dutifully upbraided herself for her lack of charity. Her thoughts jumped from one subject to another. To the chalice, to the churchwardens, to the archdeacon. There was a rumour in the diocese that Davis was dying of cancer. She hoped not, because the more she saw of him the more she liked him. She and Alec had found him a little disconcerting in the beginning, because he made a point of addressing priests and their wives by their Christian names and expected them to do the same to him.

'It's hard to know whether one should think of him as progressive or eccentric,' Alec had said after their first meeting. 'Or possibly both.'

As Mary passed the range, she touched the kettle once more: it was now lukewarm. She had nothing to do but worry. Her handbag was on the dresser. She stared at it, and her self-discipline snapped. She allowed herself to smoke two a day – one after breakfast and one after supper; and during Lent she stopped entirely, except on Sundays which according to Alec were not part of Lent; having a theologian in the family had its uses.

The prospect of feeling guilty was obscurely attractive. She undid the clasp of the handbag and God paid her out immediately: she saw the blue envelope which had arrived this morning, and the memory of the letter rushed back to the surface of her mind. Angrily she snatched a cigarette from the packet and lit it with the kitchen matches.

'All right,' she said aloud. 'I won't have one this evening. Satisfied?'

There was no answer. The tobacco tasted harsh but she forced herself to smoke on. She moved to the open window and leaned on the sill. The frame was fringed with wisteria in need of pruning. The window overlooked the narrow yard at the side of the house. On the right were the black gates that opened on to Church Street. In front of her was the old coach house, whose weathered stone tiles sagged dangerously but picturesquely. Beyond that was the roof of Mrs Abberley's cottage.

'It's not how we do things here,' Mrs Abberley had said to her when Alec had introduced incense. 'Not in Lydmouth. We like things plain and simple. Just you wait – you'll see.'

Mary looked at the cottage and shivered. Perhaps the old woman had put a curse on them. The boys said she was a witch, and half-believed it. Fear touched her for an instant, the sort of fear that lies beyond reason and deeper than reassurance, whose unchanging power is rooted in the nightmares of childhood, in the darker corners of fairy tales.

To her surprise, she heard footsteps to the left. She stood to one side of the window and peered down the yard. Two women were advancing slowly and with unmistakable wariness from the kitchen garden at the bottom. Mary swore under her breath and stubbed out the cigarette.

She recognised both of them: one was Miss Gwyn-Thomas, whom she knew quite well from church; the other was the woman journalist, Miss Francis, whose arrival at the Vicarage this morning had ushered in this train of horrible events. It was unfair, Mary knew, but for a moment she was inclined to blame Jill Francis for everything.

She took a deep breath and leant out of the window. 'Isn't this rather unusual? Most people use the front door when they come to call.'

Miss Gwyn-Thomas started, the picture of a guilty thing surprised. 'I'm terribly sorry, Mrs Sutton. I know it must look awful but the thing is, we've a favour to ask.'

Mary made the connection she should have made at once: both of her unexpected visitors worked for the *Gazette*; here was another attempt to invade the privacy of the Vicarage, even more brazen than that of the journalists massing outside the front door.

'I'm afraid I've nothing to say to you,' she said. 'My husband is busy. But I'll tell him that you've called, shall I? Now, if you don't mind, I would be grateful if you would leave.'

Mary was aware that the other woman was watching her. The journalist was very still and very elegant. Jill Francis's calm made Mary's words sound embarrassingly melodramatic in her inner ear, which annoyed Mary even further.

'And I must say,' she added, choosing to direct her anger at the weaker target, 'I'm a little surprised to see you here, Miss Gwyn-Thomas.'

'It's entirely my fault,' Jill said. 'In fact, we tried to telephone but the line was engaged.'

'We do have a front-door bell, actually.'

'You also have a reception committee waiting on the pavement. Have you thought about security?'

'What?'

'The journalists outside are just the local people. There are not very many of them yet, and they're reasonably polite. But by the end of the day you'll probably get people down from the nationals – photographers too. I'm afraid they don't have many inhibitions. We walked in through the gate at the bottom of your kitchen garden. Anyone could do the same.'

'I wondered if there was anything I could do to help?' Miss Gwyn-Thomas bleated, apparently following a different line of conversation from everyone else. 'If there is, Mrs Sutton, you have only to say.'

Jill ignored the interruption. 'I know you have a wall here but that won't necessarily keep them out. I'd lock your windows and your doors in the daytime, and draw the curtains at night. Oh, and make sure there aren't any ladders lying around.'

'Aren't you making rather a meal of this, Miss Francis?'

'I wish I were. They'll ask all sorts of things – they can be astonishingly personal. The best thing to do is just to say "no comment". You can't make much of a story out of "no comment". You can't twist it.'

'But it's absurd. You're implying that we've something to hide. But we've done nothing wrong.'

'That's not the point as far as they're concerned.'

Mary frowned. 'And what about you? I don't suppose you're here out of the kindness of your heart?'

'No. We were hoping you might allow us see Mrs Abberley without everyone knowing about it. I gather there's a back entrance through—'

Mary heard a sound behind her. She swung round. The kettle had just come to the boil, and steam was spurting from its spout in a transparent, silvery plume. On the other side of the steam shimmered an apparition: the refracted outlines of a dark-haired man standing in the kitchen doorway, with another approaching behind him.

For an instant she felt another stab of atavistic fear at the thought of strange men invading her home. Then almost instantaneously came recognition. Mary stepped easily into the rôle of hostess as if into the protection of a shell. She waved away the steam and lifted the kettle from the hotplate.

'Hello, Inspector. I'm just making some tea. Would you like a cup?'

7

Jill was glad to get away from Richard Thornhill's accusing eyes. Without saying a word he contrived to make her feel guilty. That was absurd. She had as much right to be here as he did. The police had no reason to feel possessive about the Vicarage and Church Cottage. He and Mrs Sutton stared down from the kitchen window at Miss Gwyn-Thomas and herself; and his silence was far more disturbing than his attempt to reprove her at Miss Kymin's bungalow.

Mrs Sutton gave them directions. Jill followed Miss Gwyn-Thomas into one of the Vicarage outbuildings and through a door into Mrs Abberley's domain. They were in a high-walled cottage garden, small but intensely cultivated; there were vegetables, flowers, fruit trees and a tiny lawn so green in the sunlight that it looked enamelled.

They found Mrs Abberley in her kitchen. She was cutting slabs of stewing steak rimmed with yellow fat into very small cubes. The air in the small, low-ceilinged room smelled rank and stale. It was very warm because of the heat thrown out by the gas stove and because both the door and the window were shut.

'You'll have to put up with the kitchen if you want to talk to me,' Mrs Abberley muttered to Miss Gwyn-Thomas, who hovered just inside the back door, gripping the strap of her handbag. 'I've got work to do. Can't stop for chitter-chattering, unlike some I know.'

She scooped up a piece of meat from a grey enamel dish and slapped it

51

down in front of her. The chopping board was greasy and furrowed with cracks. She began to trim the fat from the slab. Her head lowered, she glanced through bushy eyebrows at Jill.

'Who's your friend, then?'

'This is Miss Francis,' Miss Gwyn-Thomas murmured, her head swaying on her long neck like a heavy flower in a breeze. 'She works with me at the *Gazette*.'

Jill smiled at Mrs Abberley, who stared back with small bright eyes set in folds of pale skin.

'Saw you this morning.'

'That's right,' Jill agreed. 'I'm afraid I was in a hurry. I'd just had a rather nasty shock.'

'You found her.' The snout-like nose twitched, perhaps in acknowledgement of the implicit apology. 'Well, as I say, you'll have to take me as you find me.' She tossed a piece of fat on to a cracked dinner plate. 'I've got work to do.'

Miss Gwyn-Thomas blinked rapidly. 'We've got some ve*r*y bad news, Mrs Abberley. I'm afraid this will come as a terrible shock.'

'I doubt it. Someone's killed Catherine Kymin. That's what all the fuss is about outside.' The knife blade swung towards Jill. 'You and Vicar found her in church.'

'How do you know?'

'One of the reporters told me. Some people give you a civil answer when you ask them a civil question.'

'And did *you* give them civil answers too?'

Mrs Abberley glanced again at Jill, and their eyes met. 'I told you, I've got work to do. I don't have time to stand gossiping on my doorstep. Or go sneaking up to other folk's back doors.'

The message was clear enough: Mrs Abberley preferred acquiring information to providing it; but the fact she was talking to them suggested she might be willing to trade.

'Miss Kymin was in the vestry,' Jill said. 'It looked as if she'd been hit on the head.'

'Oh, aye? And how did she get in there? Vicar keeps the door locked.'

'Someone broke it open.'

'Fancy.' Mrs Abberley sniffed. 'Miss Kymin spent a lot of time in church when there weren't services. Don't ask me why. She wasn't doing anything useful like cleaning the brass or doing the flowers. Was someone after that chalice?'

Jill nodded. 'It's gone.'

'Vicar should have left it in the bank. But it's just a cup, isn't it, when all's said and done. No good to man or beast. You know what Catherine Kymin said to me the other day? She was surprised the vicar hadn't sold it already.'

'I must say she had a point,' said Miss Gwyn-Thomas. 'The Restoration Fund needs at least another—'

'Restoration Fund?' Mrs Abberley pursed her lips and then unexpectedly chuckled. 'That's not what she meant. There's no money in being a parson these days. But they're still expected to live like there was, aren't they? It was all right for my Mr Carter: he had private means. Always had a glass of wine with his dinner, and kept a bottle of whisky on the sideboard. Proper gentleman, he was.'

Keeping her voice as light as she could, Jill said, 'So Miss Kymin thought Mr Sutton should sell the chalice and use the proceeds for other things?'

'In a manner of speaking. In fact she was wondering how he managed as it was. I mean, it's not just him and his wife. They've the two boys, and they're both boarders at Ashbridge School. That's not cheap, look.'

'Perhaps the Suttons have other sources of income.' Miss Gwyn-Thomas wrinkled her nose. 'Or the boys' grandmother . . . ?'

Her voice trailed into silence, a pause crowded with wordless questions. Suspicion oozed through the overheated little room.

Jill watched the blade working its way slowly but with metronomic regularity up, down and across the meat. The knife had a long bone handle and a ring of tarnished silver where the handle met the blade; it had come down in the world, probably from a prosperous Victorian dining room.

Miss Gwyn-Thomas blundered precipitately back to the conversation. 'It's tragic. I was talking to Miss Kymin only yesterday.' She wriggled involuntarily. 'It could have been any of us.'

'I doubt that.' The old voice was disdainful. 'Trouble comes to them that seek it.'

A fly settled on the pile of meat. Mrs Abberley brushed it away with a small brown hand like a paw. Shreds of meat had lodged under her long, yellow fingernails. The fly rose unhurriedly a few inches in the air, made a leisurely loop over the plate and landed back on the meat, where it resumed its meal.

Jill looked away. 'No one else seems to have known much about Miss Kymin.'

'What makes you think I did?'

'She sits beside you in church,' Miss Gwyn-Thomas pointed out. 'Sat, I mean. She seems to have talked to you a good deal, too. And didn't she come back here the Sunday before last?'

'What if she did?'

'It shows you knew her,' Miss Gwyn-Thomas said, her face flushed with forensic triumph and her accent sliding in her excitement from an approximation of BBC English to the authentic tones of Lydmouth. 'That's what. And you had your heads together after church yesterday, mind.'

There was a clatter as Mrs Abberley threw the knife on the table. 'That's enough, Amy Thomas. I'm not being talked to like that in my own home. I remember you when you was a girl. Nasty little whippersnapper you were, too, so sour you'd turn milk. And I remember Mr Carter saying, "That Amy'll never find herself a husband, you mark my words." '

Miss Gwyn-Thomas froze, her mouth partly open.

'Listen,' Jill began in an attempt to repair the damage. 'If I could just—'

Mrs Abberley picked up the knife and jabbed it first at Jill and then at Miss Gwyn-Thomas. 'Oh – get out of my house, the pair of you. Go on. Shoo.'

PART THREE

1

'Do you take sugar, Mr Wilson?' Mary Sutton asked.

Wilson balanced his notebook on his knee and wrapped grubby fingers round the sugar tongs. He dropped three lumps, one by one, into his cup; tiny drops of tea splashed on to the polished surface of the table by his chair. He did not speak but, as he returned the tongs to the sugar bowl, his eyes met Thornhill's. In the instant of contact, the latter knew that the splashes had not happened entirely by accident.

'After you've apologised you can wipe up that mess,' he said to Wilson. 'It'll mark the table if you're not careful.'

Wilson lowered his head. 'Sorry.'

'It doesn't matter,' Mrs Sutton said.

'It does.' Thornhill kept his eyes on Wilson. 'Use your handkerchief.'

'I could fetch a cloth.'

'Thank you, Mrs Sutton,' Thornhill said. 'But there's no need.'

Wilson scrubbed the offending spots of tea. His face was pink and sweaty.

'We needn't keep you any longer, my dear,' Sutton said, holding the door open for his wife.

'Tell me if you need some more hot water.'

There was sunlight in the hall, which made the electric light in the study seem pale and insubstantial. The reporters were massing on the pavement directly outside the window, and Thornhill had advised that the study curtains be drawn.

Alec Sutton closed the door behind his wife and went over to the desk. Sounds filtered through the heavy velvet curtains and the glass of the window: faint laughter, shouting and the honking of a car horn, da-da-da-dah, the V for Victory.

Thornhill glared at Wilson to remind the younger man that his bad manners were not forgotten. Was this the new breed of police officer, he wondered, arrogant, self-possessed and convinced of his own invulnerability? Was Wilson's the face of the future?

Sutton shook a cigarette from the packet on the blotter. Belatedly he remembered his manners and offered the packet round the room. No one took a cigarette, though Wilson looked as if he would have liked to.

'You were telling us about Miss Kymin,' Thornhill prompted.

'There's nothing much more to say.'

'Did she ever visit you here, sir?'

'Me personally?' Sutton sat down behind the desk and scratched the bald patch on his scalp. 'Once or twice. When her mother died, for example. We talked about the funeral arrangements. And later she came to ask me to recommend a mason for the headstone.'

'Did she talk about anything else? Then or at other times?'

'She talked about God.'

Thornhill frowned to cover the awkwardness he felt. He noticed a smirk flitting across Wilson's face. The archdeacon sat, grey and ghostly, in an armchair in the corner.

'At one point,' Sutton went on, apparently unaware of the effect he had had, 'she wondered if she might have some sort of vocation, perhaps to become a nun.'

'Do you think she had?'

'It's hard to tell. I think probably not. Her mother had just died. Often these emotional upsets can send a person off course for a while. I advised her to wait a few weeks, and to pray. She didn't mention the subject to me again. But she did ask me about the money.'

'What money?'

'She inherited something from her mother. There was no one else – I believe she had a brother, but he was killed in the war. She wanted advice on the legal side, and about investments. She was also considering making a donation to our Restoration Fund. Once again, I advised her to wait. I also said she should discuss the matter with her solicitor, and that I wasn't really competent to give her financial advice.'

'Did you have any personal dealings with her?'

'I'm not sure what you mean, Inspector.'

'Did she visit you socially? As a friend rather than as a parishioner.' Thornhill paused, then added, 'Or Mrs Sutton, of course?'

'No.'

'Or did you visit her? Or did you meet elsewhere?'

'I went to the Kymins' bungalow only once.' Sutton's colour was rising, and so was his voice. 'That was when her mother was taken ill. And I went to visit the mother, not the daughter. I may have passed Miss Kymin in the street but I certainly didn't set out to meet her. Not in the sense I think you're insinuating.'

In the chair in the corner, Simon Davis folded his hands in his lap; he did not speak.

'We have to ask these things, sir.' Thornhill glanced at the door, making sure for the second time that it was shut. 'It's nothing personal, you understand.'

'If you'd known her you'd realise—'

From the corner came a cough. The archdeacon stirred in his chair. Sutton stopped talking and tapped the ash from his cigarette with unnecessary vigour. Looking at no one, Davis picked up his cup and saucer and took a sip of tea.

'I wonder if we might go back to the keys now,' Thornhill said.

Sutton shrugged. 'I told you everything I know this morning.'

'Keys?' Davis's high-pitched voice made the word sound like a quiet squeak. 'Are some of the keys unaccounted for?'

Between them Thornhill and Sutton explained. The archdeacon listened without interruption.

'So,' he said when they had finished. 'Even if we assume the church was locked up, almost anyone might have known that the key was in the porch.'

'It's my fault,' Sutton interrupted. 'I should have stopped that as soon as I came. I was deplorably slack.'

'In many ways it seems quite a sensible arrangement,' the archdeacon said. 'St John's is a church not a museum. One could argue that one has to strike a balance between security and allowing people reasonable access.'

'Simon, I shall always blame—'

Davis said: 'The vestry door was broken open. You and both churchwardens have keys, not that that means anything, of course.'

Sutton picked a shred of tobacco from his lip. 'I don't understand.'

'If this were a detective novel, one of the keyholders would naturally break down the door in order to create the impression that someone else was responsible.'

'The vestry lock is a Yale,' Thornhill said, feeling that the initiative had been stolen from him. 'Easy enough to have copies made.'

'And the safe door was open. Again three keys: yours, Alec; one of the churchwardens has the second, and the bank has the third.'

'We'll have to check all that,' Thornhill said. 'We'll need to talk to the manufacturers. Do you know if you have any correspondence with them?'

'Not that I've seen.' Sutton reached for the cigarettes. 'My predecessor here was – ah – not the most methodical of men.'

'That's correct, Inspector,' Davis said. 'Charles Carter believed that administration was no part of the duties of a parish priest.' His eyes were like wet pebbles behind the glasses. 'You might say that he had a moral objection to paperwork.'

Thornhill risked a small show of sympathy. 'That must have made life a little complicated.'

'Indeed.' Davis inclined his head, acknowledging the sympathy. 'The effect was cumulative. Charles came to Lydmouth in 1922. But the safe, I think, is rather older than that.'

'How can you tell?' Thornhill said sharply.

'It's a Radlett, isn't it?'

'I think so.' Thornhill riffled through his notebook until he found the note he had made in the vestry. 'Yes, Samuel Radlett & Co, serial number—'

'Just Radlett,' the archdeacon said. 'That's the point. The firm changed its name just before the Great War. It's been Radlett & Duncan ever since.'

Sutton lifted his head. 'What's that racket?'

Outside two men were shouting, the words indistinguishable but the anger unmistakable. Thornhill looked at Wilson. Wilson sat there, his face puzzled and annoyed, as if aware he had failed a test but unaware of its nature. Thornhill sighed. Sergeant Kirby would have known that the nod was a signal for him to quell the noise and investigate its cause.

There were three loud knocks on the front door.

'See who it is,' Thornhill snapped.

Wilson shot out of his chair. He almost collided with Sutton in the doorway. Sutton drew back and Wilson, his elbows out like a man in a crowd, went into the hall. There was another burst of knocking, as sharp and abrupt as gunshots. Thornhill and Davis followed the other men into the hall.

Mary Sutton appeared in the doorway of the drawing room, her hand raised to her mouth. Wilson turned the key and opened the front door.

A small man stepped into the hall. He was plump, but there was nothing soft about him: his shoulders strained against the tweed of his jacket, and his neat little head balanced on a thick, muscular neck. He removed his hat, handed it and his stick to Wilson and glared over his shoulder at the journalists outside.

On the pavement Fuggle of the *Post* waved his arms in an attempt to gain attention. 'Mr Thornhill,' he called in his fruity, port-wine voice. 'Is it true that—?'

'Shut the door,' the newcomer barked.

Wilson slammed the door in Fuggle's face and turned the key in the lock. Richard Thornhill felt a surge of anger, mixed with fear.

Alec Sutton blundered towards the new arrival. 'Sir Anthony, do come in. You know my wife, of course, and this—'

'Hello, Davis,' Ruispidge said to the archdeacon. 'Thought you might be here.' He nodded to Thornhill. 'Inspector. This is a bad business. Let's get it sorted out as soon as possible.'

He moved towards the study. His gait combined forward motion with a swaying of the body from left to right. The impression he gave was one of absolute authority in motion like the captain of a ship crossing his quarter deck.

Thornhill stood his ground in the doorway. Ruispidge stopped and scowled. He held himself rigidly straight with his head cocked at an angle.

'What is it, man?' For such a diminutive figure he had an unexpectedly deep, rasping voice. 'Spit it out.'

'I'm sorry, sir.' Thornhill forced himself not to move aside. 'I shall have to ask you to leave.'

'Are you mad?'

'No, sir. But I'm conducting an investigation, and—'

'Do you want me to take this to Mr Hendry?'

'If the Chief Constable authorises you, that's another matter. But at present it's my decision.'

'I also happen to be the patron of this living.'

'I'm afraid that doesn't change things, sir.'

Ruispidge's bright blue eyes stared fixedly at Thornhill, who stared back. Thornhill was uncertain what being the patron of a living entailed, but he knew his own rights and responsibilities as a police officer. He was also aware of what a fool he was being, and how much easier it would have been to let Ruispidge do exactly as he pleased. It rarely paid to stand on your dignity with someone who was both a magistrate and a member of the Standing Joint Committee. Thornhill was even secretly a little in awe of the fact that the little man was a baronet.

'And what are you going to do if I just walk past you? Hey? Are you and your underling going to pitch me into the street?'

'No, sir. In the circumstances, I should telephone Mr Hendry and ask for guidance.'

There was another moment of silence. Thornhill willed himself not to look away from those hard blue eyes. Ruispidge's face was highly coloured, criss-crossed with broken veins. His pink scalp gleamed with sweat. He had lost most of the hair from the top of his head; the rest was a dirty ginger-grey colour, heavily greased and plastered against the sides and back of his skull.

Ruispidge grunted. 'Have it your own way, Inspector. But I shan't forget this.'

He wheeled round. Wilson gave him back his hat and stick, and opened the front door. Outside on the pavement the expectant faces were waiting.

'Good day to you,' Ruispidge said to Mrs Sutton. He clapped the hat on his head and strode into the sunlight.

'Sir Anthony,' Fuggle said, sidling up to him. 'Can you confirm that the police are treating the case as murder?'

The other reporters gathered like flies around a jam pot. Instead of closing the door, Wilson, open-mouthed, was watching the scene outside. Thornhill walked across the hall and slammed the door.

'Ring headquarters,' he ordered Wilson, his voice chilly with anger. 'See if they've managed to trace Sergeant Kirby yet.'

2

The girl wasn't exactly a cracker, Brian Kirby thought, watching her leaving the pub with her friends. But she'd do. Her bottom almost spilled out of her camping shorts. She turned at the door to wave, and her big breasts swung lazily beneath her blouse.

'See you this evening,' he called.

She waved again and was gone. Kirby, who prided himself on his knowledge of these matters, told himself that after five years and a couple of kids she'd really start to spread, she'd be way over the hill and halfway down the other side. Still, that would be then: this was now. She and her friends came from Islington, a stone's throw or two from where he'd grown up. It had been a relief to talk to Londoners again. Their minds worked much more quickly than whatever the bumpkins down here had between their ears.

He ordered another pint. Seven o'clock, she'd said. Perhaps he'd take her to the cinema in Lydmouth. The advantage of a motorbike was that you could carry only one passenger. The three friends would have to stay behind or catch the bus.

The landlord wiped the counter. 'Campers, eh?'

'Up at Home Farm.'

'There'll be more of them soon. They've set aside the whole of Top Field. They say old Ruispidge is feeling the pinch.'

'Oh, aye. But it must be good for business as far as you're concerned.'

The man scowled. 'Half the time they bring their own sandwiches and drink bloody lemonade.'

Kirby gulped down the rest of his beer and went outside. For a moment he stood on the forecourt of the Ruispidge Arms and admired his motorbike, a second-hand BSA he had bought with the help of a loan from the bank. The sun beat down on his bare head and sweat prickled under his arms. Christ, it was only June: was the rest of the summer going to be even hotter?

Mitchelbrook was a thin, shabby village that straggled for half a mile along the road, with the river on one side and the hills on the other. The Ruispidge Arms was at the northern end. Nothing moved in the early-afternoon heat – nothing apart from the river, which slid slowly downstream like liquid milk chocolate.

Kirby turned and stared up at the ridge behind the pub. There was a pale rectangle on the green of the highest field: he guessed it was the girls' tent.

It was time to go home and build up his strength for the evening. He started the engine and rode slowly back to Lydmouth, five miles along a dusty road that followed the windings of the river. When he reached the town, he remembered to pick up his blazer from the dry cleaner's on Chepstow Road. It was a good omen for the evening.

Kirby's lodgings were nearby in Broad Lane, one of the jumble of streets between Chepstow Road and Church Street. He was lucky to have found a room so close to headquarters; Lydmouth was short of police housing of all kinds. The room was in a stone-faced, semi-detached villa owned by the middle-aged widow of a former police sergeant. The widow was stone-faced like her house; but she asked few questions, cooked a good breakfast and let him come and go as he chose. She was also semi-detached in the sense that without unseemly enthusiasm she carried on a long-standing affair with her husband's former superior officer, now retired and living in Newport.

Kirby parked the bike outside the front door and let himself into the house. As he was taking his key from the lock, the kitchen door opened. A girl appeared on the threshold. She was all wire and bones – thin shoulders, knobbly knees, round National Health glasses and frizzy black hair. She wore her school dress, blue-and-white gingham; it was tight under the arms and the hem was too high above the knees; her rate of growth outstripped her mother's ability to pay for new clothes.

'Hello, Jean.' He made his voice sound kind: he felt well-disposed to the human race in general. 'You're off school early, aren't you?'

'I didn't go into school.' A blush discoloured the pale skin. 'I had a headache.'

Which meant she had the curse, Kirby thought; and rather her than him. 'I'd like a bath,' he said. 'I'd better check with your mum there's enough water.'

'She went to Newport to do some shopping.' The blush intensified. 'She won't be back till after tea.'

'Never mind.'

'I'm sure the water's hot enough, Mr Kirby.'

'Right then.' He moved towards the stairs, anxious to get away from the girl's embarrassment; he also disliked the way she kept staring at him.

'There was a phone call for you.'

He paused, his hand resting on the newel post. 'Who from?'

'Mr Fowles at the station. He wanted you to ring him when you came in.'

'When was this?'

'I'm not sure.' Her face crumpled. 'I'm sorry, I didn't think to look at the time. It must have been two hours ago at least.'

'Don't worry.'

'But he said it was urgent.'

'It doesn't matter.'

Kirby thought quickly. He had only two days' leave. For once the weather was perfect, and for once he had a decent chance of enjoying himself. Sergeant Fowles was a stupid old woman, the sort who said everything was urgent. Ten to one he had a problem with the paperwork. Fowles wouldn't bother Thornhill with it, because Thornhill would bite his head off; he wouldn't ask Wilson because even Fowles had realised that Wilson couldn't cope with wiping his own arse. That left Kirby to deal with Fowles's problem. Or rather it would if Kirby allowed it to happen.

'Jean?' He let go of the banisters and walked down the hall towards her; she stared up at him, mesmerised, her mouth half-open. 'Will you do something for me?'

She said nothing: she simply stared.

'Listen, I'm on leave. I was going up to Hereford today. I probably wouldn't have been back till after midnight.'

Still she stared: he had an urge to slap her; anything to get a reaction, to break the concentration of her gaze.

'The thing is,' he went on, keeping his voice soft, 'it's only chance I popped in for a bath. Your mum's not in – just you and me, eh? So could you sort of forget you've seen me, do you think? I expect you were going to write the message down, weren't you? And I'll see it when I get back. Because it's not really very urgent.'

It was gloomy in the hall, but he saw her neck muscles flex as she swallowed.

'All right,' Jean said. 'But they won't find out, will they?'

'Of course they won't.' Kirby rummaged in his pocket. 'Even if they did, they'd blame me, not you.' His fingers closed on a shilling. 'Here—'

'I must go,' she said. The kitchen door closed in his face.

Brian Kirby dropped the coin back in his pocket. Jean was a funny little thing, he thought as he climbed the stairs; not quite human. He yawned. The heat and the beer had made him feel sleepy. It would be good to go to bed, preferably with a nice, obliging girl.

As he reached the landing it occurred to him there was no reason for Jean to be afraid of discovery, since by telling him of the message she had discharged her obligation. It followed that she had been afraid not for herself but for him.

Or rather it would have followed if Jean had been behaving logically. But human behaviour wasn't logical. Any police officer knew that.

3

Williamson was not a man who underestimated his own importance. He travelled the few hundred yards from headquarters to St John's in a convoy of three police cars. In Church Street he paused by the lych gate for a couple of minutes, long enough for the waiting photographers to record his image for posterity, and for him to exchange a few words with the reporters.

'We're following several promising leads, gentlemen. You'll be the first to know when we have some news.'

Thornhill waited inside the gate until Williamson had finished. Swallows and martins swooped round the tower, black streaks against the harsh blue sky. He wondered if they had been disturbed by the team of men working their way methodically among the gravestones, looking for clues among the dead. There were clouds moving in from the south-west. Rain was forecast for the evening. With luck they would have finished the search by then.

PC Porter held open the gate and Williamson came into the churchyard. The superintendent's face lost its smile.

'Any news?' he said quietly to Thornhill.

'No, sir.'

'Damn.' Williamson stared around the churchyard and up at the tower of St John's. He rubbed his large, square hands together as if washing them in the air. 'It's a big place. A lot of hiding places. A lot of exits.'

He had a point. The churchyard rose above the level of the surrounding roads, separated from them by a low retaining wall. Once the wall had been crowned with railings, but these had been torn down in an excess of patriotic fervour to make tanks and bombs. The enclosed area was a large, irregular quadrilateral crowded with memorials. The ground near the paths and around the newer graves was immaculately kept. Elsewhere, however, there were patches of weeds and long grass; and many of the older tombs and gravestones were in poor condition.

Church Street ran along the north side of the quadrilateral, linking Broad Lane with the High Street. Roads led off from the other corners as well.

'Four roads and two footpaths,' Thornhill said. 'The killer had plenty of choice.'

'Someone must have seen them. Try the almshouses over there. All those old ladies with nothing to do.'

Thornhill said nothing. As a young constable he had been astonished to discover how unobservant most people were. The two men walked slowly up the path towards the church. As Williamson talked, he darted sharp, suspicious glances from side to side as if looking for slackers among the tombstones.

'I've just had the pathologist on the blower from the mortuary, Thornhill. That new bloke – Murray – with his preliminary report. It's exactly as I thought: cause of death almost certainly a blow to the head with a blunt instrument. There's a depressed fracture on the right side of the temple, good deal of bruising, of course, and a little lacerated skin.'

'Right-hand side? So we might be looking for a southpaw?'

'Not necessarily. Might have been a back-handed blow. Murray's going to try and work out some of the possibilities.'

'How much strength was needed, sir? Did he say?'

'Not much, as long as the weapon was heavy enough. My bet is that we're looking for something like a crowbar.'

They followed the path round the west end of the church. Someone had paid for a bench to be installed against the south wall of the tower; the brass commemorative plate was illegible, worn down by the weather and the friction of hundreds of backs. Williamson sat down and pulled out a pipe and pouch. Thornhill half-closed his eyes and saw moving pictures in his mind: someone using a crowbar to break into the vestry and finding Miss Kymin there; someone lashing out. It could so easily have happened like that.

Williamson reamed the pipe with a small penknife he kept for the purpose. 'You've found no evidence that she was moved after death?'

'No, sir.'

'Nor did Murray. So we assume she was killed in the vestry. But we don't yet know when.'

'Lividity was well advanced,' Thornhill pointed out.

'You know what pathologists are like.' Williamson affected a high-pitched drawl. 'One can never tell with hypostasis. On the one hand it was a warm night. On the other hand churches can be chilly places even in summer.' His voice returned to normal. 'You pays your money and you takes your choice. When I tried to make him commit himself, he said any time between seven and midnight.'

'We know she was alive just after nine, because the neighbour saw her leaving her bungalow.'

'Sometimes I wonder why the hell we bother with pathologists. We'd have just as much chance of hearing something useful from a Ouija board.' A match rasped, and smoke rose from the bench. The next few sentences emerged between puffs of smoke as though ejected by a series of explosions deep in Williamson's interior. 'Listen, Thornhill. We need some results, see? Don't let me down, eh? We've a press conference arranged for tomorrow morning. I want something to give them.'

'So Mr Hendry isn't going to call in the Yard?'

Williamson's red face took on a purple tinge. 'I don't see why there should be any need for that. Not as things stand at present. With a bit of luck we'll have the whole thing wrapped up by the end of the day.'

Calling in the Yard, Thornhill knew, wouldn't do much for the superintendent's reputation; it might even affect his chances of promotion.

A hint of menace entered Williamson's voice: 'I hope you agree with me?'

Thornhill avoided the question. 'We've got the local knowledge, sir.'

'Precisely. Just what I told Mr Hendry. And though I say it myself, we're not a bad—'

He broke off, snatched the pipe out of his mouth and stood up. Thornhill turned. Sir Anthony Ruispidge walked round the corner of the tower with PC Porter scurrying behind him. Ruispidge flourished his stick in the air and gave a muted bellow.

'I say, Williamson.' He jabbed the stick in Thornhill's direction. 'I want a word with you.'

Snorting gently, Ruispidge joined them under the tower. He brushed aside Williamson's attempt to interrupt. 'Your inspector was damned rude to me. And in front of the Suttons, too.' He launched into a highly coloured version of what had happened at the Vicarage.

69

Meanwhile Thornhill sent Porter back to his post at the gate and stared at his shoes. What irritated him most was the fact that Ruispidge was acting as though he, Thornhill, were simply not there. Don't get angry, he told himself with increasing desperation: it won't help.

'It's a disgrace, sir,' Williamson said when he found an opening. 'Thornhill, I'm surprised at you. You'll want to apologise, I'm sure. I can't say how much I—'

'No, no, Superintendent. That's not the point.'

'Sorry, sir.' Williamson cleared his throat. 'Then – ah – what is?'

'It occurred to me on the way here, he was only doing his job.' Ruispidge transferred his bright blue gaze to Thornhill. 'Eh, Inspector? Or what you conceived to be your job. Perhaps you were right to throw me out. I don't say you were, mind: just perhaps.'

'That's very generous of you, sir,' Williamson began. 'It's true that there may have been other factors, which as an investigating officer he—'

Ruispidge was still staring at Thornhill. 'I didn't mince my words, either. Not a local man, are you?'

'No, sir.'

'Where do you come from?'

'East Anglia, sir. The Fens.'

'Well, there you are.' Ruispidge turned triumphantly to Williamson. 'So did Oliver Cromwell. Awkward lot.'

Is he going to complain, Thornhill wondered, or not? Is he going to waste any more time in the first few hours of a murder investigation?

Ruispidge moved to the bench and sat down. 'Look here, Williamson, there's something else. Mr Hendry's in a meeting, or I would have gone straight to him. You'll have to do, I suppose.'

The words were offensive, Thornhill thought, but Ruispidge's manner somehow made them seem frank rather than rude. Perhaps it was a trick they taught them at public school.

'It's all rather unsavoury.' Ruispidge shifted his position on the bench and wrinkled his nose. 'The fact is, I've had a couple of rather unpleasant letters.'

Williamson raised his eyebrows. 'Ah. They wouldn't be anonymous by any chance?'

'As a matter of fact they are. Good God – you mean there have been others? I was going to throw them away – best to ignore these things, I sometimes think. But I showed them to Giles Newton, and he thought it might be wiser to have a word with you chaps first.'

70

'Quite right, sir.'

'You'd better read them for yourself.' Ruispidge felt in the inside pocket of his jacket. 'I hope to God there's nothing in them. But I must say they made me wonder. You know what they say – there's no smoke without fire.'

4

At 3.35 p.m. Mrs Philip Wemyss-Brown pulled on her gloves, adjusted the set of her hat in the hall mirror and set out to call on her friend Mrs Giles Newton.

Perspiring lightly, Charlotte glided through the streets of Lydmouth with her handbag swinging on her arm. She nodded to acquaintances and paused briefly to chat with friends about the murder; she wasted little time on them because they knew less than she did.

She was unable to resist the temptation to make a small detour in order to visit St John's. As she walked past, she observed with well-concealed interest the line of policemen combing the churchyard, the police vehicles lining the kerb and the knot of journalists outside the Vicarage. She noticed that Sir Anthony Ruispidge was talking to Superintendent Williamson and Inspector Thornhill under the tower, and that Mrs Abberley was watching the proceedings from a dormer window on the first floor of her cottage. Poor thing, Charlotte thought charitably: the old dear probably had nothing better to do.

'I say! Mrs Wemyss-Brown! Is it true that lady reporter of yours found a poison pen letter on the corpse?'

It was that old wretch Fuggle from the *Post*, one of the reporters outside the Vicarage; as usual he looked as if he had been poured into his clothes from a great height and then slept in them for several months.

'No comment,' Charlotte called, and put on speed.

'Sorry. What was that?'

Ivor Fuggle had an irritating habit of accentuating his deafness when it suited him, and an even more irritating habit of nosing out items of news before the *Gazette*. Charlotte guessed that he hadn't expected an answer to his question: he had merely wanted to needle her.

She walked steadily on, conscious that those nasty reporters might be staring at her. Perhaps the exercise was responsible, but she found her heart beating a little faster. She wondered if there were any truth in Fuggle's suggestion that Jill had found a letter with the body. Philip had said something the other week about an anonymous letter accusing Alec Sutton of sexual misdemeanours.

It was nearly a mile from Troy House to Mill Place, the Newtons' home in Narth Road just outside Lydmouth. As Charlotte strode up the drive, she heard St John's clock striking the hour. She had timed her arrival for four: she would be certain of getting a cup of tea.

Mill Place was an L-shaped, stone-built house standing beside a broad stream which in flood times turned into a small river. Once it had been a mill, but in the previous century it had been converted into a house, first for a dowager Lady Ruispidge and later for the agents to the Estate. On two sides of the house there were lawns running down to the stream; the grass had the lush green smoothness of early summer. On the fourth was the drive, long enough for decency and privacy but short enough for convenience, and on the fourth, in the angle of L, was a cobbled yard, around which grew an enormous wisteria reputed to be over two hundred years old. Charlotte would have coveted the house had it not been so damp in winter.

A black shape moved slowly towards her across the sunlit lawn. Charlotte stopped to wait. The dog, an old and overweight black labrador, sniffed her gloved hand and waddled beside her towards the house. They found Christina Newton in the yard: she was squatting on her haunches and repotting geraniums.

'Hello, Charlotte. What brings you down here?'

'It was partly the Sweet Wivelsfield, dear. I found a packet in the shed.' She patted her handbag. 'We were talking about it a few weeks ago, and you said you might like to try some.'

'I remember.' Chrissie's long, leathery face bent over the flowerpot, and her hands pressed down the compost; she never wore gardening gloves because they got in the way. 'A cross between Sweet William and Allwoodii Pinks.'

'What a memory you've got. Super colours. They make a splendidly gay effect if you mass them along a border.'

'Hardy annuals, of course.'

'Yes – but to get the best results, our gardener says one should treat them as biennials and sow in September.'

Chrissie lifted the watering can and drenched the newly potted geranium. Some of the water splashed on her sandals, but she appeared not to notice. She wore a faded cotton dress which Charlotte would have sent to a jumble sale long ago, and her legs were bare. The dog tried to lick some of the spilled water.

'Go away, Sambo,' Chrissie said, pushing him away. 'There's plenty of water in his bowl, you know. Let's go and put the kettle on. I'm afraid it's Jane's afternoon off.'

The two women went through a half-glazed side door and down the passage to the kitchen. The Newtons no longer had live-in help in the house, but a woman came in for four-and-a-half days a week. Chrissie filled the electric kettle, a present from Giles on their twentieth wedding anniversary, and plugged it in. Charlotte noticed automatically that the sink was dirty, and the wooden draining board in need of a good scrub.

'There's bread and butter,' Chrissie said, 'and some biscuits. No cake, I'm afraid.' She opened a cupboard and peered inside. 'I must make some jam. It's a shame: for some reason it's not been a good year for strawberries.' She shut the door without taking out anything. 'Giles loves strawberry jam, and I usually make stacks of it.'

Charlotte hugged her news to herself. 'You can have some of our strawberries if you like. We've got a glut this year.'

'Are you sure you've enough for yourselves?'

'Of course. But don't leave it too long or they'll be past it for jam-making.' Suddenly Charlotte could bear the suspense no longer. 'Have you heard what happened at St John's?'

Chrissie was assembling crockery on the table. 'No – what?'

'That was my other reason for calling. You know what you were telling me about the chalice?'

'What about it?'

Charlotte took a deep, pleasurable breath and proceeded to explain. She was still talking when Chrissie carried the heavily laden tea tray out to the garden. Sambo trailed after them, his tongue dangling. Two deck chairs were already standing on the little stone-flagged terrace which ran along the south side of the house. The dog collapsed in the shade of Chrissie's chair.

'But you can't really think that Mr Sutton had something to do with it,' Chrissie said as the flow showed signs of abating. 'He's a clergyman.'

'I don't know what to think.'

'I know he has some peculiar ideas. All those smells and bells. But even so.'

'You can't deny he was determined not to sell the chalice. *Over my dead body*, those were your very words.'

'I'm sure Giles said something like that.' Chrissie stared at her hands with their bitten fingernails and a gardener's grubby skin. 'But why should he want to kill that Kymin woman?'

'Perhaps she caught him trying to take the chalice. Or perhaps they were having an affair and she threatened to—'

'Charlotte, that's absurd.'

'Is it? Between ourselves – this is utterly confidential, dear, you mustn't breathe a word, even to Giles – Philip had a letter the other week. One of those anonymous ones. Every newspaper gets a few. This one said Sutton was – well, a bit of a Casanova, apparently.'

'It's too ridiculous.'

'Is it? You know what men are like.' For an instant Charlotte allowed herself to remember that Philip had asked Jill Francis to stay in their home. Out of friendship? Or had there been another motive? She added with sudden bitterness, 'I can't believe a dog collar makes that much difference, not in that department.'

'I still can't believe it.'

There was a step on the terrace. 'Believe what?' Giles Newton said. Sambo scrambled awkwardly to his feet.

'We're talking about men, darling. Nothing you need worry about. But have you heard the news?'

Newton bent to peck his wife's cheek. 'The whole town's buzzing with it. Hello, Charlotte. You're looking blooming. Any tea in the pot?'

Chrissie went into the house to fetch a cup and the kettle. Giles opened another deck chair, sat down beside Charlotte and offered her a cigarette from his case. He was a thickset man in his fifties, with a square face and curly grey hair. He had a gentle, deliberate manner which Charlotte secretly found rather attractive.

'It must be terrible for Mr Sutton,' she said as Giles offered her a light. His hand brushed hers for an instant, and she wondered whether the touch had been intentional. 'Have you seen him yet?'

'Not yet – but we've talked on the telephone. The poor chap's at his wits' end. Tony Ruispidge was going over to see him this afternoon.'

'How very kind. I'm sure that the—'

'Kindness has got nothing to do with it. Tony's curious. He's also intending to see Williamson or Hendry in the hope of getting chapter and verse from the horse's mouth.' Giles stared at her, knitting his eyebrows. 'Everyone's doing the same: they're running around trying to find out more. It's like living in a town full of ghouls.'

'So sad,' Charlotte said, wondering whether his words should be taken as a reproof. 'Still, it's only human nature, isn't it?'

Chrissie Newton came along the terrace with the kettle in one hand and a cup and saucer in the other. 'What sort of a day have you had, darling?'

'Fine.'

'So what have you heard about this horrible business? I hope you've saved it until I came back.'

'Nothing but the bare essentials. I'm sure you two know more than I do.' Newton looked at his watch and struggled out of the deck chair. 'Actually, I think I might skip tea. I've got some work to catch up on. And I suppose I should ring Victor Youlgreave about the arrangements for services.'

'You could take a cup with you. Would you like a biscuit as well?'

'No, thanks.'

'Wouldn't it be a good idea? You didn't have much at lunchtime.'

'No – I don't want anything. Don't fuss, Chrissie.' After the briefest of pauses he smiled at Charlotte and said in a voice that tried a little too hard to sound amused, 'Now the children are hardly ever here, Chrissie's always trying to mother me.'

Oh dear, Charlotte thought. Do I detect a tiny sign of strain?

He nodded to his wife. 'I'll be in the study.'

Neither woman spoke as Giles walked along the terrace. Chrissie put on her sunglasses. He went into the house, closing the door with the quietest of clicks. The afternoon continued without him. Chrissie sipped cold tea and watched the clouds creeping slowly into the sky. Meanwhile Charlotte delivered an animated monologue on the best way of sowing Sweet Wivelsfield.

5

Jill went to the Bull because Philip had had a tip-off from Mr Quale.

'You go,' Philip said. 'But tread carefully: he doesn't like talking to the press, even to us. Luckily he's got an eye for the ladies. You're more likely to get something out of him than I am.'

'Out of who?'

'Whom, Jill dear, whom. The press has a duty to be grammatical.' Philip was as high as a kite: not because of the beer at lunchtime but because of the story. 'I meant Ruispidge, but it could also apply to Quale.'

Jill wrinkled her nose.

Philip wagged his finger at her. 'Don't be so superior. Quale is worth cultivating.'

Philip had a knack for cultivating people – little people, the sort who watched and wondered at the doings of their masters. Among his useful friends were Quale at the Bull, a sergeant at police headquarters and a disgruntled secretary at the *Post*. Philip tipped generously and remembered them at Christmas; and also, more importantly, he listened to them, asked about their families and gave them back their self-importance.

Jill collected her gloves, handbag and hat. Fortunately her frock was smart enough for a baronet. She left the offices of the *Gazette* and walked slowly along the pavement. The High Street was full of shoppers and children on their way home from school. The sky was a deep, rich blue tastefully decorated with a handful of dark clouds. The air smelled of exhaust fumes and frying fish.

LYDMOUTH CHURCH KILLING said one placard outside a newsagent. LOCAL WOMAN SLAIN said another; the manner of her death had encouraged Lydmouth to accept Miss Kymin as one of their own.

The late-afternoon sunshine warmed her. She would have liked to lie in a deckchair and close her eyes. The shock had receded, leaving her weak and muddle-headed as if she were convalescing after an illness. Sadness filled her. Miss Kymin lay in a refrigerated box in the mortuary: she would never see a summer day again.

If Jill were a proper journalist, she supposed, the sort with ink in his veins (for they were always male), she would be relishing the excitement of being at the centre of a murder case. Perhaps there had been some foundation to the masculine sneers that had dogged her professional career. But she was damned if she could find anything admirable in an attitude of mind that welcomed the unnatural death of another person.

The front door of the Bull stood open. Jill went into the cool gloom of the hallway. Quale dozed behind the reception desk beneath the head of a melancholy stag and dusty glass cases containing the corpses of fish. As Jill approached him, he raised his balding head.

'Good afternoon, Miss Francis. A pleasure to see you again.'

Quale had sat in the hall of the Bull Hotel since long before the war. Every year his neck became a little thinner and his collars a little wider. He answered the telephone, cleaned the guests' shoes and occasionally helped with their luggage. He dispensed aspirin and advice to those he liked. He had other responsibilities, but these were difficult to pin down. His striped waistcoat had faded over the years and acquired a patina, a compound of grease and dandruff, ash and miscellaneous spillages of food and drink.

'Hello, Mr Quale. Mr Wemyss-Brown told me I might find Sir Anthony here.'

Quale leant across the desk, bringing his peculiar aroma closer to her than she liked. 'His Nibs is in the office with Mr Lancaster. But don't say I told you. Sir Anthony's travelling incognito this afternoon.'

'Why is he here?'

'Looking through the books, I understand. Mr Newton does that usually.'

Jill nodded. The Bull Hotel was part of the Ruispidge Estate so Giles Newton, as Sir Anthony's agent, would be responsible for overseeing the manager's work.

'Not Mr Lancaster's favourite time of the month. But there you are: we all have our little crosses to bear.' Quale smirked, and his eyes dropped down from Jill's face to her chest. 'Sir Anthony instructed me to order the Bentley for him. Five o'clock.'

As he was speaking, Jill opened her handbag and took out her purse. She laid a ten-shilling note on the counter. A skinny hand swept it out of sight.

'You've come at a good time, miss.'

'What do you mean?'

'This is the lull before the storm. The telephone's hardly stopped ringing. Five gentlemen have booked rooms already, and I dare say there'll be more. Coming down from London on the six o'clock train.'

'Journalists?'

As he nodded, the telephone began to ring. He leaned even closer and spoke in a gabble: 'If I were you, miss, I'd wait for Sir Anthony in the yard. Then it would look as if you were just happening to come in the back way, and you could bump into him, as it were, accidentally on purpose. If you go round to the left it's the second door on the right.'

She thanked him and left him to answer the phone. The big hotel was very quiet. The door to the yard opened with a screech of protest, the bottom rail scraping against the stone floor. That was unfortunately typical of the Bull: an ill-fitting door would not have been tolerated in a better-run establishment.

The cobbled yard had a half-forgotten air about it. Two generations earlier it would have been alive with horses and grooms. Now it was empty, apart from three cars. Weeds and tufts of grass grew between the cobbles. There was a layer of green scum in the stone horse trough. Just inside the archway to the road was a barn whose double doors stood open, revealing a dusty trap, its shafts pointing like anti-aircraft guns at the sky. Propped against the nearer gable wall was a lean-to lavatory labelled GENTLEMEN, which was perhaps responsible for the faint but unpleasant smell.

It occurred to Jill that once the Bentley had arrived it would be a little awkward for her to linger in the yard and waylay Sir Anthony when he came out of the hotel. The chauffeur would see her and might tell his master that she had been lurking in ambush. It might be wiser to go through the archway into Bull Street beyond and find a convenient shop window. She crossed the yard to reconnoitre.

She had almost reached the archway when a horn blared in the street beyond. A large black car swung off the road. Swaying to the left, the

Bentley plunged towards her. Brakes shrieked. Metal scraped on stone. Still the car came on.

Jill jumped sideways. Her hat fell off. She leapt into the doorway of the barn and collided with the trap. One of the shafts thumped into her spine and she cried out. Her dress caught on something and ripped. Swallows cheeped frantically in the rafters above her head. A tarpaulin which had been covering the seat slithered to the ground. Dust billowed into the air and she began to cough. The car stopped in the yard, rocking on its springs.

'Oh, damn,' Jill said. 'Damn and blast it.'

A door opened, and there were running footsteps.

'I'm so sorry – are you all right? That bloody car just ran away with me.'

The next surprise was that the voice was a woman's: it was light and breathy, and the 'r's emerged as 'w's. *So sowwy*: like a child.

'I nearly missed the turning, you see, and I had a car on my tail practically bumper to bumper so I couldn't brake. Can you move? Oh, my God, should I get a doctor?'

'No,' Jill said, 'you shouldn't. But you could help me up.'

She gripped the hand which was offered and hauled herself up. Ruispidge's chauffeur wore well-cut jodhpurs and a tailored check shirt, an outfit which covered her body but left few of its outlines to the imagination. She was younger than Jill had thought: not a woman but a girl of about twenty. Her hair, so dark it was almost black, hung loose to her shoulders; and her eyes were enormous, the irises very blue against the pure and childlike whites surrounding them. The mouth was too large for beauty, a jagged red gash that dominated the face.

'Are you hurt? Is anything broken?'

'There may be one or two bruises. If that contraption hadn't been in the way, I'd have been fine.'

'You mean if I hadn't tried to mow you down, you'd have been fine. And you've torn your dress, too. Such a pretty one. Don't mind my asking, but it's not a Charice, is it?'

'I can't afford his prices. I bought it from one of his designers who set up on her own in Conduit Street.'

'Not Ginette?' Jill nodded and the voice rushed on at the same break-neck speed: 'Two of my friends *swear* by her. I've been meaning to go and – look, I'm so sorry, here I am chattering on. You must come inside and have a wash and a cup of tea or something. You must let me pay for having the dress mended.' She stepped back and studied the damage. 'Or perhaps it would be simpler if I bought you another.'

'There's no need. It's only a little tear. But I wouldn't mind a wash.'

'This way.'

'Should you turn off the engine? Even move the car?'

'We'll ask someone to see to that. Come along.'

The girl scooped up Jill's handbag and offered her arm. Jill grinned at her.

'It's all right. I'm not one of the walking wounded. My name's Jill Francis, by the way.'

The girl held out her hand. 'Jemima Orepool. Are you staying here?'

'No, I live in Lydmouth.' She saw the curiosity in Jemima's face and decided to pre-empt it. 'I'm a journalist. I used to work in London, but I work for the *Gazette* now.'

They went through the side door into the cool of the hotel.

'Lucky you.' The full lips briefly formed a pout. 'It must be nice to have a proper job. Though I must say I'd rather work in London. But perhaps you had to move because of your husband's job.'

'I'm not married.'

'Don't you find it a bit – well, dreary down here?'

'Not a bit. I'd had enough of London.'

Quale stared at them and leapt to his feet with an uncharacteristic display of energy. 'Miss Jemima! What's wrong?'

'Just a slight accident, Quale. Is there a bathroom Miss Francis could use?' Jemima glanced up at the clock over the desk. 'Too early for a drink, I suppose. But could we have some tea in the lounge? And ask Sir Anthony to come and join us when he's finished with Mr Lancaster.'

'Very good, miss.'

'And would you get someone to park the car? I'm not good in tight spots. The engine's still running. But see to Miss Francis first.'

Quale emerged from the shelter of his desk and contrived to bow to Jill. 'If you'd care to follow me, miss.'

Jill tried to protest that all this attention was quite unnecessary, but neither of them would listen. Quale showed her to a bathroom, provided her with a clean white towel and asked whether she would like the services of one of the chambermaids. Jill declined, unnerved by his sudden transformation into the perfect servant.

She bolted the door and examined the damage. There was a graze on her back and a bruise coming up on her arm. Her gloves were ruined but at least they were an old pair. One of her stockings was laddered; fortunately the dress would conceal the worst of the damage. The tear was another matter. It would be easy to mend but she would never feel the same way about the dress. Even if others didn't notice the repair, she herself would know it was there. That would teach her to be extravagant, she thought: seduced by the lovely lines of the skirt, Jill had bought the dress the previous summer, blowing the better part of a month's income in the process.

When she went downstairs, Quale was back behind the desk. 'Miss Jemima is waiting for you in the lounge, miss,' he said. 'Sir Anthony is still with Mr Lancaster.' He spoiled his impersonation of the perfect servant by giving her an enormous wink and adding in a murmur, 'Raised voices, I'm afraid.'

The lounge was a large, seedy room overlooking the street. An old lady was knitting by the empty fireplace. Two others, one at each end of a sofa, were leafing through magazines. Jemima Orepool was sitting by one of the windows. There was a tea tray on the table beside her, but she had a Bloody Mary in one hand and a cigarette in the other. When she saw Jill approaching she leapt up and ushered her to a chair.

'What would you like? There is tea, but I thought I might have something a little stronger.' She giggled. 'Must be the shock. In which case you'd better have at least two.'

'I'd prefer tea, actually.'

It was an indication of Jemima's influence at the Bull that she had managed to acquire a cocktail outside licensing hours. The fact that the hotel was owned by the Ruispidges no doubt had something to do with it.

Jemima poured the tea clumsily, as though it were not something she was used to doing. 'Have a cigarette.' She handed the cup to Jill and produced a slim gold case. 'Do you mind these? They're Kyprinos. Like Turkish but more so.'

Jill accepted to be sociable. While she waited for a light she said, 'I hope I'm not preventing you from—'

'Don't be silly! Uncle Tony's late so I'd be kicking my heels by myself if we hadn't met. Besides it's lovely to have someone civilised to talk to. I've been down here for almost three weeks and you cannot begin to guess how bored I am.'

'You usually live in town?'

The lips twisted into another pout. 'I'd be there now if I could. Unfortunately – well, to be blunt, I'm in disgrace. I've spent this quarter's allowance and borrowed against next quarter's – and against some of the next's, actually. It all got rather difficult. I mean, Uncle Tony has no idea what things cost these days. He hasn't spent more than two nights in London since all the girls were flappers. Anyway he turned up on my doorstep more or less with the milkman, hauled me out of bed, read the riot act and dragged me down here.'

'How long are you staying?'

'God knows. Until Uncle Tony relents and decides I'm virtuous enough to go. Either that or until I'm twenty-one. That's when they'll let me have Mummy's money.' Jemima swallowed the rest of her drink. 'I'm sorry. This must be an awful bore. Let's talk about you. Are you on this murder case? The body in the vestry. Wouldn't that make a wonderful title for a detective story?' The voice rose a little higher. 'Is it true she was *raped*?'

Three grey heads turned towards them. Silent outrage filled the room.

'Not so far as I know.' Jill stubbed out the cigarette. 'Actually I was hoping I could talk to Sir Anthony about it. My editor would like to have his opinion.'

Jemima giggled, and Jill found herself smiling again. 'As a pillar of local society? My God, you should see him in his pyjamas, before he's got his teeth in. Not that I often do, I'm glad to say – early mornings are definitely not my forte – but once seen never forgotten. When I was a kid, he—'

She broke off, her eyes on the doorway. Jill turned her head to see Ruispidge striding across the room towards them, his body rolling from side to side, his colour high. He wore what Jill recognised from her days in the male, quasi-tribal society of the Palace of Westminster as an Old Harrovian tie.

'Uncle, dear. Come and meet Jill Francis.'

Ruispidge stared at her but did not hold out his hand. 'I know you, don't I?'

'You may have seen me in court. I'm a journalist on the *Gazette*.'

'Didn't Giles Newton mention you? You used to be a political columnist or something.'

'Yes, I—'

'I'm sorry – you'll have to excuse me: I don't want to talk to journalists today.'

'Uncle, *darling*.'

He ignored his niece. 'They've been pestering me all afternoon. More of them coming down this evening. No sense of what's fitting. I've had enough of it. Come along, Jemima. We're going.' He glared at Jill. 'Good afternoon.'

He turned his back on them and stalked towards the door. Jemima stood up. Her lips moulded themselves into the pout. She ran after her uncle. At the doorway she turned: for an instant she posed, wild, graceful and as still as a statue.

'Jemima!' Ruispidge called in the distance. 'Come along.'

Jemima Orepool winked at Jill, waved to her audience of old ladies and vanished.

PART FOUR

1

'Damn it,' the Chief Constable said, his voice reduced by the intervening wires to a tinny, querulous whisper. 'The witnesses aren't likely to run away, are they?'

Williamson scowled at the telephone in his hand. 'In my opinion, sir, for what it's worth, witnesses' memories are like fresh vegetables: they deteriorate with age.'

The sentence was too carefully crafted to ring true. Thornhill wondered whether Williamson planned to use it at the press conference and had wanted a dress rehearsal; or perhaps he would save it for his memoirs. Thornhill and the superintendent were in Williamson's office; Hendry was speaking from his house.

'Yes, sir,' Williamson was saying, 'but in the morning most of them won't be there. Besides, we'll have the inquest to deal with then, and the press too . . . Yes, sir, I appreciate that the inquest will probably be only a formality . . .'

The Chief Constable wanted to delay the house-to-house questioning until the following day: he had not yet decided whether to call in Scotland Yard and was unwilling to do anything which might prejudice their approach to the investigation. The vehemence with which the superintendent put his case showed how unwilling he was to lose control over the investigation.

At last Williamson slammed down the receiver on its rest. 'Right, Thornhill.' His voice was harsh with triumph but he was careful to preserve the proprieties. 'Mr Hendry agrees with us so let's get cracking. You know what to do. I'll stay here. Someone's got to look for the wood among the trees.'

In the early evening they had their best chance of catching people at home – the children were back from school and the men were back from work. Many of them would be having their evening meal, and few of them would have yet gone out.

Thornhill briefed the five teams of officers, some drafted in from other divisions. They were to work their way along Church Street, St John's Passage, the southern end of the High Street, Fore Hill and Nutholt Lane. In order to reach the church, Miss Kymin must have come along at least one of these roads. Her attacker, too, must have slipped through this network of streets – unless, of course, he or she lived in one of them.

With Wilson half a pace behind, Thornhill left police headquarters to direct operations on the spot. There were fewer journalists in Church Street than there had been during the afternoon. Shutters covered the downstairs windows of the Vicarage. To Wilson's surprise, he walked down the length of the street and turned into Nutholt Lane. He stopped outside the house where Kirby lodged. There was a small patch of oil on the road beside the kerb. The oil was fresh enough to glisten. He glanced up at the blank windows of the house, which reflected back the evening sunlight.

'Wait here,' he told Wilson, and pushed open the gate.

The house had a front garden the size of a large double bed. Two strides took Thornhill from the gate to the front door. He rang the bell and heard it buzz somewhere in the back of the house. A moment later the door opened. A schoolgirl looked up at him, her face thin and blotchy.

Thornhill touched his hat. 'Is Sergeant Kirby in?'

The girl shook her head.

'I'm Inspector Thornhill.'

'I know, sir. But he's not here. It's his day off.'

'I saw his motorbike wasn't there, but the oil on the ground looked fresh. I wondered if—'

'He went to Hereford this morning. I don't know when he'll be back. Mr Fowles left a message for him. He – he can't have seen it yet.'

The landlady was a police widow, Thornhill remembered, dredging up the information from a canteen conversation with Kirby, and the daughter was an only child. He wished he knew how to talk to girls of this age, stranded somewhere between childhood and maturity.

'What's your name?'

'Jean Jones, sir.'

'Well, Jean – is your mother in?'

The girl flushed. 'No. She's shopping in Newport. There's a bus gets in at seven. She's usually on that.'

Thornhill half turned to go – then he paused. 'Where were you yesterday evening?'

Jean shrank back. 'At home, sir.'

'All evening?'

'I wasn't feeling well. And I had my homework to do.'

'Did you see anyone in the street?'

She shook her head. The blush darkened. 'Only Mr Kirby. I happened to be looking out of my bedroom window when he came in.'

'Ask him to phone the station when he gets back, will you?' He saw the alarm in her eyes and could not understand why it was there.

'Yes, sir. I will, I promise.'

The door was closing as Thornhill said goodbye. He dismissed the girl's alarm as immaterial. In the presence of a policeman, the most innocent people were apt to act like flustered criminals.

They walked back to Church Street. The churchyard was still cordoned off, and Thornhill stopped to talk to PC Porter who was on duty at the lych gate.

'Any trouble with the gentlemen over the road?'

'Good as gold, sir. That Mr Fuggle tried to ask me some questions, but I wasn't having any. Sent him off with a flea in his ear.' Porter glanced nervously across the road. 'Mrs Abberley gives me the willies, though. She's been watching me ever since I got here.'

Thornhill looked at Church Cottage. Something moved behind one of the upstairs windows.

Porter coughed. 'My gran says she's a witch. These old people get silly ideas, sir, don't they?'

'I think we'll have a word with her.'

As Thornhill and Wilson were crossing the road, the yellow door of the Vicarage opened. Mary Sutton appeared on the doorstep. The reporters converged on her.

'Inspector,' she called. 'Could you spare a moment?'

Thornhill and Wilson slipped through the group of reporters and into the Vicarage. Mrs Sutton wore a headscarf and a grubby pinafore. There was a smudge of dirt on one cheek, and as they entered she flicked a cobweb away from her sleeve.

'I was on the verge of telephoning you, Inspector.' She bolted the door behind them. 'Come and see what I've found.'

She led the way into the study. On the desk was a sheet of paper, yellowed with age. She picked it up and handed it to Thornhill.

'I knew I'd seen a lot of rubbish in the cellars. Trunks and tea chests and so on. I thought it was worth a try. It's rather like a time capsule down there. Everything stopped in September 1939.'

The paper felt damp. Thornhill said, 'They were afraid of the Luftwaffe?'

'I suppose we all were then. We assumed that the Germans were going to cover the whole country with bombs.'

'What else did you find down there?'

'Thirty years of the parish magazine. Old sermons. Files of PCC correspondence. Old account books. Just the things they found they didn't really need.' She stared up at Thornhill. 'It could be important, couldn't it? It's the original bill for the safe.'

'It certainly looks like it.'

'And it says that Radlett's supplied four keys with the safe. The serial number matches.'

He asked for an envelope to put the bill into. 'Does your husband know?'

'Yes, of course. He's upstairs, making sure the more accessible windows are locked. Would you like to see him?'

Thornhill declined. A moment later he and Wilson were outside again, walking towards Mrs Abberley's cottage.

'She thinks the fact there's a fourth key lets her husband out,' Wilson murmured. 'If you ask me, all it does is muddy the waters a bit.'

'She's not a fool. She realises that as well as you do.'

Thornhill knocked at Mrs Abberley's door. Thirty seconds later he knocked again, this time more loudly. After another minute she unbolted the door.

'You don't have to knock the whole house down, you know.'

Thornhill introduced himself and Wilson. Mrs Abberley demanded to see their warrant cards. Thornhill asked if they might talk to her inside, and she grudgingly consented. She ushered them into a small, airless parlour over-looking the road. The room was crowded with dark, plain furniture. Thornhill glanced at their reflections in the dusty mirror that hung above the fireplace. He opened his mouth to put the first question, but she forestalled him.

'I was in the kitchen until about half-past eight, and then I went up to bed. I didn't see no one and no one saw me. No one comes to visit you, not when you get to be my age, not unless they want something from you. And I didn't look out of the window, either. Why should I? I've got better things to do.' She smoothed her apron over her dress. 'I usually go to bed about now. So if you'll excuse me . . .'

'You were the previous vicar's housekeeper, I understand – Mr Carter's?'

She nodded and rested her hand on the doorknob.

'I dare say you were fond of him?' He waited, but she said nothing. 'And how do you like the new vicar?'

'It's not my place to like the vicar or dislike him.'

'And yet he's your landlord. You must have some feelings, one way or the other.'

'When you get to my age, mister policeman, you've had enough of feelings.'

'How about a few facts? When Mr Carter was here, do you know who had a key to the church safe?'

She shook her head.

'Mr Carter must have had one. So you'd know what it looked like.'

'I didn't. I never had anything to do with his keys.' She held the door open. 'Now, I'm going to bed. You can please yourself.'

When the two men were outside, they walked back the way they had come past the Vicarage. It was a beautiful summer evening. The street was noticeably more crowded than it had been. Many people had finished their evening meal and come out to see the show. They ebbed and flowed, chatting quietly among themselves, and watching the churchyard and the Vicarage for any sign of movement.

Two women were chatting to PC Porter. When the young constable saw Thornhill he drew himself away from them and stood in outraged official silence. One of the women pointed at Thornhill and whispered something to her neighbour, who stared at him; he quickened his pace.

At the corner of the churchyard was a small, cream-painted house with ideas above its station: it had a row of railings to separate it from the road, and there was a fanlight over the front door. The railings, the door and the woodwork of the windows were painted a dark green. The little front garden was almost painfully bright with colour. A gravel path led up to the front door.

Thornhill rang the bell. There was an immediate outburst of yapping on the other side of the door. Equally suddenly, the yapping stopped. The door swung open, revealing a small man with a white poodle struggling in his arms. The dog was the same colour as his master's hair and looked like an animated wig.

'Mr Youlgreave?'

'Good evening, Inspector. It is Inspector Thornhill, isn't it?'

'Yes, sir. We—'

'Someone pointed you out in church yesterday. And then of course I've seen you coming and going today.' He scratched the poodle's head. 'Nanki-Poo and I have been keeping an eye on the proceedings. Now come along in. I expect you want to grill me or whatever you policemen do in these circumstances.'

Tucking Nanki-Poo under his arm, Victor Youlgreave led them across a panelled hall to a square, low-ceilinged sitting room overlooking a walled garden. There were flowers and books everywhere. The walls were crowded with paintings. A half-finished piece of embroidery, a swirling design involving some sort of cup and an abundance of fruit, lay on one of the armchairs.

'Now do sit down,' Youlgreave said in his high, clear voice. 'I'd offer you some refreshment but I imagine you can't drink when constabulary duty's to be done.' He waved them to chairs, dumped Nanki-Poo on a chesterfield and sat down beside the dog. His trousers rode up, revealing a pair of dashing purple sock suspenders attached to unexpectedly hairy calves. He picked up his embroidery and laid it on his lap. 'Now, my dear chap: grill away.'

Thornhill quickly established that Youlgreave and Nanki-Poo lived alone. A housekeeper came in daily but usually left at five o'clock. Youlgreave had spent the previous evening in this room, the kitchen or in the walled garden.

As they talked, he smoothed the embroidery with his fingertips and made minute adjustments to its position, as if he were tilting it towards the light to examine the needlework.

He had not been in a position to see anyone in the street or in the churchyard. Nor could he remember hearing anything.

'Mind you, I probably wouldn't have heard if the Russians had dropped a bomb on us. I was listening to the gramophone from about eight-thirty onwards for at least a couple of hours. The divine Horowitz playing Tchaikovsky.' Youlgreave waved his hand towards a large wooden cabinet in one corner of the room. 'There's no point in paying for a good loudspeaker if one doesn't use it properly.'

'What time did you go to bed, sir?'

'Between eleven and eleven-thirty, I think.'

Wilson leant forwards. 'Do you live alone?' He managed to make the question sound mildly indecent.

'As it happens, yes.'

'And what else were you doing? You can't have been just listening to music.'

'Why not? I often do. Though last night I happened to be working on my tapestry.' He held it up to Wilson and added blandly, 'I expect you recognise it, officer. No doubt you're trained to be observant. It's a copy – a loose copy, I admit – of one of the cornucopias on Sir Thomas Ruispidge's monument under the tower.'

Wilson stiffened. 'Where the – the body was found?'

Thornhill glanced warningly at him, wondering whether Wilson was really as stupid as he seemed. Nanki-Poo scrambled up from Youlgreave's lap, jumped down to the floor and sniffed Wilson's shoes.

'No, Nanki-Poo,' Youlgreave said firmly. 'One must never bite a policeman.'

'What about Friday evening?' Thornhill said suddenly. 'Would you tell me about that?'

'Eh?' There was no mistaking the surprise on the round, pink face. Surprise or shock? 'Friday? What about it?'

'I believe there was a meeting of the Parochial Church Council at the Vicarage.'

'That's correct.'

'How long did it go on for?'

'About two hours. Giles Newton and I came back here afterwards. We had a glass of whisky.'

'What happened at the meeting, sir?'

'There were several items on the agenda, I remember. I could find it if you want. I've got it somewhere.' Youlgreave began to struggle to his feet.

'We understand there was a disagreement.'

Youlgreave fell back to a sitting position. 'There usually is, Inspector. You can't expect a group of people to see eye to eye all the time. Disagreement is a healthy sign of democracy at work. Wouldn't you agree?'

Thornhill ignored the proposed diversion. 'It would be helpful to have your account of it, sir. Just for the record.'

'In fact I was taking the minutes myself. I've not had time to write them up yet.'

'We understand that there's been some opposition to the changes which Mr Sutton has made.'

'Yes – well, there's always a transitional period, isn't there, when a new incumbent settles into his parish, where they both get used to each other. It takes time.'

'I understand that Sir Anthony Ruispidge is the patron of the living. So Mr Sutton would have been his choice?'

'Not exactly. Sir Anthony retains the right of presentation, but he asked the Bishop to make the actual appointment. Very sensible, really – for the average land owner, private patronage is nothing but a chore in this day and age. Sir Anthony still takes an interest, though. The Bishop, as you probably know, has strong views about—'

'This disagreement at the meeting, sir,' Thornhill said, cutting ruthlessly into the practised flow. 'Perhaps you would like to tell us about it.'

Victor Youlgreave blew out his already plump cheeks. He looked like an elderly cherub. 'If you insist. Though I should warn you, it's one of those incidents which is magnified in the telling. It was really just a storm in a teacup.' He sat back and clicked his fingers. Nanki-Poo scrambled up on to the chesterfield and settled down beside his master. Youlgreave scratched the dog's head: the well-kept fingernail moved very slowly to and fro and the dog yawned with pleasure. 'As I'm sure you know, the parish owns a large and rather valuable mediaeval chalice. We also have a particularly fine church which is in desperate need of repair. I and several other members of the council feel that the chalice should be sold to pay for these repairs. Mr Sutton does not agree. He feels that it should stay in Lydmouth.' Youlgreave looked at Thornhill. 'Of course we will have to sell the chalice sooner or later. It's a matter of economics. On the one hand it's a white elephant – we hardly use it because we can't afford to insure it properly. On the other hand, the church is unique – we simply can't let it fall down. If we had a sensible government, there would be a central restoration fund one could apply to. But we don't and there isn't. So we have to raise the money by other means. And as far as St John's is concerned, the only method available is selling that chalice.'

'Would it be fair to say tempers were lost, sir?'

'I certainly lost mine,' Youlgreave said with a touch of smugness. 'And so one should, if one's architectural heritage is at stake. And I must say that Sutton himself was rather outspoken. If that's the word I want. Sometimes I wonder if incense does something to the brain. Kippers those little grey cells.

I mean, look at where it's got the Roman Catholic church.' He snorted, and Nanki-Poo gave a small supportive yap. 'Papal infallibility indeed.'

'You do know that the chalice has been stolen?'

Youlgreave nodded. 'But you're not toying with the idea that Alec Sutton might have pinched it, are you?'

Thornhill glanced at Wilson and stood up. 'I'm not toying with anything, sir. I'm merely collecting facts.'

Youlgreave stood up. His head came up to Thornhill's shoulder. 'Look here, Inspector. Sutton may be misguided in some respects, but he's not a criminal. As Giles Newton said only last night, you can't help liking the man. Respecting him, even. He's the sort who's too honest for his own good. If he'd been alive in the sixteenth century he'd have managed to get himself burnt at the stake.'

'You talked to Mr Newton last night? On the telephone?'

'Oh, no. He came over here for a sandwich and a pow-wow at about seven o'clock.'

'You didn't mention this before.'

'You didn't ask, Inspector.' Youlgreave smiled up at Thornhill, his unlined face empty of guile. 'We needed to have a chat about this PCC business. Co-ordinate our strategy, as it were. The upshot was, we agreed that Newton should go and see Sutton today – unofficially as it were. Once all our tempers had had time to cool. The truth is, the patronal service went so well that we thought that Sutton would probably be in a good mood, and therefore anxious to seize any olive branches that might be passing. One has to use diplomacy on the PCC. Tact will get you everywhere.'

'And when did Mr Newton leave?'

'About eight o'clock. It was such a fine evening he'd walked over. He said something about going back via the Bull. I think he wanted to have a word with Mr Lancaster, the manager.'

Youlgreave took Thornhill and Wilson back through the rose-scented hall. As he opened the door, he looked up at Thornhill. The light fell on his face and Thornhill saw that there was a film of sweat on his forehead.

'Now you really mustn't waste time over us, Inspector. You can't really think that Sutton or Giles Newton or I would steal the chalice, can you? It's just not the sort of thing we'd do.'

2

For the third time that evening, Brian Kirby checked that the packet of contraceptives was still in his wallet. He was growing worried.

The contraceptives were still there, of course. The trouble was, it was becoming increasingly possible that he might not be able to find a use for them during the evening. He restored the wallet to the pocket of the heavy leather flying jacket that he had draped over the back of his chair. He had chosen the jacket because he knew it made him look dashing, and there was also the point that it was comfortable to lie on; it had served him well in the past. He looked at his watch again. Only three minutes had crawled by since he had last checked the time. He seemed to have been waiting in the garden of the Ruispidge Arms for a small eternity.

It was partly his own fault: he had left Lydmouth just after six, unable to face being cooped up any longer in his hot little bedroom. There had been the possibility, which now seemed merely a bad joke, that the girl would be early. He flicked ash from the sleeve of his newly cleaned blazer and adjusted the set of his cravat. He was very proud of the blazer and did not want to spoil its lines; that was why he kept his wallet and his cigarettes in the flying jacket.

He was waiting for her outside. There was a garden containing three ruined lime kilns, a dilapidated kitchen table and an assortment of elderly seats. Kirby had dragged one of the more robust-looking chairs to a lime kiln. Leaning back against the rough, warm stonework, he sat smoking and drinking in the evening sunshine. Behind the kilns, the ground sloped steeply up to the ridge behind the village.

He had chosen his position with care: he had a view along the frontage of the pub and of the road in both directions. His motorbike was parked outside the pub – the girl could hardly miss it, whatever direction she came from.

At first the waiting had been a pleasure. Kirby visualised the girl as she'd been that afternoon; not her face because he hadn't liked that much, but the pink thighs and the full breasts, the swaying walk and the quick sense of humour. He had not started to worry until a quarter past seven. She should have been here by now: he had assumed she would be desperate to get away from the rustic amenities of Mitchelbrook. He finished his second pint and wondered whether he should fetch himself another.

It was then that he heard the rattle of a stone. It was somewhere behind him where the ground sloped sharply up to the ridge. The stone bounced twice on the lime kiln and hit Kirby's glass, making a loud ping. He leapt to his feet and stared up the slope.

He hadn't noticed before that a footpath ran diagonally down behind the pub to join the road. There was a girl walking down it. She was only about ten yards away, separated from him by a steep scree partly covered with saplings and weeds. Kirby flung away his cigarette and instinctively smoothed his hair.

'I'm so sorry,' she said. 'Have I broken your glass, or knocked it over?'

'No, it's fine.' As Kirby looked up at the girl, all thoughts of the camper from Islington vanished from his mind. Black hair framed blue eyes and a big, loose red mouth. She was wearing a blue summer dress and from where he was standing he could see well above her knees. She couldn't pronounce her 'r's properly, which made her sound disconcertingly childlike. The accent was top drawer, the real thing.

'You haven't seen a man coming down the path, have you?' she asked. 'Or even going up?'

'No. I might not have seen him but I would have heard him.'

'What about a car?' She pointed to a small car park beside the river on the other side of the road, and as she raised her arm Kirby admired the curve of her breast which the gesture revealed. 'Did you happen to notice if anyone has been parked there?'

Kirby shook his head. 'I've been here over an hour. There was a lorry there when I arrived, and that Morris turned up about five minutes ago. Apart from that there's been no one else.' There were times, he thought, when a policeman's training had its uses. As he was speaking he could not keep his eyes off her. If you don't ask, he thought, you don't get. 'Is there anything I can do to help?'

She looked down at him and smiled. 'I was meant to be meeting someone about twenty minutes ago. I was hoping he might buy me a drink.'

The smile told him he was in with a chance. 'That's funny. I was meant to be meeting someone too but they haven't turned up either. Do you think we'd better cut our losses?'

She rested her hands on her hips. 'And how exactly do you think we should do that?'

'You could let me buy you a drink.'

'Here?' With the tiniest lift of an eyebrow she showed what she thought of the Ruispidge Arms.

'I've got a motorbike. Why don't we go somewhere a bit better?'

She looked hard at him, and then glanced at the rocky slope that separated them. 'If you were to help me, I think I could manage that.'

Hardly believing it could be so easy, he clambered a few steps up the rocky slope and held out his hands to her. Her face solemn with concentration, she placed her hands in his and let him guide her down. She was wearing high-heeled shoes more suitable for a Mayfair pavement than a country walk. Loose stones shifted beneath her: she slid forwards, putting more of her weight on him than he was ready for, pushing him backwards down the slope. Automatically he drew her down after him. She stumbled against a tree root and collided with his chest. He almost lost his balance. For a moment her body, warm and alluring, rested lightly against his. He smelt her perfume, and saw very clearly that one of the long black lashes that fringed her eyes was bent out of true. A moment later she was several feet away from him, demurely smoothing down her dress.

'I'm Brian Kirby.' His voice was jerky and breathless; his habitual assurance had deserted him. 'Look – are you going to be okay on the back of a bike?' He eyed her thin, short-sleeved dress, then quickly looked away as it occurred to him she might misunderstand his reason for staring. 'It could get quite cold. Especially on the way back.'

'You can lend me your leather jacket. I'm Jemima Orepool.' She paused, letting a silence develop; he sensed that she was waiting for a reaction but he didn't know what it was. Then she said slowly, 'You're from London, aren't you? Are you on holiday?'

'I work down here.' He did not want to tell her what he did – not yet, perhaps never; some girls found his job put them off. 'There's a new place just opened on the Gloucester road. Do you know it – the Golden Fox? A sort of roadhouse. Shall we go there?'

'If you like.'

The Golden Fox was rumoured to be ridiculously expensive; but it had an air of American sophistication, and Jemima was a girl who obviously expected the best.

Kirby picked up the heavy jacket and they walked together down the steps from the bedraggled garden to the little forecourt in front of the pub.

Jemima stroked the seat of the motorbike. 'It's beautiful. Is it very fast? It looks as if it should be.'

'I did a ton once on the Great West Road,' he said modestly. He had nearly got booked for speeding, too: only his warrant card had saved him on that occasion. 'Have you got a scarf or something?'

'No, but it doesn't matter. I like to feel the wind in my hair.'

She turned and raised her arms. He understood at once that she wanted him to help her into the jacket, that she automatically assumed that someone would always be there to help her. He had no objection – quite the contrary: it gave him another opportunity to stand near her.

She watched as he climbed on the motorbike and started the engine. The jacket came down far below her waist, dwarfing her body and magnifying her attractions. There was something indecently sexual about the incongruity. He revved the engine higher than he needed. She climbed on to the bike and put her arms around his waist as if it were the most natural thing in the world.

Kirby took the road north, which was the longer way; he did not want to go through Lydmouth because someone he knew might see them. He took the bends a little faster than he would normally have done, and on one occasion he nearly killed them both when he overtook a lorry and narrowly avoided a collision with a car coming in the opposite direction.

On one or two of the sharper bends her hands tightened round his waist. When they nearly smashed into the oncoming car, she gripped him so hard that he almost cried out. The cool air ruffled his hair and blew through the thin material of his shirt and blazer. He was suspended helplessly in a condition that was neither joy nor agony but oscillated frantically between the two. If he had to die, though he was secretly unconvinced that death could ever take a personal interest in him, this would be a good time to do it.

The Golden Fox was a long, low building with an immense car park separating it from the main road. The owners had painted the building white and equipped the exterior walls with a lattice of black planks. Half a dozen cars were parked near the entrance, a door of baronial proportions studded with blackened nails. Kirby sent the bike into a long, roaring curve round the car park and coasted to a halt near the cars. As he switched off the engine, Jemima released him and climbed off the motorbike. Dance music was playing, just audible above the noise of a lorry on the road behind them.

'It looks a bit dead, doesn't it?'

'It's only Monday.' His voice sounded defensive, even to himself. He had wanted her to be impressed. 'Let's go and find that drink.'

The heavy door was standing open. Jemima led the way inside. The music was much louder in the foyer. There were wall lights disguised ineffectually as candles. A woman in a black dress, perhaps the manageress, came towards them, her mouth tightening in disgust as she saw Jemima – without a hat, a scarf, gloves or a handbag; wearing a man's flying jacket.

Jemima peeled herself out of the jacket and handed it to the woman, who was too surprised not to take it.

'I don't suppose you could lend me a comb?'

Jemima's vowel-mangling drawl and the assurance which lay behind it worked a magical transformation on the manageress. Her mouth relaxed and she led Jemima away to a cloakroom, leaving Kirby to go on to the bar.

'Would you get me a gin-and-french, Brian?' called Jemima as she disappeared. Kirby liked to hear her voice saying his name. It implied a miraculous intimacy between them, and demonstrated it for all the world – or at least the manageress – to see.

The bar was a cavernous room with few windows. The carpet had a pink background and the chairs and benches were upholstered with purple velvet. At one end was a long counter where a white-coated waiter chatted with a moon-faced barman. At the other end of the room was a small dais, empty except for an upright piano. The dance music boomed from a large radio fixed to a bracket on the wall. The centre of the floor had been cleared for dancing but no one was out there.

Only four of the twenty-odd tables were occupied. Middle-aged couples, all of them – businessmen, probably: two with their wives, one with his mistress, and one with a woman who might be either. Kirby was relieved to see there was no one there he knew. It was always a risk. That was one reason why he'd wanted to take Jemima to a place so far from Lydmouth.

The waiter, a tall thin man with a perpetual sneer welded to his face, showed Kirby to a table and took his order. He tried in the manner of his kind to make Kirby feel inferior. Kirby was more than equal to that challenge, and demanded nuts and a clean ashtray. Then Jemima came into the room, and the waiter's attitude – and indeed the attitude of most of the men in the room – subtly changed. The waiter pulled out a chair for her and asked if she would like olives as well as nuts.

Jemima ignored him. 'I thought you might need these,' she said to Kirby. 'They were in the jacket.' She laid his cigarette case, his lighter and his wallet on the table.

She had done something to her hair, he thought, and her eyes seemed brighter than before. He offered her a cigarette, which she accepted. When he lit it for her, she held his hand to steady the flame. She let the smoke trickle slowly from her nostrils.

'You didn't tell me you were a policeman.'

Kirby choked on his beer. So she had been through the wallet. He ought to feel aggrieved about that. She'd found his warrant card, obviously. Oh, Christ – the thought suddenly hit him – she must have found the contraceptives as well. At least she didn't seem upset by either discovery.

She put her elbows on the table. 'I've never met a copper before, not properly, I mean. I've always thought that dark blue uniform is very dashing. Like the Navy, but more so.'

'I don't wear the uniform much these days.'

'You're a detective? How thrilling. You must meet all sorts of interesting people.' She looked up at him through the long lashes. 'Tell me, is it true what they say, that there's honour among thieves?'

'Not that I've noticed. Most of them would nick their granny's last sixpence and not think twice about it. Are you staying down here?'

'In a way. I'm spending a month or two up at Clearland Court.'

Kirby tried to conceal his shock. 'Are you related to old Ruispidge, then?'

'He's my uncle. Mummy's brother. Why? Do you know him?'

'I've come across him,' Kirby said carefully. 'He's a magistrate and all that.'

'You don't have to tell me. You should hear him on the subject of law and order. It's all part of the country going to the dogs. The rot set in when we stopped flogging poachers.' She ground out the cigarette. 'Who were you waiting for at the pub?'

'Just someone I met this afternoon.' In his present company, the thought of a camper from Islington was worse than ludicrous.

Jemima was merciless. 'Who?'

'This girl. She said she might come down for a drink – she's camping with friends somewhere near the village – and I was at a loose end, so—'

Jemima let out a squeal of laughter. 'Not one of those fat slags in the tent?' Heads were turning towards their table. 'Oh Brian. You couldn't.'

Suddenly relaxed, he grinned at her. 'As it happens, I didn't.' He thought of the contraceptives and changed the subject. 'What do you think of this place?'

'Ghastly, isn't it?'

'Do you think so?'

She didn't bother to lower her voice. 'Terribly vulgar. Like one of those fake American roadhouses in darkest Surrey.'

'There's not much choice around here on a Monday evening.' He leant a little closer to her and tried to turn the Golden Fox to his advantage. 'The trouble is, with my job it can be hard to find somewhere for a drink where they don't know your face.'

'Must be awful for you, darling.'

He didn't know whether she was mocking him or not: he was out of his depth, and to his surprise he rather liked the sensation. 'So where do you usually go when you're in this part of the world?' His voice came out more roughly than usual, as though she were a witness in need of intimidating.

'Around here? Chance would be a fine thing. Uncle Tony doesn't believe in letting me gad about. He thinks it's bad for my character. Anyway I haven't any money.'

'But surely—'

'I'm absolutely *skint*, Brian. Besides, Uncle wouldn't approve of me coming out to places like this. It's not the sort of thing one does. By and large one doesn't get pissed in public. One does it in private instead.'

He shied away from the savagery in her voice, not knowing whether it was directed at him. 'London's a different kettle of fish, I suppose?'

'London's a very different kettle of fish,' she replied, mimicking his accent.

He pointed at her empty glass. 'Do you want another one of those?' he said curtly.

'All right.'

He summoned the waiter and ordered another round. When they were alone again, she touched his hand with one finger.

'Sorry. I must sound like a bitch. I got out of bed the wrong side today.'

'That's OK.' Her apology was harder to handle than her rudeness.

'It's not OK. It's Uncle Tony – it's all his fault. He's so mean. He caught me having a tiny cocktail before dinner yesterday. So then he spent the entire evening lecturing me about the evils of drink. And practically all the time he had a glass in his hand himself. Can you believe it? The hypocrite.'

The waiter arrived with their drinks.

'So you don't like Clearland Court very much?'

'I loathe it. I've not been down here since I was about ten. And the only reason I'm here now is because I haven't any money. As soon as I can, I'm going back to London.' She took a cigarette from his case without asking and waited for him to light it for her. 'I'm not really such a cow. Uncle Tony can be quite a sweetie, really. But he's so Victorian – no, much worse than that, Neanderthal or whatever it is. In his heart of hearts, he really thinks that men ought to drag their womenfolk along by their hair.' She sucked in the smoke. 'But that's enough about me. Let's talk about something interesting. Why did you want to become a policeman?'

'My dad said it was a good job. Secure, you get a pension at the end of it.' There had been other reasons, too: people had to look up to you if you were a policeman; sometimes they had to take orders from you, and sometimes you knew things about them which they would rather you didn't know. Buried far beneath the adult reasons were other motives, all the more potent because he'd never examined them – the stories he used to read of Sexton Blake and Sherlock Holmes, the Saint and Bulldog Drummond.

'Have you ever met a murderer?'

'One or two.' The girls who knew what he did almost always asked him this question sooner or later. It was a relief to find Jemima running true to form, in this at least.

She leaned across the table, so close that he could feel her breath on his cheek, and said in that confiding child's voice, 'What were they like, Brian? Were they different? I mean, could you tell afterwards that there was something strange about them?'

'Not really.' He stared at the wide mouth, the teeth glistening behind the red lips, and wondered what it would be like to kiss it. 'They were just ordinary folk.'

'Of course they weren't. They *killed* people.'

'Yes, but there were reasons. They got caught up in things. They had problems.'

'You mean anyone could be a murderer? I could? Or you?'

He shrugged. 'God knows.'

'But that's horrible,' she said. 'And I bet it's not true, either. I think it must be something you're born with.'

'It's something we're all born with, more or less.' His voice was irritable despite his efforts to conceal how he felt. He didn't want to talk about murderers or about being a policeman: he wanted them to talk about each other. 'Some people are much more likely to do it, of course. Maybe their minds were messed up from the start, or maybe they saw lots of violent grown-ups when they were a kid. I don't know – ask a trick cyclist. But if you ask me, anyone could be a murderer – if they're pushed hard enough, in a place where it hurts.'

He was surprised to hear himself talking like this: he had never formulated how he felt about murderers. But Jemima's reaction surprised him even more.

She sat back and pulled his cigarette case towards her. 'I want to go back now.'

'I thought—'

'Then I expect you thought wrong.' She had stubbed out the last cigarette after a few puffs, but now she took another and began to roll it round and round between her finger and thumb. Automatically he picked up his lighter. 'I'm bored,' she went on coldly. 'I want to go home.'

Kirby lit her cigarette. She stared into the middle distance, paying him as much attention as she would a waiter. Anger slid through him like a strong, cold drink.

'Then I'd better pay the bill.'

'Do what you like.' She stood up, pushing back her chair with the back of her legs. 'I'm going to the lavatory.'

She left the bar, the blue skirt swinging, drawing the eyes of the men after her. Kirby, aware that almost everyone in the room must know they'd had some kind of quarrel, strolled with exaggerated nonchalance towards the bar counter. It seemed to him that the barman and the waiter were studying him with undisguised scorn on their faces.

What angered him most of all was the injustice of it. He'd not felt like this since his eighth birthday, when his greatest enemy had kicked his new football, made of real leather, into the green, slow-moving canal, and he had watched it floating slowly downstream.

There were newspapers on the bar, and he picked up one of them at random while the barman was calculating the bill. It was a reflex gesture to avoid having to meet anyone's eyes. He didn't want to see mockery or, even worse, pity. The newspaper was the *Lydmouth Gazette*. He stared at the big black letters of the headline.

Jemima, he thought, how could you? It's so unfair. I'd like to teach you a lesson, my girl, I'd like to bloody kill you.

Then the sense of the headline sank in: LYDMOUTH CHURCH KILLING, he read. LOCAL WOMAN BRUTALLY SLAIN.

The barman put down a saucer carrying the bill on the newspaper. Kirby pushed it aside and continued reading, winnowing the few useful facts from the welter of background detail, local colour and speculation. So that was why Sergeant Fowles had been trying to get hold of him; the CID was under strength as it was, and Thornhill had the additional problem of that young blockhead Wilson to deal with. It was all of a piece – all part of this ruined day: the camper failing to turn up, Jemima raising hopes only to destroy them and now a murder investigation on his doorstep, an investigation that Kirby should have been part of from the start.

The barman cleared his throat. 'Haven't got all night, you know.'

Kirby slowly looked up, his face breaking into a small, unpleasant smile. He opened his wallet, angling it so that the man could see the warrant card. He heard a gratifying intake of breath on the other side of the counter as he laid a pound note on the top of the bill. The saucer returned with a little pile of change on it. Kirby scooped the coins into his hand, deciding not to leave a tip.

'You ought to be careful, mate,' he said, glancing up at the flat white face of the barman. 'You could be very vulnerable here. You know that?'

'I don't know what you mean,' the barman said in an undertone.

Kirby walked away, knowing that in these situations it was almost always wiser to say less rather than more. It was generally safe to assume that people behind any kind of bars had guilty consciences. He swayed slightly as he walked, the beer catching up on him at last.

The foyer was empty apart from the woman in the black dress who was listlessly painting her nails. Jemima hadn't even bothered to wait for him.

Despair rose inside him, sour like bile, pushing aside the murder case: that would teach him to fancy an upper-class bitch.

'I hope we'll see you again, sir,' the manageress said.

'I doubt it,' Kirby said savagely. 'Not if I have any choice in the matter.'

He went outside. It was still light, though the sun had gone and grey shadows had crept across the car park. Jemima was not beside the bike. For all he knew she had found herself another mug, someone prepared to drive her home in more comfort than the motorbike offered. What did it matter? The sooner he returned to Lydmouth and found Thornhill the better.

At that moment Jemima jumped up like a jack-in-a-box. She had been crouching behind the long bonnet of the nearest car. Bewildered, Kirby stared at her. She had his jacket over her shoulders and looked about fifteen. He opened his mouth to ask her what the hell she thought she was playing at.

'Boo!' she shouted.

The evening dissolved. Jemima ran towards him. The jacket fell to the ground.

'Jemima?' he said. 'Jemima?'

'Hush.'

Bare arms slid around his neck. Her hands drew his head down to hers. She began to kiss him with soft, warm lips. Her mouth tasted of gin-and-french. When she bit him, he gasped and tasted blood.

3

Charlotte looked doubtfully at the aspidistra on the table at her elbow. 'I knew I should have repotted it in the spring. It looks positively sickly.'

'Perhaps it's the heat.' Jill fanned herself with a newspaper.

'I don't think so. They thrive on warmth.' She glanced at Jill over the top of her glass. 'Did you say why you were at the Bull in the first place?'

Used to Charlotte's methods, Jill took the question in her stride. 'I was trying to have a word with Sir Anthony,' she said. 'We wanted a quote for the *Gazette*. But then his niece drove into the yard and nearly knocked me down.'

The two women were waiting for Philip, who was late for dinner. They were drinking sherry in the drawing room at Troy House. Jill was in the throes of explaining how she had ruined her best summer dress. She felt as though she were being interrogated by a hostile secret policeman.

'Jemima Orepool?' Charlotte said, temporarily diverted. 'Typical. Not a girl who looks before she leaps.'

'You know her?'

'Not to speak of. And I can't say I want to. How shall I put it? She has a certain reputation.' Charlotte smoothed her dress over plump thighs, her face wrinkling as if in the presence of an unpleasant smell. 'She was such a sweet thing when she was a child. She used to come down here in the early years of the war. Not often, but one saw her about occasionally.'

'What happened?'

'What always happens to children. They grow up.' Quite unconsciously Charlotte continued to stroke herself. 'She's an orphan now: Papa was killed at Dunkirk – he was in the Welsh Guards, I think – and the mother died in the Blitz. Sir Anthony's sister,' she added in passing. 'Rather flighty, but no malice in her.'

Jill had been following another line of thought. 'She seemed – she seemed very vulnerable.' She was finding it hard to match thoughts with words. 'Jemima, I mean.'

'Hard as nails in my opinion. They say she was living a very rackety life in London. Enormous debts, I gather.' Charlotte stopped stroking. 'And I believe there were other problems, too.' She lowered her voice. '*Men.* Chrissie Newton told me that her uncle had to drag her down here by the scruff of her neck. She—'

She broke off, hearing Philip's key in the front door.

'Sorry, I'm late. It's chaos at the office.' He rubbed his hands happily together and advanced on the drinks tray. 'Another drink for either of you? No?' He poured himself some whisky and squirted soda into the glass. He sat down and took one of the *Gazette*'s advertising forms from his pocket. 'This came in as we were closing. Any good to you?'

Jill skimmed through the advertisement. 'Perhaps.' She passed it to Charlotte.

'It looks wonderful,' Charlotte said, making up for Jill's lack of enthusiasm. 'Spacious room in family house. Well, you don't really want more than a room, do you?'

It was a rhetorical question, but Jill did her best to answer it. 'I was hoping to find a flat or a cottage, actually. Somewhere self-contained.'

'I'm sure you will, dear, one day. But for the time being, this might suit you very well. It's off the Chepstow Road – a very nice part of town, I always think. Of course it's a bus route, which is always so convenient. Telephone – excellent. Meals by arrangement. Happy family atmosphere. And the rent's not unreasonable, is it, when you think of all they're offering.'

Jill couldn't concentrate on what was being said. In her mind she saw Miss Kymin, a huddle of flesh and bone and clothes beneath the cherubs and cornucopias of the Ruispidge monument. She put down her glass and accepted the inevitable. 'I'll go and see it tomorrow.'

'I'd go this evening, dear.' Charlotte smiled impartially at the space between her husband and Jill. 'Otherwise you'll get lost in the crowd. This sort of advertisement always attracts a host of applicants.'

Philip offered his cigarette case. 'Seems a bit unethical. Well, almost.'

'Nonsense. If Jill takes this room, these people won't have to pay a penny for the advertisement. Anyway, it's one of the few perks we have. One might as well make use of it occasionally.'

Philip rummaged in his pocket, looking for his lighter. 'I'll run you up in the car after dinner, if you like.'

'No,' Jill said quickly. 'I can manage quite—'

Simultaneously Charlotte burst into speech: 'I was hoping we could discuss the accounts this evening, Philip. We really should have done it over the weekend.'

'I'd like the walk. I need the exercise.'

Her point won, Charlotte beamed. 'Why don't you take my bicycle? It's no trouble. Philip will bring it round from the shed, won't you, darling? You may need to put a teensy bit of air in the tyres.'

After dinner, Philip wheeled round a heavy, sit-up-and-beg bicycle with a sturdy basket slung between the handlebars, but without gears. Jill suspected Charlotte hadn't ridden it since the war: she was the wrong shape for cycling. Philip pumped up the tyres. He and Charlotte waved goodbye as Jill pushed the bike on to the road, making her feel like an undutiful daughter.

'I hope it's a super room,' Charlotte called as Jill cycled away. 'And remember, one can always make changes.'

Pedalling was hard work, especially uphill. Heavy grey clouds blanketed most of the sky, holding in the heat of the day. There was no wind. Soon Jill felt sticky and breathless. Her nose would be glowing like a beacon. Depression crept steadily over her.

After all Charlotte's excitement, the room was not a success. The house lay down a mud track on the outskirts of town. The room itself was poky. The furniture should have gone to the rag-and-bone man. The landing smelt of dirty lavatories and old fried food. Three children, each with a halo of jam around his or her mouth, ran up and down the stairs continuously while she was there, apparently engaged in a competition to see who could make the most noise. Their mother talked about her ailments, and their father squeezed Jill's bottom as she passed through a doorway in front of him.

Jill extracted herself with difficulty from the woman's medical history and rode back into town. The thought of Charlotte's likely reaction did not encourage her to go straight back to Troy House. On impulse she turned left into Broadwell Drive and cycled briskly along the road to the four bungalows at the end.

Miss Kymin's bungalow had already acquired a forlorn air. The curtains were drawn, the grass seemed longer than it had in the morning, the paintwork seemed to have lost its lustre.

Mrs Milkwall was pruning the roses in her front garden. As Jill approached, she straightened up and dropped the secateurs in her trug. Jill dismounted and propped the bicycle against Miss Kymin's gatepost. Mrs Milkwall's dog ran out of the porch and barked vigorously.

'Ollie! Shut your mouth!' shouted Mrs Milkwall; the dog wagged its tail and went back to the porch.

'Hello,' Jill said. 'Has all the excitement died down?'

'Had the police here all day, just about.' Mrs Milkwall sniffed but her face was pleased. 'It's not nice, is it? Broadwell Drive will be in all the newspapers. It will give people quite the wrong idea.'

'I'm sure no one would—'

'My Ern says it will mean our place is worth less. Folks won't want to live next-door to a house whose owner was murdered.'

'It could work the other way. But I wouldn't worry if I were you. After all, Miss Kymin wasn't killed here. And people have very short memories.'

'That nasty young man was poking around all over the place,' went on Mrs Milkwall, refusing to be comforted. 'Not the older one, the inspector: the other one, who looks about sixteen. Had a nasty look in his eyes, he did. I wouldn't like to meet him on a dark night.'

Jill glanced at the bungalow next-door. 'I thought the police might have left a guard here.'

'No point. They'll have taken anything they want.'

'What about the cat? Has anyone taken that?'

'It was around at teatime, wailing its head off in the back garden. Anyway, who'd want a scraggy little thing like that?'

Jill opened her handbag, which was in the basket hanging from the handlebars, and took out her purse. 'If I give you some money, would you feed it for a day or two? I'm sure – Alice, was it? – would eat whatever your dog eats. And perhaps she might like a saucer of milk occasionally.' She took out a ten-shilling note and held it loosely between her fingers.

Mrs Milkwall frowned. 'What d'you mean – go into her garden? Feed it in the shed like she used to?'

Jill glanced at the dog lying at his ease in the porch. 'That would be best, I imagine.'

'Just for a day or two, mind.'

'Just for a day or two.' Jill handed Mrs Milkwall the money over the gate. 'But why do you want to do it?'

Jill knew that she would find it hard to answer that question even to herself, let alone to Mrs Milkwall. 'I was wondering about getting a cat,' she lied.

Mrs Milkwall teased the note through her fingers. 'Plenty of nice kittens around. Our Ern's sister—'

'I wanted a full-grown cat. A house-trained female.' Jill sensed she was getting into far deeper waters than she'd intended. 'Just an idea, you see. I've not made up my mind. But if you feed her for a day or two I'll have a chance to think about it.'

Mrs Milkwall tucked the ten-shilling note down the neck of her blouse and worked it into some recess in her undergarments. 'I'll go over there when I've finished the pruning.'

Jill said goodbye, mounted the bicycle and rode away. She didn't want a cat. In any case, you needed a home if you were going to have a pet. She briefly entertained the possibility of asking Charlotte if she would like to have Alice. The thought of Charlotte's likely response made her want to giggle and shudder simultaneously. She turned into the Chepstow Road and cycled towards town. Charlotte was going to be annoyed enough as it was, not that she would dream of saying so, because the room had failed to suit.

The front wheel of the bicycle jolted through a pothole, and the handbag shifted in the basket. Jill glanced down at the bag, noticing that it was not closed; the catch was defective, and she made a mental note to have it seen to. At that moment the first few drops of rain splashed down from the lead-coloured sky.

She swore. The raindrops were large and heavy, the sort that usher in a downpour. She had almost reached the war memorial, where she would turn right off the main road towards Troy House. By the time she reached it, she would be soaked.

The idea came to her fully formed. Why not ride up to the Bull Hotel, which was no distance away? It would have the additional advantage of further postponing the need to break the news to Charlotte. She could shelter at the Bull and have a drink; perhaps it would be worth asking Quale a few questions, or perhaps she would know some of the journalists who had come down from London. Suddenly she yearned to be among her own kind in the sort of smoky Fleet Street pub she had loathed when she worked in Town.

Jill pedalled hard up the High Street. The rain drummed on the road in front of her, raising clouds of dust like miniature explosions. Men were sheltering from the rain under the big pillared porch of the hotel, and one of them whistled at her. She turned left into Bull Lane, and right under the archway of the hotel's yard.

No one was about. A clatter of saucepans came through the open window of the kitchen. Someone was whistling 'We'll Meet Again'. She dismounted and wheeled the bicycle through the doorway of the barn. It was dark in here apart from the area immediately inside the doorway. She propped the machine against the abandoned trap and turned to leave. A long drink, she thought, that's what I need: something with a good deal of gin in the bottom. The rain pattered on the roof above her head, and puddles were already forming among the cobbles of the yard.

There was no warning, or none that she knew about. No footsteps, no darkening of the light. Not even a sense of displaced air moving behind her.

The last thing she felt was the unbearable brightness of pain.

PART FIVE

1

Mrs Abberley was restless. When the policemen left her she returned to her little sitting room and sat there staring out of the window.

'Papist bastards,' she muttered to herself. 'I'll learn them a lesson.' In her heart she blamed the Suttons for Mr Carter's retirement and death; she knew she was being unreasonable, and she gloried in her irrationality.

Slowly light and colour seeped away, and slowly she became calmer. She watched the people waiting on the pavement in the hope that something sensational might happen. She watched the policemen moving to and fro, growing younger by the minute as policemen tended to do.

The wallpaper lost its pattern and the rain came. Still she did not move. The leaves in the churchyard blurred into the generalised green of the trees; soon the greenness turned to shadows. Water ran down the window, sending ripples of distortion through the world outside. The people left. Soon there was only a uniformed constable huddled in his cape in the shelter of the lych gate. There would be other policeman out there, she guessed. Perhaps they would keep watch all night.

Mrs Abberley sat and thought and waited. The rain stopped. The church clock began to strike ten. She stood up slowly; she had been sitting so long that her muscles had stiffened. There was no hurry. Perhaps she would have a cup of tea before she went.

To her disgust she found that this would not be practical: the milk in the larder had turned sour, even standing on the marble slab. The weather was to blame. It occurred to her that a refrigerator might have its uses.

Grumbling to herself, she put on her coat and hat. Purse in one pocket, torch in the other: then she was ready. She let herself out of the back door.

The garden smelled of fresh earth. The light from the kitchen window glistened on the path that led down to the compost heap. Here, squeezed between the compost heap and the corner of the wall, was a door half-hidden beneath a curtain of ivy. It opened quietly – she had taken the precaution of oiling the hinges.

Immediately on the other side was more ivy and a screen of self-seeded saplings. Mrs Abberley slipped round them and into the wider walled expanse of the Vicarage kitchen garden. The garden stirred up her anger. The Suttons were allowing it to revert to a wilderness. She remembered it before and during the war when there had not been a weed in sight.

Mrs Abberley followed the broad path down the middle of the garden. She dared not use the torch because there was a chance it might be seen from one of the upstairs rooms at the back of the Vicarage.

The path brought her to another gate. To her surprise she found that it was bolted. The Suttons never bolted any of the gates; sometimes she wondered whether they even bothered to lock their doors at night.

She drew back these bolts and let herself out into the unmetalled path beyond. The path ran behind the gardens on the Vicarage side of Church Street and was wide enough for a car. She switched on the torch; it was very dark here because there were no street lights – only a dim radiance filtering down from the solitary street lamp in Bull Lane. Hugging the left-hand wall, she followed the path to its end at the bottom of Bull Lane.

She walked slowly up to the High Street. She passed a row of shuttered shops and, on the other side of the road, the archway into the yard of the Bull Hotel. Two cars swished by, and she heard loud masculine voices in the distance.

On the corner of the High Street and Bull Lane was a red telephone kiosk set back on a plot of ground it shared with the new public lavatories. With difficulty she pulled open the heavy door of the box and went inside.

With her back to the High Street she fumbled through the directory until she found the entry she wanted. It was just as well that they had modernised the local exchange and installed the automatic one after the war. As the telephone was ringing at the other end, she realised that she was crossing the fingers of both her hands, a practice learnt in childhood and never discarded on the principle of better safe than sorry. At last the ringing stopped.

'I saw you last night,' Mrs Abberley said when she was connected, and when she had made sure whom she was talking to.

'What's that? Who's speaking?'

'I saw you last night. I saw her go in first, and then you. Must have been about five minutes later.'

'I don't know what you're talking about.'

'Please yourself. I saw you coming out too. Down the path and through the lych gate. And then—'

'I'm going to put the phone down.'

'You nearly fell over once, didn't you? And you were trying to hide something under your jacket.'

'That's utter nonsense.' There was a click at the other end of the line, as if someone had snapped open a lighter.

'So I'll tell that policeman, shall I? The one that came to see me tonight.'

'He'd never believe you.'

'Why not? Of course there's no reason why I should tell him. Not necessarily. After all, I might have been mistaken. At that time of evening, it's easy to think you see things moving. At my age I sometimes doze off, too. And when I sleep I dream. Did you dream last night?'

'It sounds to me as if you imagined it. Perhaps you need a holiday? I might be able to help, I suppose.'

'I don't want a holiday.'

'I'm not in a position to offer—'

'And I don't want money, either.' As she spoke, it occurred to her that in fact a little money would come in very handy. There was the refrigerator, for example. But first things first.

'Then what the hell do you want?'

She played with him for a little longer and then she told him.

2

'You wouldn't have credited it, Sarge,' Wilson was saying to Fowles. 'Some of her underwear was – well – like a tart's.'

Fowles, older and warier than Wilson, cleared his throat in warning; he had heard Thornhill's steps on the stairs.

'Known many tarts, Wilson, have you?' Thornhill said. 'How interesting. When you have a spare moment, you must tell me what other areas of expert knowledge you have.'

Both Fowles and Wilson, who had been leaning on either side of the counter, straightened up and took a step backwards.

'Anything from Sergeant Kirby?'

'No, sir,' said Fowles. 'He hasn't called in yet. Do you want me to send someone round?'

Thornhill shook his head. 'There's not much more we can do until the morning.'

'But there was a call from the hospital just now,' Fowles said, darting a sly glance at the inspector. 'About Miss Francis.'

'What about her? What's she doing there?'

'Sorry, sir – I thought you'd have heard. Quale found her in the yard at the Bull about an hour ago. Just lying in the barn at the back – very groggy. He thought she'd fainted or something so he called an ambulance. But we've just had a call from the hospital to say they've found a bruise on her head.'

'Could it have been an accident?'

Fowles shrugged.

'Is she all right? Has she come round?'

'She came round almost immediately. But apparently she can't remember anything apart from the fact that she was going to have a drink at the Bull because it was raining. She had a bike – that was in the barn with her.'

'Who's been down there?'

Fowles licked his lips. 'No one yet, sir. Uniformed are overstretched because of the house-to-house.'

'Dear God,' said Thornhill, who rarely swore. 'Why wasn't I told?'

'You were in a meeting with Mr Williamson, sir, and—'

'With a murder case, anything could be relevant. Was she robbed?'

'The hospital said her handbag went with her in the ambulance.'

Thornhill looked at his watch. He knew Wilson was watching him with interest, eyes half-closed, mouth pursed. 'You had better cut along home,' Thornhill told him. 'I want you back here at seven-thirty sharp.' When Wilson hesitated, Thornhill snarled, 'Go on – off you go. I've had enough of you for one day.'

Wilson slipped away, his expression startled and unexpectedly vulnerable. Fowles said nothing and kept his face wooden. He'd learned in the last six months that it was worth handling Thornhill with caution.

Thornhill went back upstairs and into his own room. He sat down behind his desk. For an instant he had an overwhelming desire to put his head on his arms and go to sleep. Instead, he told himself sternly that this wouldn't do, and reminded himself that he'd had nothing to eat since his sketchy lunch with Williamson, and nothing to drink since a cup of tea in the middle of the afternoon. He picked up the telephone and dialled the hospital.

The sister in charge of Jill Francis's ward confirmed what Fowles had told him. There appeared to be little wrong with her apart from a bruise and headache, but the doctor wanted to keep her in for a night for observation; it was always wise to err on the side of caution where head injuries were concerned. When Thornhill suggested that the police might need to question her, the sister told him crisply that Miss Francis was asleep and that no one would be asking her any questions until the morning. She could tell him nothing about the nature of the bruise, and suggested that he should discuss it with the doctor who had examined her. Unfortunately, she went on, the doctor had gone off duty.

Thornhill stood up and picked up his hat. When he reached the door, he hesitated and went back to the desk and the telephone. He dialled his own number. It was answered on the second ring, which meant that she had been waiting by the phone.

'Edith? It's me.'

'Are you all right?'

'I'm fine.' He was irritated by his wife's concern.

'There's no news?'

This was an old arrangement between them. 'Yes' would mean the case he was working on had reached an arrest. 'No,' he said. 'I'm not sure what time I'll be back – I have to go out now. You might as well go to bed.'

'Yes,' Edith said.

'Are the children OK?' he added, now feeling obscurely guilty. 'And yourself?'

'They're asleep.'

'Goodnight then. I'll try not to disturb you when I come in.'

Thornhill put down the telephone, knowing that whatever time he came in she would be awake, waiting. On his way downstairs he noticed that there was a line of light under the door of Williamson's room. He persuaded himself that it wasn't worth interrupting the superintendent to tell him about the possible attack on Jill Francis, not at this juncture. Fowles looked up as he walked down the stairs.

'I'll be at the Bull, Sergeant. I may go straight home after that. I'm not sure.'

'Yes, sir. Would you like me to tell Mr Williamson?'

'Not unless he asks.'

Thornhill went out into the street. The rain had done little to clear the air. The pavements were empty and most of the shop windows were in darkness. The Bull Hotel, however, was still vigorously alive. A wedge of light spilled across the pavement from its open front door. Several men, some with glasses in their hands, were standing under the porch and talking loudly. More cars than usual were parked outside. Thornhill overheard scraps of conversation as he went into the hotel. They were discussing the Kymin case and drinking shorts. Journalists, probably, from London.

In the hall, the manager, 'Bomber' Lancaster, a harassed expression on his flushed face, was talking about train times to London with an aggrieved guest. Quale, who was leaning across the reception desk, openly eavesdropping, was the first to see Thornhill. He straightened up, and his face went blank. It was as if his mind were an infernal calculating machine, Thornhill thought; you could almost hear the whir of the wheels turning.

'Mr Thornhill,' Lancaster said with enthusiasm, scenting a chance to escape. 'What can I do for you? Shall we go up to the office?'

'I'd like a word with Mr Quale, if I may.'

Lancaster smoothed his handlebar moustache and emitted a jerky but conciliatory series of syllables, of which only 'of course' and 'my dear fellow' were distinguishable.

'Let's go outside,' Thornhill said to Quale.

'A lovely evening now the rain's stopped.' Lancaster abruptly discarded his rôle as mine host. 'About Miss Francis, is it? I thought she'd fainted or something.'

Thornhill smiled and said thank you. He put his hand on Quale's elbow and steered the old man down the hall towards the back entrance. 'Who's that?' he heard the man with Lancaster ask. The door scraped against the floor as Quale opened it.

As soon as they went outside, Quale pulled out a packet of five Woodbine and lit up. 'What's all this then, Mr Thornhill?' His head swayed like a questing tortoise's from side to side. 'Miss Francis? I thought it might be a fit.'

'Probably was. We're just checking. Routine.' Why the hell was he here? Thornhill asked himself. It was half-past ten at night and he was in the middle of a murder investigation. Of course there might be a connection. It was arguably his duty to make sure that there wasn't. 'Tell me what happened.'

'I slipped out for a fag about half-past nine. I'd just got outside when I heard something.' He waved the glowing tip of his cigarette towards the barn. 'Over there. Sort of moaning, it was. I went over and there she was – half under that old trap. There was enough light to see who it was, so I called her name, shook her shoulder. She mumbled something but she wasn't well, so I thought I'd better get Mr Lancaster. So I went back inside. He thought an ambulance would be the best thing.' Quale edged a little nearer to Thornhill. 'He doesn't like doctors on the premises: bad for business, you understand.'

'I would have thought an ambulance would be worse.'

'He told it to come round the back. And got me to lock the back door until it had come and gone.'

'And?'

'I put a blanket over her and waited until the ambulance came. It was about ten minutes.'

Thornhill moved towards the dark entrance of the barn. He took out his torch and panned the beam round the barn. The light was too feeble to do much more than emphasise the shadows at the back and the sides. The place was full of rubbish: so much wasted space. He wondered why Lancaster hadn't had it converted into garages.

'Where was she? Show me exactly.'

Quale pointed at the trap. 'Sort of on her side down there. Beside the bike and with her feet towards the door.'

'Handbag?'

'Just there – by the wheel of the trap.' Quale hesitated. 'Is that what this is about? I never touched it, I swear.'

Thornhill walked round the barn, shining the torch up into the rafters and into the crumbling cracks of the masonry and down to the dusty flagged floor.

'If there's something been nicked, it must have been those ambulance men. Like bleeding magpies, that lot. Or maybe someone at the hospital.'

Thornhill turned back to him. 'Who said anything had been stolen?'

'In my job you can't be too careful.' Quale drew himself up to his full height of five foot three. 'My reputation is very precious to me, Mr Thornhill.' He dropped his cigarette end and ground it under his heel. 'Let's face it, if it got around that I was light-fingered, I wouldn't have a job.'

'As far as I know, there's nothing missing.' Thornhill hitched up his trouser legs and crouched beside the trap. He poked at the rubbish which had accumulated beneath and around it. Dust swirled on the floor. 'Who else came in here besides you and the ambulance men?'

'One or two of the kitchen staff.' Quale raised his hands, palms out. 'Well, why not? They wanted to see what had happened. It's only natural. Oh, and three of the gentlemen of the press poked their noses inside too. That was before we locked the back door. Just in case there was something there for them. But they decided there wasn't.'

The torch beam touched something which gleamed of gold. Thornhill edged further underneath the trap and stretched out a hand. It was a slim, round powder compact, made of gold, with a blue enamel lid decorated with flowers.

Quale bent down. 'What is it?'

'Something Miss Francis may have dropped.' Thornhill stood up and slipped the compact into his pocket.

'I hope she's all right, sir. Very nice lady, Miss Francis. I was thinking that only this afternoon when she was here with Miss Jemima.'

'Who's Miss Jemima?'

'Sir Anthony's niece.' Quale's voice was incredulous. 'I thought you'd know. They had tea in the lounge. Leastways Miss Francis had tea and Miss Jemima had a Bloody Mary. There'd been an accident. Miss Jemima almost knocked her down when she drove into the yard.'

Thornhill had had enough of the Ruispidges for one day. He was wasting his time here. He heard the scrape of the back door and footsteps in the yard.

'All serene, eh?' said the manager. There was an undercurrent of anxiety in his voice. He stood in the doorway and leaned against one of the door posts as if his weight was too much for his legs to cope with. 'No problems, I hope?'

'I don't think so. Thank you, Quale.'

Quale scuttled past the burly figure of Lancaster and disappeared through the back door.

'Are you going off duty now, Inspector? If you are you're welcome to join me for a nightcap.'

'That's very kind, sir, but I can't spare the time at the moment.'

Lancaster moved with him towards the gate out of the yard. 'The poor lady just fainted, didn't she? What they're prone to do, eh? The ladies, God bless them!' The stumbling flow of words trickled into silence.

'I'll say goodnight, sir.'

'I say, there's nothing funny about this, is there? I have to think of the reputation of the hotel and all that.'

'This was just a routine call, sir.'

'I have to be especially careful, you see, with all these journalists in the house. My God, they're quick. One of them was asking me who you were the minute you came in.'

'You have a lot of them staying with you?'

'Six tonight, and four more booked in for tomorrow. It's bloody marvellous for trade.' Lancaster sighed and Thornhill could smell the whisky on his breath. 'The trouble is, between ourselves, it's the wrong sort of publicity.' He twitched, looked over his shoulder, as if fearful someone was eavesdropping. 'Still, mustn't grumble. Goodnight.'

Thornhill thanked him and said goodbye. He left the hotel by the front door, intending to collect his car from the yard behind police headquarters. As he was negotiating his way through the knot of drinkers on the pavement outside the Bull, one of them recognised him.

'Hello, it's Mr Thornhill, isn't it?' He and the others clustered round in a vaguely threatening formation of glasses, cigarettes and red faces. Thornhill continued walking.

'Anything you can tell us, Inspector? Got any clues?'

'No comment.' Thornhill was past them now. He walked steadily along the pavement, his eyes on the comforting light above the front door of the police station.

Someone laughed. 'It was the vicar did it. Makes a change from choir boys.'

Thornhill walked on. Journalists were like that, he told himself: prepared to jettison all standards of decency for a good story; they measured their success by the circulation figures of their newspapers. They were all tarred with the same brush.

Rather than go through the front entrance, which would have meant meeting Fowles and running the risk of meeting Williamson, he turned down the side road which led to the car park at the back. It was darker here and no one was about. He pushed his left hand into his jacket pocket. His fingers closed round the smooth, hard outlines of the powder compact. He should have mentioned it to Lancaster. It might not belong to Jill Francis. It could be anyone's.

He saw no one as he climbed into the little Austin. He put the key in the ignition. His left hand was still in his jacket pocket, and the metal was growing warm, feeding off the heat of his hand. He took the compact out and sniffed it. He thought that he recognised the smell, faint but unmistakable, of Jill Francis.

3

Charlotte Wemyss-Brown lowered a tent-like nightdress over her head. It billowed towards the floor. Eventually her pink, scrubbed face emerged from its folds.

'I don't see what all the fuss is about,' she said. 'She fainted or slipped – then she fell and hit her head.'

Philip sat down heavily on the bed and took off his slippers. 'That doctor thought it was odd that the bruise was at the back of the head.' He put the slippers together and aligned them with his bedside table; Charlotte liked things to be neat.

'I'm sure he's just making things complicated. I expect there's a perfectly simple explanation. Perhaps the door has a low lintel. If you ask me' – she tugged back the eiderdown viciously from her side of the bed – 'everyone's making rather a lot of fuss about a relatively minor accident. I can't stop thinking about what happened to poor Catherine Kymin only last night. It rather puts things into perspective, doesn't it?'

'It does indeed.'

'It's most inconvenient, too – that it should happen now, I mean. Just when you need all hands on deck.'

'We'll manage.'

'I'm sure you will.' Charlotte climbed into bed and picked up her book and her glasses. She settled the glasses on her nose. 'We'll have to finish the accounts tomorrow evening. It was such a shame having to rush up to the hospital just as we were beginning to see light at the end of the tunnel.'

Philip got into bed beside her. He rested his hand on her thigh. 'I thought you were wonderful this evening, dear – the way you dealt with that staff nurse.' He chuckled. 'The look on her face.'

'I believe in speaking my mind. And Jill was cold – she needed an extra blanket at once. After all, we're paying for it.' She smiled grimly. 'It's our National Health Service.'

Philip slowly stroked the thigh. Charlotte's thin nightdress grew warm under the palm of his hand.

'I wonder how Jill got on with that room she went to see.' Charlotte edged her body a little closer to her husband's. 'I forgot to ask.'

'We'll find out tomorrow.' Philip twisted his torso and brought his other hand into play. What had begun as a means of distracting Charlotte was also distracting him. Jill, pale and small in a high hospital bed, was very far away. 'Did you – um—?'

'Yes, dear.' Charlotte effortlessly understood that Philip was referring to her Dutch cap. She turned her body towards him. 'Philip,' she said in a voice that had suddenly become soft and low, 'you do love me, don't you?'

4

Banished to the kitchen, Sambo whined at the door that led to the hall. He was an old dog and the training he had acquired so painfully as a puppy was beginning to desert him.

Like dog, like master, Giles Newton thought. He walked slowly along the hall and hesitated outside the study door. He was tempted to have a nightcap but knew if he did he would find it hard to stop. He had had far too much to drink the previous evening. The resulting hangover was too fresh in his memory. He needed to keep a clear head, now more than ever.

Turning out the lights as he went, he went upstairs with dragging steps. There were some of Chrissie's sleeping tablets in the bathroom cupboard: they would do instead. He noticed that there was still a line of light beneath the door of the room he shared with his wife. He went into the bathroom to find the tablets and do his teeth.

Chrissie was sitting up in bed waiting for him. She wasn't even pretending to read. Christ, Newton thought, she looks like a horse with colic. It was a warm night but she was hugging herself. He forced himself to smile at her. One of the sleeping tablets had caught in his throat. Keeping his back to her, he emptied the contents of his pockets on to the dressing table and began to undress. His neck muscles were stiff with tension.

'Giles, we have to talk.'

He simulated a yawn. 'Must we? It's been one hell of a day. Can't it wait until morning?'

'No. It can't. Anyway, you'd just find another excuse for putting it off. You're like a little boy, Giles. You think if you ignore something it will go away.'

He climbed into his pyjama trousers and knotted the cord, noticing the way his waist was thickening and his belly was beginning to bulge. His pubic hair and the hair on his chest was grey.

Chrissie blinked rapidly several times. 'I saw that letter from the school. The one which arrived this morning.'

In a way it was a relief. He put on a show of anger: 'You've been prying in my desk.' The thought of what she might find – might have found – made him feel weak. 'Is this an old habit or one you've developed recently?'

'I was dusting. I couldn't help seeing it – it was on the blotter.'

'It was in its envelope.'

'I knew it was from the school.' She waved away the objection as though it was irrelevant. 'Why haven't you paid the fees this term?'

Newton picked up his cigarette case and lighter from the dressing table. 'Because it's not important. When I was at school, my father was often several terms in arrears. It was perfectly common – well, at least it used to be. The trouble is, even the decent schools seem to be run by accountants these days. It's all happened since the war. Damn it, they run the place like a pawn shop.'

'Can we pay?'

'Of course we can. It's just that it will be more convenient next month when my salary comes in.'

'But shouldn't we do it sooner than that?'

He shrugged.

'Giles, *could* we do it sooner?'

'It's more a question of convenience.' He drew deeply on his cigarette. 'It's not been a good year. Several of our investments haven't been behaving very well, largely because of what the Chancellor's up to. In fact, I was wondering if the housekeeping need be quite so lavish in future.'

'But I don't understand. I thought we were quite comfortable.' She was sitting straight up in bed now, her face creased and ugly, like a monkey's. 'What with what Daddy left me and—'

'Don't you understand anything?' He slammed his hand down on the dressing table. The coins jumped up and down. 'Things have changed. What was comfortable in 1939 can be bloody uncomfortable now.'

'Don't be like that, Giles. I only want to know what's happening. Then perhaps I could help.'

'Help? And what do you think you could do? Find a job?'

For a long moment he watched her face disintegrate. He wished the words unsaid. More than that, he wished he was the young man concealed within his ageing body. Does she know, he wondered at the same time, that crying makes her look even uglier? He felt angry with her for putting him into this invidious position. He also felt enormous pity for himself.

In the end the anger triumphed -- that and the desire to make a gesture, and most of all the need to get away from her accusing face. He scooped up his cigarette case, lighter and clothes and stalked to the door, injured masculine dignity in a pair of patched pyjamas.

'I think I shall sleep in the spare room tonight.'

She said nothing as he went out of the room. She did not even cry. In a way her silence was the worst thing of all.

5

Shortly after half-past eleven on Monday evening, David Thornhill sat up in bed and searched increasingly wildly for the baby's vest which contributed so much to his emotional security. A moment later, he called for his mother, his voice high and wavering, nearing the brink of panic. She was already padding on her bare feet down the landing.

Richard Thornhill, who had just got into bed, sat up and turned on the light. He was glad to have an excuse not to try to go to sleep. After a while, Edith came back.

'He wants you.' She slid into bed beside him. 'I was almost asleep.'

He went along to David's room. The light was still on, and his son was watching the doorway with large bright eyes. The vest was locked into both hands and pushed up against his nose, obscuring most of his mouth.

'Daddy. Will you take me to the park to play football on Saturday?'

'If I can.' Even as a boy, Thornhill had found football tedious, an opinion partly based on lack of aptitude for the game.

'Promise?'

'I will if I can. I promise that.'

'Other people's dads promise to. Why can't you?'

'You know why I can't. It's time to go to sleep now.' He turned out the light and sat on the edge of the bed until David's breathing grew slow and regular. While he waited, Thornhill found himself wondering how he would feel if Edith or David or Elizabeth were murdered. He tried to imagine the dull, grinding horror of it, the desire for revenge, the knowledge that the victim was now permanently absent, a part of oneself lost for ever. Perhaps Miss Kymin's case was worse still: she had no close relations; no one had admitted even to liking the woman. There was no one to mourn her.

He went back to bed. Edith was lying on her back. As he went in to their bedroom, the light from the landing gleamed on the whites of her eyes. He slipped into bed. It was a warm night and they had only a sheet and a blanket over them.

'It's too hot to sleep,' Edith said.

'I don't feel sleepy in any case.' Thornhill, who was also lying on his back, reached out his hand and found hers. Her fingers tightened around his.

'I hate it when you're on a murder case.'

'So do I.' This was only partly true. A murder case made him feel useful and necessary; it was the ultimate justification for the long, tedious hours he devoted to unravelling petty crimes and satisfying the whims of bureaucrats, perhaps the ultimate justification for being alive. For much of the time, too, he relished the excitement and the sense of importance it gave him.

'How is it going?'

'There's not a shadow of a lead yet. If we don't get something soon, Hendry will have to call in the Yard.'

'I wish he would.'

'It would mean we'd still do most of the work but get none of the glory. Assuming there is any glory to be got out of this.'

'There's something horribly personal about all this. Because we were at church with her yesterday. Oh my God.'

'What?'

She let out a breath in a tremulous sigh. 'It's only just occurred to me. I suppose the murderer might have been there too – sitting in the congregation.' She turned her head on the pillow; her face was a blur. 'That makes it worse.'

'Perhaps it would be best if Hendry did call in the Yard.' Thornhill was following his own line of thought, which ran alongside Edith's without actually touching it. 'We're too close to see it all objectively. Then we have the added problem of people like Ruispidge throwing their weight around.'

'Have you seen his niece? Jemima somebody. Someone pointed her out to me after church. She's awfully pretty.'

Thornhill found himself thinking of Jill Francis: not a pretty woman — pretty was quite the wrong word for her.

'If I turn over,' Edith said, 'will you hold me? I can't stop thinking of that poor woman.'

6

Jean Jones was afraid of the dark. Despite her mother's scorn, she slept with her door open and the landing light on. The alarm clock ticked like a bomb on her bedside table. She stretched out her hand and tilted the clock so the light fell on its face. It was almost midnight.

'Brian,' she whispered. 'Brian.'

Her mother's snores penetrated the partition wall between them. Brian Kirby still wasn't back. Jean guessed he was with a girl. Jealousy filled her, burning deeper and deeper inside her, twisting and turning until it found its way into every cranny. She had a brief but agreeable fantasy in which the faceless girl fell in the river; she surfaced long enough to beg Jean to throw her a life belt ('I can't swim!'); Jean smiled aloofly at her and slowly shook her head; and then the girl began to plead as the waters closed above her head, abasing herself in a most satisfactory manner, but to no avail; and finally she drowned.

Jean slipped out of bed and drifted across the chilly linoleum to the window. She looked down on the road below. All was quiet. She stared at the place where Brian usually left his motorbike, willing him to arrive like a genie in a puff of smoke.

In the next room, the snores slipped into a deeper register. The cow was properly asleep, tired out by her long day in Newport. Jean shied away from the implications of that. They had had a dreadful row this evening after her mother returned, on the subject of yesterday evening. They hadn't seen each other for almost twenty-four hours because at seven-thirty on Sunday evening her mother had gone next-door to watch their neighbour's television, leaving Jean with strict instructions to stay at home, finish her homework and go to bed. She had come back late, by which time Jean had been pretending to be asleep, and left early in the morning for Newport. Jean had had no inkling of the storm that was waiting to burst over her head.

'Where were you last night, young lady?' her mother had shouted, waving a copy of the *Gazette* in her face. 'I popped back for a minute and the house was empty. And *now* I hear there was a flaming murderer on the loose.'

'What murder? I don't understand.'

'What are you trying to do, Jean?' Her mother dropped the newspaper on the table and pointed dramatically at the big headline. 'Look at that. Do you want to get yourself killed?'

Jean had taken refuge in silence. In her mind she was shrieking with panic. She had told Mr Thornhill, Brian's boss, that she had been at home all evening. At the time Jean hadn't known that someone had been killed. That wouldn't make any difference. They could probably put you in jail for lying to a policeman investigating a murder.

'Where did you go?' her mother said.

'Nowhere. Just out for some fresh air.'

How could Jean tell them the truth? That she liked to see Brian Kirby coming home? That she had left the house just after nine o'clock on Sunday and run to the churchyard, where there was a place where you could lie in the long grass between the yews and watch the length of Church Street. While she was waiting, someone had come out of the church. Jean had taken little notice at the time, except to hope that she wouldn't be seen, because she was watching for Brian. She had been in the middle of a daydream. ('Fancy seeing you here,' Brian had said. 'It's a lovely evening for a stroll. Won't you take my arm?')

But Brian hadn't come. She'd waited and waited, sick with disappointment. He almost always walked back this way. Finally she had crept home. He had come in much later, and afterwards the bathroom had smelled strongly of beer.

'And what about the homework?' her mother had shrieked, working herself up into a frenzy. 'It's still not done, is it? I looked in your satchel. You say you're too ill to go to school, but what the heck have you been doing with yourself all day?'

Most of the time she had lain on her bed, tortured physically by the pain of a heavy period and mentally by her thoughts of Brian Kirby.

'Why, Jean? I try to bring you up properly, and just look at you. What have I done to deserve it?'

Jean couldn't answer the questions so she kept silent, which had stoked her mother's rage to an even greater heat. Her mother was often in a state after a Newport trip. In any case the anger meant nothing in comparison with what Jean felt now. Between them, the worry, the guilt and the jealousy were tearing her into little pieces.

When Jean had been a child, she had looked forward to falling in love. Now she knew better: love was a terrible thing, a wild animal that stalked through the cage of your body and forced you to do dreadful deeds.

Brian, she thought. Help me. What shall I do?

Shivering, she moved away from the window. The hope of comfort drew her; though she knew that the comfort was false, even false comfort was better than none. She padded on to the landing and listened. The snoring continued unchanged. Holding her breath, she slowly opened the door of the third bedroom, Brian's room. It was almost as familiar as her own.

She came here as often as she dared. Even its smell reassured her. She tiptoed to the wardrobe. There was a mirror inside the door. In the dim light from the landing she was pale but beautiful. She reached in and touched Brian's new suit, the blue double-breasted one which made him look like a film star. She lifted out the arm of the jacket and draped it across her shoulder. In the mirror it was a dark shadow against the white of her nightdress. She adjusted the sleeve so that it fell between her breasts.

In the looking-glass world Brian stood behind her. She stroked his arm, holding it close to her. His breath was warm on her neck and her skin tingled.

'Jean,' he whispered. 'Jean, darling.'

143

7

The stable clock was striking midnight, which meant that it was about ten minutes after that. Tony Ruispidge knocked on his wife's door, opened it and put his head into the big room beyond.

'She's not back.'

His wife put down the detective novel she was reading. 'There's nothing you can do about it so you might as well stop worrying.'

'I'm not worrying. I'm just bloody angry. She treats this place like an hotel.'

'Why don't you come into the room and shut the door? There's a draught.'

'There can't be a draught. There's no wind.' Nevertheless Ruispidge came into the room and closed the door behind him. 'She hasn't even taken a car, you know. Pinson says he saw her walking down to Mitchelbrook.'

'Yes, dear.' His wife turned a page. 'But I'm sure she's all right. She always is.'

He wandered across to the tall window and stared down at the fountain in the drive, ghostly in the moonlight. 'I'll be glad when today's over, I don't mind telling you.'

Lady Ruispidge picked up her book. 'Then why don't you go to bed?'

He ignored this suggestion. 'I've been trying to ginger up Hendry and his chaps. You can't have something like this hanging over the town for a minute longer than you have to. Poisons the whole atmosphere. The place is crawling with journalists, too. Wretched little hacks.' He turned from the

145

window and faced the bed, squaring his shoulders. 'Can't help feeling responsible.'

His wife lowered her book again. 'Why? You didn't kill her, did you? I thought you said that you didn't even know who the Kymin woman was.'

'It's no joking matter, Soph. The thing is, the woman allowed herself to be killed in St John's.'

'That's ridiculous. Just because your family has been choosing the incumbents for the last few generations, you're not responsible for all that goes on there. Anyway, you let the Bishop or someone do the choosing, didn't you? And so you should. It's an absurdly archaic system. So by your reasoning, if anyone's responsible the Bishop is.'

Ruispidge wandered through the shadowy room, touching pieces of furniture as if they might bring him luck, straightening pictures and glancing up at the ceiling. The only light came from the lamp by the bedside. His wife watched him, her finger marking her place in her book. She was a long, stringy woman with a plain face and beautiful hands.

'It's that girl, really, isn't it?' she said at last.

Ruispidge dug his hands into the pockets of his dressing gown. 'Ferndale sent me another of her bills today.' Ferndale was the Ruispidges' London solicitor. 'Brings the running total to a little over twelve hundred pounds. We may have to sell something if it gets much worse.'

'I've always said that girl needed a good spanking. I see no reason to change my mind now that she's grown up.'

'That's the point, Soph. You can't blame her. Not with that dreadful father of hers. And then there was the war. I know she's wild, but it's just a stage she's going through. Some day soon she'll meet a nice chap and settle down.'

Sophia Ruispidge looked at her husband and wisely held her tongue. Then the silence of the night was broken by the roar of a motorcycle coming up the drive of Clearland Court.

PART SIX

1

The Reverend Alec Sutton was one of those fortunate people who, when life becomes too much for them, are able to take refuge in sleep. His wife was not. For most of the night she lay wakeful beside his sleeping body, listening to his heavy breathing and staring at the rectangle of the window. Sometimes she dozed, but the condition was more akin to trance than sleep. Her thoughts moved wearily in circles, returning at intervals to the same question: *Should she or should she not tell the police?*

Alec woke as he always did at six-thirty. He slid out of bed, trying not to wake her, pushed his feet into slippers, took his dressing gown from the end of the bed and slipped out of the room.

Routine comforted Alec; it was essential in a way that Mary did not understand to his spiritual life. The distant sounds of his movements formed a familiar pattern which for once she found reassuring rather than mildly irritating.

The creak of the stairs was followed by the flushing of the downstairs lavatory. A rhythmic scraping and rattling signified that he was dealing with the range in the kitchen. A few minutes later, she heard the click of the study door opening. It was his habit to say the morning office while the kettle came to the boil.

At this point on Tuesday morning, Mary Sutton fell deeply and inexplicably asleep. She was awakened ten minutes later by her husband bringing her a cup of tea. He put the cup and saucer down on her bedside table.

149

'I wonder if we shall see the Bishop today.'

'I think we should tell him,' Mary said, sitting up and returning to a conversation they had begun at bedtime. 'Or even Simon Davis.'

Alec picked up his clothes and moved towards the door. 'I don't see why. It's none of their business. It isn't anyone's business apart from ours.'

His wife looked out of the window in the direction of the church. 'When something like this happens, everything comes out. Everyone's secrets.'

'Nonsense.'

'We can't afford to give the appearance of hiding something.'

'We'll talk about it later,' Alec murmured, which was his way of postponing something unpleasant permanently to the future.

Jam tomorrow, Mary thought, never jam today: it won't do. She said, 'I've made up my mind.'

Alec stopped at the door. He had his clothes over one arm, his towel over the other, and a cup of tea precariously held in his hand; he was unshaven and his hair stood up on end. She loved him very much. He smiled at her, and for a moment she thought she glimpsed relief in his face.

'If you've made up your mind, my dear,' he said slowly, 'there's no point in our talking about it.'

He went to have his cold bath. Mary Sutton drank her tea and listened to her husband splashing vigorously in the distance.

For a while the familiar routine made Tuesday feel like any other morning. Soon, however, the day had lost all semblance of normality. By half-past seven the reporters were beginning to congregate in the street outside. Two policemen were on duty outside, one by the lych gate, the other patrolling solemnly round the churchyard. The telephone rang again and again; and the callers were all imbued with a sense of urgency which overrode good manners and common sense.

Some of the people who telephoned were journalists. Some were friends and parishioners, full of concern and anxious to relay offers of help. Others were harder to deal with, and harder to excuse: they brought malicious and usually anonymous innuendo, silences filled with heavy breathing, and on one occasion a burst of high, uncontrollable laughter.

'I feel like something in a horror film,' Mary said to her husband as they washed up after breakfast. 'A freak. I'm going to try to see Inspector Thornhill, I think.'

'Why don't I phone Ruispidge instead? After all, he's our patron, and he knows the Chief Constable very well, I believe. Might as well go in at the top.'

'No. I'd rather talk to Thornhill.'

'Why?'

'Because I don't want to go to the top.' She dried her hands on the towel. 'I'd rather be ordinary. That's what we are. Anyway, I'm not sure that going through Ruispidge would do any good.'

'I merely thought that—'

'You thought that if we went through Ruispidge, there was a chance the whole thing could be hushed up, didn't you? Sort of gentlemen's agreement? Let's draw a veil over it, chaps.'

'It might be the best thing.'

She glared at him. 'It might be the most convenient thing, you mean.'

He put his arms around her, squeezed her bottom and kissed her soundly on the lips. Afterwards they shared a cigarette in companionable silence, broken only by two more telephone calls. Alec was unwilling to leave the phone off the hook in case one of his parishioners needed him.

Mary phoned Inspector Thornhill and asked if she could see him. He offered to come to the Vicarage but she said that she preferred to come to him.

'I need to do some shopping. In any case, if I stay much longer in this house I shall start feeling like a besieged army.'

There was a silence at the other end of the line, and Mary wondered whether it was bad form to make mild jokes to policemen on duty. Or perhaps policemen only had a sense of humour in detective fiction. Perhaps their job was not compatible with humour. She hurriedly said goodbye to him.

The journalists threw questions at her as she left the house. Remembering Jill Francis's suggestion, she parried them all with 'no comment'; the tactic seemed to work. She walked down Church Street and turned into the High Street. Quale was sweeping the steps outside the Bull in the morning sunshine, a cigarette dangling from the corner of his mouth. He sketched a salute as Mary passed.

'Any news, ma'am?'

'Not that I've heard,' she replied. 'Have you?'

He leaned on his broom. 'You know Miss Francis went into hospital last night?'

'No – but why?'

'She fainted or something in the barn in our yard. Mr Lancaster thought it best to call an ambulance.'

'Was she badly hurt?'

'I wouldn't know, ma'am. Best to be on the safe side.' Quale was watching her carefully, hungry for a reaction. 'Mr Thornhill popped in later. Had a look around.'

'How conscientious of him.'

Mary gave him the unrevealing smile she had perfected in fifteen years of parish work, said goodbye and walked on. She suspected that he was staring after her. If so, he wasn't the only one. She glimpsed from the corner of one eye a woman pointing her out to her husband. A man she had met at one of the Newtons' cocktail parties crossed the road, perhaps to avoid having to speak to her. Dear God, Mary Sutton murmured to herself, are we ever going to live this down?

She went into the police station. The hall was crowded. She had dreaded having to explain her business in front of strangers, but this proved not to be necessary. The desk sergeant recognised her and waved her forward.

'Mr Thornhill's expecting you, ma'am. I'll send a constable up with you.' He opened a door behind him and shouted into the room beyond, 'Porter!'

Thornhill's office proved to be a poky little room with too much furniture in it. To her dismay he was not alone. He introduced the other man as Detective Sergeant Kirby and offered her a chair.

'Oh, dear. This is rather difficult.' She glanced at Kirby, who stared back with hard eyes. He was a younger man than Thornhill; he had yellow, slicked-back hair and wore a cheap suit and a flashy tie. 'I had assumed . . .'

'You'd prefer to talk to me alone?' Thornhill made it sound a perfectly natural request.

'Yes, please,' she said gratefully. She smiled at Kirby as he stood up. 'It's nothing personal, you understand.'

Kirby grinned unexpectedly at her. The effect was like walking from a cold room into a warm one. The door closed behind him.

'You do realise—' Thornhill began.

'That I'm not talking to you under the seal of the confessional? Yes, of course.'

She opened her handbag and took out a blue envelope, which she laid on the desk between them. Rather to her annoyance, Thornhill made no move to take it.

'When did you get this?'

'First post yesterday morning.' He knows what it is, she thought: so there must have been others. 'You may look at it if you want to.'

He pulled the envelope towards him and picked it up, holding it between the palms of his hands by the edges. He shook the letter out of the envelope and gingerly unfolded it. It occurred to Mary that he would have acted in the same way if the letter had been physically hot. She stared at the smudges of black and white newsprint on the blue paper. She was too far away to be able to read it but there was no need.

YOUR ALEC PUTS HIMSELF ABOUT DOESN'T HE. THAT COW KYMIN DOWN HERE AND ALL THEM TARTS UP IN LONDON. HOPE HE HAS SOME LEFT OVER FOR YOU. TARTS DON'T COME CHEAP. HAVE YOU NEVER WONDERED WHERE HE GETS THE MONEY FROM.

Thornhill studied the letter. At last he looked up.

'We've had quite a rash of these, Mrs Sutton.'

'About my husband?'

'Yes. Making much the same sort of allegations.'

She waited, but he said nothing else. His manner was detached, like a doctor's or a dentist's – or for that matter a priest's.

'It's foul,' she burst out. 'How would you like it if someone went around writing letters like that about you? And sent them to your wife?'

'I should hate it. It hasn't happened to me yet, but I wouldn't be surprised if it does. Policemen are rather prone to attracting that sort of attention, just like clergymen.'

'I'm sorry.' Mary Sutton wished he wouldn't be so beastly nice about it. 'How many letters have there been? Who's had them?' The idea that half Lydmouth had been reading this sort of smut about Alec without her knowing made her even more furious and upset than before.

'I'm afraid I can't tell you that. Not yet, in any case.'

She frowned at him. 'But why? Oh, I suppose it's under investigation. You can't talk about things you're investigating, obviously. But you don't think there's a connection, do you?'

'With what?'

'With Miss Kymin's murder, of course.'

'It's early days yet.' He smiled at her, taking some of the sting out of his avoidance of the question. 'Is there something more you want to tell me?'

He was sharp, Mary thought. She said delicately, 'This business about Alec's going up to town, and needing money . . . I thought it might help if I explained.' She waited, but he said nothing. She plunged on, floundering.

'It's so silly – talking about it like this makes it seem shady, but it isn't like that at all.'

Thornhill's face, though still polite, was now looking frankly bewildered. Suddenly Mary lost patience – with herself as much as with him. She snapped open her handbag and took out a large brown envelope. She removed a book from the envelope and laid it on the desk. It was a hardback with a brightly coloured dust jacket. A man with a striking resemblance to the late Benito Mussolini was threatening a beautiful blonde girl with a revolver. The title was emblazoned in red capitals across the cover: *INSPECTOR COLEFORD STRIKES A MATCH.*

'I don't understand,' Thornhill said, his calm at last showing signs of evaporating. 'What is this?'

'It's a book,' Mary Sutton snapped. 'And I wrote it.'

2

Never one to shirk her more obvious obligations, Charlotte brought clothes, a detective novel, grapes and roses to the hospital. She bulldozed her way through the hospital regulations, considerably assisted by the fact that the ward sister was one of her colleagues on the flower rota at St John's.

They had given Jill a room of her own. She was staring out of her window at the blue, distant hills when Charlotte arrived. 'How are you, dear?'

'I've still got an awful headache. But they tell me nothing's broken.'

'Well, that's a blessing. Can you remember what happened?'

Jill shook her head slowly, wincing. 'I can't remember anything after cycling down the Chepstow Road. It was starting to rain.' Her fingers picked at the blanket. 'I'm sorry I'm being such a nuisance. How's Philip? The police are having a press conference this morning, aren't they?'

'You mustn't worry about anything. You know Philip – this is just what he likes best: a really good excuse to play the ace reporter.' Charlotte smiled at Jill, who found herself smiling back. 'Now where shall I put the roses?'

Charlotte found a vase on the windowsill, filled it with water and stuffed it with stiff, pink roses. Jill ate a grape, just for the look of the thing, and glanced at the detective novel, an old Ngaio Marsh. Charlotte was in a good mood this morning, Jill thought, and she wondered whether the cause of the cheerfulness was the fact that she and her husband had their house to themselves.

'I went to see that room last night,' Jill said, on the principle that the

Andrew Taylor

sooner she got it out of the way the better.

'What was it like? Blast.' Charlotte had pricked her finger on a thorn. She sucked greedily at the wound. 'Can you remember?'

'It was foul. The woman was a slut, the children were hooligans and the husband pinched my bottom.'

'Don't you worry about that now.' Charlotte took a grape and popped it into her own mouth. 'Just concentrate on getting better.' She opened the wardrobe and began to unpack the little suitcase. 'Have they said when you can come out?'

'No. A doctor's meant to be coming this morning.'

'When you know, ask them to phone us. Philip will come and fetch you.'

Jill's eyes filled with tears. She turned her head away from the window, away from Charlotte's kindness. 'I think I should go to the Bull. I've already imposed on you both too much.'

'Nonsense. We've got bags of space.' Sometimes it was hard to know whether Charlotte was being genuinely insensitive or merely pretending to be for tactical reasons. 'Besides,' Charlotte rushed on, perhaps aware that she was treading on thin ice, 'besides, I doubt if you could get a bed at the Bull for love or money. It's packed to the seams with journalists.'

A staff nurse plodded into the room. She had a narrow head, slim shoulders and swollen legs; her skin was pale and slightly grubby, and her face suggested that smiles were subjected to severe rationing. 'Time for a rest.'

Jill nodded, and felt her head grow heavy on the pillow. I would agree to anything at present, she thought; if someone told me I'd killed Miss Kymin, I'd probably believe them.

Charlotte closed the wardrobe door. 'Is there anything else you need?'

'Some face powder, perhaps. I can't find my compact. I thought it was in my handbag.'

'Sister's in her office if you'd like a word,' the nurse said to Charlotte. She held open the door.

Charlotte blinked and for once bowed without protest to another's authority. She bent and kissed Jill clumsily on the cheek, surprising Jill and perhaps herself as well. Her face was a little pinker than usual beneath its layer of powder. She straightened up, looped her handbag over her arm and turned to go. Then she hesitated.

'I forgot to mention, Jill. Philip sends his love.'

3

'Next one.' Superintendent Williamson's voice cut through the babble of questions. He stabbed his forefinger at a man at the far end of the table. 'You.'

'Farnham of the *Daily Sketch*. Is there any truth in the story that the lady may have been at the church for an assignation?'

'We don't yet know why Miss Kymin was there,' Williamson said. 'We are investigating several possibilities, and keeping our minds open.'

As Williamson's voice droned on, Thornhill's attention wandered. They were in the Conference Room on the ground floor of the police station. Reporters from the nationals were there as well as the usual men from the provincial press. The room was high-ceilinged and the windows were open, but already the air was thick with smoke.

Thornhill could not help noticing Jill Francis's absence. That was perfectly natural, he told himself, because she stuck out like a sore thumb at these otherwise entirely masculine gatherings. His left hand slipped into his jacket pocket: he felt the hard, smooth outlines of the powder compact he had found at the Bull.

Sometimes he wanted to blush for her, for he considered that the things she heard in this room were often unsuitable for a woman's ears. Part of him was surprised that Philip Wemyss-Brown allowed her to come. Philip was making notes; he looked up, caught Thornhill staring at him and gave him the ghost of a smile.

'Superintendent! Superintendent!' Ivor Fuggle waved his hand in the air. 'Over here.'

At last Williamson could ignore him no longer.

'Fuggle of the *Post*.' He introduced himself unnecessarily solely to irritate Williamson. 'Can you confirm that the police are investigating anonymous letters which have recently been received in Lydmouth?'

'We investigate everything that is brought to our attention,' Williamson said heavily. 'Everything that needs it, that is.'

'But there have been letters?'

'I'm not at present in a position to comment on that.'

'What about the Yard, then? Are you calling them in?'

Williamson rapped out, 'Next.'

Simultaneously Thornhill remembered the Chief Constable's ultimatum twenty minutes earlier: *You and your people have twenty-four hours, Williamson. After that I'll call in the Yard.* And then, in a lowered voice that Thornhill had not been meant to hear, *They don't have Tony Ruispidge breathing down their necks.*

The press conference struggled towards its predictably inconclusive conclusion. Afterwards Thornhill followed Williamson up the stairs. Sergeant Kirby was waiting for them outside the superintendent's office. He was colourfully dressed in a blue double-breasted suit and a bright American tie adorned with baseball players. He was carrying something wrapped in a folded newspaper.

'Sergeant,' Thornhill said. 'You usually walk home down Church Street, don't you? Did you notice anyone when you went off duty on Sunday night?'

'Sorry, sir – not on Sunday. I went down to the Bathurst Arms for a couple of beers, seeing as Monday was my day off. Came back the other way, and that was after closing time.'

'What have you got there?' Williamson demanded.

'Would this fit as the weapon, sir?' Kirby unfolded the newspaper, revealing a tyre lever, its surface pocked with rust but still perfectly usable.

'Where did it come from?'

'Quale's just come in with it. He says he found it in a bin in the yard of the Bull. He's downstairs if you'd like to talk to him.' Kirby jiggled from one foot to another, the energy bursting to escape. 'I think he's hoping for a reward.'

'We won't get a decent print off a surface like that,' Williamson said grumpily. 'Maybe the lab will find something. But I wouldn't bank on it.

And I'd have been happier if it had been found in the churchyard. Somewhere nearer.'

Thornhill said, 'Remember that incident last night with Miss Francis. Could there be a connection? To my mind, you don't throw away a perfectly serviceable tyre lever just for the hell of it.'

Williamson grunted. 'I wouldn't put it past Quale to plant the bloody thing and then find it himself. Not if he thought there was money in it.' He paused. 'Has anyone talked to Miss Francis?'

'No, sir,' Thornhill said. 'Not yet.'

4

Jill was on the verge of sleep when she became uneasily aware that she was not alone.

Charlotte's Ngaio Marsh novel had held her attention only as far as the list of characters at the front. She was lying propped up against the pillows with her eyes half-open; her mind occupied with longing to be out of hospital and with wondering what had happened to her at the Bull the previous evening. Then she caught a flicker of movement on the edge of her field of vision and was instantly awake.

She turned her head. A cleaner was in the act of tiptoeing into the room. There was a furtive expression on her broad, pink face. She wore overalls and her hair was concealed under a scarf. In her hand she carried a cast-iron bucket with a mop poking out of it. Unaware that Jill was awake, she stared slowly round the little room as if fearful of discovering witnesses lurking beneath the bed or beside the little wardrobe.

'What do you want?' Jill asked.

The woman almost dropped the bucket; the mop swung out and clattered against the iron rail at the foot of the bed. 'Oh my God, oh my God.' She seized the mop and lowered her voice to an aggressive whisper. 'If that staff nurse catches me she'll have my guts for garters.' She fished out a small bundle of damp newspaper from her bucket. She held this up and added brusquely, 'It's for you.'

Jill recognised something about the gesture. 'Mrs Milkwall. How kind.'

161

She heard the relief in her own voice and wondered just what she had been afraid of.

'I happened to be passing,' Mrs Milkwall said accusingly. 'Thought I'd look in.'

'How did you know I was here?'

'One of our neighbours is working nights on this ward. She knew I'd met you yesterday, and she told me you'd been admitted. What a day, eh? First Miss Kymin, then you.'

'I'm not dead,' Jill pointed out. 'It's very kind of you . . . kind of you to drop in.'

'It's only that damn cat. That's why I'm here. I thought you should know, seeing as you're taking an interest. I put some food down for it last night, but it didn't come back. Hadn't eaten a mouthful by the time I came to work this morning.'

'Perhaps she's scared,' Jill said. 'Perhaps she needs time.'

'I reckon it's gone. Either it's buggered off or it's been run over.'

'You'll keep putting food down, won't you?'

'It's up to you.' Mrs Milkwall dumped the bundle on the bedside table. She unwrapped the newspaper, revealing a bundle of glorious tea roses. 'They were past their best anyway. The petals are just about beginning to fall off. I thought you might as well have them.'

'They're lovely.'

'Shouldn't have bothered, should I?' Mrs Milkwall nodded at Charlotte's pink, tight buds on the windowsill, arranged with stiff symmetry in the tall vase. 'I see someone's already brought you some.'

'Yours are nicer,' Jill said with perfect truth. 'There's another vase over there – at the end of the windowsill. Do they smell of tea? May I have them on my bedside table?'

Mrs Milkwall tossed the newspaper into the wastepaper basket and arranged the roses in the vase. 'Nothing like roses, I always say. Mind you, they're more trouble than they're worth. Like pets, really.' She hesitated a moment. 'Were you serious about taking that cat?'

Before Jill could answer, the door swung open to its full extent and the staff nurse filled the doorway. Her colour was high and her eyes protruded from her face. Mrs Milkwall seized her bucket and mop. She looked defenceless and miserable.

'And what do you think you are doing here?' the nurse asked. 'You're meant to be at the other end of the ward.'

'It was my fault,' Jill said quickly. 'I dropped my handbag and I asked her in to pick it up.'

The nurse appeared to accept this excuse, albeit reluctantly. She chivvied Mrs Milkwall out of the room. Jill was wide awake now. The unscheduled visit seemed to have had the effect of a tonic.

She swung her legs out of bed and stood up. She felt less shaky than she had earlier in the morning when she had gone to the bathroom. One sheet of Mrs Milkwall's newspaper had fallen behind the wastepaper basket. Jill stooped cautiously, one hand on the bedside table, and picked it up.

Automatically she smoothed out the wrinkled paper and folded it. It came from the *Gazette*, she noticed – she recognised the headline of a story she had written at the end of the previous month: MOTORIST KNOCKS DOWN SHEEP. Next she noticed, at first without interest, that someone had been cutting or poking holes in the paper. She sat down heavily on the bed. Her head swam; it was as though her brains had turned to liquid and were slopping to and fro inside her skull. Perhaps she was trying to do too much too soon?

Poking holes?

No, not poking holes, but cutting neat little windows. Jill studied the newsprint, trying to see what was missing. Individual words mainly, it seemed, though in some places a group of words had been lifted out – and in others only a few letters. What struck her most of all was the extreme neatness of the work. Such meticulous snipping had surely been unnecessary.

Her head steadied. Such neatness only made sense if the work had been a labour of love.

5

Mrs Abberley crept out of her cottage and locked the door behind her. Blinking in the morning sunlight, she crossed the road to avoid the journalists and walked westwards in the direction of Nutholt Lane. She carried a shopping basket and an umbrella.

Four journalists were chatting and smoking outside the Vicarage. The youngest of them, a dark-haired youth with a red face and the beginnings of a pot belly, threw away his cigarette and crossed the road to join her.

'Hello, love. It's Mrs Abberley, isn't it?' He gave her a boyish smile. 'Is it true this vicar's not a patch on the old?'

Mrs Abberley stared up at him for a moment with her blank, black eyes. Then she bent her head and spat on the pavement between them. The young man recoiled.

'Hey! There's no call for that.'

She walked on. As she passed the green railings of Victor Youlgreave's house, she heard the dog barking. She assumed, for once wrongly, that it was barking at her. Nasty animals, dogs – worse than a child in some ways, and unlike most children liable to bite at unexpected moments. She glanced towards the trim front door with its burnished brass knocker. If you only knew, she thought, hugging her knowledge to herself, if you only knew.

She collected a pair of shoes from the cobbler's in Nutholt Lane, spending an agreeable five minutes disputing the price and criticising the quality of the repair. Then, her pulse beating a little faster, she walked down the lane to the phone box at the far end.

She had meant to delay this stage of the affair for a day or two, but the temptation to exercise her newfound power was irresistible. She wondered how much she should start with. She didn't need the money particularly, but then this wasn't really a question of money.

Twenty pounds, she thought: that's it: neither too much nor too little. Later on she would ask for more. She knew instinctively that it would be not only more effective but more enjoyable to begin by asking for small amounts; gradually, as the weeks and months passed, she would raise the demands.

Her mind filled with a picture of a hand squeezing an overripe orange. The peel split under the pressure, and juice spurted through the cracks and trickled through the fingers. The hand squeezed tighter and tighter, and finally there was no juice left, only a soggy mass of peel and pith, flesh and pips.

Mrs Abberley dialled the number. As she listened to the ringing, she wondered whether oranges would keep indefinitely in a refrigerator.

6

The next and as it happened the last anonymous letter arrived by special delivery in the middle of Tuesday morning. No one realised the letter's real significance until later in the day.

An alert post office sorter had noticed the envelope and was sensible enough to show it to his supervisor. The supervisor rang police headquarters, and Kirby went round immediately to collect the letter. He took it to Williamson's office and laid the envelope carefully in the middle of the superintendent's blotter. Thornhill was out.

'Bloody hell,' Williamson said. 'I'd forgotten we had this joker to deal with too.'

The letter had been posted locally, probably at the main post office in Lydmouth, and it was addressed simply to CID, LYDMOUTH. The writing was in pencil; the capital letters were poorly formed and sloping backwards, as if written with the writer's left hand.

Williamson pulled on a pair of gloves and picked up his paperknife. Inside the blue envelope was a single sheet of matching paper. Kirby craned over the desk to read the message on it.

KYMIN WAS GOING TO TELL ABOUT THEIR AFFAIR. THAT IS WHY SUTTON KILLED HER. TOOK CHALICE TO MAKE IT LOOK LIKE ROBBERY.

Williamson made a face. 'Same envelope, same paper. Woolworth's best, eh? And it looks like the newsprint comes from the *Gazette*. I could do without this.'

Kirby said nothing.

'What are you waiting for, Sergeant?' Williamson asked. 'Get the lab to look at it. Then carry on with your work.'

Kirby disposed of the letter and returned to the CID Office. The large, awkwardly shaped room was on the second floor of police headquarters. It had been formed by removing the partition walls between a corridor and what had once been two bedrooms. Two rows of pale wooden Utility desks faced each other down the longer axis of the room. Other desks were against the walls. The office was more crowded than usual because Williamson had brought in detectives from other divisions to help with the murder enquiry.

Kirby sat down and lit a cigarette. Detective Constable Wilson leaned across the aisle that separated their desks.

'Why's Thornhill gone to see the Francis woman?' he said. 'Why not you or me? That's what I want to know.'

'None of your business.' Kirby picked up a report and began to flick through it. Standards really were slipping, he thought: when he had been a young detective constable, he would never have dared to talk like that to his sergeant.

'And why's he gone by himself?'

'Get some tea, will you?'

'Maybe Thornhill's sweet on her. Wants to see her in her negligée.'

'Tea,' Kirby said. 'And why haven't you finished the filing yet?'

'I will. It won't take long.'

'No, you're right: it won't. Not when you actually get going. But first make the tea.'

Wilson cast his eyes up and down the long room. There were no women CID officers in the entire county force. But several uniformed WPCs were attached to the CID. They supplemented the efforts of the civilian clerical staff, and it was grudgingly admitted even by Williamson that they had their uses when an investigating officer needed to deal with women and children. They also were traditionally expected to make the tea, an expectation elevated to the status of a moral imperative by their male colleagues. Unfortunately for Wilson, the only WPC present was taking an incoming call on the temporary switchboard.

Kirby tapped his pencil on the desk. 'Look sharp. Two sugars.'

Wilson slouched out of the room, the back of his neck glowing an angry pink above his stiff white collar. It was generally agreed that Williamson had made a mistake in allowing Wilson to join the CID. The trouble was, Williamson did not have to live directly with the consequences.

Kirby returned to the pile of reports he was sifting through. In a murder investigation, particularly in the early stages before routine set in, even the dreariest jobs had an urgency and an interest about them. Thornhill had told him to collate the results of yesterday's interviews. The tedium was vital, Kirby knew, because gradually a detailed picture of people's movements on Sunday evening would emerge. There would be gaps, as there always were, but no more than necessary. Vital or not, the job was making him yawn.

'Bloody little tyke,' said the elderly sergeant at the next desk, one of the officers brought in from another division. 'Is it true what they say, his dad's a mate of Williamson's?'

'Afraid so.'

'Makes you sick. Bet he's a bleeding Mason. They all stick together on the square. You lodge with old Jonesie's widow, don't you?'

'That's right.'

'Case in point in a manner of speaking.' The old sergeant tapped his teeth with his pencil. 'Jonesie always claimed he never made inspector because he couldn't do the funny handshakes.'

At last the sergeant went back to his work. Kirby thought briefly of young Jean, his landlady's daughter. The kid had looked terrible this morning. She had scuttled past him on the landing, her eyes red and her bony shoulders poking out of her nightdress. Ill or unhappy? His mind slipped back to Jemima.

'My mother named me after one of Job's daughters,' she'd told him last night. 'The bitch! No wonder I had an unhappy childhood.'

Kirby himself was too happy to bear a grudge against anyone, even Wilson. He had hardly slept last night. At times it had seemed to him that he would never need to sleep again. He had been too happy to sleep, or indeed to eat. He pulled another file towards him and allowed the memories to drift through his mind. He felt like a miser counting his gold, picking up and gloating over each coin in turn. He wished he could escape from the racket around him.

The air was full of smoke and the clatter of typewriters. There was a continuous roar of talking, the sound ebbing and flowing like surf. Telephones rang, their shrill sound slicing through the conversations. The

noises around him receded. Gradually they blended into one comforting mass. Kirby felt his eyes closing.

'Sarge!'

Irritated, he swung round in his chair. The WPC at the switchboard waved her hand at him. 'For you,' she called over the hubbub. 'Do you want it on that phone?'

She pointed to the telephone on the next desk, Wilson's. The temporary switchboard was still a novelty. Usually the CID shared the main switchboard downstairs, but Williamson had ordered another to be installed in the CID Office for the duration of the murder investigation. It had been in operation only since yesterday evening, and there were still a number of problems, among them the fact that there were not enough telephones to go round.

He picked up Wilson's phone. 'Kirby,' he said into the mouthpiece.

'Brian darling,' Jemima murmured. 'How deliciously laconic.'

Delight warred with dismay. 'I'm afraid that may not be entirely relevant, miss,' he said, turning away from the old sergeant.

'People are listening? Not easy to talk?'

'There may be some truth in that.' He saw Wilson coming back into the room with a cup of tea in each hand. That was all he needed: little Mr Nosy.

'At least I can talk to you, darling. It was marvellous, wasn't it? I can't wait to see you again.'

He was shocked that she had rung him at work – and in the middle of a murder investigation, too. Oddly enough, this added to the excitement he felt: the more illicit a pleasure, the more enjoyable it was.

'Uncle Tony was waiting up when I got back. In rather a crusty mood, I'm afraid. Did you miss me last night?'

'That's correct.'

Wilson had put down the tea and was now pretending to sort out his cards for filing. In reality, Kirby suspected, he was trying to overhear the telephone conversation.

'I've got to see you,' Jemima said in a voice that turned his legs to jelly. 'I need you, Brian. Can you come and pick me up before lunch? We could have a drink somewhere, and then—'

'In the circumstances, that wouldn't be easy.'

'Oh, Brian.' She pronounced his name Bwian, and spoke in a voice that suggested she was on the verge of tears. 'Then when can you come?'

'I don't know, miss. Perhaps this evening.'

'Ring me as soon as you know when you can get off,' Jemima said. 'I'll walk down to Mitchelbrook and meet you there.'

There was an obvious difficulty even about this, and Kirby strove to find a way of saying it that was suitable for Wilson's ears. 'We need to be sure that the right person will be available.'

She laughed. 'Don't worry. I'll see that Uncle Tony doesn't answer. I'll be waiting beside the phone all day.'

'It may be later than that.'

'I don't care how late it is. Or rather, I do because the sooner the better. But I want to see you. Brian, I need you.'

There was a click as she hung up on him. Wilson looked up at Kirby with pale, knowing eyes.

'Your tea's getting cold, Sarge.'

7

It was a ward for women. Thornhill had not anticipated it would make him feel so uncomfortable. He wished he had had the sense to bring a WPC with him. In normal circumstances, he would have done; but the demands of the murder enquiry were stretching their resources to the limit.

It was not, he had told himself, as if he was going to interview a complete stranger, or a woman who might have to be arrested, or a child. This line of reasoning had made perfect sense at police headquarters. Here at the hospital, however, it no longer seemed quite so convincing.

An obliging clerk had arranged for him to meet the doctor who had examined Jill in the sister's office of the ward she was in. The doctor was a young, ginger-haired man with pink-rimmed eyes. A large, unfriendly staff nurse introduced him to Thornhill. It was a small room, and when the two men sat facing each other on hard wooden chairs, their knees almost touched.

'There's not much I can tell you, Inspector. Miss Francis had a bang on the head. It put her out for a moment or two, but she seems to be making a good recovery. No sign of anything broken. Her pupils react to light. She's slightly concussed, perhaps, but that's only to be expected. We'll probably let her out today.'

'What about her memory?'

'There's a little retrograde amnesia but that will probably fade.'

'How long will that take?'

'Who knows? Could be weeks or even months. Or it could be before lunch.'

'Where did the blow fall?' Thornhill asked.

The doctor touched the back of his head on the left-hand side just below the crown. 'About there.'

'Could you tell anything from the bruise? I take it the skin wasn't broken?'

'That's correct. But a bruise is a bruise. This one was a bit longer than it was wide, if I remember rightly.'

'Any idea what might have caused it?'

The doctor stared at him as if he'd asked for the moon. 'How should I know? She could have hit her head on something – the bottom of a sash window perhaps. Or someone could have hit her. Your guess is as good as mine, Inspector.'

'But the skin wasn't broken.'

The man smothered a yawn. 'Which might mean something or nothing.'

'Suppose you were a gambling man,' Thornhill said with increasing desperation. 'What would you guess had caused the blow?'

'As it happens, I disapprove strongly of gambling in all forms. But since you ask, if I had to guess, I would say that the bruise was caused by something long and thin and hard. Not much more than half an inch wide, if that. And I doubt if it had any sharp edges. It was probably rounded. Like a poker, perhaps.'

'Or a tyre lever?'

'Or a tyre lever.'

The doctor glanced at his watch. Thornhill took the hint and stood up. They went out into the corridor that ran the length of the ward. The staff nurse bore down on them. Despite her bulk, she moved quietly and with surprising speed.

'Thank you, doctor.' Thornhill turned to the staff nurse. 'I'd like to see Miss Francis now.'

The nurse looked stonily at him. 'I'll see if that will be possible,' she said. 'Wait here.'

The doctor slipped away, leaving Thornhill stranded in the middle of the corridor. He watched the staff nurse waddle purposefully down to a door at the end. She opened it and went into the room beyond. He felt acutely uncomfortable. To him the ward smelled of disease and death. Through half-open doorways he caught glimpses of women in various stages of undress. A nurse pushed a trolley laden with medicines down the corridor, and he had to move out of the way. He had to move again when two porters wheeled a bed in the opposite direction and out through the double doors at the end. He averted his eyes from the person on the bed, from the white, slack-mouthed face on the crisply starched pillow.

He tried to divert himself by thinking about the case. Nothing made sense about it. It was all loose ends. Usually you could see, or at least infer, a pattern behind every crime: when you knew the how and the why, you generally knew the who as well. In this case, however, they knew only one thing for sure: that a woman was dead, killed by a blow to the head. All the other facts, even the missing chalice, might have nothing to do with the case at all.

The possible attack on Jill Francis was one of the loose ends. Typical of the woman, Thornhill thought, always barging in where she isn't wanted. He still found it hard to forgive her interference in another case at the end of last year. Now here she was again, wasting his time when his time was most in short supply.

'Inspector.' The staff nurse beckoned him down the corridor. 'Just five minutes, mind.' She poked her head back into the room behind her. 'Ring the bell if he gets tiresome.'

The first thing he saw were the splashes of colour – the pink roses on the windowsill and the yellow on the bedside table. In a fraction of a second he had time to wish he had brought something himself; after all Jill Francis was not exactly a stranger, and it would have been only civil. Hard on the heels of that thought was a less generous one: once again she had managed to put him in the wrong; that she'd done so unintentionally was entirely beside the point. Then he saw Jill.

Her face turned towards him as he came in. She looked so small that for an instant he thought he had been shown into the wrong room, that a child with a face like Jill's was lying in the bed. She was very pale; he wondered whether this was due to the blow or to lack of make-up. There were smudges of tiredness under her eyes. He opened his mouth to ask how she was. But she spoke first, and once again she took him by surprise.

'I'm sorry,' she said.

'What?'

Her fingers twitched on the sheet. Today she wasn't wearing any rings. 'For dragging you out here. You must be terribly busy.'

'It's all right.' The aggression seeped out of him. She reminded him of how his children looked when they were ill: physically diminished, their colours faded, in need of comfort; the best thing to do was to put your arm around them. 'We – Mr Williamson and I – thought that someone should see you – just in case.'

'In case this has some bearing on the other business?' Her voice, never loud, was softer than usual, and he had to come close to the bed to hear what she was saying. 'I'm afraid I can't tell you anything about how it happened. I can't even remember deciding to go to the Bull.'

'Is this yours?' Thornhill put his hand in his jacket pocket and took out the powder compact.

Her eyes widened. 'How did you find it? How did you know?'

'I was at the Bull just after this happened. They found you lying near a cart in that barn in the yard. I shone a torch underneath – and there this was.'

'But how did you know it was mine?'

Thornhill thought, Because it smelled of you. He said, 'It seemed a reasonable guess to make in the circumstances.' He held it out to her. When she took the compact one of her fingers brushed the side of his hand. Her skin felt dry, soft and warm.

'It must have fallen out when I fell down. The catch on my handbag is faulty.'

'I don't suppose it jogs your memory?'

She shook her head.

Thornhill said, 'I'm tiring you, I'm afraid. I'll let you rest.'

'Don't go.' For an instant he thought he had misheard her. She stared up at him with huge eyes. 'There's something I have to tell you.'

'Time's up, Inspector,' said the staff nurse from the doorway.

'Just a moment, please.'

At the same time, Jill sat up in bed. 'Pass me my handbag,' Jill said to Thornhill, her voice suddenly much firmer. It was on the bedside table. Automatically he handed it to her.

'Inspector – doctor's orders, I'm afraid.'

'I've got something for him, Nurse.' Jill opened the handbag and took out a folded sheet of newspaper. 'You'd better have a look at that.'

Frowning, he took the newspaper, a double-page from the *Gazette*. The paper felt damp. The nurse cleared her throat, and the noise sounded like a knife being whetted on a grindstone.

'Someone's been cutting out letters and words,' Jill said to Thornhill, her voice rapid and desperate. 'Now why should they want to do that?'

PART SEVEN

1

'I say, Newton!' Bomber Lancaster trotted down the wide stairs of the Bull: the motion made the ends of his handlebar moustache jiggle up and down, creating the impression he was preparing for takeoff. 'Have you got a minute?'

Newton paused. He had been walking through the hall, a briefcase tucked under his arm, on his way from the front door of the Bull to the back. This was a recognised short cut among the older inhabitants of Lydmouth, enabling one to go from A to B via one side of a triangle rather than two. He glanced upstairs. Lancaster thought, a little smugly: my God, the old boy's showing his age.

'Of course.' Newton's voice was the same as ever. 'No time like the present.' He nodded to Quale behind the reception desk and came up the stairs. Newton had cut himself while shaving, Lancaster noticed, and he looked as if he'd slept in his trousers; not that Giles Newton was what one would call a snappy dresser.

Lancaster held open the door of his office. The room overlooked the High Street. Lancaster spent a good deal of his time standing at the window, staring down at the scene below, which was how he had come to see Newton hurrying along the pavement. The walls were panelled in dark-stained wood. The furniture was severe, shabby and masculine. There were hunting prints above the fireplace; and on the wall behind the desk were framed group photographs showing, among other people, an improbably youthful

179

Lancaster at school and in the RAF. There was a small safe on the floor in one corner with a tray of bottles on top.

Lancaster hovered over the tray. 'Not too early for a little something, is it?'

'Not for me, thanks.' Newton dropped his briefcase on the window seat and sat down in the leather armchair in front of the desk. 'I think my liver needs a rest.'

'Personally I believe in hair of the dog.' Lancaster poured himself a large, pale sherry, the colour of bleached straw. He held the glass up to the window and examined it approvingly. 'Still, each to his own.' He sat down behind his desk, picked up a pipe and blew down it. 'How is it one can never find a clean pipe when one wants one?'

Newton, who had been patting his jacket pockets, brought out a cigarette case. 'What's the problem? I imagine that business is booming.'

'This Kymin murder has been a godsend. I don't mean to sound callous, but there it is. Mind you, journalists make exacting guests. The London ones especially.' Lancaster's face, already pink, became a little pinker. 'I can't say they're a very well-mannered lot either. However, I suppose one shouldn't grumble. Most of them seem to have unlimited expense accounts, that's the important thing.' He suspended cleaning operations on his pipe and picked up his glass. 'Cheers.'

'Is there any news on that front?'

'Our murder? Not that I know of. The inquest was adjourned, I gather. Then the police had a press conference but I don't think anything came out of it.'

'Are they going to call in the Yard?'

'Apparently not.' Lancaster threw the pipe cleaner in the wastepaper basket, wiped his fingers surreptitiously on his trousers and began to fill his pipe. 'The received opinion downstairs seems to be that the police must have something up their sleeve.'

'You mean we may have an arrest soon?'

Lancaster shrugged. 'It's anybody's guess. But you'd think they'd have to call in the Yard unless they were pretty sure of what they're doing. Wouldn't you agree?'

Newton, his head in silhouette against the window, nodded slowly. 'Could be.' He selected a cigarette from his case. Lancaster pushed a lighter across the desk to him. 'Now what did you—?'

At the same time Lancaster began, 'Difficult to make rhyme or reason of it.' He stopped. 'Sorry, old chap. After you.'

'No – after you.'

'I was only going to say, why should anyone want to kill an old bat like that? Seems inexplicable.' He took another mouthful of sherry.

'She disturbed some tramp, I imagine, probably looking for whatever he could find. I don't suppose he meant to kill her. Just lashed out at her and made himself scarce. I expect he's halfway to London, now. Or gone to ground in Cardiff or somewhere.'

'But why was she there in the first place?'

'Who knows? It sounds as if she was one of those unmarried ladies who get religion. The most likely thing is that she just popped into the church to commune with the Almighty.'

'So you don't believe this story about the vicar that's going around?'

'That Sutton was having a fling with her? Seems a little implausible.' Newton shrugged his heavy shoulders. 'But who knows?'

A silence settled over the room like a cloud. Lancaster drained the rest of his sherry and puffed vigorously on his pipe. Newton rubbed the right knee of his trousers with a fingertip, as if trying to erase an invisible spot. Through the open window came the sounds of passing traffic, of someone whistling shrilly at a girl, of fragments of conversation. Lancaster wondered dully why he was finding it so hard to get to the point. Newton would help if anyone could. Old Giles was a friend as well as the representative of the hotel's owner.

'The thing is,' Lancaster said suddenly, 'I had rather an awkward session with Sir Anthony yesterday. Has he mentioned anything?'

Newton shook his head, darkness moving against the light. 'What's the problem?'

'Something and nothing probably. It's the quarterly figures. He thinks he's found a discrepancy between cash received and cash paid into the bank. Not cheques, you understand – actual cash.'

Newton tapped ash from his cigarette. 'I wouldn't have thought the figures would have meant much to him. He's not an accountant.'

'I think he got a friend of his to cast an eye over them. Chap he was in the Navy with. He's a bursar now, at some Oxford college.'

There was a pause. Then Newton said, 'I know. Fred Wingfield.'

'Ah, there you are.' Lancaster looked relieved. 'So you know about this already.'

'No. But I've met Fred Wingfield. What exactly is the problem?'

Lancaster fiddled with the ends of his moustache. 'Well, I don't mind admitting record-keeping's not my forte. I've never pretended it was. I'm more the sort who leads from the front, if you know what I mean, so there it is. I've been wondering if something wasn't quite right for a month or two. Almost mentioned it to you on Sunday night, as a matter of fact. But it wasn't the right time for talking about the accounts, eh? Need a clear head for that sort of thing.'

He hesitated, realising slowly that he might not be making himself understood. 'You know the system as well as I do. We have separate books for the restaurants, the bars, the hotel side and the petty cash. And people enter things in, and the cheques and the cash go in there.' He waved towards the safe in the corner. 'And every few days someone goes down to the bank and pays it all in. Could be me, you, Quale – anyone. Simplicity itself. But the trouble is, it looks like we've received rather more money than we've actually paid into the bank. It's a pretty sizeable sum, too – running into hundreds over the last few years.'

Newton slowly stubbed out his cigarette. 'What does Sir Anthony intend to do about it?'

'Naturally he wants to find out what's happened to the money. I did suggest – tactfully, of course – that he or his friend might have made a mistake. Perfectly natural, if you're not used to the way we do things here. I'm afraid that didn't go down too well.' Lancaster picked up the sherry decanter. 'Sure you won't change your mind?'

Newton shook his head. Lancaster absentmindedly gave himself a refill.

'Is he going to call in the police?' Newton asked.

'He said nothing about that to me.' The neck of the decanter trembled against the rim of the glass. 'Surely there's no need? Just a simple mistake. It's easily done. One leaves out a nought here or there. I've done it myself, sometimes. I was wondering – would you mind? – do you think if you and I were to sit down with the books and the bank statements and the cheque stubs and so forth, make an evening of it, lots of black coffee, eh? – I'm sure we could sort it out.' He swallowed half of the sherry. 'At least, I hope so,' he added. 'You see, Sir Anthony says that otherwise he'll have to hold me responsible.'

2

The archdeacon looked worse this morning, his skin almost transparent. The Bishop, he said, had been detained at Lambeth Palace overnight but hoped to be back in the diocese tomorrow; in the meantime the Bishop felt that the most important thing was for them to make arrangements to carry on the spiritual life of the parish.

Mary Sutton knew that in practice this would mean sharing St Thomas's Church, an arrangement which would please neither the congregations nor the incumbents. Alec had said over breakfast that he thought God was trying to teach him humility. Mary thought this might well be true; but she was not looking forward to the effects of the lesson because she knew from experience that when God was teaching Alec humility, Alec tended to become dreadfully bad-tempered.

Davis made it clear that he wanted to talk to Alec alone. This suited Mary very well. Alec intended to tell the archdeacon about the life and crimes of Inspector Coleford. At the best of times, Mary found Inspector Coleford acutely embarrassing, and she had no wish to be present when Alec explained the facts of his creation and continuing existence to the archdeacon.

There was another reason why she did not want to be in the study with the men. She had a plan. It was not the sort of plan she could share with Alec, or not until she had carried it out, for he would be sure to object to it. Sometimes – especially when his self-interest was concerned – he was inclined to be too scrupulous for his own good. That was one reason why Mary had married him: he needed someone to save him from himself.

She left the men to their coffee and went back to the kitchen. Her handbag was on the table, sorely tempting her to have a cigarette. She promised herself one as a reward if she was successful.

She locked the back door behind her, something which would have been inconceivable only twenty-four hours ago. In the past they had occasionally forgotten to lock the front door at night, and until yesterday they had never once bothered to bolt the gates. All that had changed for ever, a small side effect of the murder.

The coach house was cool and dark. The only light came from the open doors, and from the bright blue oblongs above her head where tiles were missing. Mary negotiated her way round Alec's ex-Army Vauxhall and reached the low door at the back. She slid back the bolts and stepped with no outward sign of hesitation into Mrs Abberley's garden.

The high walls retained the heat. The air was still and smelt cloyingly of new-mown grass. Mary had never been here before; on her rare visits to the cottage, she had knocked on the front door out of politeness, but that would not have been wise this morning with the journalists camping on the doorstep, and in any case Mary had no wish to be polite.

Over half the ground was given over to vegetables arranged in neat, well-hoed rows. Two espaliered fruit trees, an apple and a pear, grew against one wall. There was not a weed to be seen on the little lawn. By the back door was a stone horse trough containing an enormous honeysuckle with white, pink and yellow flowers. The door itself was ajar, and in the doorway stood Mrs Abberley.

In one hand she held a knife with a grey, tapering blade. In the other was a large potato. For a moment, neither of them spoke.

'What do you think you're doing here?' The words were indignant but the tone was conversational. 'Barging in like this. And what do you mean by letting Amy Thomas and her friend come through yesterday morning?'

Mary felt anger creeping over her. She welcomed it. 'I think it's high time we had a chat, Mrs Abberley.' There was a bench on the other side of the door. She seized the initiative and sat down.

'There's nothing to talk about.'

'I think there is. Keys, for example.'

Mrs Abberley emerged into the sunshine. 'It's trespassing, that's what you're doing. Some people would call the police.'

'Only very stupid people, I imagine. How can I possibly be trespassing? I'm your landlady.'

The knife hanging slackly in her hand, Mrs Abberley stared at Mary. 'Mr Carter said I could have this cottage for as long as I wanted.'

'It was a verbal arrangement. In any case, Mr Carter is dead. He has no power to bind his successors. The cottage goes with the Vicarage.' Mary offered up a silent apology to heaven and plunged into her first major lie. 'You may need to make alternative arrangements. A lady who was Mr Sutton's nurse is about to retire.'

'You can't turn me out of here. It's my home.'

'Not necessarily for ever.' Mary left a small pause to allow the 'not necessarily' to sink in. Then she produced her next lie. 'We were under the impression you've been looking for somewhere else to live. Surely you didn't expect to stay here?'

'You'd never do it.' Mrs Abberley's voice lacked conviction. 'You'd never dare throw me out. I'd raise such a stink.'

'On that front, things couldn't get much worse for us than they are already,' Mary pointed out cheerfully. 'I expect a few members of the PCC would make a fuss, but there again they always do. I'll think you'll find that the legal position is quite clear.'

Mrs Abberley's face was expressionless. Very carefully she put the knife down on the windowsill and the potato alongside it. She wiped her hands on her apron. Mary waited, disliking herself intensely. To her surprise, she found herself feeling an unwilling admiration for Mrs Abberley. The old woman had nothing left but her silence, and she wrapped herself in it like a cloak. In the end it was Mary who had to speak first.

'I might be able to persuade Mr Sutton to reconsider his decision. But the letters would have to stop.'

'Letters? What letters?'

'You know very well what I mean.'

'I don't see why I shouldn't write to the newspapers. It's a free country, isn't it?'

'I don't mean those letters.' Mary felt the situation was slipping out of her control. 'I mean the other ones.'

'What other ones?'

'I think you know. And also I think you know that they have to stop. Is that clear?'

Mrs Abberley shrugged.

'And then there's the keys.'

'What keys?'

'Don't start that again.' Mary fought off the beginnings of panic; following your hunches was all very well, but what happened when they didn't come off? 'There were four safe keys made. Mr Sutton has one, Mr Newton has the second, the bank has the third – where's the fourth?'

Mrs Abberley said nothing, but the quality of her silence had changed.

'I shouldn't be surprised if a vestry key has gone missing, too,' Mary went on. 'They are just Yales – easy enough to have copies made.'

A jet fighter screamed across the sky. The silence below continued. 'You kept a spare set in the cottage,' Mary suggested.

'I never.' The little eyes flickered between the folds of skin. 'I didn't have anything to do with the church. It wouldn't have been right. Mr Carter had all the keys for the church.'

'Did he have two sets of keys?'

Mrs Abberley slowly nodded. 'For the vestry and the safe. Never bothered about the church, mind. He hardly ever remembered to lock it. Not latterly, any road. He got a bit forgetful.'

The words said one thing, but other meanings floated below their surface. 'Forgetful?' Mary repeated carefully. 'Did Mr Carter sometimes forget his keys?'

'In his last few years he could have forgotten anything,' Mrs Abberley said with a certain pride. 'Even his own name.'

'Sometimes I expect he went over to church and found he'd forgotten his keys?'

Mrs Abberley grunted, a sound which on the whole seemed to signify agreement.

'Perhaps he decided it would save time if he left a set over there?' Another grunt. 'He wouldn't leave them anywhere, though. Not in full sight.' Mary stared thoughtfully at Mrs Abberley. 'He'd hide them somewhere – somewhere safe from the cleaners. The organ loft?'

Mrs Abberley pursed her lips, pushing them forward as if imitating a pig's snout. A negative?

'Somewhere in the sanctuary?' Mary went on. 'No – I don't think so. The boiler house would be more likely, but that's outside and Mr Carter wouldn't want to walk halfway round the church to fetch his spare key. The pulpit then – or perhaps his stall?'

'There's a lot of carving in that canopy thing over the vicar's stall,' Mrs

Abberley said. 'Mr Carter was a tall man.'

'He kept it there?' Mary resisted the temptation to give Mrs Abberley a good shake and ask her why she hadn't said so straight away. 'And when he left, the keys just stayed there?'

'He forgot them. Like he forgot everything else.'

There was a hint of bitterness in the voice, and Mary remembered hearing that Mrs Abberley had not been mentioned in Mr Carter's will. 'Who else knew where he kept the keys?'

'How should I know?'

'But we know one thing, don't we?' Mary took a deep breath. 'Mr Carter left Lydmouth before Miss Kymin arrived. He didn't tell her where the keys were, did he? You did.'

3

They had prayed, they had finished their coffee and they had agreed the main features of the temporary alliance between St John's and St Thomas's.

'There's something else, Simon,' Alec Sutton said.

'I rather thought there might be.'

Sutton left the shelter of Mary's bureau and came to sit in the armchair opposite the archdeacon's. They were in the large, shabby drawing room at the back of the house, where the furniture stood on an island of carpet in a sea of linoleum. The study was too uncomfortable to sit in for any length of time – the shutters were still up because of the journalists outside.

'It's one of those silly things. I should have told you ages ago. The thing is, in a way it was Mary's secret and not mine.'

Simon Davis watched him with pale, unblinking eyes magnified to the size of pennies by the lenses in the tortoiseshell frames. There was no help there, Alec thought. Damn the man.

'It started about six years ago, when we were at Champney. As you know, it's not a very wealthy parish, and we had the boys growing up, and at that time Mary's mother was living with us.' He stared at his hands, thinking how thin and shabby the excuses sounded when he spoke them aloud. 'It was a very strait-laced, old-fashioned place. The villagers didn't think that the rector's wife should work, not for money, and nor did the old couple in the manor house. Just not the sort of thing ladies were supposed to do. In any case, there weren't any jobs in Champney. The nearest town was six miles away, and there weren't many more jobs there either.'

He paused, but Davis said nothing. There was nothing for it but to go on.

'One day, Mary told me she was writing a book – a detective story. She'd always liked the things and she thought she'd have a stab at one herself. I'm no judge, but I thought it seemed quite good, so when she'd finished, we sent it off to a chap I knew from university.' Alec risked a glance at the archdeacon, who stared blankly back. 'This chap works at a publisher's now. We just wanted his opinion, really. It was almost a joke, do you see? But two weeks later he wrote back and said his company would like to publish the book, and were there any more in the pipeline? He said he was awfully sorry he couldn't offer more but would Mary accept an advance of eighty pounds against royalties?'

He stopped talking for a moment and stared miserably at the empty fireplace, remembering what an enormous windfall the money had seemed; talk about pennies from heaven.

Davis took off his glasses and rubbed the red mark across the bridge of his nose. 'Forgive me, Alec, but I'm not sure I understand the problem. Why the need for subterfuge?'

'I told you – if they'd found out, most of the village would have cut us dead. The rector's wife – writing detective stories for money? It would have put us quite beyond the pale. There were a pair of farmers' wives who really ran the show, real old battle-axes, and what they said, went. If they'd stopped calling on Mary, their employees would have stopped coming to church.' He shrugged. 'That's how it seemed to me at the time. Perhaps I was making excuses. Perhaps I didn't like the idea of my wife having to work. And we needed the money. We were drifting into debt.'

'Did you consider discussing the matter with your bishop?' The reproof was there, buried in a question. Alec fought an urge to squirm.

'Of course I did. But the bishop in question was Bastable-Cairns. Do you remember him? He used to be the Dean of Rosington in the thirties.'

Davis nodded. 'I see. He had a row with Dorothy L. Sayers on the wireless: rather a childish affair, I seem to remember, and it went on rumbling in the newspapers for months afterwards.'

'They disagreed,' Alec said slowly, 'on the ethics of writing detective fiction.'

The archdeacon nodded again, acknowledging the point without necessarily accepting it. Alec patted his pockets, looking for cigarettes which weren't there. He stood up and unlocked a cupboard in the panelling on the left of the fireplace. The shelves held an assortment of books in brightly coloured jackets. He chose two at random and handed them to the archdeacon.

'To make matters worse, Mary's books are a little on the sensational side. A chap on the *Sunday Times* even compared her to Edgar Wallace, though I think that's unfair. You see the difficulty – it's almost respectable if you write detective novels which are like articulated crossword puzzles. But as soon as you breathe a breath of excitement into them, they become tinged with immorality.' His voice trailed into silence.

Davis examined the covers. *A Bullet for the Inspector* featured an elderly gentleman in a dinner jacket tastefully arranged on the hearthrug in front of a fireplace of baronial dimensions; in the centre of his forehead was a neat red hole. *Inspector Coleford and the Hand of Death* had a more impressionistic cover with swirling shadows, drops of blood and a hangman's noose. The author's name was Denton Carbury.

'Mary put her mother's surname together with my mother's.' Alec shut the cupboard door. 'It seemed a good idea at the time.'

'May I borrow these?'

'Of course. You'll need to advise the Bishop about their contents. You could keep them if you wanted to, but I dare say you don't.' He rushed on, unwilling to hear the offer formally turned down. 'There are five altogether. The last one, *Inspector Coleford Strikes a Match*, was published last month.'

'In this diocese we're a little less conservative. But you didn't mention Mary's writing when you came to be interviewed for this living. And nor did she. Why was that?'

'Because we wanted to come here so badly. If one person on the diocesan board didn't approve of an incumbent's wife writing detective stories, it could have been enough to destroy my chances.' Alec flushed and went on rapidly, 'That's the reason for all this, but I know it's not an excuse. I'm sorry, Simon. I've been telling lies to myself, you see, little lies for what I thought were the best of motives. And they've had a cumulative effect. I've ended up with a major lie, a sort of dishonesty.'

'And what do you think you should do about it?'

Sutton sank back in his chair. 'It's not for me to say. If the Bishop wants me to resign my living, then of course I shall.'

'And Mary?'

'She was hoping to carry on with her writing. But I don't know how she will feel now. We couldn't manage the boys' school fees without the royalties.'

191

Davis was leafing through one of the books. He did not look up.

'It's astonishing what one can make oneself believe when one wants to.' Sutton examined his fingernails. A page rustled as it turned. 'I can't take any credit for finally being honest, either. Mary had one of those anonymous letters yesterday. It made a number of nasty allegations, and asked where we got our money from. If people are wondering where we get our money from, far better to get it out in the open. So Mary took the letter to show Inspector Thornhill this morning. And she also took a copy of the latest book.'

He waited. Davis turned another page.

'What happens now? I imagine you'll want to discuss it with the Bishop.'

The archdeacon looked up. 'Of course. I'm glad this is out in the open. I'm sure you are, too.' He inched himself forward on the seat of his chair and with painful slowness raised himself to his feet. 'I wonder – might I swap one of these for *Inspector Coleford Strikes a Match*? I've not read that one yet.'

4

'Not in front of the servants' was one of those sayings which had come down to Chrissie Newton from her mother, who had probably had it from her mother before her. It was more than a saying: it had the moral force of advice written in stone and delivered by hand to Moses on Mount Sinai. There were a number of similar sayings, all essential to the conduct of life. A man should not wear tweeds in Town. One was not rude to servants because they could not answer back. Displays of emotion, whether positive or negative, were almost always suspicious, being intrinsically vulgar, unBritish and unhelpful.

As Chrissie lay in the darkened bedroom pretending to have a headache, she wondered whether perhaps she had been mistaken for all those years. She had seen Anthony Ruispidge wear tweeds in Jermyn Street. She had heard him shouting at his niece Jemima in front of Pinson, the increasingly inefficient butler. But of course Anthony Ruispidge always did whatever he pleased. It would never occur to him to worry what others were saying about him.

The front door slammed. Chrissie slithered off the bed and padded in her stockinged feet across the floor to the window. She peered through the crack in the curtains.

Giles was walking steadily down the drive, with a briefcase under his arm and Sambo ambling after him. It was a shock to see her husband looking so normal, at least from the rear. Part of her would have liked to see external corroboration of the process working away inside him – his hair turned suddenly white, for example, or his right arm in a sling; an outward symptom of the disintegration within. Giles's apparent normality made ner wonder, just for an instant, whether she'd imagined the whole thing.

But she hadn't imagined what she had found in his desk yesterday morning. The tangle of bills and bank statements, the emptied deposit accounts, the investments long since sold – put together, they seemed to add up to a mystery: how had their expenditure apparently increased while their income had apparently diminished?

Chrissie sat on the bed and slipped on her shoes. Giles was walking, which meant he must be going into Lydmouth rather than up to Clearland Court this morning. She pulled back the curtains with a jerk, and light flooded into the room. The photographs sprang to life on her dressing table: John Anthony doing his national service with a hussar regiment before going up to Cambridge; Edwina at that terrifyingly expensive establishment in Paris where they taught one how to construct menus and reply to invitations; and Michael, her baby, still at Harrow.

'How could you?' she said to Giles, watching her lips move soundlessly in the looking glass. 'These are our children.'

The hum of the vacuum cleaner filtered up the stairs. Mrs Turner was getting on with the domestic grind in her special way: 'Me, I'm like one of them clockwork engines. Just wind me up and off I go.'

Chrissie opened the bedroom door. By the sound of it Mrs Turner was dragging the vacuum cleaner round the dining room by its hose, banging it against the legs of the chairs and the table.

Not in front of the servants. At half-past four this morning, Chrissie had crept downstairs to leave a note for Mrs Turner on the kitchen table: the note explained that she, Chrissie, had a headache and would try to sleep late.

The vacuum cleaner masked her footsteps on the stairs. When she reached the hall, she hesitated. Giles's walking sticks stood stiffly in the brass cartridge case by the front door. There were two letters on the table under the mirror – brown envelopes, almost certainly more bills. The vacuum cleaner roared on. Chrissie gripped the knob on the study door and gently twisted it. The knob turned but when she pushed the door nothing happened. Giles had locked it, damn him, to prevent her from finding out more. She shook the knob angrily.

When she turned round, she found that Mrs Turner was watching her through the open door of the dining room, standing stock-still, while her right arm swung to and fro, automatically running the vacuum cleaner over the same piece of carpet. Mrs Turner stamped on the button at the back of the machine and the sound slowly died away.

'Feeling better?'

'Not too bad, thanks.'

'There's some tea in the kitchen if you want it. Bit stewed, mind.'

'Thanks.'

Chrissie fled down the hall towards the kitchen. Mrs Turner pressed the button and the vacuum cleaner began to devour everything in its path. She should be grateful, Chrissie told herself, that Mrs Turner was only interested in her grudges and her grandchildren; otherwise the story of Mrs Newton's headache and Mr Newton's failure to say goodbye to his wife, adorned with suitable embellishments, would be all over Lydmouth by teatime.

The teapot was the next-best thing to cold. Chrissie couldn't be bothered to make any more. She went out into the garden, hoping to find comfort. For once its magic failed to work on her. She saw the jobs that needed to be done and had no desire to do them. Her eyes drifted over her achievements and saw them for precisely what they were: the handiwork of a lonely woman with too much time on her hands.

'Damn you,' she shouted, frightening a pigeon and two blackbirds into the air.

Sambo, who had left Giles by the gate, padded round the corner of the house to investigate. He stabbed his grey muzzle against Chrissie's thigh, demanding affection. All she could remember was that Giles was the only significant person in Sambo's universe.

'And damn you, too.'

Chrissie went back into the kitchen and swept the keys of the Alvis from the dresser. 'I'm going out,' she called down the hall, careless of whether Mrs Turner would hear her above the vacuum cleaner. She tucked her handbag under her arm and walked with her head down through the sunshine of the yard. The Alvis was kept in a lean-to shed at the end.

The engine rumbled into life. Chrissie reversed slowly out of the garage. The car unnerved her – it smelt of Giles, of pipe tobacco and, more faintly, of the shaving cream he used. The floor in front of the driver's seat was thick with ash, because he was in the habit of using the car as an ashtray. One of the stubs in front of the passenger seat had lipstick on it. The car stopped with a jolt which threw her against the back of her seat. Glass tinkled and the engine stalled. She glanced in the rear-view mirror. The car had collided with a gatepost.

Giles would be furious. Her husband considered the car to be his, and only allowed her to drive it on sufferance. He claimed it was essential for his work so she required his express permission to borrow it. To have damaged the car when she should not have been driving it in the first place amounted to one of those offences which turned him for days, at least behind closed doors, into a white-lipped stranger. Chrissie knew all this intellectually but for once it did not seem to matter; it was as if her thoughts were individually wrapped in cotton wool in case they should jostle against one another and cause damage with their hard edges.

She did not bother to inspect the damage. She lit a cigarette and drove north out of Lydmouth. The car seemed almost to take care of itself. She followed the main road through the outskirts of the town and into the country. She turned right into a lane which wound upwards between high, overgrown hedges. Sometimes she glimpsed through gateways the landscape beyond the hedges: a secret country of swelling hills and small sinuous valleys. The morning sun beat down from a clear blue sky on a pastoral world populated with sheep and cows.

Clearland Court lay on a high tongue of land enclosed on three sides by the river. The lane levelled out and curved through a patch of woodland; the branches of the trees met overhead, turning the road into a green, claustrophobic tunnel. Suddenly terrified, Chrissie pushed down the accelerator as far as it would go. In her panic, she overshot the wrought-iron lodge gates and had to reverse back to them.

The gates were open. The car clattered over a cattle grid, shaking her entire body as Giles had once done when he came home drunk and in a temper; she could not remember the reason for his anger, only its effects.

The drive curved round and up to the house which sat on a bluff overlooking a green bowl of parkland. The grass was dotted, apparently casually, with elms, oaks and more cows. The line of the drive lifted the eyes up to the house, preventing one from noticing the potholes in its surface until it was too late.

Chrissie let the car drift to a halt beside the fountain, lichen-streaked and waterless. Above her reared the house, a tall, stone-faced rectangle of pale yellow stone with small, low wings disguised as classical temples; not so much a home as a statement of position.

After a while, she got out of the car, leaving the door open and the engine running. She walked slowly across the weed-infested gravel and up the wide, shallow steps. The outer doors stood open. There were glazed doors inside.

Chrissie pulled the bell. She heard nothing, which might be because it wasn't working or because the servants' end of the house was so far away.

Out of the sunshine and just inside the house, she was cold and she began to shiver. She turned round, hoping to draw warmth from the view, and noticed the car door dangling open. Terror struck her once again: how odd they would think her, if they were looking out of the windows. She ran across the gravel, turned off the engine and slammed the door. She turned round and saw Pinson waiting in the doorway, his face like a supercilious sheep's.

'Good morning, madam.'

'I want to see Sir Anthony,' she said in a rush. 'Is he in?'

Pinson held open one leaf of the glazed doors. 'If you would like to wait in the library, I will see if he is at home.'

The hall was floored with marble, and the clack of his heels rose into the still air and set off a chattering army of echoes. Pinson was long past retirement age, practically gaga according to Giles. He was, Chrissie thought miserably, one of those servants who give the impression of being able to peer deep into not only one's soul but one's genealogy, and to pluck out all the failures and inadequacies.

She would have been in awe of him had not Giles, when drunk, once told her that Pinson was a man with a past; before the war he had worked for years at one of Ruispidge's clubs, Brooks's, until he had been sent to prison for soliciting boys in the public lavatory at Piccadilly Circus. Such behaviour puzzled and disgusted her; Giles had been amused rather than disturbed. 'You wouldn't have thought he had it in him, would you?' he had said. Brooks's had sacked Pinson as a matter of course, but when he came out of prison Sir Anthony had offered him a job at Clearland Court. Perhaps, Chrissie wondered, Tony Ruispidge liked to have around him people who were obliged to him? What did that say about Giles?

Pinson opened the library door and stood aside to let her enter. There were egg stains on the sleeve of his old black coat, and he smelled of sweat and stale milk. The door closed behind her.

The library was a long, thin room with a bay window at the far end, bookshelves in oppressively dark-stained wood, and a chimneypiece like the west front of a small cathedral. Sir Anthony's grandfather had had an unfortunate taste for the gothic. There was a flash of black and white, like a startled magpie, at the far end of the room.

'Hello – it's Mrs Newton, isn't it?' Jemima Orepool said. 'What do you want?'

197

She had been sitting in a high-backed armchair in front of the fireplace. On the desk beside the chair, a copy of *Picture Post* was propped against the telephone.

'Pinson showed me in here.' Chrissie knew her voice sounded defensive.

'Aunt Soph isn't in. She's at a committee meeting somewhere.'

'I've come to see Sir Anthony.' She was afraid of Jemima Orepool because the girl was young, beautiful and Sir Anthony Ruispidge's niece. 'I'm sorry to disturb you.'

'I can't think why he didn't put you in the drawing room. It's much more comfortable there.'

Jemima moved down the library as if planning to herd Chrissie into the drawing room herself. In order to frustrate this manoeuvre, Chrissie sat down on the nearest chair. Jemima stared at her but said nothing. With shaking hands, Chrissie opened her handbag and offered her a cigarette.

'No, thank you.'

Chrissie took one herself. The flint in her lighter was giving trouble, and the wick refused to light. She flicked the wheel again and again, imagining that Jemima was staring scornfully at her. The door opened and Sir Anthony came into the room. To her immense mortification Chrissie promptly dropped the cigarette on the carpet and had to scrabble for it on her hands and knees.

'It's not alight,' she said brightly. 'It won't damage the carpet.'

Ruispidge helped her up. 'Chrissie, my dear. What can I do for you?'

'I – I wanted a word about something.'

'By all means.' He glared at Jemima. 'See if you can persuade them to make some coffee, will you?'

Without a word, Jemima slipped out of the room, leaving the door open. Chrissie listened to the sound of her footsteps receding across the hall, raising echoes which were lighter and crisper than Pinson's had been.

'Do sit down.' He picked up the big lighter on the desk and lit her cigarette. 'It wasn't Soph you really wanted, was it? Pinson said it was me, but sometimes he gets a bit muddled. If it's Soph, I'm afraid you're out of luck. Had to go to Cheltenham today. Something about lifeboats, I think.'

'I didn't want to see Soph.' She hated using the Ruispidges' Christian names; they sounded presumptuous on her lips, though the two couples had been on first-name terms since before the war. 'I wanted to see you.'

'Splendid.' Frowning slightly, Ruispidge stamped down the room and lowered himself into a high-backed armchair whose seat was a little too tall for his short legs. 'What's this about?'

'I'm worried about Giles. Would you mind if I talked to you about it?'

Sir Anthony stared at the carpet. 'Of course not. But – ah – are you sure it's any of my business?'

'He's been very short-tempered recently. I wondered if there might be something on his mind.'

The blue eyes swung upwards and stared at her. 'Always had a short fuse, Giles did. I remember at school—'

'No,' Chrissie said. 'It's not like that. This is serious. I think there may be money problems.'

There was a silence. Ruispidge's colour darkened a little further. Chrissie knew then that any good will he felt for her would always come a poor second to his loyalty to Giles. He stirred in his chair.

'There's not a lot I can do, Chrissie. I don't know the facts, you see.'

'That's the problem. Nor do I, not really. But—'

'There's your answer, if you ask me. Have a chat with Giles. It's easy to get things out of proportion when one doesn't have the facts.'

'I've tried that. He won't tell me anything.'

'Perhaps there's nothing much to tell, eh? Ten to one it's a storm in a teacup.'

Ruispidge launched into an anecdote on the theme of storms in teacups. Chrissie had heard it more than once before: the story involved Giles and Tony Ruispidge and culminated with an explosion in the school chemistry laboratory.

After a decent interval he glanced at his watch and pantomimed surprise. 'Good God – is that the time? They're expecting me at Home Farm.' He slipped off the chair.

Chrissie remained where she was, perched on the edge of the fat leather armchair. Suddenly she saw him for what he was: a pugnacious little man running away from her. Why had she ever been in awe of him?

'Now don't dash off, will you? Jemima will be along with the coffee in a moment. Do her good to have a chat with another woman. I think she finds us rather dull down here.' By now he was moving towards the door. 'I'm sure all this will blow over. Talk to Giles when things have calmed down, eh?'

'He's not even paying the school fees,' Chrissie burst out. 'I'm worried about the children.'

Sir Anthony hesitated. 'I'm not sure how I could—'

She cut through his embarrassment. 'You could talk to him. Try to find out what's the matter.'

'Of course, if you think it would help.'

'I've no idea if it'll help.' Chrissie stood up and snatched her handbag from the arm of the chair. 'All I know is that he's more likely to talk to you than me.'

Ruispidge automatically opened the door for her as she strode down the room. As she passed, he muttered something about being delighted to do his best.

'*Why* won't he talk to me?' She glared at him. 'He never would, you know, not properly.'

He shuffled his feet, weaving like a boxer trying to avoid an anticipated blow. 'I've always had a lot of time for old Giles.'

The telephone began to ring, its bell tinny in the vast empty spaces of the library. Chrissie crossed the hall. Sir Anthony followed her, almost trotting in his effort to overtake her before she reached the front door. She remembered that she had left her lighter on the arm of her chair in the library. Let them keep it. She wanted to leave this house as quickly as possible. Ruispidge opened a leaf of the front door.

'There's something wrong,' Chrissie said as she passed him. 'Really wrong – can't you see? You're meant to be his friend.'

Jemima Orepool ran across the hall on sandalled feet and into the library, slamming the door behind her. A moment later, the ringing of the telephone stopped.

5

There were early peas in the Vicarage kitchen garden. Mrs Abberley, a small, squat shadow under the hard blue sky, made sure they were still there, half-hidden behind an elder tree near the door to the lane. She made a mental note to pick them on her way back. They wouldn't take long to prepare, and they would go nicely with the beetroot and the cold tongue. She enjoyed a bit of colour on the plate.

She unbolted the door in the wall and slipped into the alley. A moment later she was walking up Bull Lane, her umbrella tapping on the paving stones. No one was about. When she reached the High Street, even that had a deserted air, for most people were either eating their midday meal or preparing it.

She went into the phone box by the public lavatory and fumbled in her purse for change.

'Leave the parson alone,' she was going to say. 'I've changed my mind.'

Better the devil you know, Mrs Abberley thought; that Mary Sutton wasn't quite the mealy-mouthed niminy-piminy miss she appeared. Mrs Abberley respected few things but strength of character was one of them. It would be wrong to say that the two women had declared a truce: it was rather that they had decided that their individual interests were better served by a state of armed neutrality. If the Suttons stayed at the Vicarage, then so would Mrs Abberley at Church Cottage. But if the Suttons went, anything could happen.

As for the other one, the poor weak fool, he would have other uses. Nothing dramatic, mind, but a pound here and a pound there would smooth life's rough corners. It was another hot day and Mrs Abberley found her mind returning to the merits of refrigerators. He would hardly notice the cost if she did it on the never-never.

The ringing went on. Mrs Abberley let it run to twenty-five rings before she broke the connection. She would try again in the evening. Sooner or later she would reach him. That was the advantage of a town like Lydmouth. There was nowhere to run to, nowhere to hide.

She walked slowly back the way she had come. The air shimmered in the heat and the tarmac in Bull Lane seemed to ripple, a black river. As she walked, her lips moved, sending out a silent stream of words.

'She was a fool, look, asking for trouble. And he's another, giving it her. Nice little peas. Sweet little peas. Peas would keep longer if I had a refrigerator.' She opened the door in the wall and went into the walled warmth of the kitchen garden. 'Milk wouldn't go off so quickly. And I could have my own ice, too, as much as I wanted.' She imagined elderflower cordial with ice cubes on a hot afternoon; the ice chinking in her glass. She said aloud in a voice filled with wonder: 'It'd be like something in a film.'

She stuck the umbrella in the earth. With her ears straining in the direction of the Vicarage, for there was always the possibility that one of the Suttons would appear, she began to gather peas with greedy hands. A large succulent-looking pod caught her attention. She stretched out her hand and plucked it.

Butter too, she thought, milk and eggs and God alone knew what else. In her mind she visualised the gleaming interior of a refrigerator she had seen in the window of the electricity showroom. With an enormous effort of imagination she transferred its Arctic purity from the showroom to her kitchen. It would fit so neatly between the dresser and the wall.

Every now and then she turned her head towards the Vicarage. As far as she knew, the Suttons rarely came down here, but you couldn't be too careful. If the worst came to the worst and they caught her red-handed – *green*-handed – she had her defence ready-made.

'It's one of them traditions. Old Mr Carter said the tenant of the cottage could take what he wanted from the kitchen garden. Just for himself, mind, not for selling or giving away: that wouldn't be right.'

It was always best to act not guilty.

6

Williamson filled the doorway of Thornhill's office. He had just returned from briefing the Chief Constable on their lack of progress. He took his pipe out of his mouth and pointed it at Thornhill. 'Where've you been? Got lost on the way to the hospital?'

'No, sir. I saw Miss Francis—'

'Can she remember what happened?'

'No, sir.'

'You do surprise me. That's wonderful. Bloody marvellous.'

'The doctor says it's possible that someone gave her a bang on the head.'

'Possible? We need something better than that, Thornhill.'

'The bruise would fit the tyre lever that Quale brought in.'

'I know some people don't like reporters, but knocking them on the head seems a bit extreme.'

'There was another thing, sir.' Thornhill knew that when Williamson was in this mood, the only way to cope was to ignore it.

'We've got further on the letter-writing front. Miss Kymin's neighbour turned up with some roses for Miss Francis. You remember – Mrs Milkwall? She's a cleaner at the hospital. The roses were wrapped in a sheet of old newspaper. Someone had been snipping words out of it.'

Williamson frowned. He came into the room and shut the door.

'Mrs Milkwall?'

Thornhill shook his head. 'I've been to see her. That's what took me so

203

long. She's not a churchgoer. And she's not too good at reading and writing, either: I asked her supervisor at the hospital. She says she found the newspaper in the Kymins' shed. Apparently she'd gone there to feed Miss Kymin's cat. She wanted something to wrap the roses in and took the paper from the top of the pile. Didn't notice anything odd about it.'

'Miss Kymin? But what about the letter in her handbag? Why should she write to herself?'

'I don't know, sir. An insurance policy, perhaps – just in case anyone grew suspicious?' Thornhill remembered Miss Kymin's unexpectedly exotic collection of lingerie and wondered whether there might have been another explanation: perhaps accusing herself of having an affair with the vicar had been pleasurable in itself.

'Are you sure the papers weren't a plant?' Williamson demanded.

'They were copies of the *Gazette*. They used to get the papers delivered. Each one was marked Kymin.'

'You'd better check that.'

'I've told Wilson to go round the newsagent's this afternoon.' It was the sort of job, Thornhill thought, that even Wilson would be able to manage. 'And there's something else, sir.'

Williamson, his mind running ahead to lunch, had already turned to go. 'Yes? Make it snappy.'

'If Miss Kymin was writing the anonymous letters, who sent the one Mr Hendry had this morning? The one that accused Sutton of Miss Kymin's murder?'

7

In the CID Office they took their lunch in three shifts between twelve-thirty and two. Sergeant Kirby allotted Norman Wilson to the third shift.

This annoyed Wilson considerably. He objected not to the time but to the company. In all organisations there exist hidden hierarchies, and even as a child Wilson had been inordinately sensitive to them. In his opinion the three shifts reflected the unofficial pecking order of the CID. He should have gone with the first shift, whose members included Kirby, people who were going places in the force and who had a correspondingly high opinion of themselves. Many of them had trickled back to the CID Office before their time was up.

Wilson would not have minded too much had he been attached to the second shift. These were the rugby players and the beer drinkers, often better at making arrests than writing reports or passing promotion exams; they might not be career-minded, but they had an undeniable rough glamour. The men on this shift came back a little later than they should have done, smelling of alcohol and boasting about their rate of consumption.

The third shift had nothing to recommend it, Wilson considered, apart from himself, who was obviously exceptional. Here were the no-hopers, people like PC Porter who had been attached to the CID Office in a vague but lowly capacity for the duration of the enquiry.

One day he would show them all, Wilson told himself, and that would teach them to undervalue him. The fact that the grievance was such an intangible one served only to increase his irritation.

When Kirby told him he could go, Wilson stalked out of the room, determined to find a way of proving himself. Most of the others on this shift went down to the canteen, but he had no intention of sharing his lunch with them. Instead he went out into the sunshine, lit a cigarette and walked briskly along the pavement to Lyd Street. On the corner down the hill was the Bathurst Arms. He would pick up a sandwich in the bar; he didn't have time for one of their lunches.

To his dismay the saloon bar was crowded. Between the press of bodies he glimpsed his other reason for coming to the Bathurst Arms – the landlady, a well set-up woman encased in her charms like a suit of armour; she was rather older than Wilson, but exerted a disturbing fascination over him.

He tried to insinuate his way through the bodies to the bar. They wouldn't let him through. He was on the verge of giving up when a man at the counter turned and waved. It was old Fuggle from the *Post*.

'Mr Wilson,' he called, his fruity voice clearly audible over the hubbub. 'What can I get you?'

'Half of mild, please.'

Flattered by the attention, Wilson retreated to the bay window and stood smoking and looking out at the river. A moment later, Ivor Fuggle joined him. He had apparently misheard what Wilson said, because in his hand were two large whiskies. He handed one to Wilson.

'Cheers.'

'Cheers,' Wilson echoed. There seemed to be very little soda in the whisky. The alcohol stung the back of his throat. He didn't like to say anything in case Fuggle thought he could not take his drink. Best to swallow it quickly so it didn't linger in the mouth. He noticed that the journalist had already almost finished.

'You've had a busy morning, I bet,' Fuggle said. 'And I expect the rest of the day won't exactly be a rest cure. You need something to build you up. Drink up and I'll get you another one of those.'

'I couldn't – anyway it's my round.'

'The paper's paying. What's the use of having expenses if you don't use them? Every job has its perks, eh?' He poked Wilson lightly in the ribs and laughed immoderately. Wilson joined in. Soon he discovered that his glass was empty but that did not matter because Fuggle waved his hand and refills appeared as if by magic.

'This is the life,' Fuggle was saying. 'Not that I mean I'm glad the lady's dead, far from it, but something like this makes the whole town come alive. Gives a bit of interest to life. Don't you agree?'

Norman Wilson agreed fervently.

'I'm glad you boys in the CID are handling it yourselves,' Fuggle went on. 'Damn it, it's a local murder – so of course the local chaps are going to be the best people to sort it out.'

A whisky-flavoured glow was spreading through Wilson's empty stomach. It was true: he did feel more alive – standing here, cigarette in one hand, whisky in the other, a man among men. He glimpsed the landlady behind the counter and fancied she was staring admiringly at him. Maybe I should try my luck there, he told himself. If you don't ask you don't get.

'Never rains but it pours, does it?' Fuggle said.

'What do you mean?'

'You must have a lot on at the moment. So have we.' Fuggle twirled the glass in his hand. 'Not just this murder case, is there? There's this poison pen writer, as well. And the stolen chalice.'

'They may all be parts of the same thing,' Wilson said casually. 'We can't afford to ignore that possibility.'

'I can see the murder and the theft being connected – that's common sense. But the letters?'

Wilson lowered his voice. 'Between you and me, there may be developments there.'

'You don't say.' Fuggle looked admiringly at him. Then the journalist tapped the side of his nose. 'Yes, but anyone can have an idea. Mr Williamson is always getting bees in his bonnet. But what we all need is facts.'

'But we've got facts, evidence that will stand up in court.' Wilson realised what he was saying and added in a rapid undertone, 'This is strictly between you and me, you understand. Not for the paper.'

'Of course.' Ivor Fuggle looked solemn. 'You have my word. I've been a journalist for nearly forty years, and believe you me if there's one thing I've learned it's this: there's never any advantage in getting on the wrong side of a policeman. Or in trying to fool him, come to that.'

Wilson felt obscurely flattered. He had not realised that Fuggle was such a shrewd old chap. Someone – a friend of Fuggle's? – insisted on buying them more drinks, but, having bought them, faded back into the crowd, leaving the two of them alone.

'It beats me,' Fuggle was saying. 'I just don't see how the two cases could be connected.'

'It's obvious,' Wilson heard himself saying. 'I thought of it almost at once. And old Thornhill managed to prove it this morning. That Kymin woman wasn't just the murder victim. She was the letter-writer too.'

Fuggle let out a long, respectful whistle. 'Good God. But that puts a different complexion on the whole thing. No wonder someone topped her. But when you say you've got proof, what exactly do you mean?'

Norman Wilson was not listening. In his mind he heard the last words he had spoken, repeated over and over again. His mouth was dry and foul-tasting. He had a stomachache. According to the clock on the wall, it was ten past two.

'Mr Fuggle—'

'Call me Ivor, dear boy. No need for formality between friends.'

'All this is confidential. And I can't be quite sure of the facts. Not – not yet. It will go no further, will it?'

Fuggle waved his glass in an expansive gesture. 'You know me, Norman. The soul of discretion. Wild horses could not force me to betray a friend's confidence.' He bent down, bringing his head close to Wilson's; there were flecks of food on his regular and very white false teeth. 'Besides, now we know what we're looking for, we can maybe get to it by another direction. So don't you worry about a thing. Not that it really matters. You'd be surprised at how many stories are attributed to "a source within the police".'

'You promised. Please – you won't let on?'

'Of course I promise. Don't worry. Trust me, lad. Tell you what, perhaps we could meet for a jar this evening. On the paper, naturally. It's a shame not to use your expenses when you can, eh?'

Wilson was already pushing through the crowd towards the door. He burst out on to the pavement. He began to run up Lyd Street. Halfway up the hill, his stomach revolted. He stopped, and to the surprise of the pedestrians vomited neatly into the doorway of Masterman's, the jeweller's.

8

'Late back from lunch at·a time like this,' Kirby said, twisting his features into an expression of outraged virtue. 'That lad knows how to impress.' He glanced at Thornhill, who was walking down the High Street at his side. 'I expect Mr Williamson will have something to say about it.'

'There's also the point that he managed to miss those newspapers in the Kymins' shed.' Thornhill grinned at his sergeant; they both knew that Wilson would not be allowed to forget the failure. 'Still, it's Mr Williamson's decision.'

The two men walked on in a friendly silence, having made their feelings perfectly plain to each other without deviating from the respect due to rank. The clock chimed a quarter-past two as they turned into Church Street. Thornhill had a hollow feeling in the pit of his stomach, an uneasy sense that the investigation might be nearing its climax. On the other side of the road, a uniformed constable stood on guard at the lych gate and another patrolled the churchyard. Three journalists and two photographers were leaning against the wall of the Vicarage. Thornhill slowed his pace.

'It's not watertight,' he said to Kirby, speaking his thoughts aloud. 'I know that.'

'What isn't?'

'The idea that there's only a small circle of suspects now.'

'Why not? It seems clear enough to me, sir.'

'The person who sent the letter to Hendry this morning couldn't have been

Miss Kymin. But he or she knew about the letters, their appearance as well as their contents.'

'That means he must have seen at least one of them,' Kirby said. 'He might even have had one sent to him.'

'Yes, but the trouble is, we don't know everyone who's had one of those letters, and we don't know who they might have shown them to.'

Kirby grinned. 'It's still simpler than having to think of most of Lydmouth as in the frame.' He was walking buoyantly along the pavement, rising slightly on the balls of his feet at each step, hands in pockets, head thrown back. 'And the second letter-writer could well be the murderer.'

'Not necessarily,' Thornhill objected. 'You're assuming the writer's trying to shift the blame away from himself and on to Sutton. But the motive might have been just malice.' Or even, he thought, a warped desire to see justice done: suppose Sutton was the killer after all?

'All right, sir. But you agree it's possible that the killer was the second letter-writer?' In his excitement Kirby sprayed spittle into the air. 'Because if so, we know who likes writing letters, we know who was friendly with Miss Kymin, and we know who hates Sutton. One and the same person. Mrs Abberley has to be the front runner.'

Thornhill wished he could share his sergeant's optimism. But life wasn't like a detective novel where you could safely assume that one of the dozen characters listed for easy reference at the front would prove to be the murderer. People were messy, and so were their lives; half the time they didn't know the reasons for their actions and half the time they were quite capable of acting out of character; throw in the enormous rôle of chance and you were left with the situation in which the principles of rational deduction had only a very limited application.

The two detectives stopped outside the door of Church Cottage. Kirby knocked three times. The reporters and the photographers moved in a body towards them.

'Any developments, Inspector?'

'Mr Thornhill – this way please.' A camera shutter clicked. And to Kirby: 'Are you a police officer too?'

'What do you think?' Kirby knocked again. 'I'll give you three guesses.'

'Why do you want to see the old lady? Do you think she saw something on Sunday night?'

The third burst of knocking brought no response. Damn the woman, Thornhill thought: answer that door.

'Do you want to come back later?' Kirby said in an undertone.

'I'd rather not. Not in the circumstances.' *Not if Mrs Abberley's the killer.* Thornhill touched Kirby's arm. The two policemen walked on to the yellow door of the Vicarage. The journalists trailed after them without unseemly enthusiasm.

'Any news of this chalice yet? Is it true it's a Welsh national treasure? When will you call in Scotland Yard?'

Thornhill rang the doorbell. A moment later the flap of the letterbox was lifted from within.

'Who is it?' Mary Sutton asked.

'Inspector Thornhill. May we come in?'

Bolts slid back and a key turned in the lock. Finally the door opened and the two men slipped inside the Vicarage.

'Sorry to be so unwelcoming.' Mrs Sutton relocked the door and pushed the bolts home. 'I thought you were one of those beastly men. Either that or Mr Youlgreave – not that he's beastly, but we are expecting him. Did you want my husband? He's in the study. He's on the phone, so he may be a while unless I tell him you're here.'

'There's no need to disturb him.'

Thornhill introduced Sergeant Kirby. She smiled at him and led the way to the panelled drawing room at the back of the house. Kirby, smiling vaguely at no one in particular, began unobtrusively to examine the room.

'I've just tried to phone you,' she said.

'Really?'

'I found something out. I think it might be rather important. I had a chat with Mrs Abberley this morning.' Her face turned a delicate shade of pink beneath her powder. 'You remember that the manufacturers supplied four keys for the safe? And that we only have three of them? Well, it seems that Mr Carter had the fourth key. Apparently, in his later years he became a little forgetful, and he would sometimes go over to church without his keys. So he decided to keep spares for the safe and the vestry actually in the church.'

'Where did he put them?'

'Mrs Abberley said that he hid them in the canopy over his stall in the choir. You may not have noticed, but it has some rather elaborate carving.'

Thornhill remembered the dark carved wood of the choir and thought about the possibility of fingerprints. 'And they were left there when he died?'

'I think so. No one knew they were there. Except Mrs Abberley, of course.' Mrs Sutton hesitated. 'Their existence seems to have slipped her mind. Of course she had a lot to think about and she's not as young as she was. But she thinks that she may have mentioned the keys in passing to Miss Kymin.' The pink darkened to a colour approaching red. 'You know how things can slip out when one's chatting away.'

'Then why didn't she mention them to me when I saw her yesterday?'

'Perhaps she forgot. Or perhaps she felt that it would be confessing her own guilt, that you'd whisk her off to prison. You must remember that her friend's death, and in those dreadful circumstances, must have come as a tremendous shock.'

Thornhill looked steadily at her. Left to himself he would have said that Mrs Abberley had the emotional fragility of a Tiger tank. There was a sense of compromise – reconciliation would have been too strong a word – in the air. Possibilities churned rapidly through his mind. If Miss Kymin had had a full set of keys at her disposal, she would have been able to open the vestry door; if she had pulled the door shut behind her, the Yale lock would have automatically engaged. Had her attacker broken his way in to find her cowering against the wall under the Ruispidge monument? And had he made the most of this unexpected opportunity and used her keys to open the safe on the off-chance that it contained something worth stealing?

He realised that Mrs Sutton was looking blankly at him and brought his mind abruptly back to the present. 'Thank you for telling me. I shall need to talk to her about that. In fact I wanted to see her rather urgently about another matter. But she's not answering her door. I wondered if you'd seen her go out?'

'She was there at midday.' Mary Sutton straightened an ornament on the mantelpiece, a manoeuvre that allowed her to turn her back on the two policemen. 'She was peeling potatoes, and I rather assumed she was getting ready for lunch. In which case, one wouldn't have thought she'd have gone out.'

'Would you have seen her if she had?'

'Not necessarily. Even in normal circumstances, I don't spend much time looking out of the window.' Mrs Sutton turned back to face the room. 'Besides, if she's going out, she often sneaks out the back way. There's a gate from her garden into what used to be the Vicarage kitchen garden. There's a door in the far wall which leads out into the alley behind.'

Kirby nodded. 'I know. It runs into the bottom of Bull Lane.'

'There are a few vegetables in the kitchen garden, and sometimes she helps herself. Don't think I'm complaining – it doesn't matter a hoot. I think she only does it for the principle of the thing. She likes the idea that we don't know she's putting one over us.'

'So there's a way to get from here to her back door without going into the street?'

'Yes. Would you like me to show you?'

Mrs Sutton led the two policemen down the long hall into the kitchen and through the back door into the yard.

She pointed to the left. 'The kitchen garden's down there. On the other side of that wall. But we can cut through the coach house.'

'You've a surprising amount of land here,' Thornhill said.

'Much more than we need. It's over two acres in all. We mow the lawn below the terrace but we've had to let the rest run to seed. We grow a few vegetables, but only in a hit-or-miss way. Mr Carter could afford a gardener but that's beyond our means.' She pulled open one leaf of the coach-house doors. 'Still, it's a paradise for the boys when they're home from school.' She nodded towards the door in the back wall. 'The cottage is through there.'

Kirby tugged the door open. Sunlight poured into the interior of the coach house. The doorway acted as a frame for the colours of the garden beyond.

'Such a pretty garden,' Mary Sutton said unexpectedly. 'And the cottage itself isn't bad, either, though it needs work done on it. The rooms are quite a good size.' She led the way into the garden, calling, 'Mrs Abberley? Mrs Abberley?'

There was no answer. The three of them walked warily towards the back door. Framed by the honeysuckle it was standing open. Mrs Sutton stood in the doorway and once again called out Mrs Abberley's name.

'That's odd,' she said. 'Something's burning.' Kirby and Thornhill followed her into the kitchen. The air smelled of smoke, and there was a layer of condensation on the windows and other smooth surfaces.

'She's left a pan on the ring.' Mary Sutton moved quickly to the stove. 'Pass me that towel, will you?'

Thornhill's uneasiness was growing. He watched Mrs Sutton turning out the gas under the saucepan. Kirby handed her a towel. She wrapped it round the handle of the pan and lifted it off the stove.

'Potatoes. She must have left them simmering. It's boiled dry.'

Thornhill glanced round the room. A place had been laid at the kitchen table. A piece of tongue sat on a plate beneath the grey mesh dome of a meat cage. There were beetroots in a small bowl beside it. The air was full of flies.

'Check the other rooms,' he said to Kirby.

213

Kirby slipped like a well-trained dog through the kitchen door into the hall beyond. The others listened to his footsteps moving briskly first in the parlour at the front of the house and then on the stairs. A moment later he returned to the kitchen.

'No sign of her, sir. The bolts are across on the front door.'

'Peas,' Mary Sutton said suddenly. 'Or possibly lettuce.' She saw Thornhill's expression. 'That's probably what happened. She was obviously making lunch, and perhaps she popped out for some vegetables. I know there are some peas in the kitchen garden. And Alec found a lettuce there the other day. Or she might have run out of something. Salt, say. There's a little general shop before you get to the Bull. Going through the kitchen garden is much quicker than going through the front door and up to the High Street. But what's delaying her?'

Kirby and Thornhill were already in the garden. 'Which way would she have gone?' Thornhill asked. 'The way we came?'

'No – through there: the gate beyond the compost heap. You can hardly see it because of all the ivy.'

Thornhill noticed in passing that on Mrs Abberley's side there was a pair of heavy bolts on the gate, but no lock; the bolts had been recently oiled, as had the hinges. Immediately on the other side was a small forest of sycamore and ash saplings which had colonised what had once been a soft-fruit bed.

'I suspect she thinks we haven't realised the gate is there,' Mary Sutton said as she followed the policemen into the kitchen garden. 'It's not obvious from this side – not unless you're a small boy playing hide and seek.'

The broad, weed-strewn path led down the middle of the kitchen garden to the door in the far wall. It was very quiet. The walls were of stone, with the top courses built of crumbling brick which had weathered to a faded russet. Against one wall was a lean-to greenhouse now given over to empty plant pots and shards of glass.

The three of them walked down the path towards the door. Thornhill was hot, worried and irritated. Time was too valuable to be wasted in looking for old ladies who might have wandered off to the shops. Kirby was whistling a jaunty little tune. Thornhill wished his sergeant were not so cheerful. Perhaps it was because they were in the middle of a murder investigation: some detectives found murder a tonic.

Mary Sutton stopped abruptly. 'What's that?'

They were almost at the door now. Thornhill's eyes followed her pointing finger. Standing in the bare earth was an umbrella, originally black but now green with age. He took a couple of steps towards it. The movement brought into sight something else: a woman's black shoe, much worn and with a slight heel. The ends of the laces were frayed. He could also see an ankle and part of a calf encased in a thick grey woollen stocking.

Beside him, Kirby sucked in his breath. 'Oh, Christ.'

'Stay here,' Thornhill said to Mary Sutton.

She was looking up at him, her eyes huge. 'Please. No. *No.*'

He put his hand gently on her arm and gave her a little push. 'Would you fetch Mr Sutton?' He didn't want to see Sutton, not at this moment, but he knew that at a time like this any action was preferable to none.

'Not again,' she said. 'Oh, God, not again. I can't *bear* it.' She walked up the path towards the Vicarage. There was something blundering and unco-ordinated about her movements, like those of a person just awakened from a deep sleep.

Thornhill turned back. He pulled aside the branch of an elder tree and looked down at Mrs Abberley.

She lay on her back, staring at the bright blue sky with bloodshot eyes. There were pea pods around her, some even on her black dress, jaunty splashes of green. One of the pods had burst open and peas nestled in the folds of the dark material. Her glasses had fallen off; they were lying unbroken on the path. There was a handbag too, which lay an inch away from her outstretched fingers on the hard earth.

'Oh, bloody hell,' Kirby said at his shoulder. 'Just look at her face.'

Mrs Abberley's lips and ears had darkened to a bluish-purple. Froth and flecks of blood caked her nostrils and the corners of her mouth. Her tongue had been forced out, dislodging the false teeth.

The worst thing was the flies. They crawled over Mrs Abberley's face, sucking the blood, the saliva and the froth. Her head, Thornhill thought, was more in need of a meat cage than her lunch.

PART EIGHT

1

'She had her dinner. And about time too.'

Startled, Jill looked up. Mrs Milkwall loomed above her left shoulder. She stared challengingly first at Jill and then at anyone else who would meet her eyes. The waiting room was to the left of the main reception desk, a limbo full of anxious-looking people stranded between everyday life and the purgatory of the hospital.

'Alice?' Jill asked.

'Couldn't have it in Miss Kymin's shed, though. Crawling with coppers, look. So I asked that man in charge, the inspector, and he said try leaving the bowl outside the back door. And I said, I hope all those clod-hopping constables will mind their feet.'

'Are you sure it was Alice?'

'Saw her with my own eyes. The coppers were off having *their* dinner. She sneaked over the wall and came along when the coast was clear.'

Mrs Milkwall's voice was naturally loud, and in moments of excitement it became even louder. Jill sensed the attention of the other people in the room like the heat from an electric fire. They were pretending to be immersed in magazines or knitting or the view from the window; but the half-hearted conversations had now stopped because the talkers had turned into eavesdroppers.

Jill glanced up at the clock on the wall, conscious of her lack of make-up, and conscious that her dress wasn't as fresh as it had been yesterday.

219

'It was kind of you to come and tell me.'

This was the wrong thing to have said. Mrs Milkwall drew back, pressing her lips together in a half-moon of disapproval. 'I didn't come here in particular. Just happened to be passing and there you were.' She patted her string bag, which appeared to contain balls of old newspaper peppered with earth. 'I promised I'd bring my friend Doreen a couple of lettuces. She works in the kitchens here. And then I'm going into town, look – so it's just on the way to the bus stop.'

'Thank you again for the roses.' Jill had them on her lap, Charlotte's and Mrs Milkwall's, the discreet pink buds smothered by the mass of yellow petals.

The shrewd little eyes examined her. 'You're looking peaky. I don't reckon they should be letting you go. Easy to have a setback, you know. When you've worked in this hospital as long as I have, you get to know the signs.'

Jill picked at the roses. A yellow petal fluttered to the floor. Her head ached dully. 'I'm sure they wouldn't let me out unless they thought it would be all right.'

'Don't you believe it.' Mrs Milkwall shook her head with gloomy relish. 'The stories I could tell you.'

'Please don't. Or at least not until I feel a little better.'

'You've got people to take care of you?' Mrs Milkwall demanded, her tone suggesting that if the answer was no Jill had only herself to blame.

'Oh, yes. I'm staying with friends at present.'

'Make sure they look after you proper. Take your time, that's my advice. Tell them to give you camomile tea. My mam swore by it: good for the nerves. And don't worry about that cat. It probably won't bother to turn up, but if it does, I'll see it doesn't go hungry.'

'Thank you. I—'

'No more than that, mind. I haven't got time for cats. Anyway our dog would eat it as soon as look at it. Cats aren't company like dogs, are they?'

Mrs Milkwall left without formally saying goodbye. She was still talking as she went out of the room, apparently telling Jill or an invisible companion an anecdote that showed conclusively that cats spread disease if you were foolish enough to let them into the house. In the doorway she almost collided with Philip Wemyss-Brown. Philip swept off his hat and said what a pleasure it was to see her again. The back of Mrs Milkwall's neck flushed a dark purple; she said that she hadn't time to stand around gossiping to all and sundry and fled down the corridor.

Philip's concern enveloped Jill like an eiderdown. He took her bag in one hand, offered her his arm and walked her slowly out to the Rover, which was parked just outside the doors in a spot marked AMBULANCES ONLY.

Already the familiar feel and smell of the car's interior had become something to notice and relish, rather than to accept unthinkingly; it didn't take long in hospital to make one feel a stranger in one's own life. Philip fussed over her, asking whether she would like a blanket over her legs.

'Don't fuss, please – I'm not an invalid.' She saw his face and added quickly, 'I'm sorry to sound so ungrateful. It's just the reaction, I expect.'

At this he showed signs of fussing even more. Jill diverted him with Mrs Milkwall and Alice.

'Charlotte doesn't like cats much.' Philip started the engine and the car rolled slowly down the drive towards the guard post at the gates. 'Says they play hell with the furniture.'

'I'm sure she's right.'

'Also their fur makes her cough or something.'

'I wasn't going to ask you to have it at Troy House,' Jill said meekly as they turned into Chepstow Road. 'But perhaps when I find a place of my own . . .' She fell silent wondering why she had been so foolish as to abandon her flat in London before she had found somewhere permanent to live in Lydmouth. The answer was that she had been in a hurry. By coming here she had hoped to start a new life; and you couldn't start a new life unless you relinquished your old one. She said, 'Let's not worry about it now.' Tears filled her eyes and she fished in her handbag for a handkerchief. 'You don't know how relieved I feel. It's as if I've just been let out of jail.' She turned her head aside to blow her nose and surreptitiously dab her eyes.

'There's old Ruispidge's Bentley.' Philip might have been creating a diplomatic distraction or simply pointing out an item of interest; with Philip it was often difficult to know what went on beneath the surface and how it differed, if at all, from the part of him he left on display. 'The girl's driving him – that niece of his.'

'Jemima?'

The Bentley had been travelling in the opposite direction to the Rover. The big car turned into the High Street, halting the oncoming traffic with a fine disregard for the usual rules of the road. Jemima Orepool looked very small behind the wheel. Sir Anthony was sitting beside her in the front passenger seat.

'I'm surprised he lets her drive after yesterday. It's like letting a child play with a loaded revolver.'

'It was an accident,' Jill said. 'It could have happened to anyone.'

'You shouldn't be making excuses for her.'

'Why not? She's very young. And rather sweet in her way – she couldn't have been nicer after the accident.'

'Probably terrified you'd complain to Uncle.' For a second Philip took his eyes off the road and glanced at Jill. 'Though I expect he's used to hearing complaints. By all accounts the girl's always upsetting people. The trouble is, she's got enough sex appeal to fill the Albert Hall twice over.'

Jill wondered if Philip felt it too. The possibility that he found Jemima attractive made her feel obscurely uneasy. Surely it couldn't be jealousy? She said: 'You can't blame her for that. It's something you're born with.'

'It's not just what you're born with that counts. It's what you do with it.'

They drove on. They had known each other so long that they were accustomed to each other's silences. Jill stared out of the window and wondered how anyone could find Philip sexually attractive. When she tried to imagine going to bed with him, she found herself thinking of an enormous teddy bear she had seen in Hamley's window the year before the war.

'No news on the investigation,' Philip said suddenly, his voice unexpectedly harsh. 'If they don't get results soon, Hendry will have to call in the Yard.'

Jill realised how strange it was that neither of them had mentioned Miss Kymin's murder before this. It was as if they were trying to push it to the back of their minds. 'It's such a messy business.' She heard a querulous tone in her voice and thought that she must sound like Charlotte complaining about the quality of the cod the fishmonger had sent up. 'It's like a tangle of string. You think that if you find an end and pull it, it will all sort itself out, but it doesn't – it just makes the tangle worse.'

'Damn.' Philip braked gently, and the Rover rolled slowly along the frontage of Troy House. 'We've company. That's the Newtons' car.'

An Alvis was standing at the kerb. Jill wondered if her invalid status meant that she would be expected to take refuge in her room. In fact the idea of company seemed almost attractive: she had had enough of solitude in hospital.

When Jill climbed out of the car she was surprised how normal she felt. Philip offered her his arm again. She took it more to please him than because she needed his support. The front door opened before they reached it and there was Charlotte framed in the doorway. For an instant Jill thought she glimpsed irritation in Charlotte's face, but almost before she had identified the emotion, it had been wiped away and replaced with solicitude.

'How are you feeling? Now come and sit down. Philip, what were you thinking of? You could have brought the car nearer the door than that.'

Behind Charlotte in the gloom of the hall, Chrissie Newton bobbed up and down. 'Shall I come back later?' she murmured as Jill came into the house. 'The strawberries aren't important, not at all. There's no hurry. I just happened to be passing. Of course if I'd known—'

'Come and sit down, Jill.' Charlotte pushed open the door of the drawing room. 'Perhaps you'd like to take Jill's bag upstairs,' she suggested to Philip. She put an unnecessary hand under Jill's elbow and turned to Chrissie: 'It's no trouble at all. Besides, it's most unwise to wait with strawberries. They go bad so terribly quickly.'

Once inside the drawing room Jill broke away from Charlotte. 'I'm all right. Otherwise they wouldn't have let me out.'

Charlotte shook her head vigorously. 'Head injuries are notoriously difficult to predict. Now you sit down and I'll see about some tea.' On her way to the door she passed Chrissie, who was hovering just inside the room. 'You'll stay for a cup, won't you?'

Charlotte's heavy footsteps pounded down the hall towards the kitchen. Chrissie sat down and smiled, her long head slightly averted like a shy horse sizing up a stranger in the hope of earning a sugar lump. Jill had met her several times since coming to Lydmouth because the Wemyss-Browns and the Newtons saw a good deal of each other. Jill liked what she knew of her though the conversations between them tended to be hard work; Chrissie Newton's main interests in life were her garden and her children, and since Jill had neither she sometimes found it hard to make the appropriate responses.

'You're feeling better, I hope.' The long fingers picked at the faded cotton of the dress. The nails were grubby and the skin was dry, the cracks ingrained with dirt. 'Such a horrible thing to have happened, for a woman to be attacked like that – and in the middle of town. Coming on top of the murder, too – I simply don't know what's happening to Lydmouth. Everything's changed since the war.'

'I suppose that's true of everywhere.'

'Giles blames the Americans. He says all those GIs with their nylons and chocolates had a very corrupting influence. Most of them may have gone home, but their films are almost as bad.' Chrissie leant a little closer and automatically lowered her voice; her breath smelled of peppermints and halitosis. 'Did you know that there are several children in Templefields with black faces?'

Jill tried to look suitably shocked.

'I just popped in for some strawberries,' Chrissie went on quickly, in full retreat from the potential minefield of discussing miscegenation with a near stranger. 'Charlotte's got a glut.' A shadow passed across Chrissie's face. 'I don't know why it is but she seems to have a way with strawberries. She always has more than I do, and they tend to taste nicer too. She claims it's all in the guano but I think it must be more complicated than that. Something to do with the soil, perhaps, or where the beds are sited.'

Jill recalled Charlotte talking interminably about the cultivation of strawberries. 'Do you use different varieties? Could that be it?'

'I don't think so. Charlotte goes in for Royal Sovereign. I've tried them but I have better results with Bedford Champion myself. We both grow Givons' Late Prolific as well – that's one of the last varieties to ripen.' Chrissie raised her head and stared at Jill with blue bewildered eyes. 'Strawberries have such a short fruiting season, don't they? It's so sad.'

'Yes,' Jill said. 'I suppose it is.'

'I'm going to make jam with most of Charlotte's. There are far too many to eat. Besides, Giles is very partial to strawberry jam. So are the boys.'

There were voices outside the door. Charlotte wheeled in the tea trolley. Philip strolled into the room after them.

'How are you feeling now?' he asked Jill.

Jill noticed Charlotte's glance at him. 'I'm fine, thank you. Are those your home-made ginger biscuits, Charlotte? You're spoiling me.'

Philip blundered on, blinded by his concern: 'Perhaps you should have some sugar in your tea. That's good for shock, isn't it?'

'I'm not in shock,' Jill said tartly. 'And I don't like sugar in tea.'

Charlotte said comfortably, 'My grandmother used to have cream in tea. Can you imagine?'

The awkwardness sank into the depths but did not dissolve. The drawing room was like a pool with too many undercurrents swirling below the surface. Jill watched Charlotte pouring the tea and thought of weeds stirring and eddies of silt rising into dark water; then she wondered whether her mind really was back to normal.

Philip handed round the cups and plates. Everyone tried hard to act normally and nobody quite succeeded. Conversation sputtered and flared like a candle with an untrimmed wick.

'And how's old Giles?' Philip said.

'Fine.' Chrissie hesitated. 'Working very hard, of course. Things always get busy around Quarter Day.'

'It's when the rent falls due,' Philip explained unnecessarily to Jill.

'Giles says it's like trying to get blood out of a stone with some of the tenants,' Chrissie said. 'And what makes it worse for him is that they all know Tony Ruispidge isn't going to turn them out if it comes to a pinch. Not if they've got a halfway decent hard luck story.'

Charlotte dropped a biscuit crumb daintily into her ashtray. 'It must make Giles's job rather difficult.'

'It's not so bad with the farmers. Town tenants tend to be the worst. Some of them are awfully feckless. The men get their pay packets on Friday and it's off to the betting shop and then to the pub. By Monday there's nothing left.'

Charlotte nodded her head. 'Templefields,' she said darkly. Templefields, an area of Lydmouth near the station, had a reputation as a nursery for poverty and crime.

'I think Giles may be there today. He's somewhere in town.' Chrissie put down her cup and saucer, the tea untouched. 'I really should go. The sooner I get started on the jam, the better.'

The telephone began to ring in the hall. Philip muttered an apology and went to answer it. Charlotte launched into a disquisition on the folly of making jam with damaged fruit. Jill could distinguish the sound of Philip's voice on the other side of the closed door, but not the words he was saying. She guessed the other women were trying to listen too. A moment later, he came back into the room. Charlotte glanced at his face and cut herself off in mid-sentence.

'That was Amy Gwyn-Thomas.' He added for Chrissie's benefit. 'My secretary.' As he was speaking, he was advancing swiftly into the room, scooping up cigarettes and lighter. 'I shall have to go into the office, I'm afraid. There's been another murder.'

No one spoke. It seemed to Jill that the four of them were frozen in time. Appropriately enough, she felt very cold.

'It's Mrs Abberley.' Philip said – casually, as if mentioning the winner of the sweepstake at the St John's Fête; but his face had lost much of its colour. 'She's been strangled.'

'Where?' Jill asked. For some reason it was desperately important to know, desperately important that it should not have been in the yard of the Bull Hotel.

'In the Vicarage garden. That's all she knew.' At the door he turned back to Charlotte. 'I'm not sure when I'll be home. I'll try to ring.'

Jill started to stand up. 'I should come too. Perhaps there's something I can do.'

Charlotte's chair creaked loudly.

'No, you must stay here.' Philip glanced back at Charlotte. 'Goodbye, darling.'

2

'LADYKILLER STALKS THE STREETS OF LYDMOUTH,' Williamson said to Thornhill, his voice low and menacing. He flung himself down on the visitor's chair in front of Thornhill's desk. 'Headlines like that, they terrify the Chief Constable. Two murders and one attack, all with women victims.' He slapped one of the telephones on the desk. 'And there's another thing. Mr Hendry has had a call from a man he knows on the *Daily Telegraph*. Is it true, this chap wanted to know, that Miss Kymin was sending anonymous letters to all and sundry? All about the vicar? And are we considering the possibility that she and the vicar were using the vestry for romantic assignations?'

'What?' Thornhill blurted out, startled out of his defensive silence. 'Where did he get that from?'

'Someone's been talking out of turn. Apparently the *Telegraph* man bought the story as an exclusive from a local journalist acting on his own. The Chief Constable twisted his arm till he told him who it was: Ivor bloody Fuggle. Surprise, surprise. What Mr Hendry wants to know is who told *him*? And so do I.' Williamson took out a pipe and blew down it, producing a rich bubbling sound. 'Two possibilities. An officer in this building. Or that Francis woman. And I—'

'How could it be her?' Thornhill interrupted. 'She didn't know that the newspaper she gave me had come from Miss Kymin's shed.'

'She could have worked it out. She's no fool, that one.'

'But she's in hospital, sir,' Thornhill persisted. 'How would she be able to talk to Fuggle? In any case, if she wanted to sell the story, she'd go through Wemyss-Brown.'

'He's her boss.' Williamson stabbed the pipe bowl with his penknife. 'She wouldn't go to him if she wanted to moonlight. But whoever it is, I want his or her head on a plate, all right? You should have a little more time on your hands in the next day or two. Mr Hendry's called in the Yard.'

Thornhill had guessed that this was coming. The Chief Constable couldn't let Williamson hang on to the case for ever. Hendry was under fire himself – from the press on one side and the Standing Joint Committee on the other. What Thornhill hadn't expected was his own sense of disappointment. Failure had an unpleasant taste.

At last Williamson lit the pipe, sending smoke billowing across Thornhill's desk. 'What's the latest on the second corpse?'

'Probably manual strangulation, sir. I've phoned Cardiff and the pathologist is coming back. There's a possibility that Mrs Abberley may have marked her attacker. You can see something under her nails. Could be blood and bits of skin. The lab will be able to give us a blood group, of course.'

'That's something, I suppose. Get it in writing for the super sleuths, eh? Mr Hendry wants, and I quote, "these chaps in London to find everything in apple-pie order". So what are you waiting for? Go and count our bloody apples.'

Williamson wandered away in the direction of his own room. A moment later, Thornhill walked along the corridor to the CID Office. He could hear the hum of activity inside before he opened the door. The noise was a compound of typewriters and telephones, talking and movements: it was a formidable, almost alien sound which made him think of an industrial process – in this case one which would continue to churn relentlessly on whether the men pulling the levers came from Lydmouth or London.

The quality of the noise changed as Thornhill went into the room: it became less excited, more disciplined. Kirby, whose desk was near the door, raised his head. Look at him, Thornhill thought: we're in the middle of a murder investigation and he's as happy as a sandboy. Kirby came over to him.

'Had a phone call from Mr Masterman.'

'Who?'

'You remember, sir. The old jeweller in Lyd Street.'

'Relevant?'

'To the case? Not really.'

'Then can't it wait?' Thornhill asked, already moving down the long room.

'Maybe.' Kirby lowered his voice. 'But it's a complaint against a police officer.'

Thornhill swung round. He jerked his head towards the door. Neither of them spoke until they were outside.

'Who is it?' Thornhill asked.

'Young Wilson. Apparently he's just plastered the doorway of Masterman's shop with vomit.' He made an unsuccessful attempt to imitate Masterman's cantankerous wail: 'Drunk as a lord, but not so polite about it.'

Thornhill hesitated. For once duty and inclination marched side by side. 'What time was this?'

'About a quarter-past two.'

'It's a very serious allegation, Sergeant. Where's Wilson?'

'He's been in the WC for the last half-hour. Told Sergeant Fowles he had an upset stomach.'

Thornhill considered the geography. There was only one pub at the bottom of Lyd Street. Wilson wouldn't have gone further afield because he had had only thirty minutes for lunch – though it seemed that in the event he had taken rather longer. 'Ring the Bathurst Arms. Find out if Wilson was in there at lunchtime, and see if they can remember what he had.'

'Yes, sir.' Kirby's face was blank and respectful, but Thornhill sensed the inner enthusiasm behind the mask. 'Shall I do it straightaway?'

'Why not? While their memories are fresh. By the way, the Chief Constable's called in the Yard.'

He heard Williamson's door opening behind him.

'I'd like a word, Inspector. In my office if you please.'

'Treat that as urgent, Sergeant,' Thornhill said over his shoulder. 'If the results are positive, let me know at once.'

Williamson's room was much larger than Thornhill's, though clumsy partitioning had made it too narrow for its height. It smelt of old tobacco, old paper and old sweat. Thornhill shut the door. Williamson was standing by the window staring down at the High Street beneath.

'Take a pew,' he said without turning round.

Thornhill sat down. The offer of a seat was in itself significant. Williamson was alive to the respect due to senior officers and preferred to keep his subordinates standing.

'Mr Hendry has just informed me that the Yard can't get down here before early evening,' he said. 'Quite possibly later. So we've a few hours' grace. As you know, he wants us to do what we can beforehand.' He glowered at Thornhill, who knew enough not to take it personally. 'Apple-pie order. Now wouldn't it be nice if we could sort out the whole case before the gentlemen from the Met arrive? And we might just manage it. We'll leave a team here to deal with the paperwork and make the apple pies. We'd better get down to the Vicarage garden. Ginger them up. If there's going to be a breakthrough, that's where it'll be.'

'What about the Bull?'

'What about it?'

'I think it would pay to find out exactly who was there on Sunday evening. And what they were doing.' Jill Francis's face, as he'd last seen it, wan against the hospital pillows, rose unwanted in Thornhill's mind. 'And for that matter on Monday evening. There may be a connection.'

Williamson walked to the desk and rapped his pipe like a gavel against the ashtray. 'What are you getting at?'

Thornhill wasn't sure. He said: 'There may be useful witnesses we haven't talked to yet. Newton, for instance. On Sunday evening he had a bite to eat with Youlgreave, the other churchwarden. And then he went off to the Bull at about eight o'clock. I know Miss Kymin was killed at least an hour after that, but he might have seen someone hanging about the church. He might have seen someone at the Bull that night.'

'More likely Quale would have done. Got eyes in the back of his head, he has.'

Thornhill nodded. 'Then there's the incident on Monday night – the attack on Miss Francis.'

'No evidence of a connection.'

'I know, sir. But suppose there were.' Thornhill stood up and moved to the map of Lydmouth on the wall beside Williamson's desk. 'If the killer was leaving the church on Sunday night, where would he go? The light's fading and there're not too many people around. But he still wouldn't want to risk being seen near the church. He's got the weapon on him and the chalice. We know the chalice was too big to slip in a pocket. Probably the same was true of the weapon.'

Williamson moved nearer to the map and stabbed at it with the stem of his pipe. 'But if he turns left he has to go past Youlgreave's house, and then Nutholt Lane. And if he turns right he has to pass those cottages at the western end of Church Street, and then he comes out in the middle of the High Street. Not very clever in my opinion.'

Thornhill's finger traced a line from the south porch of the church round the west tower and down to the lych gate on the northern boundary of the churchyard. 'Suppose he goes down here. Up near the church, the yews shield him from the south-west. Apart from that, his only real problem is the windows of Church Cottage and the Vicarage.'

'He still has to turn right or left.'

Thornhill ran his fingertip from the Vicarage to the cottage. 'But why couldn't he have gone through there?'

'You think the second letter-writer told the truth?' Williamson sounded genuinely interested in the possibility. 'That Sutton killed her?'

'I doubt it. It's far more likely it was someone else. Someone who knew his way around the Vicarage and its garden.' Thornhill talked faster, warming to his theme. 'As far as I can see, the Suttons didn't bother to lock the Vicarage gates, not until this happened. They live mainly at the front of the house. The kitchen window doesn't overlook the gates. If the killer knew all this, he would also know that all he had to do was slip through the wicket and go down the yard and into the kitchen garden. Then he could let himself out of the door in the wall into the lane.' Thornhill's finger followed the possible route. 'Not perfect, but less overlooked than any other way. And if he did go through the Suttons' garden, he probably came that way, too. Which would explain why the house-to-house questioning failed to turn up anything useful.'

'And the chalice and the weapon? The lab's drawn a blank on Kirby's tyre lever, by the way. Or rather they won't commit themselves.'

'He might have hidden them somewhere in the garden – but if he did, I'm surprised we haven't found them yet.'

'He might have retrieved them.'

Thornhill nodded, accepting the point. 'On the other hand he might have hidden them somewhere else. On neutral territory – somewhere where they'd be easier for him to pick up.' His finger inched along the lane and into the side street which ran up to the High Street. It paused at the entrance to the yard of the Bull. 'He could have put them in that barn and then he'd pop into the hotel the back way – have a drink, maybe, or just walk through to the High Street. No one would bat an eyelid.'

'People use the Bull as a public footpath.' Williamson scratched his head. 'All right, it's feasible – but no more than that, mind.'

'Yesterday evening when Miss Francis left her bike in that barn, suppose she disturbed the murderer. Suppose he'd come back for the chalice and the weapon. He could have had them in his hands when he heard her footsteps in the yard. He'd try and hide – then perhaps he panicked – knocked her on the head and ran off. And he dropped the tyre lever in the litter bin where Kirby found it this morning.'

'All a bit far fetched. Just one bloody hypothesis after another.'

'But it fits in with what we know already.'

Williamson rapped his pipe on the ashtray again and came to a decision. 'We've got so little time that we have to take chances. I want you to—' There was a tap on the door. Williamson scowled and bellowed 'Come!'

Kirby came into the room. 'Excuse me, sir.'

'What is it?'

'Message for Mr Thornhill, sir.' Kirby handed Thornhill a piece of paper. On it he had written, *Fuggle bought Wilson four double whiskies at dinner time.*

Thornhill looked across the desk at Williamson. 'There's something else I have to tell you, sir.' He glanced up at Kirby and said formally, 'Thank you, Sergeant. That will be all.' He waited until the door had closed behind Kirby. 'I think we've found the source of our leak.'

3

Lydmouth drowsed through the long, hot summer afternoon. Even two murders had had little apparent effect on its calm. Here and there were flurries of activity, but the town as a whole proceeded at its usual leisurely tempo.

Jemima Orepool wandered slowly down the High Street. Sheltered by dark glasses and the broad brim of her hat, she stared with distaste at the world around her. Boredom stretched like a desert in every direction as far as the eye could see. How could people live here, she wondered, year in, year out? Why didn't they wither up and die from the sheer tedium?

She had come into town with her uncle because Clearland Court was even more tiresome with no one but Aunt Soph and a few cows and sheep for company. She had also come because underlying the boredom was a layer of fear, only half acknowledged. If there were any news to be had, she would find it here. She drifted to a halt in front of Madame Ghislaine's window. THE SHOP GIVING PERSONAL SERVICE, said the advertisement in the *Gazette*. FASHIONS DIRECT FROM PARIS. Jemima stood under the shop's striped awning and yawned at the provincial frumpery on display. How could people wear such ghastly things?

She heard footsteps and the sharp intake of breath. The shadowy reflection of a man joined hers in the glass of the shop window. She turned her head and said without enthusiasm, 'Giles.'

'Darling, I knew you'd come. I've got to talk to you.'

'Someone might notice.'

'Why? We meet by chance in Lydmouth – it's perfectly natural for us to stop and chat.'

He towered over her, making her feel trapped. Jemima began to walk along the pavement in the direction of the Bull. Giles padded along beside her like an enormous dog. As a rule she rather liked older men – they tended to be more interesting, more considerate, and able to make up for their lack of youth in other ways. She had never found Giles sexy, but in the absence of serious competition he had at least been a challenge. She had known him since she was a child. It wasn't the man she had found sexy but what he stood for.

'It went wrong. There was nothing I could do about it. But as long as we keep our heads, it'll be all right.'

'I hope so – for your sake.'

He lifted his arm, as if intending to touch hers.

She veered away from him. 'What have you done to your hand? Those scratches.'

He snatched his hand back and put it in his trouser pocket. 'A cat. I was talking to one of our tenants in Templefields. Tried to lift a cat off a chair and the bloody animal went for me. Darling, what shall we do with the chalice? Shall I give it to you as planned?'

She stared up at him. 'Are you mad?'

He recoiled from the fury in her face. 'I suppose if you let me have that chap's address, I could post it to him. Not from here, of course. I'd better go to Bristol or Cardiff.'

'I don't want anything to do with it. Not now. Everything's changed – don't you understand?'

'I thought you needed the money.'

'I do. But it's even more important not to get dragged into a murder case.'

It was the first time either of them had said the word aloud. For a moment neither of them spoke.

Giles murmured in a voice so low she could hardly hear him, 'I need the money, too.'

'That's your affair.'

They had reached the pillared porch of the Bull Hotel. They lingered on the sun-filled pavement, unwilling to enter the gloom of the hall where Quale would be waiting, watching and listening.

'Why don't we just go away?' Giles burst out in an agonised whisper.

'Just as we'd planned. A chap I know has a villa near Menton, and I'm sure he'd lend it to us.'

Jemima stared at him, noting that when he'd shaved that morning he had missed a triangle of stubble at the corner of his mouth. His eyes were bloodshot, and the muscles in his face were jumping and twisting quite independently of their owner's control.

'Sooner or later,' he was saying, 'Chrissie would give me a divorce – I know she would. Then we could get married.'

'You must be joking.' Her surprise was genuine.

'But, darling, you promised.'

She made to move away from him. 'That was then, Giles.' And even then she had not been serious. Discussing marriage had been a way of raising the emotional stakes, of making what they were doing more fun. It surprised her that Giles had taken the conversation seriously. It had been only a game.

His hand pounced on her forearm. She gasped and tried to pull herself away. She stared, half-fascinated, half-terrified, at the scratched, hairy skin and the powerful fingers.

'Is there someone else?'

'Let me go. Someone will notice.'

He released her and took a step backwards, his face dark red with embarrassment. 'Sorry. I—'

'I'm sorry, too. Can't you understand, it's over? And it was never very much to begin with. And to be frank, I wish to God we'd never begun.'

She went into the cool of the Bull's hall. She felt a certain pride. As these things went, it had been a neat little speech. Quale beamed at her from behind his desk, and she wondered whether he had heard anything.

'Good afternoon, Miss Jemima.' He leaned closer to her. 'Have you heard the news? There's been another murder.'

4

'A pleasure, Sir Anthony. Always a pleasure.' The bank manager squeezed Ruispidge's hand with the faint, flabby pressure of a person whose job entailed too many handshakes. 'Anything I can do to help, you must just let me know.'

The heavy door closed between them with a click. Ruispidge tucked his stick under his arm and walked slowly across the banking hall. The high barrel vault bounced back the sound of his footsteps, blurred and distorted. There was only one other customer. He noticed but barely registered that the two cashiers were covertly watching him from behind their grilles. He would have felt odd if they hadn't noticed him – in Lydmouth he had been accustomed to being the centre of attention since childhood; he was not used to being ignored. Then Giles Newton appeared in the doorway that led to the street. He had a briefcase under his arm.

'Hello, Tony.' Newton's voice sounded normal – if anything slightly more offhand than usual. 'Pretty warm, isn't it?'

'Weather won't last.' Ruispidge joined Newton in the doorway. 'There's low pressure coming in from the Atlantic. Any luck with the late payers?'

Newton squeezed the briefcase. 'I managed to persuade a few of them to make at least a contribution towards their arrears. You wouldn't believe the stories I've heard.' He edged away. 'They'll be closing soon. I'd better pay this in.'

Ruispidge said abruptly, 'Leave it for a moment, will you? I want a word.'

Newton hesitated for an interval like a missed heartbeat. 'Where? We could wander along to the Bull if you like.'

'I'd rather be outside. Need a bit of fresh air. Let's go down to the river. If there's a breeze, that's where we'll find it.'

They walked in silence down the steps from the bank, along the High Street and into Lyd Street. The hill sloped down to the river, a broad, brown ribbon streaked with silver. Ruispidge had known Giles Newton for most of his life; usually the silence between them was a comfortable thing, the fruit of a long friendship. But today everything was different.

Ruispidge glanced up at Newton and thought: My God, how he's changed. Giles Newton had reached his glorious peak when he was eighteen – as head of house, captain of cricket and the acknowledged social leader of his year. That was the Giles whom Ruispidge usually saw. This large, shambling middle-aged man was a stranger inhabiting the shell of someone he had once known.

Harrow had proved not to be a microcosm of the real world, after all: what happened there had no relation to what happened later. The only thing that Tony Ruispidge valued from his schooldays was his friendship with Giles Newton. Now he realised with reluctance that Harrow and Lydmouth, like youth and middle age, belonged on different planets and conducted themselves according to different laws.

Below the Bathurst Arms there was a slipway to the river with a small quay stretching downstream from it; two warehouses with a yard between them rotted quietly behind the quay. Once, before the coming of the railways, this had been a thriving little port with bargeloads of coal and timber slipping downstream towards the Bristol Channel. The Ruispidge Estate owned both the warehouses and the quay but they hadn't generated any significant income since the 1920s.

In the middle of the quay was a solitary cherry tree which Ruispidge had allowed the Council to plant in a vain attempt to make the area more attractive to visitors. Beneath the tree was a wooden bench chiefly patronised by youthful louts with nothing better to do and by drunks ejected from the Bathurst Arms.

Ruispidge sat down with a sigh and clasped his hands round the silver-mounted top of his walking stick. Giles Newton followed suit, his hands still in his pockets and his briefcase tucked under his arm. He looked ill, Ruispidge thought, as well he might. Giles sat with his head thrown back, apparently absorbed in staring at the seagulls which wheeled and dipped above their heads.

'Look here,' Ruispidge began. At the last moment, his resolve faltered. 'Had you heard there's been another murder?'

Newton nodded. 'Quale told me.'

'That man hears everything first. But I imagine the news is all over town by now. The Abberley woman from Church Cottage, I understand.' He stretched out his legs in front of him and looked for comfort at the immaculate surface of his gleaming brown brogues. 'A bad business.'

Newton said nothing. His very stillness was unnerving. He wasn't even smoking. Ruispidge wished that he would take his hands out of his pockets: he looked sloppy and ill-kempt, like a farm labourer drunk on market day.

'Giles – there's no easy way to do this, is there?'

Newton turned his heavy head and looked blankly at him. Ruispidge felt a terrible pity seeping into him. Newton had been expecting this: one could tell by his face.

'We all know things have been difficult since the war. During the war, too. It's like Scylla and what's-its-name – Charybdis? If the taxman doesn't finish you off then the bloody bureaucrats will. And I dare say I've been a bit slack about these things myself.'

Newton stirred on the uncomfortable seat and sat up a little straighter.

'No point in beating about the bush,' Ruispidge went on doggedly. 'I know the Estate's turnover has gone down in all areas, but I gather that less is being banked than should be coming in. The paperwork for cash receipts doesn't match up. The problem goes back three or four years at least.'

He scratched his bald patch and waited for Giles to say something – to defend himself or explain: or even to apologise.

'I thought it was Lancaster, at first. The Bull's finances are in a mess – don't know what's coming in or going out from one week to the next. He's a nice chap, means well and all that, but he hasn't got a head for the business side. His elder brother did, though: best first lieutenant I ever had, anything he touched ran like clockwork. That's why I gave young Lancaster the job.'

He ran out of breath and stopped, conscious of the temptation to ramble round the point which had to be made rather than go straight towards it. Giles was no help at all.

Ruispidge forced himself to continue. 'But it's not just the Bull. It's anything involving cash transactions. Some of the rents, for example. Overtime at Home Farm. Stock sales.'

At last Giles turned his head towards Ruispidge. 'I'm afraid the bookkeeping's in a bit of a tangle at present.' His voice was light and level. 'I've had a lot on my mind.'

'Of course – I quite understand.'

'Could you give me a month or two? I can sort it out. It's been a matter of cash flow. I was going to have things balanced up in a month or two.'

'I'm sure you were.' Ruispidge looked away because Newton's face was working, and he was afraid that his friend might cry. He tried ineffectually to spear the wrapper from a bar of chocolate with the tip of his stick. After a while he said, 'I thought it would be something like that. But best to get it all straightened out and in the open, eh? Tell you what, you can have until the end of the quarter to do it. Would that give you enough time?'

Giles nodded slowly.

'I wonder if it would be useful if Shipston gave you a hand?' Shipston was the solicitor to the Ruispidge Estate. 'You know – many hands make light work.' He watched Newton carefully, trying to gauge his reaction to what amounted to a vote of no confidence in his, Newton's, competence and honesty. 'And then there's the future.' He hesitated. 'We'll have to see what seems most appropriate.'

The gulls shrieked above their heads. Children with home-made rods and lines had arrived on the slipway and were trying to catch fish. Giles had withdrawn into his privacy once more.

Ruispidge said quickly: 'I didn't want to come over to Mill Place. I thought it better to have a chat by ourselves – didn't want to worry Chrissie. Though – I don't know if you realise – she is a little concerned.'

Giles looked round and smiled. 'I'll have a word with her, don't worry.' He sounded almost like his normal, familiar self.

'It's queer how women pick things up. Their famous intuition, eh?'

Newton seemed not to have heard. 'I'm sorry I've been such a nuisance, Tony. I'll soon have it sorted it out, I promise.' He stood up. 'Thanks for being so patient. If you don't mind, I might go back home now. Make a start on the paperwork.'

'Good idea.'

'Some of it's in my study, you see. And the rest of it's up at the Estate office. First thing to do is to bring it all together, wouldn't you say? You remember what old Markby used to tell us?' Markby had taught them trigonometry in the Upper Fourth. ' "Organisation, boy: that's the key." '

'Old Markby – good lord, yes. He used to keep his bicycle clips on when he was teaching.' Ruispidge slowly stood up, flexing the joints which had already grown stiff and glad of the stick's support. 'I wonder what happened to him.'

They began to walk up Lyd Street. Ruispidge had never noticed before that one could see St John's from down here, and the lie of the land made the church tower seem much taller than it really was, like a mast on a ship.

'Markby?' Giles said. 'I think someone told me he was killed in the Blitz. Of course, he must have been getting on by then.'

'Funny old chap – I'd almost forgotten him. "Organisation, that's the key." He was rather on the muddle-headed side himself, wasn't he?'

Giles stared into the past. 'I think you're right. He may well have been.'

The two men had reached the top of Lyd Street. They slowed and stopped, turning to each other as if they had agreed that it was here that they would say goodbye.

'I might walk home,' Ruispidge said. 'Need to stretch my legs.' What he actually needed was time by himself, time to come to terms with the unthinkable. 'But the Bentley's at the Bull. I'm sure Jemima would run you back to Mill Place if you liked.'

'Don't bother her, the exercise will do me good. But first I must go and pay this into the bank.'

Ruispidge glanced down at the worn leather briefcase. 'Ah, yes – the rents.'

Giles raised a hand in farewell and walked slowly towards the bank. Ruispidge could not bear to let him go.

'Giles – you and Chrissie must come to dinner. Our turn, isn't it?'

Newton turned, his face breaking into a smile. 'I'd like that.'

'Splendid. I'll ask Soph to give Chrissie a ring, shall I?'

Newton raised his hand in a half-salute. Ruispidge lifted his stick, acknowledging the signal. The two men walked briskly away from one another. Ruispidge fought the temptation to look over his shoulder. It was a relief when he reached the sanctuary of the Bull's dark hallway.

Quale snapped to full alertness behind the desk. 'Miss Jemima is in the lounge, Sir Anthony.'

Ruispidge dropped his stick in the receptacle at the base of the hat stand. He found Jemima reading *Vogue* and smoking a cigarette. There was no one else in the big room. She had a tray of tea at her elbow. Trust Jemima, he thought: the girl had a genius for making herself comfortable. She had her feet up on a low table, and one could see more of her legs than Ruispidge considered desirable.

'Hello, Uncle. Would you like some tea? There's a spare cup. Or would you rather go straight home?'

Her thoughtfulness was uncharacteristic. Ruispidge said: 'I just looked in to say I'm going to walk back. I rather fancy a stroll along the river.'

She dropped the magazine on the empty chair beside her and swung her legs off the table. 'In that case I'll go now.'

The smell of her cigarette reached his nostrils, reminding him that he hadn't had a smoke since after lunch; and after that tricky interview with Giles, he felt he deserved one. He felt in his jacket pocket for the cigarette case. It rattled against something hard.

'Damn,' he said, taking out his case and opening it. 'I forgot to give Chrissie's lighter to Giles.' The thought of meeting Chrissie was not appealing. He hated women who made scenes. 'Would you drop it in on your way back home?'

Jemima pushed out her lower lip. 'Must I?' She stared at Ruispidge's face for a moment and added: 'Oh, all right.'

Her eyes widened slightly and her face changed: it reminded him of tuning a radio, the way a touch of the fingers changed a previously blurred signal to clear reception. Ruispidge turned. Inspector Thornhill was standing in the doorway. Ruispidge's first thought was that the man had been eavesdropping. It was with difficulty that he kept the rawness of his anger out of his voice.

'Yes? What is it?'

'I'm looking for Mr Lancaster, sir. Quale said he came along here.'

'Why do you want to see him?' Ruispidge scowled. 'No, don't tell me. I know what you'll say: none of my business.'

Another man appeared in the doorway – younger than Thornhill; a flashy dresser; Ruispidge had seen him often enough in court but couldn't remember his name, only the whining Cockney accent overlaid by a thin veneer of what these days they were pleased to call education. Jemima yawned and sank back into the armchair. Ruispidge selected a cigarette and tried to light it with Chrissie Newton's lighter.

'Try the kitchens – use the service door in the dining room.'

'Thank you, sir,' Thornhill said gravely. 'Good afternoon.'

The two policemen disappeared. Jemima stretched her arms above her head.

'On second thoughts, I think I might finish my tea before I go home.' She picked up the magazine. 'You don't mind, do you? There's no hurry with Mrs Newton's lighter, is there?'

'Please yourself,' Ruispidge said, placing the lighter on top of Jemima's gloves. And as he walked out of the room with the unlit cigarette in his hand, he added silently to himself: You usually do.

5

Dapper in a linen suit and a brightly striped silk tie, Victor Youlgreave breezed into the Vicarage after lunch. He had come by arrangement to discuss the temporary amalgamation of St John's with St Thomas's. Under his arm was a snakeskin attaché case which proved to contain his detailed proposals, page after page of foolscap covered with his small neat writing in turquoise ink.

The Suttons had been dreading his visit, expecting polite disagreement and interminable negotiations. Since the discovery of Mrs Abberley's body, however, they had simply forgotten that he was coming. Youlgreave arrived to be met by a uniformed constable outside the door.

With gentle patience he argued his way past the police. Neither Williamson nor Thornhill was in the house, and the sergeant co-ordinating the search of the Vicarage itself was inclined to play it by the book. Youlgreave persuaded him that the superintendent and the Chief Constable would want the vicar to see his churchwarden. He achieved this in such a way that the sergeant was later convinced that the idea had come from himself. Mary Sutton knew all this because the drawing-room door was open a crack, and she was standing out of sight behind it.

By the time Youlgreave bustled into the room, she was sitting with her husband in the huddle of chairs near the empty fireplace. The police presence made them feel like strangers in their own house. Alec was smoking incessantly, throwing butt after butt into the empty grate, and occasionally complaining of a pain in his stomach: Mary hoped that this was due to tension.

Youlgreave took both of Mary's hands in his. 'My dear Mrs Sutton. This is a very bad business. You must find it terribly distressing.'

Mary laughed shakily. 'I'm beginning to wonder if we've brought bad luck to the parish.'

'Nonsense.' Youlgreave gave her hands a little shake. 'You mustn't even think such a foolish thing.' He released her hands and turned to Alec. 'Does the archdeacon know about the second murder yet?'

Alec shook his head. 'I tried to ring him but he was out. I rang the palace too, but the Bishop's still in London. I left a message with his chaplain.'

'Then we shall have to manage by ourselves for the time being. Have they any idea who was responsible? Are they working on the assumption that the same person killed both women?'

Alec Sutton shrugged. 'Who knows? They don't tell us anything.'

Mary remembered her manners. 'Do sit down.'

The doorbell rang as they were settling themselves. There were voices in the hall.

'Who was the last person to see Mrs Abberley alive?' Youlgreave asked.

'I was.' Mary Sutton hugged herself, trying to prevent herself from shivering. 'They probably think I killed her.'

'Of course they don't,' Alec said.

'Why not? It's no secret that we didn't get on.' She looked at Youlgreave. 'Though in fact when I saw her just before lunch we'd just concluded a sort of non-aggression pact. Like Hitler and Stalin in the war.'

'No,' her husband said gently. 'Not like them.'

'What do you mean?'

'Hitler reneged on the agreement and attacked Stalin.' He paused as the doorbell rang once more; and this time the caller knocked on the door too. 'It's like Piccadilly Circus here,' he said to Youlgreave. 'Complete bedlam.' After a pause he went on: 'When we have an opportunity, I should like to talk to you and to Newton. I'm seriously wondering whether I shouldn't resign the living.'

'You mustn't do anything of the kind,' Youlgreave said. 'It would give people quite the wrong idea. Besides, the parish wouldn't want to lose you.'

In the silence that followed, Mary glanced at her husband. He was examining a hole in the arm of his chair, his face absorbed.

'Look here,' he said. 'This business about the chalice. I've been rather wrong-headed about it.'

'I think we all got a little carried away at the PCC meeting on Friday.' Youlgreave hesitated and then added, 'Myself included. Midsummer madness, eh?'

'If we ever get the chalice back, I think we should reopen the issue. I'm beginning to appreciate the strength of some of your arguments. After all, of all the parish's material possessions, the church is far and away the most important. And we have a responsibility to look after it as well as we can.'

'At present it seems a little academic.'

'You mentioned something about taking soundings from all the interested parties, from people in the parish to the Bishop himself. Perhaps that's the way forward.'

'Alec, dear,' Mary interrupted. 'The chalice hasn't been recovered yet. Isn't it a little premature to be talking about what you are going to do with it?'

'Not really.' Sutton's smile embraced both his wife and their visitor. 'After all, it's not really the chalice we're talking about, is it? The real issue is what it stands for. It should be a symbol of unity, not a cause of war.'

Youlgreave smiled. 'That sounds like the rough draft of a sermon.'

'It probably is.' There was another ring on the doorbell, and Sutton's face lost its good humour. 'It's so difficult to settle to anything at present.'

'This must be most unpleasant for you. The constant stream of visitors – you must feel like prisoners in your own house.'

'The advantage of the police is that they keep the journalists away, or at least at arm's length,' Mary said. 'The superintendent says that the press have heard that there was bad blood between us and Mrs Abberley.'

Youlgreave edged his bottom forward on the seat of his chair until he was perching on the front edge. He clasped his hands and stared earnestly at Mary. 'This really won't do, will it? You can't stay here.' As if to emphasise his point, there was another burst of knocking on the door. 'Would you like to spend the afternoon at my house? At least you'd have a little peace and quiet. You could stay to supper if you liked – nothing elaborate; I might see if I could arrange a soufflé.'

'Thank you, but I have to stay here,' Alec said. 'Somebody might need me.'

'Besides,' Mary added, 'if we walk down the road to your house, the journalists will simply follow and picket your front door instead of ours.'

'The police would redirect any callers on genuine parish business.' Youlgreave pursed his lips. 'And as for your other point, you needn't go to my house. I know – shall we pay a call on Charlotte Wemyss-Brown?'

'We don't know her very well.'

'She'll be delighted to rectify that. And a change of scene for the rest of the afternoon would do you both good.'

Alec cleared his throat. 'The thing is – I don't want to seem ungrateful or suspicious . . .'

'You're thinking that Wemyss-Brown edits the *Gazette* and his wife owns it? I promise you needn't worry about that. Just think of them as two of your parishioners who would like to help.'

Mary said quickly: 'I think we should go. I can't face staying here.'

Alec nodded agreement at once; Mary knew that he did it for her sake, not realising that the main reason why she couldn't face staying at the Vicarage was the effect it would have on him.

Youlgreave stood up. 'Why don't I ring them up?'

Mary thought later that their lack of resistance to this proposal showed how profoundly the events of the last two days had shaken herself and Alec. Youlgreave hurried away to the telephone. He also cleared the plan with the police, who indeed seemed almost indecently eager to see the back of the Suttons; Mary suspected their presence inhibited the search of the premises.

At other times, Mary would have enjoyed the circumstances of their departure: they had elements of romantic adventure, as if lifted from a novel by John Buchan or Dornford Yates. As Youlgreave's car, a pre-war Daimler, drew up outside the Vicarage, a policeman opened the front door while two of his colleagues escorted the Suttons across the pavement and into the car. One of the policemen slammed the door and Youlgreave let out the clutch before the Suttons had time to sit down.

The windows at the back and side of the car were curtained, but Mary could not resist the temptation to pull aside the curtain at the back window and watch the journalists milling like agitated insects outside the Vicarage. Three cameras were pointing at them. One youthful reporter was even running after the car. It was most exciting, and Mary wondered if she could somehow work the scene into the next Inspector Coleford, always assuming she would write another. It would be a shame to waste the material.

Youlgreave turned into the High Street and then into the Chepstow Road, where he put his foot down hard on the accelerator.

'Where are we going?' Mary said suddenly. 'This isn't the way to Troy House.'

Youlgreave's eyes met hers in the rear-view mirror. 'I'm just checking that we've got no one on our tail.'

She did not know whether to take him seriously. Was he too a devotee of the works of John Buchan and Dornford Yates? Or were his actions founded on experience? That had been one of the unexpected legacies of the war: one often had very little idea what people had done in those six years, what they were still capable of doing now.

No one spoke for the rest of the journey. Alec stared out of the window. She wondered what he was thinking. Her hand crept across the back seat and touched his. His fingers closed around hers, but he did not look at her.

The Daimler pulled up outside Troy House. Charlotte Wemyss-Brown was standing at the bay window of the drawing room. She waved and came to meet them.

'You need some tea,' she announced.

'That's very kind,' Mary began, 'but—'

'Mr Youlgreave, you'll stay, won't you?'

'With pleasure.'

Charlotte turned back to the Suttons. 'You must both be shattered. Perhaps you'd like a rest? The beds are made up in the spare room. I could bring you up some tea, if you like?'

Alec was looking dazed under the onslaught of so much good will. He glanced over his shoulder as if fearing that an army of journalists was in pursuit.

'Or perhaps you'd like something a little stronger, Mr Sutton?'

As the wife of a parish priest, Mary knew all about making people feel useful. 'I'm too keyed up to sleep, I think. But we'd love a cup of tea, wouldn't we, dear? We weren't able to have one after lunch because the police were all over the kitchen.'

'It must be awful having them in one's home. I know they're only doing their job, but even so. Such an imposition.' As Charlotte was talking she led them into the drawing room. 'You've met our friend Jill Francis, haven't you?'

Jill, rather pale but otherwise unchanged, at least on the surface, was standing by the fireplace. She smiled at the Suttons. Mary wondered how on earth the woman managed to look so graceful after a bang on the head and a night in hospital.

'I hadn't realised they'd discharged you,' Alec said, his professional manner suddenly to the fore. 'You must need peace and quiet. I wonder if we should—'

'I'm so glad you're here,' Jill said firmly. 'There's nothing really wrong with me. I'm delighted to have company. Charlotte will tell you that I'm no good at sitting around doing nothing.'

'Then we shall have to entertain you,' Mary said. She wished she could take back the words as soon as she'd spoken them. Nervousness was making her gush; she sounded like a stranger to herself.

Her embarrassment was lost in a flurry of activity. Spurning offers of help, Charlotte went to make the tea or at least to ask her housekeeper to do so. Alec and Victor Youlgreave drifted over towards the window in the drawing room and were soon involved in a highly technical discussion about the relative merits of St John's and St Thomas's as church buildings; it appeared to be giving them a good deal of satisfaction. That left Mary with Jill Francis. They sat in adjacent chairs, separated only by a table bearing a large aspidistra in a glazed pot.

'Are you living here permanently?' Mary asked, automatically batting the conversational ball over the net. 'At Troy House, I mean.'

Jill peered round the aspidistra. 'Charlotte and Philip have asked me to stay as long as I want to, but I'd rather find somewhere of my own. I've grown too used to having my own independence.'

How nice it must be, Mary thought, to have only oneself to consider: to get up when one wanted, eat when one wanted, work when one wanted. 'What are you looking for? Furnished rooms, a flat?'

'I used to rent a bedsitter in Castle Street but that wasn't very satisfactory. I had a minority share in the kitchen and bathroom. I'd really like somewhere self-contained and preferably unfurnished – all my things are in store at present, and it's costing a fortune. But you know what it's like: there's just not enough housing to go round. I knew London was like that, but I had no idea it was so bad in Lydmouth too.'

Jill talked gently and slowly, drawing them through safe, neutral topics. She left openings for Mary, but seemed satisfied with the monosyllabic replies which she received. Jill was not, Mary thought, one of those people with a pathological need to talk mainly about themselves: the flow of chatter was designed to give Mary time, if she needed it, to return to normal, or something which would pass for normality. Mary found a wry amusement in the situation: she was more used to exercising tactful control than to receiving it. It was also strangely relaxing: she had a similar sensation when she was a passenger in a car with a good driver behind the wheel.

The conversation moved to Jill's former home in London, a flat in Maida

Vale. Mary listened with half her attention to a description of how difficult it had been to find a cleaning woman who was both trustworthy and competent. Her mind leapfrogged from cleaning women to retired servants in general to the late tenant of Church Cottage in particular.

'It's strange,' she interrupted. 'Talking of cleaners and servants – Mrs Abberley and I did not get on, but I think I shall miss her.'

There was a tiny pause then Jill plunged smoothly into the new subject. 'She'll leave a void, I suppose. It's the same when you lose a friend, isn't it?'

Mary nodded, grateful for the understanding. The departure of an enemy left a gap in one's life just as the departure of a friend did. And Mrs Abberley, despite their recent truce, had been an enemy.

'I wish I could feel sad for her. Not just this terrible blankness.'

'That's a common reaction to death, isn't it?'

'Not this sort of blankness.' Mary hesitated, then said abruptly: 'It's worse than blankness, actually. I can't help feeling if anyone can deserve to die like that, she did.'

Jill said nothing. Mary looked towards the window, and was relieved to hear that the men were absorbed in the pros and cons of underfloor heating. She touched one of the blade-like leaves of the aspidistra.

'I know that sounds awful. Most unchristian. But she was dreadfully malevolent. Did you know that she told Miss Kymin where to find the keys of the church on Sunday night? That's how Miss Kymin got into the vestry.'

'What was she planning to do?'

Mary hugged herself. 'I shouldn't have told you that. Would you forget it? I don't know what I'm saying at present.'

'The last time we met I was working,' Jill said slowly. 'I'm not now.'

'I hardly know you.'

'Perhaps that's a good thing. Talk if you'd like to. Or not. But if you do, anything you say won't go further – not unless you want it to.'

Mary stared up at the clock on the mantelpiece. The ticking seemed unnaturally loud. Time slipped away, every beat measured; then, for each person, suddenly it stopped, and its essential irrelevance was cruelly exposed as one was pitchforked into eternity. No wonder everyone was so worried about time. To be timeless was to be dead. She imagined Miss Kymin and Mrs Abberley floating like a pair of airborne witches among the stars in a measureless tract of space.

'Miss Kymin wrote those letters.' Jill waited; and Mary felt the shock slipping like a shadow through her mind. A moment later Jill went on: 'The police found the newspapers she used. I suppose going to the vestry was all part of the same impulse to make mischief.'

Mary looked at her. 'Everyone will know sooner or later, if they don't already: I think Miss Kymin planned to steal the chalice, or perhaps vandalise it in some way. She must have wanted to make life difficult for my husband.'

'Hence the letters?'

'Yes.' Mary swallowed. 'There may have been an element of genuine misunderstanding, but she misinterpreted everything. Wilfully. It all makes sense now. She must have seen Alec in Soho. Mr Thornhill told me that one of the letters claimed he was visiting prostitutes in London.' She shivered. 'And that he was going to steal the chalice to pay for his . . . his pleasures.'

Without warning, the conversation coasted to a halt. Mary heard the murmur of the men's voices in the bay window. 'Their monuments aren't a patch on ours, either,' Youlgreave was saying. She wondered whether Jill would want to know why Alec had been in Soho, and thought how difficult it was to break her self-imposed vow of silence.

Mary said: 'She was in love with Alec, I suppose. It's not uncommon for lonely women to fall in love with their parish priest. Only usually they don't go so far.' She felt furious with Miss Kymin for her impertinence; the fact that Miss Kymin was dead made no difference. She made herself add, 'She must have been very unhappy.'

'Hence the letters. And the attempt to steal the chalice.'

There were footsteps in the hall and a hard object banged into the door of the drawing room. The door swung back into the room and Charlotte nudged a heavily laden tea trolley through the doorway. The men rushed to her assistance.

'I thought we could all do with a cup of tea,' Charlotte announced, 'Except you, dear,' she added to Jill. 'I've brought you some beef tea. You need building up, not stimulation.'

Mary was looking at Jill. She glimpsed a flash of mutiny in the other's face, instantly suppressed. The men helped Charlotte dispense the tea, Youlgreave with dainty efficiency, and Alec with his mind obviously elsewhere, a condition which made Mary worry constantly that he was on the verge of dropping something. She guessed that there was strain between Charlotte and Jill and wondered about its cause. The men withdrew to the window and Charlotte left the room to fetch the kettle.

'Why was Miss Kymin in London?' Jill asked in what Mary suspected was an attempt to distract herself from the prospect of beef tea. 'When she saw Mr Sutton, I mean.'

'Probably something to do with her mother's estate. Her solicitor was in London, and she had to go up several times. She asked Alec's advice about one or two things, in fact.' Mary paused, mindful of the archdeacon's advice that there should be no more secrets. 'Alec was in Soho to take my latest book to the publisher's. Their office is in Brewer Street.'

'I didn't know that you wrote.'

'Nor do many people. I've tended to keep quiet about it. But I think that was a mistake.'

Jill nodded, and Mary thought how agreeable it was to talk with an intelligent woman again. One didn't have to spell out the fact that secrets made one vulnerable, especially when people like Miss Kymin were about.

'What do you write? Novels?'

'It depends how generous your definition of the novel is. I write detective stories.'

'Under a pseudonym?'

Mary said with a sense of pride which surprised her, 'I am Denton Carbury.'

'Inspector Coleford?' Jill's face lit up, perhaps relieved that she'd actually heard of Mary's detective stories. 'He's quite a charmer, isn't he?'

'Do you think so? Some people think I've given him too much of a sense of humour.'

'Oh, no. Anyway, why shouldn't policemen have a sense of humour?' Jill frowned. 'Mind you, I'm not sure the ones in Lydmouth have. Tell me, how do you feel about publicity?'

'Terrified.'

'If you liked, we could do a feature on your writing in the *Gazette*. But perhaps you'd rather we didn't?'

'It would get it over with, I suppose. Once it was in the *Gazette* everyone would know.' Mary shuddered inwardly at the thought. 'I'd better see what Alec thinks. But in principle it seems a good idea.' Another thought struck her. 'But would people be interested?'

'Oh, they'd be interested all right. Have you got a new novel coming out soon?'

'Not until the beginning of next year. The provisional title is *Inspector Coleford Runs Away*. Which is exactly what I feel like doing.'

Charlotte returned with the kettle; she also brought a plate of éclairs to supplement the sandwiches, the toasted tea cakes and the Victoria sponge.

As Youlgreave fussed with teacups, plates and knives, Mary surreptitiously observed Jill. To think of practicalities so soon after Mrs Abberley's death seemed almost sinful. But the fact remained that Alec would soon have to find a new tenant for Church Cottage. And how pleasant it would be if the new tenant was someone one could actually talk to. It was of course far too soon even to think of broaching the subject to Jill, but Mary made a note to have a word with Alec. Out of evil might come a little good, she thought; and then she felt disgusted with her levity in the face of two barbaric killings. It occurred to her, not for the first time, that her mind was a wild, ill-disciplined thing that needed all the control she could give it. Perhaps that was why she needed to write: it gave her the illusion that it was possible to tidy up experience, whereas in reality one could no more tidy it up than one could the boys' bedrooms.

'Runs away,' Jill murmured, frowning at the brown liquid in her cup. 'Running away.'

'*Inspector Coleford Runs Away*,' Mary said. 'No – it isn't much of a title, is it? I might call it *Inspector Coleford's Ghost* instead. Only that would worry my editor because the catalogues have already gone out.'

'It's not that.' Jill put the cup and saucer down on the table beside her chair. 'It's just you jogged my memory. I couldn't remember exactly what happened in the ten minutes or so before I was knocked out last night. I still can't, not entirely, but I have remembered something: someone was running away.'

'When?'

'A few seconds afterwards, I think. I wasn't unconscious for very long. No more than a few seconds, perhaps. And then I was lying there face down in that barn, feeling neither one thing nor the other. You know how it is sometimes, when one's not quite awake and not quite asleep: it was like that, only much more painful because my head was hurting so much. The point is I heard someone running away, and a door being opened – it made a sort of scraping noise.'

Mary's professional curiosity was aroused. 'I wonder why you were hit on the head? It couldn't have been to kill you, otherwise they would have made a better job of it.' She felt herself blushing and added hurriedly: 'I didn't mean to sound so callous.'

'It doesn't matter. I've been wondering the same thing. I presume he didn't want me to see his face.'

'And possibly the chalice.'

'What do you mean?' Jill asked.

'Suppose the killer hid the chalice in the barn on the previous evening. Suppose he came back for it on Monday, only to find you there. Or he might have been already there, with the chalice in his hand. He might have been hiding in the shadows.'

Jill shivered.

'A door scraped on something,' Mary went on dreamily. 'What sort of door? A car door?'

'Not that sort of noise. More like a house or shed door.'

'Well, that implies that your attacker didn't run away into the street. It's much more likely he went into the Bull.'

'Is everything all right?' Charlotte asked. 'Jill, you haven't touched your beef tea. Come along now, drink it up: it's good for you.'

For a moment Mary thought that Jill was about to object to being treated as if she belonged in the nursery. Then Charlotte surged out of the room in search of more milk. The men were still talking in the bay window, their voices lowered to an inaudible rumble.

Jill said softly: 'I'm going out.'

'Where?' Mary asked.

'I want to see Quale at the Bull. The person who attacked me was probably there. And the person who attacked me is almost certainly the murderer.'

'Are you all right to go by yourself?'

Jill nodded. 'But the sooner I go, the better. Otherwise I shall have to deal with Charlotte and that could take hours.'

The two women exchanged smiles of perfect complicity. Jill slipped out of the room. As the door closed, Mary lifted Jill's cup and in one swift movement poured the beef tea into the pot containing the aspidistra.

PART NINE

1

It was very warm in the yard at the back of the Bull. Brian Kirby was sweating, though that was as much from desire as from the heat.

'How long have we got, darling?' Jemima whispered.

'God knows. Not long – when Thornhill's finished with Lancaster, we'll be off to the Vicarage.'

He was standing by the open driver's window of the Bentley. The bulk of the car screened him from anyone who might be watching from the hotel. Jemima had one arm on the wheel and the other resting on the sill of the window. He stared into her face and thought quite seriously that he would like to do this for ever. But not just this: sooner or later she had to let him make love to her again.

'If only we knew exactly how long.' She moistened her lips. 'We could do it on the back seat of the car.'

He touched the arm that lay on the windowsill. The skin was speckled with soft, pale down. He sketched a cross for a kiss on the warm flesh. Her other hand left the wheel and squeezed his. He felt sick with lust.

'But why are you here?' she went on. 'I'd have thought you'd all be sleuthing away at the Vicarage.'

'We need to check the movements here on Sunday night,' he said absently, wondering if it would be safe to translate the kiss from symbol to reality. 'There's a chance that Miss Kymin's killer came back this way.'

'So the murderer was someone who was here on Sunday night?'

'Not exactly.' Between them, desire and conscience were making him decidedly uncomfortable. He shifted his weight on his feet, trying to summon up the moral courage to step back from her.

'Who was here, Brian? Anyone I know?'

Kirby ran the dozen or so names through his mind. 'Only Mr Newton, probably.' There could surely be no harm in telling her that. According to Quale, Newton had been drinking heavily that night, which was uncharacteristic of him. Drowning his sorrows? But you wouldn't think a bloke like Newton would have any sorrows. In any case half a dozen people would probably be able to give him an alibi. Lancaster had even walked part of the way home with him.

'Are you any nearer finding out who did it?'

'Not really.' He looked away from her eyes. 'I shouldn't be talking to you like this.'

She laid a warm soft hand against his cheek. 'You don't have to worry. I won't tell anyone.'

'Jemima, I—'

There were footsteps on the other side of the car, much too close for comfort. Jemima snatched her hand away. Someone had entered the yard from the side road. Kirby took a couple of steps backwards and collided with the wall behind him.

'No, Sergeant,' Jemima said in a high, carrying voice. 'I'm afraid my uncle's walking home. If I were you I'd telephone Clearland Court and leave a message.'

Jill Francis appeared. Jemima leant out of the window and called, 'Hello – how are you?'

She came towards the car. Kirby made rapid and anxious calculations. It was just his luck that it was someone who knew them both, and a journalist at that. Coming into the yard from the side road, she might well have seen Jemima touching his cheek.

'Right, miss,' he said to Jemima, wondering if his feelings for her were as obvious as they felt. 'Sorry to bother you.'

'Not at all, Sergeant.'

'Is Inspector Thornhill here?' Jill asked.

'Yes, miss.'

'That's very convenient. I assumed he'd be at the Vicarage. Do you think I might be able to have a word with him?'

'He's busy at present, miss, but perhaps you could speak to him when he's finished.' Kirby was now convinced that she had seen them touching. And why did she want to see Thornhill? To tell him what she had seen? 'If you don't mind waiting, that is.'

'How's your head, Jill? You don't mind if I call you Jill, do you? I'm Jemima.'

'Of course I don't mind. I'm fine, apart from a bit of a headache.'

'When did they let you out?'

'After lunch.'

'You are brave. It actually happened here, didn't it?'

'Yes.' Jill Francis took a step towards the back door. 'Perhaps I should wait in the hall. I'd like to have a word with Mr Quale as well.' Kirby did not know whether to be thankful for her tact or distressed by its implications – if tact it was.

Jemima said: 'Why don't we meet for a drink or something? Are you doing anything this evening?'

He had time to feel jealous of Jill – for if she was with Jemima, he could not be. She was opening her mouth to answer when there was the familiar screech of wood on stone as the back door opened. Automatically the three of them looked towards the direction of the sound.

Jill said softly, 'That's it. The noise I heard.'

Inspector Thornhill came into the yard. For an instant he stood blinking in the sunshine. Then he saw them.

In that moment of recognition, Kirby saw something too. When there was no call to be professionally alert, he was usually self-contained to the point of self-absorption; but since meeting Jemima, all his faculties seemed unbearably sharp. He saw how Thornhill's head went up in shock, how the eyes widened fractionally, how the face became suddenly wary. In that moment, the realisation flooded over him.

Christ, he thought, Wilson was right: the Guv'nor fancies her.

2

Laborare est orare, the nuns at school used to say, to work is to pray. Nonsense, Chrissie Newton thought; to work is to forget. The best thing about work was that you didn't have to think.

Working in the house usually bored her. Jam-making, however, was one of those indoor jobs that almost qualified as a form of honorary gardening. It was a messy but productive job with a beginning and an end. And you only had to do it once a year.

It was tiring work too. She had started by cleaning the large preserving pan; since last year it had been gathering dust at the back of the tall wooden cupboard in the scullery. The pan had been her mother's, and every time Chrissie used it she remembered the great jam-making sessions of her childhood when her mother and the aunts had turned the kitchen of their house near Leatherhead into a cross between a production line and a war zone.

She worked quickly. During the morning, she had washed the jam jars ready to be sterilised and made sure that she had enough sugar in the store cupboard. Charlotte had given her just over six pounds of strawberries. Chrissie drove back from Troy House with them on the back seat. At Mill Place she left the Alvis in the drive. She noticed as she went into the house that the car's offside tail light was broken, and there was a dent in the rear bumper. With an effort she cast her mind back to the morning, to reversing out of the garage on her way to Clearland Court. The damage did not seem to matter. The important thing was to get on with the jam.

She sat at the kitchen table to hull the fruit. Much of it was a little underripe, just as it should be. She picked over the individual berries, one by one, discarding the over soft and the bruised. The stalks of the less ripe fruit broke off as she tugged them, leaving their bases embedded in the fruit. This was something she found intensely irritating even though she knew it was inevitable. Her hands grew red with strawberry juice. She remembered the red lipstick on the cigarette butt she had seen in the Alvis. My hands are like a servant's, she thought: no wonder Giles doesn't want me.

Sambo sensed her mood. He lay under the kitchen table, breathing heavily and somehow reproachfully. At one point Chrissie was tempted to tread on one of his paws, which lay resting against the leg of the table. She resisted the temptation, but the impulse had been so wild and inexplicable that it shook her considerably.

When she weighed out the sugar, she spilled some on the floor. Sambo looked up at her enquiringly. 'You stupid dog,' she said and left the spilled sugar where it lay. It crunched beneath her shoes as she worked.

She buttered the base of the preserving pan and began to layer the strawberries and lump sugar inside it. She lit the gas and lifted the pan on top of the stove.

'The lemon,' an aunt's voice said in her memory. 'With strawberry jam, lemon is essential.'

Chrissie had completely forgotten. Fortunately there was a large lemon in the fruit bowl on the dresser. The knife she had used when hulling the strawberries had vanished. She opened the drawer in the table where she kept the kitchen cutlery. There should have been two or three knives in there but she couldn't see them.

Taking herself by surprise, she swore aloud, using words she'd heard Giles and her brothers use, but had never used herself. It was as if a stranger were inside her, speaking through her mouth. It was the inner stranger, too, who pulled the drawer out from the table and threw it on the floor. There was a satisfyingly loud clatter. Sambo's claws scrabbled on the tiles as he retreated towards the door to the hall. The back of the drawer came adrift from the sides.

Among the débris she saw two knives which would be suitable for cutting the lemon, three if one counted the bread knife. She stooped and picked up one of them. She sawed violently at the lemon. The room darkened fractionally.

'What the hell are you doing?' Giles said. He was standing in the doorway to the yard. Sambo padded towards him.

'What does it look like? Making jam. Where have you been?'

He ignored the question. 'What happened to the car? The tail light's smashed, and there's a bloody great dent in the bumper.'

'I know.'

'How did it happen?'

'The gatepost was in the way.'

He took a step towards her, raising his arm. For a second, she was convinced he was going to hit her. She swung round to face him. She still had the knife in one hand and the lemon in the other.

'What's happened to your hand? All those scratches.'

He lowered his arm. 'One of the tenant's cats.' His voice was much calmer. 'Why's that drawer on the floor?'

'Because I put it there.'

Sambo thrust his nose against his master's leg. Giles ignored him.

'You've been talking to Tony,' he said quietly. 'What exactly did you say?'

She turned away and finished cutting the lemon in half. 'You've seen him then?'

'Of course I have. But I could have done without your interference. It makes a man seem so stupid.'

She squeezed the juice and pips out of the lemon into an earthenware bowl. She used such force that she tore the skin. 'I wasn't interfering. It's my business too.'

'Don't be ridiculous.'

She tried to pick out the pips from the bottom of the bowl with her fingers. The lemon juice stung the cracks in her roughened skin. 'Of course it is.' She was amazed by her own temerity. 'You've spent all my money. How can we afford to keep going?'

'You can leave that sort of thing to me.'

'No, I can't. It's not just my future I'm worried about – it's the children's. You've ruined my life, but you've got no right to ruin theirs.'

'Don't be so melodramatic.'

She turned to face him. 'Why on earth not?'

'Because it makes you sound like a hysterical parlour maid.'

'Look, I can put up with a lot, Giles. I don't mind your moods—'

'If you only knew how ugly you look when you're angry. You should take

265

more care of your appearance.' He walked towards the kitchen door, Sambo trailing unhappily after him. 'But it's too late for that now.'

The words sickened her. 'What does it matter how I look?' She slammed the knife down on the table. 'After all, you've got your lady friend to console you. Is *she* pretty?'

He turned, his face whitening. 'Who told you?'

'You did. If you think you could hide the signs, you're more of a fool than I thought. My God, do you think I'm stupid? You've been having these little flings for years, ever since I was pregnant with Michael.'

'You don't know what you're talking about.'

'Don't I? I've known about this one for weeks. Her cigarette ends are in the car. Sometimes I can smell her stink on you. And when I sort your clothes for the laundry – well, what does it matter? At least it keeps you from pawing me. As long as you're discreet about it, it won't harm me and the children.' She paused and her voice became calmer and colder. 'But this business with the money is quite different. If Tony gives you the sack, where are you going to find another job? Who would want to employ you?'

He looked down at his hands and said softly, 'And why should I need to look for another job?'

'Because this time it's not just inefficiency: it's embezzlement, isn't it?'

'Is that what Tony told you?'

'No one told me. I worked it out for myself. I went through your desk yesterday morning. I used to do Daddy's accounts, remember? I know how to add up a few figures and make them balance. Except that ours don't balance, do they? The only possible explanation is that you've had your hand in the till.'

'You're mad,' he said without conviction. 'Stark, staring—'

'What happened? Has your lady friend got expensive tastes? I shouldn't be at all surprised, judging by the scent she uses. Quite classy, I'd say, unlike your usual bits of skirt. You tend to go for the cheap and vulgar.'

'Shut up,' he shouted, opening his mouth so wide that she could see the pink cavern at the back of his throat. 'Shut up! Shut up!'

Sambo growled.

'Who is it, anyway?' she enquired. 'Anyone I know? A man with decent manners would choose a stranger, but we both know what your manners are like.'

He kicked the drawer with his foot and sent it flying across the floor. Sambo yelped as it clipped his paw and retreated to the shelter of the dresser.

Chrissie put the table between herself and her husband. He took a step towards her. She seized the knife, its blade still sticky with lemon juice.

Giles bent down and stroked Sambo between the ears with a scratched hand. Then he looked at Chrissie.

'Bitch,' he said softly. 'Bitch, bitch, bitch.'

3

When Victor Youlgreave found her, Jill was sitting in the lounge of the Bull Hotel and talking about London nightclubs with Jemima Orepool. Or rather Jill was sitting there smoking one of Jemima's cigarettes with angry concentration while Jemima, her eyes gleaming with remembered excitement, did most of the talking. They had the room to themselves.

'Miss Francis – I was hoping to find you here.' With his Panama hat tucked under his arm, Youlgreave trotted towards them, weaving his way among tables and chairs. 'Hello – it's Miss Orepool, isn't it? I hope I'm not interrupting a tête-à-tête.'

Jemima briefly examined him with a curiosity so open that it was almost inoffensive.

'Do you know Mr Youlgreave?' Jill said. 'He's one of the churchwardens at St John's.'

Jemima nodded. 'How do you do?' She did not bother to waste a smile or a handshake on him.

Youlgreave turned back to Jill. 'I've just taken the Suttons back to the Vicarage. I promised Mrs Wemyss-Brown I'd look in here on the way back and see if I could find you.'

'How kind of her,' Jill said, thinking the opposite.

'Perhaps I could give you a lift back to Troy House?'

'Unfortunately, Inspector Thornhill asked me to wait here. I seem to be helping the police with their enquiries. I'm not sure how long I'll be.'

She was unable to keep the bitterness from her voice. Thornhill's manner had been intolerable – pompous, arrogant and ungracious. She had brought him a useful piece of information and his only response had been a curt nod, implying that she had told him something he already knew, and an order, thinly veiled as a request, to await his pleasure in the lounge. She had found his manner all the more offensive because she had been feeling unusually well disposed towards him. He had been very gentle when he had visited her at the hospital, and she had found herself almost liking him. But now it was clear she had allowed herself to be fooled by his bedside manner. She felt angry with herself as well as with him.

'I thought the Suttons were staying longer.' Jill wondered whether they'd had enough of Charlotte.

Youlgreave bounced up and down on the balls of his feet as if trying to make himself taller. 'The archdeacon rang. He'd just heard the news and was coming into Lydmouth.' Youlgreave hesitated. 'Alec thought it would be wiser to see him at the Vicarage.'

Jill noticed Youlgreave's use of Sutton's Christian name. 'And Mrs Sutton went too?'

'Yes. As one would expect.' His eyes met Jill's and she guessed that they were thinking the same thing: that the Suttons' was a good marriage, and in a good marriage you shared the bad things as well as the good things. 'Interesting that she's an author, don't you think?'

Jemima yawned. She stood up in a graceful wriggle, murmured something about powdering her nose and glided out of the room.

'I hope I haven't frightened her off,' Youlgreave murmured.

'I don't think she's the sort that gets frightened.' Jill stubbed out her cigarette. 'Do sit down, Mr Youlgreave.'

He collapsed into a chair with a wheeze of relief. He sat well forward on the seat, turning his hat round and round in his hand. 'She and Mrs Wemyss-Brown were talking about her novels after you left. Most interesting. Mrs Wemyss-Brown is very keen that the *Gazette* should do a feature on her. Is that the word one uses? The Suttons seemed to like the idea – no point in hiding one's light under a bushel, eh?'

Jill saw movement on the edge of her range of vision. She looked up. Inspector Thornhill had come into the lounge and was making his way quietly towards them. He and Youlgreave exchanged greetings. He turned to Jill.

'Sorry to keep you waiting, Miss Francis.'

'I'm afraid I've remembered nothing else about the attack.'

'In that case there's no need for you to stay any longer.'

'Thank you so much for letting me know.'

Jill glanced at her watch. Thornhill compressed his lips. She picked up her handbag and gloves.

'You must allow me to give you a lift,' Youlgreave said. 'My car's outside at the front.'

Thornhill cleared his throat. 'Don't hesitate to ring if you happen to remember anything else.' He made it sound as if she were to blame for the gaps in her memory. 'Anything at all about the attack. Even if it seems trivial to you.'

She nodded, suspecting condescension and resenting it.

He lowered his voice. 'You're absolutely sure that you heard the back door opening?'

'I wouldn't have said it if I had not been absolutely sure.' As she stood up, Jill's headache worsened. She made herself smile at Youlgreave. 'I hope I'm not putting you to too much trouble?'

'Not at all. It's all working out rather nicely, in fact. After I've dropped you off at Troy House, it'll be just time for Nanki-Poo's walk. I shouldn't like to be late for that. He's a creature of habit, you know. He becomes inordinately tetchy when his routine is upset.' Youlgreave glanced from Jill to Thornhill. 'Just like a human being, in fact.'

Thornhill stood aside to allow Jill and Youlgreave to precede him through the doorway.

Youlgreave paused. 'I do hope you catch this chap soon, Inspector. He's done terrible things to this town. What he needs is a short sharp shock.'

'From a chopper, sir?'

'Ah – another Gilbertian. We may consider choppers out of date in these enlightened days, but personally I've no objection to the use of their modern equivalent.'

Jill watched Youlgreave smiling up at Thornhill. She suddenly realised that the churchwarden's pink, pleasant face was no more than a mask. And she wasn't sure that she liked the man within.

'Yes,' said Youlgreave, rubbing his little hands together. 'I'm thoroughly in favour of the Lord High Executioner. How else can one deal with a murderer?'

4

By the time Jean left school, almost everyone else had gone home. The weekend's half-completed homework had earned her a detention, not just for this afternoon but every afternoon for the rest of the week.

'Now mind you come straight back, Jean,' her mother had said at breakfast. 'Don't dawdle like you usually do. There's a murderer around. You don't want to end up under a hedge with your throat cut, do you?'

Once she had finished her work she spent the rest of the detention drawing hearts pierced with arrows, with BRIAN at the top and JEAN at the bottom. When each drawing was complete she scrubbed it out with her pen, the nib digging deep into the paper and the ink leaking through to the page beneath.

While she was drawing she weighed all the considerations in her mind and came, slowly and painfully, to a decision. If she kept her head it would be possible to tell them what she had seen on Sunday evening without revealing that she had been watching for Brian. Even better, if she played her cards right, she would earn Brian's gratitude and respect. ('You're wonderful, Jean. We couldn't have solved the case without you.')

'Bugger the old cow,' Jean muttered to herself, thinking of her mother. 'It's my life, isn't it?'

The detention gave her an excuse to be late. When she left the school, Jean did not take the quickest way home but her usual route, which was considerably longer. In normal circumstances, she liked to linger in the High Street, pretending to look at shop displays but in reality watching the police

273

station in the hope of seeing Brian Kirby.

On this afternoon she marched boldly up the steps of the police station and went inside. Sergeant Fowles was behind the counter. It was a good omen: he had known her father well in the old days.

'Hello, Jean. How are you and your mother keeping?'

'All right, thanks. Is Mr Kirby in?'

'Yes.' Fowles looked gravely at her. 'But he's busy. We're all rather busy at present.'

She wanted to shout at him, Don't treat me as a kid. I'm not a baby.

'If you've got a message from your mum, I'll see that he gets it.'

'It's not that. Can I see him, please?' She found a phrase from a film waiting in her mind: 'I have some important information for him.'

'What's it about?'

'I have to tell Mr Kirby.'

Fowles stared at her. At last he picked up the telephone. He waved her to the bench against the wall. She strained to hear what he was saying but could not make out the words. She sat rehearsing her speech and drawing the strap of her satchel through her fingers. If only her mother would allow her to wear make-up. Men preferred girls who wore make-up.

There were footsteps on the stairs. She looked up. Brian came over to her. He looked so beautiful in his new blue suit with the wonderful American tie. She wished he would smile at her.

'What's this about, Jean? Make it snappy, will you?'

'I went out for a stroll on Sunday evening,' she said in a rush. 'It was about nine o'clock. I know I told Mr Thornhill I didn't go out, but that was because I thought he meant the Sunday before.' She glanced up at Brian Kirby, trying to discover whether or not he believed the lie. 'I was in the churchyard for a bit. I saw a man coming out of the church.'

He took her forearm and squeezed it until she yelped. 'Who was it?'

'Mr Newton.'

'You stupid girl. Why the *hell* didn't you tell us before?' He put his hot, angry face close to hers. 'You're sure? This isn't some silly story?'

'Of course it isn't. I *saw* him.'

Brian released her and ran upstairs without even saying goodbye. Her eyes burned. Tears spilled down her cheeks. She was making what her mother called 'a public spectacle of herself'. In the middle of her despair she heard Sergeant Fowles speaking, his voice coming to her across a great void.

Haven't you heard? Jean, there's been another murder today.'

5

Sambo lay under the desk, smelling strongly of old dog; his slow breathing rasped like a sheet of sandpaper being rubbed to and fro. His head rested heavily on Giles Newton's left foot.

Newton was writing letters. The door was locked. Through the window he could see the green of the lawn sloping down to the stream at the bottom of the garden. The world was very beautiful, full of rich, bright colours that hurt the eyes.

The first letter was addressed to the coroner.

I have decided to kill myself. I apologise for any inconvenience that this may cause. No one else is in any way responsible or to blame for my decision. I have been experiencing a number of financial problems, and this seems the best way out, all things considered.

The letter to the coroner had been the easiest one to write. Next he had written a note to Chrissie, not because he wanted to, but because it would have seemed odd if he had not done so. There was a right way to do everything, even to kill oneself.

The letter proved unexpectedly difficult. He managed it in the end by pretending that they were two quite different people.

. . . so you must not blame yourself in any way. Sometimes the best way

to deal with a difficulty is to walk away from it. I suggest that you ask Tony for advice. I think things will be much easier once I'm out of the way. Darling, I'm sorry for the trouble I have caused. With my love to you and to the children . . .

The letter to Tony Ruispidge was even harder to write. Tony need never know that there had been a double betrayal. That was one advantage with choosing this way out. Another was that there were worse scandals than suicide. He wished he did not have to write to Tony. But Tony deserved a letter, even an inadequate one. Here at least he did not have to pretend, or not very much. What he wrote was almost entirely the truth, though not the whole truth.

Sorry, old man. I know this must seem a poor return for all you've done. The fact that I have in many ways mismanaged the financial side of the Estate upsets me very much. I hope you will realise that this was due to nothing more than my incompetence.

Giles felt that he could rely on Tony to minimise the scandal. The word embezzlement wouldn't be mentioned, or not in public at any rate. The one thing that hadn't turned sour in life, Giles thought, was friendship.

As you know, my will names you as my executor. I hope in the circumstances you will be able to accept the job. I would feel happier knowing you were doing it. I have tried to sort things out so everything will be as straightforward as possible. As old Markby used to say, organisation is the key.

Lack of organisation – that had been the problem for the last forty-eight hours. He had been forced to improvise all the time. He had never been much good at improvising. It was all the fault of that bloody Kymin woman. He'd planned the theft of the chalice so carefully. The risk of being seen was minimal if he came through the grounds of the Vicarage. The south door had been unlocked – at the time, he had assumed that Alec Sutton had forgotten to lock it. He had checked, of course, that no one was in the church. He had even rattled the door handle of the vestry to make sure that it was locked. Sutton wouldn't lock himself in the vestry.

Following the plan, he had not used his copy of the vestry key but had wrenched the door open with the tyre lever. He remembered the cracking of wood, how loud and violent it had sounded in the quietness of the church. He pushed open the door and then, at that precise instant, everything had gone wrong. He had had filthy bad luck all his life, but this was the crowning example of it.

'No,' Miss Kymin had screamed. 'Stay away from me.'

She had been cowering under the Ruispidge monument, her arms thrown up to ward off an attack which hadn't yet begun; he'd seen the whites of her eyes. Fear had made her even more ugly than usual. She disgusted him.

'Don't touch me, you monster. Oh, please, please, please.'

Her panic had triggered his own. She had seen him breaking in. He did not stop to think how she had got in herself, or what she was doing in the vestry. This foul little woman would ruin him if she didn't stop screaming.

He had lashed out with the tyre lever, a swift backhand blow with all his weight behind it. He hadn't even made a conscious decision. It had simply happened. The blow was nothing to do with him on one level. It was even untrue to say that he had improvised: his body had done the improvising, not his mind.

The bloody woman had squawked and fallen over in a huddle. He had almost felt relief: now there was no need to improvise – he could simply follow the plan. The whole point of breaking open the vestry door was to imply that someone without a key had stolen the chalice, perhaps a passing tramp. A tramp had found Miss Kymin in the church and had killed her in a fit of panic: that's what everyone would believe.

His hands had been shaking so much that he dropped the keys when he tried to unlock the safe. It took him almost a minute to get it open. Follow the plan, he had thought, follow the plan. He took the chalice from its case and ran through the shadowy church. He knew that he could not walk back to the Bull with the tyre lever in one hand and the chalice in the other. The chalice was too large to go in a pocket. He tucked the tyre lever and the chalice inside his jacket, holding them in place with his arms. Their chilly hardness penetrated his shirt and vest.

It was neither day nor night. The windows of Church Cottage were in darkness. There was nothing to show that the Abberley hag was watching from her bedroom, waiting for Miss Kymin to return. In the Vicarage, the only light showing had been behind a curtained window on the first floor, probably the Suttons' bedroom. Outside there was still enough natural light to see where he was going.

Newton walked quickly through the churchyard and over the road; running footsteps might attract attention. He had left one leaf of the Suttons' gates ajar. He slipped inside, latched the gate behind him and made his way stealthily down the long, thin yard at the side of the Vicarage. On this side of the house the windows were in darkness. That was a relief: he had been worried about the kitchen, whose window overlooked part of the yard.

The Vicarage garden was almost as familiar to him as his own. He walked as quickly as he could without making unnecessary noise, but had the sensation he was trying to stride through treacle. The twilight played tricks on his eyes: it brought shadows alive and twisted shapes into creatures from dreams. He had felt then what he felt now: that this could not be true; that there had been some dreadful mistake. The horror of what he'd done was increased by the fact that he could not believe it. It could only be a nightmare, and nightmares by definition could not be real.

When he reached the old kitchen garden, he had tried to run, driven by the fear that something or someone was dogging his footsteps. He was still capable of interludes of rational thought. For example, he had considered hiding the chalice and the tyre lever in the garden, but decided in the end to keep to his original plan; it was always safer not to improvise.

Two minutes later, he had reached the yard at the Bull. He rolled the chalice and the tyre lever into the piece of sackcloth he had left in the barn. No one was around. He could hear someone washing up through the open windows of the kitchen. He peeled off his gloves and walked into the gentlemen's lavatory at the end of the barn. There he pulled the chain in one of the cubicles and washed his hands thoroughly. He was glad that he hadn't had to touch Miss Kymin.

He went back into the hotel, nodding to Quale behind the reception desk, and returned to the bar. Nothing had changed, or at least nothing that mattered. When Newton had slipped away, Lancaster had been in the throes of ordering another round. There was a pint of beer by Newton's chair, but Lancaster himself had got no more than halfway down his treble whisky. He and the other men in their group, three of the Bull's regulars, were still criticising with a wealth of anecdotal detail the composition of the county cricket team. Their voices were loud and slurred.

Newton slipped back into his seat and picked up his glass. His hand was perfectly steady, which struck him as odd and rather admirable. The conversation ebbed and flowed around him. No one appeared to notice his arrival any more than his departure. According to the clock on the wall, he'd been away for eleven minutes. He slipped back into the conversation with a slightly risqué joke involving sticky wickets and the MCC's selectors, and was rewarded with a gust of laughter.

He was not usually a heavy drinker, but that night he had had too much without noticing. He had planned to walk home at closing time, collecting the chalice and the tyre lever on the way. Bomber Lancaster had frustrated this intention. It was a beautiful night, Lancaster had said, just the sort of night for a walk and a pipe. He would go part of the way home with Newton.

Lancaster was more than a little the worse for wear, too. He had wanted to talk about the accounting problems at the Bull, but had managed only to skirt round the subject.

'It's unaccountable, old man,' Lancaster kept saying. 'Figures just don't add up. Unaccountable. Get it? It's a joke.'

That was Sunday evening, the beginning of the nightmare. Yesterday, Monday, Giles had woken in the early hours with a hangover and the sense of a terrible weight pressing him down into the mattress. He dragged himself out of bed and searched without success for the aspirin.

The day went rapidly from bad to worse. He had been so fearfully unlucky. Everything had come together. First there had been the shock of discovering that Mrs Abberley, that ghastly old crow, had seen him coming out of the church the previous evening and proposed to blackmail him: she wanted him to write an anonymous letter framing Sutton for the murder; like Jemima, she liked a man to do her dirty work.

Next, in the evening, when he had returned to the Bull to pick up the chalice, Jill Francis had barged into the barn. He had followed his impulses. What else could he have done but improvise? His first thought had been that somehow she knew the chalice was there. She knew too much and therefore he had to stop her talking. Allied to this was the knowledge that as soon as she turned, she would see him, his back pressed against the wall just inside the doorway. Fear has its own logic, and he had followed it almost to the bitter end. At least she hadn't died.

He hadn't meant to kill Mrs Abberley this morning, either, despite the fact that she had begun to demand money he didn't have. He had wanted to talk to her, even plead with her. He had followed her down Bull Lane and into the kitchen garden. He blamed her reaction for what had happened. He had seen the fear in her face, seen her mouth opening to scream. He wouldn't have killed her if she hadn't screamed and struggled. She had scratched like a cat and spat in his face. He had not meant to kill her, only to quieten her down.

It was not his fault that she would not stop struggling and screeching. She had been a stupid woman as well as a wicked one.

And now, even if he escaped a double murder charge, there was nothing left. To all intents and purposes he no longer had a job or a home: Tony Ruispidge would expect him to resign. There was the risk of a criminal prosecution when Tony discovered the precise nature of the Estate's financial entanglements.

Last and worst of all, Jemima had rejected him. Without intending to, he said aloud, 'She gave me a glimpse of heaven, and she threw me down to hell.' Sambo whined under the desk and was silent. The words sounded trite and unbearably vulgar, as if they belonged in a romantic novel written for kitchen maids and shop girls.

The thought of Jemima filled him with yearning: his heart wanted to break out of his chest. Everything was over, everything was destroyed. He thought of himself as Samson imprisoned by his enemies and chained to the pillars. He would tear the house down and destroy them and him in the same catastrophe. He stared out of the window at the green of the lawn, the blue of the sky and the silver of the stream. He felt calm and extraordinarily noble. They might guess about the murders, but they could never be absolutely sure; and he would keep Jemima's name out of it. He owed that to her and to Tony. It occurred to him belatedly that perhaps he also owed it to Chrissie and the children.

He sealed up the letters and wrote the names of the recipients on the envelopes. He arranged them in a neat pile in the centre of his blotter. He pushed back his chair and stood up. Sambo struggled to his feet, but when his master showed no signs of leaving the room, slowly collapsed back on to the floor.

Newton took out his keyring and unlocked the cupboard on the right of the fireplace where he kept his guns. He chose one of the round-bodied Boss 12-bores which his father had given him on his twenty-first birthday. Sambo stirred again at the sight of the gun.

Out of habit Newton took two cartridges from the box. He put them carefully beside the envelopes on the blotter. He sat down in the chair by the desk and considered the practicalities of the situation. If he bent forward and put the muzzles in his mouth, which he understood was the best way to do it, he would not be able to reach the triggers: his arm simply wasn't long enough. He experimented with ways to extend his reach, first with a ruler and then, more successfully, with a brass Indian paperknife whose handle was a seated Buddha and whose blade was like a scimitar's; the curve between the two tips formed a shallow hook which fitted securely over the trigger. Out of habit he loaded both barrels.

He made himself smoke a last cigarette. The tobacco made him cough and brought him no satisfaction, but it was the thing to do. He considered fetching himself a glass of brandy from the dining room, but he didn't want to run the risk of meeting Chrissie.

He stubbed out the cigarette. He held the barrel with his left hand and put the muzzles in his mouth. He leaned forward in his chair and picked up the paperknife with his right hand. He stretched down the length of the gun and slotted the double tips of the knife into the trigger guard.

Everything was ready. He wondered whether he should say a prayer. 'Almighty and most merciful Father; we have erred, and strayed from thy ways like lost sheep.' Then the memory of Jemima flooded into his mind and he almost cried aloud with the pain of it. He looked down the long, familiar barrel towards the trigger. There would be blood all over the place, he thought, and bits of brain and bone and hair. He tried to gauge the likely trajectory of the shot: the worst of the mess would be on the wall and the ceiling just behind the desk. Some of the mess would hit the engraving of Clearland Court which Tony and Soph had given him the Christmas before last.

Sambo lifted his head and whined once more. The poor bloody animal knew that something was wrong but not what. Newton wondered if he should kill the dog before he killed himself; it would be kinder to Sambo to do it that way. But he couldn't face seeing the mess on the study floor. Besides it might distract him from his purpose, and the sound of a shot would bring Chrissie running.

The metal was cold and oily in his mouth; the muzzles tasted faintly of cordite and jarred against his teeth. They said it was a quick death, that one felt nothing; it was all over before one had time to feel. His eyes smarted with unshed tears for himself. He watched his hand tightening round the handle of the paper knife.

Oh Jemima, he thought, Oh darling Jemima.

The dog nudged his foot. Newton almost welcomed the distraction. He sat up and propped the gun against the desk. He bent down and stroked Sambo, who in the ecstasy of his pleasure stuck out his tongue, waved a hind leg and dribbled on the carpet.

There was no hurry, Giles Newton thought, not with all eternity waiting for him. Perhaps he would smoke another cigarette.

6

The ritual of jam-making soothed her; it made things slightly less unbearable, just as rituals were designed to do.

It was very nearly time now. Chrissie picked up the chipped cup she used as a ladle and scooped up a sample of the red, bubbling jam. She emptied half the contents of the cup on to a plate. Frowning with concentration, she blew away the steam. The kitchen clock ticked loudly. As she watched, a skin slowly formed on the jam: it was ready at last. She turned back to the pan. The jam jars waited in two ranks beside the stove. She plunged the cup into the pan.

'Hello,' said a voice from the doorway.

Chrissie glanced over her shoulder. A woman was silhouetted against the sunlight from the yard beyond. Recognition came almost immediately, with dislike chasing after it.

'Jemima – what can I do for you?'

The girl came into the room, carrying her jacket over her arm. 'Uncle Tony asked me to drop by with your lighter. You left it at Clearland Court this morning.'

'How kind of you.' Chrissie gave the jam a slow stir with the cup; she wished that Jemima had come a little earlier or a little later, if she had to come at all. 'I'd offer you some tea, but as you can see—'

'I've just had some at the Bull, thanks.' The girl came into the kitchen and put the lighter on the table. 'I'll leave it here, shall I?'

She was so young and so pretty that Chrissie could not help hating her.

'Oh – do you make jam yourself?' Jemima made it sound like some strange anthropological rite otherwise practised only by a handful of primitive tribes in the interior of Borneo. 'How fascinating.'

She came a little closer to the stove. The shirtwaisted dress outlined the curves of her figure. Her complexion was perfect – smooth, unlined and creamy. She leant forward to sniff the jam simmering in the pan. And as Jemima smelt the jam, Chrissie smelled Jemima.

Chrissie heard herself saying in a gentle, conversational tone, 'So it was you. I should have guessed.'

Jemima drew back, frowning. 'What do you mean?'

'You've been carrying on with that stupid husband of mine, haven't you?'

Jemima glared at her. 'He's old enough to be my father.' The fingers of her left hand pleated the material of her dress. Without warning her face became an ugly stranger's. 'All right. If you must know, we had a little fling. Anything to stop him making sheep's eyes at me.'

'Why did you do it?' Chrissie said quietly, her eyes on the jam again.

'Why? Why does one do anything? Because it seemed a good idea at the time. But in this case, I soon realised it wasn't such a good idea. What does it matter? It meant nothing.'

'Of course it did.' Chrissie thought about herself, the children, Giles's job, this house; and behind them lurked other possibilities so dark that she dared not articulate them to herself. She watched jam oozing into the cup. When the cup was full, she automatically poured its contents slowly into the nearest jam jar. Wisps of steam rose into the air.

'Don't worry,' Jemima drawled. 'It's all over. If the truth were known, he's not much good at the mechanics of the business. But you must know that already. At least, I assume you do.'

'You'd better go.'

The cup was full once more. Chrissie lifted it slowly out of the pan.

'Actually I wasn't intending to stay.' Jemima hesitated. 'Look, he's a man. Men are always doing stupid things.' She turned to leave. 'One has to be grown up about it. If you ask me, it's best for a wife to turn a blind eye.'

'Jemima?'

She looked back. Such a pretty face, Chrissie thought. With a flick of her wrist, she sent the contents of the cup flying through the air. For an instant the strawberry jam, red and bubbling like anger made visible, hung between them.

Jam splattered against the left side of Jemima's face and neck. A few drops fell on the shoulder of her dress. The jam looked like blood – not real blood, but the sort Chrissie remembered seeing in plays, as comfortingly artificial as the rest of the little world beyond the proscenium arch.

For an instant everything was silent: it reminded Chrissie of the terrifying absence of sound after one of her children had suffered a hurt when they were babies; and the longer the silence, the worse the hurt.

Jemima clawed at her face as if trying to scratch out her eyes and tear off her cheek. Then the screams began. The boiling jam dug deep into the perfect skin.

Still with the cup in her hand Chrissie blundered towards Jemima. 'Oh my God. I'm so sorry.'

The girl made a strangled sound deep in her throat. She turned and stumbled through the doorway.

'Jemima, come here. Come to the sink.'

If Jemima heard, she took no notice. She ran into the yard. From behind she looked unblemished. Chrissie dropped the cup, realising belatedly that Jemima had run away because she expected another shower of molten jam. The cup shattered on the tiled floor.

There were footsteps, much heavier than Jemima's, in the house. The kitchen door opened so violently that it banged against the dresser. Giles burst into the room.

'Ring for an ambulance,' Chrissie snapped at him.

She ran after Jemima. The girl was out of sight. But it wouldn't be hard to find her. All Chrissie needed to do was to follow the screams.

EPILOGUE

'Midsummer madness,' Alec Sutton said. 'That's what Victor Youlgreave called it.'

'I don't want to disturb your evening, sir.' Thornhill sounded tired. 'I just wanted to—'

'No, no – come in.'

Sutton ushered Thornhill into the huge drawing room, where Mary and Jill were sitting among the huddle of furniture near the fireplace like survivors from a shipwreck surrounded by their salvage. 'You'll have some coffee with us, Inspector? I'll fetch another cup.'

'Come and sit down.' Mary put down her cup. 'I know it will take us all weeks to absorb the shock, but thank heaven it's over.'

They heard Alec whistling a sprightly version of 'All Things Bright and Beautiful' on his way to the kitchen. Jill watched Thornhill walking towards them from the doorway. He was very pale, but he looked much more relaxed than he had been earlier in the day. As he drew nearer the fireplace, he hesitated, and Jill guessed he was wondering where he should sit. There were two chairs, one on either side of the fireplace; Mary was sitting in one of these and it was obvious from the cigarettes on the arm that Alec had been sitting in the other. That left the sofa, directly in front of the fireplace. Jill was leaning against a pile of cushions at the end nearer Mary.

Thornhill gingerly sat down at the other end, pulling up the knees of his trousers to avoid them bagging at the knees. 'I'm sorry to call on you so late,' he said to Mary. 'I didn't realise you had a visitor. But I thought you'd like to know what's happening.'

'Should I go?' Jill asked, making a half-hearted attempt to move.

'There's no need.' He looked at her, a grave expression on his long, thin face. 'I don't want to disturb you.'

Jill glanced at him, wondering if the words had another meaning beyond their obvious one. She decided she was imagining things.

Sutton came back into the room with a cup and saucer in his hand. He and Mary fussed gently round the coffee tray, pouring Thornhill's cup and refilling the others, dealing with the sugar bowl, the cream jug and the spoons. Jill noticed that they worked without consultation but in harmony; part of her found this domestic teamwork enviable, and another part wondered whether she herself would find such a relationship claustrophobic.

'Yes, Midsummer madness.' Sutton offered cigarettes which only he accepted. 'Nonstop for two days.'

'It feels more like years.' Mary raised her eyebrows at Thornhill. 'And I suppose we haven't finished?'

He smiled at her, his face for once unguarded. 'At least it won't be as bad as today and yesterday. But you may well be needed at the trial. And I'm afraid we shall have to keep you out of your kitchen garden and Church Cottage for a while.'

'I'd be quite happy if I never went into the kitchen garden again. Let nature do its worst in there.'

'I'll leave a constable here overnight. In the garden, I mean. He'll keep an eye on things. You may hear him moving about.'

'This has been most educational, Mr Thornhill. I'm afraid Inspector Coleford will never be the same. I shall have to make some changes.'

'Don't make him too real, Mrs Sutton.'

She said softly, 'None of us can bear too much reality.'

He put down his coffee cup. 'Or so Mr Eliot tells us.'

Jill had had enough. Her headache was coming back. She had enjoyed having supper with the Suttons but Thornhill's arrival had put an end to that. He had interrupted their conversation. It irritated her to see him behaving like a visitor, not a policeman. It irritated her that he should apparently be familiar with *The Four Quartets*. Most of all, it irritated her that Mary Sutton should be almost flirting with him. Jill acknowledged that flirting was too strong a word for whatever was happening between the two of them, and that in any case it was nothing to do with her. Alec Sutton was smiling complaisantly at them and puffing on his cigarette. The truth was, Jill told herself, she was out of sorts, still suffering from the after-effects of that blow.

She looked at her watch. 'I really must go.'

Alec Sutton threw his cigarette end into the grate. 'I'll run you back.'

'No, I'll walk.' Jill stood up. 'It's a lovely evening.'

Thornhill looked up. 'I should be leaving as well. May I give you a lift?'

'That's very kind, but—'

'I really think you should accept,' Mary interrupted, destroying at a stroke the darker suspicions Jill had been nursing. 'You mustn't overdo things for the next day or two.'

It was true that now she was standing, Jill felt more tired. She forced a smile and said to Thornhill, 'Thanks. If you're sure it won't take you too much out of your way.'

The Suttons escorted their visitors into the hall. The vicar helped Jill into her coat.

'Now, about Alice,' Mary said to Jill. 'Would it be best if I collected her?'

'I think we should liaise with Mrs Milkwall first.'

Sutton unlocked the front door. 'Are you two trying to be mysterious on purpose?'

Mary patted his arm. 'Alice was Miss Kymin's cat, darling. Miss Francis is going to have her if no one else will. I said we'd look after her until Miss Francis has a place of her own. You don't mind, do you? It seemed quite a sensible idea in the circumstances.'

'This is a big house. I dare say Alice and I won't have much to do with each other. Not unless we want to.' Sutton opened the door. He smiled at Mary and nodded outside. 'Look at that.'

Mary frowned at the empty pavement. 'At what?'

'Precisely. Not a reporter in sight.'

'Except Miss Francis.'

'Not at present,' Jill said firmly. 'I'm off-duty.'

The four of them exchanged goodnights. A moment later Jill was alone on the pavement with Thornhill.

'Would you mind if we go via Church Cottage? I should tell them I'm going off-duty myself.'

They walked the few yards along the pavement to what had until this morning been Mrs Abberley's front door. Sergeant Kirby answered Thornhill's knock. His eyes swung from Thornhill to Jill and back again. His face looked tired, and his mouth was a tight straight line. Jill guessed that he might have put the wrong interpretation on her presence: he might think that she had told Thornhill about seeing him with Jemima Orepool in the yard of the Bull.

'I'm signing off now,' Thornhill said easily. 'You can reach me at home if you need me.'

Kirby stared at Jill with hard, flat eyes. When Thornhill wished him goodnight he grunted a reply and shut the door a second earlier than politeness would have dictated. Thornhill looked disconcerted, Jill thought, but made no comment.

They crossed the road. The sightseers had gone as well as the journalists. It was not quite dark. It occurred to Jill that it must be almost exactly forty-eight hours since Miss Kymin was murdered.

'My car's over there,' Thornhill gestured past the church.

'Shall we walk through the churchyard?'

'You don't mind?'

She led the way through the lych gate. 'I don't believe in ghosts, Miss Kymin's or anyone else's. Do you?'

'I don't know.' He closed the gate behind them.

'Mrs Sutton does. We were talking about it over supper. Her next book might be called *Inspector Coleford's Ghost.*'

'Are you going to do an article on her work for the *Gazette*?'

'Yes. They asked me to supper for a preliminary talk about it. Also I think they wanted a distraction.'

'We all need that sometimes.'

Again she had the sense that his words meant more than they said. They walked slowly up the path. It was darker here, because there were yew trees on either side. Gravestones glimmered in the dusk. Jill thought about Sergeant Kirby and wondered what had been going on between him and Jemima Orepool. She had been stroking his cheek. It was none of Jill's business. It could have no direct bearing on the case, and she didn't intend to mention it to Richard Thornhill. Jemima Orepool had left a trail of unhappiness in her wake. There had been enough suffering already.

The tower loomed up in front of them. They were walking more and more slowly. Jill wasn't sure why. She was very conscious of Thornhill's nearness in the darkness. If she moved her hand a few inches to the right, she would touch the sleeve of his jacket. She wished he didn't have such an upsetting effect on her. At least they weren't squabbling this evening. Perhaps the half light of the long midsummer evening, neither day nor night, enclosed them in a Tom Tiddler's ground where the ordinary rules were temporarily suspended.

His head turned towards her. 'Mr Hendry and Mr Williamson have decided to have a press conference in the morning. Will you go?'

'I don't think so. I'm really on sick leave so I'll leave it to Mr Wemyss-Brown.' Her tiredness and the comforting almost-darkness allowed her to add, 'Besides, a murder case is meat and drink to him. It's real journalism.'

Thornhill snorted with what she realised, a second later, was amusement.

Feeling that speech was safer than silence, she went on, 'I imagine that you – the police as a whole – must feel rather pleased with yourselves. You haven't had to call in the Yard. And you've solved the case very quickly.'

Thornhill stopped. They had reached a fork in the path. The left-hand tributary ran up to the rarely used north door. The path on the right ran round the tower at the west end of the church. His silence unnerved her.

'I'm sorry. Perhaps you'd rather not talk about it.' Suddenly she was annoyed with him. 'Damn it, I wasn't speaking as a journalist.'

'I know you're not. And I don't mind talking about it. The trouble is, we didn't solve the case: it solved itself.'

'Rather like a splinter.'

'What?'

She knew the blood was rushing to her face and hoped there would not be enough light for him to notice. 'It's as if the consequences of murder work their way out into the open of their own accord. Like a splinter works its way out of one's finger.'

'Yes: that's it. In any case, I don't think we've much to congratulate ourselves about. We failed to prevent two people from being killed. And it's not over yet, is it? You know what the aftermath of a murder case is like. In a way the whole town's on trial.'

As if reacting to a signal, they walked on. It was lighter here because there were no yews. But there was not enough light to show the broken flagstone. Its edge rose above the level of the surrounding path. Jill tripped over it. She stumbled forwards. She was not in the least danger of falling and regained her balance almost instantly. For a moment she thought Thornhill was going to take her arm, but he didn't. She felt simultaneously relieved and cross.

He said abruptly: 'Are you all right?'

'Yes, thank you.'

'You don't sound it.'

'Actually I feel a little shaky.'

'Shall we sit down for a moment? Over there.'

He herded her towards the bench under the south wall of the tower. Jill sat down more suddenly than she had intended. She felt very tired. Thornhill sat down too, as far away as possible from her. Disjointed thoughts flashed through her mind like pictures on a magic lantern screen: this was the Suttons' sofa all over again, with him at one end and her at the other, and never the twain shall meet; directly behind them, on the other side of the wall of the tower, was the Ruispidge monument, beneath which Miss Kymin had been found; why didn't Thornhill say something?

She blundered into speech again. 'Have you found the chalice?'

'It was in the old mill pool in Newton's garden, tied up in a sack. He'd taken the collection money too: that was there as well, and so were Carter's spare keys, the ones Miss Kymin used. He told us where to look.'

'Why did he steal it? How do you sell something like that?' She hesitated. 'Sorry – forget that: I'm sure you don't really want to talk about the case.'

'Most of it will come out at the press conference tomorrow morning.'

'I dare say I could keep a secret until then.'

'I'm sure you could.' His voice sounded amused. 'Mr Newton has made a full confession. According to him, Miss Orepool has a friend in London who's an antique dealer. Not a particularly scrupulous one by all accounts. Many of his customers are Americans with private collections. We've traced him, and as a matter of fact, the chap has a record for receiving stolen goods. And he admits to knowing Miss Orepool.'

Jill remembered Brian Kirby's bleak, betrayed face. 'So she egged Newton on?'

'That's what he says now. At first he claimed she had nothing to do with it. But his chivalry was only skin-deep. Now he's desperate to find someone to share the blame.'

'And what does Miss Orepool say to that?'

'Not very much at present – or nothing that makes much sense. They've had to pump her full of morphine. She's lucky to be at the RAF hospital. One of the consultants there has done a lot of plastic surgery.'

'It's that bad?'

'She's probably lost the sight of her left eye. And that side of her face and neck may well be permanently scarred.' He stirred; the bench creaked and moved slightly beneath her. 'I'm afraid Mr Newton will probably hang.

Two murders. Also he wrote an anonymous letter trying to frame Mr Sutton for Miss Kymin's murder. That will weigh heavily against him. His only hope is if they can prove he's not fit to plead.'

Thornhill had told her more than would become public knowledge at the press conference tomorrow. He hadn't even asked her to treat it as confidential: he had simply assumed that she would.

'Mr Sutton went to see Mrs Newton,' Jill said. 'I understand Newton tried to kill himself.'

'Yes.'

'He couldn't cope with that, either. He had it all arranged but couldn't bring himself to pull the trigger.'

'No.'

Jill wondered whether Thornhill was regretting having spoken so frankly. She went on: 'The man was a failure. I suppose you could say that is one definition of a murderer.'

'He wasn't unique in being a failure. Most of us are in some respect.'

A silence grew between them. The sky was darkening rapidly. She was aware that Thornhill had turned his head towards her.

He said in a voice so low it was almost a whisper: 'Before all this happened I really rather liked him.'

'So did I. What will happen to her?'

'Miss Orepool?'

'No. Chrissie Newton.'

'It depends – on Sir Anthony, among other things, and on what sort of recovery Miss Orepool makes. It's clear that Mrs Newton acted on impulse, and immediately tried to do what she could to help the girl. She also seems to have had a good deal of provocation.'

'In her position I might well have done the same.' Jill wondered how Edith Thornhill would react if her husband betrayed her and his lover taunted her with the fact. She shivered.

'You're cold. I should take you home.'

'Yes.'

Neither of them moved. Troy House wasn't home, Jill thought. Mary Sutton had hinted that after a decent interval she, Jill, might be able to lease Church Cottage if she wanted it. Jill wasn't sure. She wanted a home, but only if there were no ghosts. She didn't believe in ghosts, of course, but one could never be absolutely sure.

Richard Thornhill's hand lay on the bench between them. She could stretch out her own hand and touch it. It was even possible that he'd left it there in the hope that she'd do just that. She was beginning to feel cold. His hand would be warm.

Thornhill stood up so suddenly that the bench rocked. 'I mustn't keep you out any longer, Miss Francis.'

Automatically, she rose to her feet. With her head high and her back straight, she walked beside him with eighteen inches of emptiness between them. On this occasion, instead of branching left to the south door of the church, they took the path that sloped downhill to the far gate.

'It's a beautiful evening,' Thornhill said carefully. 'I wonder how long this weather will last.'

'Not long.' She wondered if they were really talking about the weather. 'It never does.'

He reached the gate before her. He held it open, keeping well back so there was no danger of her brushing against him as she passed. She looked up at him and murmured a word of thanks. His face was a polite, pale mask.

The little Austin was parked at the kerb. She was so tired she could hardly walk towards it in a straight line. Time is running out, she thought, and nothing I can do will stop it or even slow it down. Her eyes pricked with tears and her vision blurred. Mentally she gave herself a good shake. There was a simple physiological explanation for the way she felt: the blow on the head had left her weak and vulnerable; what she needed was a good night's sleep.

I will not cry, she ordered herself. Once before she had cried in Thornhill's car, and he had lent her a handkerchief. Never again. Once was too often. He opened the passenger door and waited for her to climb in. She paused to gather strength, one hand resting on the roof of the car.

'Jill?'

Astonished, she stared at him. He had used her Christian name. She could hardly believe her ears. The shock was half disturbing, half pleasurable, like the lurch of the stomach when one's car went over a humpbacked bridge. His eyes were dark and gleaming. He looked angry. Perhaps that was a trick of the light.

'I'm sorry,' he said hurriedly, taking a step backwards. 'I must apologise. I don't mean to . . .' His voice tailed away.

'What did you want to say?' she asked.

'Oh – nothing.'

After a moment she folded herself carefully into the car, and he shut the door.